EVERYMAN,

I WILL GO WITH THEE,

AND BE THY GUIDE,

IN THY MOST NEED

TO GO BY THY SIDE

EVERYMAN'S POCKET CLASSICS

RUSSIAN
STORIES

EDITED BY CHRISTOPH KELLER

EVERYMAN'S POCKET CLASSICS

Alfred A. Knopf New York London Toronto

THIS IS A BORZOI BOOK
PUBLISHED BY ALFRED A. KNOPF

This selection by Christoph Keller first published in
Everyman's Library, 2019
Copyright © 2019 by Everyman's Library
A list of acknowledgments to copyright owners appears at the back
of this volume.

All rights reserved. Published in the United States by Alfred A. Knopf,
a division of Penguin Random House LLC, New York, and in
Canada by Penguin Random House Canada Ltd., Toronto.
Distributed by Penguin Random House LLC, New York. Published
in the United Kingdom by Everyman's Library, 50 Albemarle Street,
London W1S 4BD and distributed by Penguin Random House UK,
20 Vauxhall Bridge Road, London SW1V 2SA.

www.randomhouse.com/everymans
www.everymanslibrary.co.uk

ISBN: 978-0-525-65603-6 (US)
978-1-84159-627-3 (UK)

A CIP catalogue reference for this book is available from the
British Library

Typography by Peter B. Willberg
Typeset in the UK by Input Data Services Ltd, Isle Abbotts, Somerset
Printed and bound in Germany by GGP Media GmbH, Pössneck

Contents

FOREWORD

Russian Blizzards

Blizzards, both real and metaphorical, are a recurring theme in this selection of classic Russian stories. Elemental, mysterious, uncontrollable forces of nature, blizzards are *fate*, changing the lives of individuals and the destinies of nations. If it weren't for Russia's really bad weather, the armies of Napoleon in the nineteenth century and of Hitler in the twentieth might have conquered this bear of a country. Blizzards stir up dreams and nightmares and blow doors wide open: into memories, mysteries, madness. They are portals to the fabled Russian soul that has so intrigued readers around the world for the past two centuries.

It was Russia's greatest poet, Alexander Pushkin (1799–1837), tired of poetry at least for the warm fall of 1830, who introduced *weather as fate* to Russian fiction. In Pushkin's "The Blizzard," the titular "snow event" thwarts the bridegroom's plan to abduct his bride; all it takes to transform two lives are those icy crystals whirling around them at the wrong time. Then, in 1842, comes Nikolai Gogol's "The Overcoat," the story of a poor clerk splurging on a luxurious winter coat only to be robbed of it after he shows it off for the first time – yes, during a blizzard. From then on, as amply demonstrated in the stories gathered in this volume, Russian literature could be described as an unendingly beautiful – sometimes blissful, sometimes tragic – encounter with the chaos of the storm, whether on one-horse sleighs, in elegant troikas, on trains and in black limousines, on foot or inside someone's head.

In 2010, Vladimir Sorokin, one of modern Russia's most resonant literary voices, dedicated an entire novel, *The Blizzard*, to a surreal sleigh ride through an unrelenting snowstorm that is, at the same time, a phantasmagoric trip through the history of Russian literature. The stakes couldn't be higher: if Sorokin's Dr. Garin can't make it through with a vaccine, a virus will turn everyone into zombies. Sorokin's award-winning novel is ideal further reading, but in this collection he is represented by "Start of the Season," a story from 1985 that charts the whirlwind of *perestroika*, the reforming of the Soviet Union that turned out to be the system's undoing.

Blizzards may be one of the most endearing, as well as enduring, features of Russian literature. Did anyone *not* fall in love with Russia during the poetic "frozen dacha" scene from Boris Pasternak's novel *Doctor Zhivago*, so irresistibly portrayed in David Lean's movie? The dacha was a winter palace for Zhivago and Lara, ready for romance but also for writing: the first drawer the good doctor opens reveals paper and frozen ink. Their love will thaw the ink, but the snow, backed by the storms of twentieth-century history, will determine the lovers' fate.

Naturally, not every personal upheaval in these stories is caused by weather. But in the way that American culture is unthinkable without the literature of "the road," blizzards are in the DNA of Russian literature. Even in a story like Tatyana Tolstaya's "Sweet Shura," in which an elderly woman recalls a long-lost lover over tea with a neighbor in a

8

stuffy, weather-free living room, a blizzard nevertheless intrudes. The hostess's prosaic question "More tea?" prompts the seemingly out-of-context thought: "A blizzard."

It may not be a coincidence that women writers, more than their male colleagues, focus on blizzards of the soul, of human passions and intentions. This collection features an unusually high number of women writers, including some who have been unjustly overlooked in the male-dominated Russian canon – Teffi, Nina Berberova, Marina Tsvetaeva – and some who emerged during the 1980s and 1990s to stand as tall as their male counterparts: Petrushevskaya, Tolstaya, Sadur, Palei, Ulitskaya.

It is only fitting to close this tour of great Russian writers with a female voice – one that also *collects* voices – Svetlana Alexievich, the Belarusian winner of the 2015 Nobel Prize in Literature. Technically, Alexievich's prose isn't fiction; she writes the stories of real people in what she calls the "genre of actual human voices and confessions." It is a genre that is both modern and deeply rooted in Russian oral tradition – called *skaz* in Russian – a genre elevated to literature by writers from Gogol to Petrushevskaya and Tolstaya. The "voice" chosen here from Alexievich's "Landscape of Loneliness: Three Voices" tells us about storms of love both hot and cold: "You can't live at that temperature. Delirious. In a dream."

But in great Russian stories you can. Just as Gogol's poor clerk met his heartbreaking fate, caused by unforgiving weather and an even more unforgiving society, "through the blizzard that whistled down the streets, blowing him off the sidewalks," so, too, do inner and outer storms drive the fates of our most beloved characters. Is there anything more honest and decent, more universally true, more touching and soul-nourishing than a great, classic Russian story? Yes, there is. A generous collection of them

More tea?

Blizzards.

Christoph Keller

ALEXANDER PUSHKIN

THE BLIZZARD

Translated by Paul Debreczeny

Over hillocks deep in snow
Speeding horses trample,
In a clearing off the road
Winks a lonely temple.
. . .

All at once a blizzard flings
Drifts across the way,
And a wheeling raven's wings
Rasp above the sleigh.
Sorrow spell the gusty wails,
And the hasting horses
Scan the darkness, manes and tails
Bristling in their courses . . .

ZHUKOVSKII

TOWARD THE END OF THE YEAR 1811 – a memorable time
for us – there lived in his own village of Nenaradovo a good
man called Gavrila Gavrilovich R. He was renowned
throughout the region for his hospitality and cordiality:
neighbors came to his house all the time, some to eat and
drink well, others to play Boston for five-kopeck stakes with
his wife, Praskovia Petrovna, and still others to see the
couple's daughter, Maria Gavrilovna, a slender and pale girl
of seventeen. She was considered a good match, and quite a
few men marked her out either for themselves or for their
sons.

13

Maria Gavrilovna had been brought up on French novels and was consequently in love. The object she had chosen for her affections was a penniless sublieutenant of infantry, who at the time was staying in his village on a furlough. It goes without saying that the young man was aflame with an equal passion, and that the parents of his beloved, as soon as they noticed the young couple's mutual inclinations, forbade their daughter even to think about him. They began receiving him at their home with less kindness than they would have shown a retired assessor.

Our lovers were engaged in correspondence, and they met alone every day either in the pine grove or by the ancient chapel. There they swore eternal love for each other, lamented their fate, and discussed different possible courses of action. As a result of such correspondence and meetings, they arrived (which was quite natural) at the following consideration: if we cannot breathe without each other, yet the will of cruel parents stands in the way of our happiness, should we not disregard that will? It is easy to guess that this felicitous idea occurred to the young man first and was then heartily embraced by Maria Gavrilovna's romantic imagination.

Winter set in and put a stop to the young couple's meetings; their correspondence, on the other hand, grew all the more lively. Vladimir Nikolaevich entreated Maria Gavrilovna in each letter to give herself to him and wed him in secret; they would remain in hiding for a while, then throw themselves at the feet of her parents, who of course would at last be moved by the lovers' heroic constancy and unhappy state and would inevitably say, "Children! Come to our bosoms!"

Maria Gavrilovna hesitated for a long while; many a plan for elopement was rejected. At last she gave her consent: on an appointed day she was to miss supper and retire to her room on the pretext of a headache. Her maid was in collusion with her; they were both to go into the garden by way of the back porch, find the sleigh waiting for them behind the garden, get in and ride five versts from Nenaradovo to the village of Zhadrino, and once there, go straight to the church, where Vladimir would be expecting them.

The night before the decisive day Maria Gavrilovna could not sleep a wink; she packed, tied up her linen and clothes into bundles, wrote a long letter to a friend – a sentimental young lady – and another one to her parents. She took leave of them in the most touching terms, excused her act by the irresistible force of her passion, and concluded with the assertion that it would be the happiest moment of her life if she were allowed to throw herself at the feet of her dearest parents. Having sealed both letters with a seal from Tula that showed two flaming hearts with an appropriate inscription, she threw herself on her bed just before dawn and dozed off, but terrible dreams kept waking her even then. At first she fancied that just as she was getting into the sleigh to ride to her wedding, her father stopped her, dragged her across the snow with excruciating speed, and threw her into a bottomless pit ... She was falling headlong with indescribable palpitations of the heart ... Then she saw Vladimir lying in the grass pale and bloodied. Dying, he begged her in a piercing voice to hurry up and marry him ... Still other visions, equally hideous and absurd, flitted before her in quick succession. At last she got up, paler than usual and with a genuine headache. Her father and mother noticed her anxious state; their tender solicitude and never-ending questions – "What's the matter with you, Masha?" "Are you ill, Masha?" – lacerated her heart. She tried to reassure them, tried to appear happy, but could not. Evening came. The thought that she was spending her last day in the midst of her family weighed on her heart. She was more dead than alive; in her mind she was saying good-bye to all the people and objects surrounding her. Supper was served: her heart began to beat violently. She declared in a trembling voice that she did not feel like eating supper, and wished her father and mother good night. They kissed her and, as usual, blessed her, which almost made her cry. On reaching her room, she threw herself in an armchair and burst into a flood of tears. Her maid pleaded with her to calm herself and summon up her courage. Everything was ready. In another half hour Masha was to leave forever her parents' home, the tranquil life of a maiden ... Outside a blizzard was whirling; the wind howled, the shutters shook and rattled; all of which seemed a threat and a bad omen to her. The house soon grew quiet: everybody was asleep. Masha wrapped herself in a shawl, put on a warm coat, picked up her bandbox, and went out on the back porch. The maid came after her, carrying two bundles. They descended into the garden. The blizzard was not letting up; the wind met Masha head-on as if trying to stop the young malefactress. They could hardly reach the other end of the garden. The sleigh was waiting for them on the road. The horses, frozen through, could not stand still; Vladimir's coachman walked up and down in front of the shafts of the sleigh trying to restrain the restless animals. He helped the young lady and her maid climb in and find room for the two bundles and the box, then he took the reins, and the horses dashed off. But let us entrust the young lady to her lucky stars and to the skill of Tereshka the coachman, while we turn our attention to our young paramour.

Vladimir had been on the road all day. In the morning he went to see the priest at Zhadrino and could just barely prevail on him; then he went in search of potential witnesses among the landowners of the neighborhood. The first one he called on, a forty-year-old retired cavalry officer by the name of Dravin, consented with pleasure. This adventure, he kept saying, reminded him of his earlier days and his pranks in the hussars. He persuaded Vladimir to stay for dinner, assuring him that finding two more witnesses would be no problem at all. Indeed a land surveyor named Schmitt, wearing mustachios and spurs, and the son of the police superintendent, a boy of sixteen who had recently joined the uhlans, appeared on the scene right after dinner. Not only did they accede to Vladimir's request, but they even swore they would sacrifice their lives for him. Vladimir embraced them with fervor and went home to get ready.

It was already quite dark. He sent his reliable Tereshka to Nenaradovo with his troika and with detailed, thorough instructions. For himself he had a small one-horse sleigh harnessed, and set out alone, without a driver, for Zhadrino, where Maria Gavrilovna was due to arrive in another couple of hours. He knew the road well, and it was only a twenty-minute ride.

But no sooner had he left the village behind and entered the fields than the wind rose, and such a blizzard developed that he could not see anything. In one minute the road was covered over; the surrounding landscape disappeared in a thick yellowish mist driven through with white flakes of snow; the sky merged with the earth. Vladimir found himself in the middle of a field, and his attempts to get back on the road were all in vain. The horse trod at random, now clambering up a pile of snow, now tumbling into a ditch; the sleigh kept turning over; all Vladimir could do was to try not to lose the right direction. It seemed to him, however, that more than half an hour had passed, yet he had still not reached the Zhadrino woods. Another ten minutes or so went by, but the woods still did not come within his view.

He rode across a field intersected by deep gullies. The blizzard would not let up; the sky would not clear. The horse began to get tired, and Vladimir perspired profusely, even though he kept sinking into the snow up to his waist.

At last Vladimir realized he was going in the wrong direction. He stopped, began to think, to recollect, to consider, and became convinced that he should have turned to the right. He started off to the right. His horse could hardly move. He had already been on the road for over an hour. Zhadrino should not have been very far. Yet though he rode on and on, there was no end to the open country. Snowdrifts and gullies at every step; the sleigh kept turning over; he had to lift it upright every minute. The time was passing; he began to worry in earnest.

At last something dark came into his view on one side. He turned toward it. Coming closer, he could make out a wood. Thank God, he thought, I am close now. He drove along the edge of the wood, hoping presently to meet the familiar road, or else to go around the wood and find Zhadrino right behind it. He soon found the road and advanced into the darkness under the trees bared by winter. Here the wind could not blow quite so fiercely; the road was even; the horse perked up, and Vladimir felt reassured.

He rode on and on, however, yet there was no sign of Zhadrino; nor was there an end to the woods. He realized with horror that he had driven into an unfamiliar forest. Despair took possession of him. He whipped the horse; the poor animal tried to break into a trot but soon gave in to fatigue, and within a quarter of an hour slowed down to a snail's pace despite every effort on the part of the unfortunate Vladimir.

Gradually the trees thinned out, and Vladimir emerged

from the forest, but there was still no sign of Zhadrino. It must have been around midnight. Tears gushed from his eyes; he drove forward haphazardly. The weather had by now grown calm, the clouds were breaking up, and a broad, flat field, covered with a white undulating carpet, stretched out before Vladimir. The night was quite clear. A short distance away Vladimir saw a hamlet consisting of four or five houses. He rode up to it. At the first hut he jumped out of the sleigh, ran up to the window, and started knocking. In a few minutes the wooden shutter opened and an old man thrust his gray beard out of the window.

"What d'ya want?"

"Is Zhadrino far from here?"

"If Zhadrino's far?"

"Yes, yes. Is it far?"

"Not that far; it'll be ten versts or thereabouts."

Hearing this answer, Vladimir clutched his head and remained motionless like a man condemned to die.

"And where would you be coming from?" continued the old man.

Vladimir was not in a state to answer questions.

"Listen, old man," he said, "can you procure some horses that will take me to Zhadrino?"

"Horses, here?"

"Could I at least take a guide with me? I will pay him as much as he wants."

"Wait," said the old man, letting the shutter down. "I'll send my son out. He'll show you the way."

Vladimir waited a little, but scarcely a minute had gone by when he started knocking again. The shutter was raised, and the beard came in view.

"What d'ya want?"

"What about your son?"

"He'll be out in a minute. Tying up his shoes. You're frozen, I trow; come inside to warm up."

"No, thank you, just send your son out as soon as possible."

The gate creaked; a lad came out with a cudgel in his hand; he went ahead of Vladimir, either leading him along the road or searching for it where it was covered by snowdrifts.

"What is the time?" Vladimir asked him.

"It'll soon be getting light," answered the young peasant. Vladimir no longer said anything.

The cocks were crowing, and it was already daylight by the time they reached Zhadrino. The church was locked. Vladimir paid his guide and drove to the priest's house. His troika was not in the courtyard. What news awaited him!

But let us return to the good proprietors of Nenaradovo and take a look: what might be happening at their house?

Well, nothing.

The old couple woke up and came down to the living room. Gavrila Gavrilovich wore his nightcap and a flannel jacket, Praskovia Petrovna was in her quilted dressing gown. The samovar was lit, and Gavrila Gavrilovich sent a little handmaid to find out how Maria Gavrilovna felt and whether she had slept well. The little girl came back with the answer that the young mistress had slept badly but was by now feeling better and, so please Your Honor, would soon come down to the living room. Indeed, the door opened, and Maria Gavrilovna came up to her papa and mama in turn to wish them good morning.

"How's your head, Masha?" asked Gavrila Gavrilovich.

"It's better, papa," answered Masha.

"It must have been the fumes from the stove that made you feel poorly last night," said Praskovia Petrovna.

"It may have been," answered Masha.

The day passed without any incident, but during the night Masha fell ill. They went to town for the doctor. He arrived toward evening and found the invalid in a state of delirium. A high fever had developed, and the poor girl hovered on the brink of the grave for two weeks.

Nobody in the household knew about the intended elopement. The letters Masha had written the night before were burned, and her maid, fearing the anger of her masters, did not breathe a word to anybody. The priest, the retired officer, the mustachioed land surveyor, and the juvenile uhlan were all discreet, and for good reason. Tereshka the coachman never used an extra word, even in his cups. Thus the secret was kept by more than half a dozen conspirators. It was only Maria Gavrilovna who revealed her secret in her continual state of delirium. Her words, however, were so incongruous that her mother, who never for a moment left her bedside, could make out only that Masha was fatally in love with Vladimir Nikolaevich, and that her love was probably the cause of her illness. She consulted her husband and some neighbors, and they all came to the unanimous conclusion that this was evidently Masha's destiny, that marriages were made in heaven, that poverty was no shame, that you have to live with the man, not with his money, and so forth. Moral maxims are surprisingly useful on occasions when we can invent little else to justify our actions.

In the meanwhile the young lady began to get better. Vladimir had not been seen at Gavrila Gavrilovich's house for a long time. He was afraid of getting the usual reception. They decided to send for him and notify him of his unexpected luck – their consent to his marriage to Masha. How immensely astonished were the proprietors of Nenaradovo, however, when in answer to their invitation they received a half-insane letter from him! He declared he would never set foot in their house again and asked them to forget the unhappy man for whom death was the only remaining hope In a few days they learned that he had returned to the army. This was in the year 1812.

For a long time they did not dare give the news to the convalescent Masha. She never mentioned Vladimir. She did faint, a few months later, when she saw his name on a list of those who had distinguished themselves and been severely wounded at Borodino, and it was feared that her fever might return, but, thank God, her fainting had no consequences.

Another grief was visited on her; Gavrila Gavrilovich died, leaving his whole fortune to her as his sole heiress. Her inheritance did not console her; she sincerely shared poor Praskovia Petrovna's grief and vowed never to part with her; together they left Nenaradovo, the scene of so many sad memories, and settled on an estate in N. Guberniia.

Here, too, eligible young men came whirling around the charming rich maiden, but she did not give the slightest encouragement to any of them. Her mother would try on occasion to persuade her to make a choice, but Maria Gavrilovna would only shake her head and grow pensive. By this time Vladimir was not among the living: he had died in Moscow on the eve of its occupation by the French. His memory seemed to be sacred to Masha; at least she faithfully kept everything that could remind her of him – books he had read at one time, his drawings, the music or poetry he had copied out for her. The neighbors, hearing all about it, wondered at her constancy and awaited with curiosity the appearance of the hero who would eventually triumph over the sad fidelity of this virginal Artemisia.

Meanwhile, the war had come to a glorious end. Our regiments were returning from abroad. Crowds rushed out to meet them on the way. The bands were playing songs captured in the war: "Vive Henri Quatre," Tyrolean waltzes, and arias from *Joconde*. Officers who had left for the campaign almost as adolescents were returning as men seasoned in war and decorated with crosses all over their chests. Soldiers chatted gaily, constantly mixing German and French words into their speech. Unforgettable time! A time of glory and ecstasy! How mightily beat the Russian heart at the word Fatherland! How sweet were the tears of reunion! How unanimously did we ally our feeling of national pride with our love for the Emperor! And what a moment it was for him!

The women, Russian women, were inimitable then. Their usual coldness disappeared. Their enthusiasm was truly intoxicating when they met the victors, shouted "hurray!"

And tossed their caps into the air.

Who, among the officers of the time, will deny that he was indebted to Russian womanhood for the best, most precious reward he had ever received?

Maria Gavrilovna and her mother lived through these glorious days in N. Guberniia and did not witness how the two capitals celebrated the return of the troops. But the general enthusiasm was possibly even greater in the provincial towns and villages. Arriving in one of these places was a veritable triumph for an officer; and a lover in a frock coat fared poorly in his vicinity.

We have already mentioned that her coldness notwithstanding, Maria Gavrilovna was surrounded by suitors as before. All had to give up, however, when a wounded hussar colonel called Burmin – with the St. George Cross in his buttonhole and an *interesting pallor* on his face, as young ladies of the time used to say – presented himself at the manor house. He was about twenty-six. He came to spend his furlough on his estate, adjacent to Maria Gavrilovna's village. Maria Gavrilovna bestowed special attention on him. In his presence her mood, usually pensive, grew lively. You could not say she was flirting with him, but a poet observing her demeanor with him would have said:

Se amor non e, che dunque?

Burmin was indeed a very appealing young man. His mind was just the kind women like: it was a mind at once delicate and observant, without the slightest pretensions, and with a penchant for light-hearted banter. His mien with Maria Gavrilovna was simple and free; he followed with his eyes and all his feelings whatever she said or did. He seemed to be of a quiet and modest disposition, but the gossips insisted that in his earlier days he had been a frightful rake, which actually did not lower him in Maria Gavrilovna's opinion because she (like almost all young ladies) readily excused mischiefs that revealed a daring and ardent nature.

But the aspect of the young hussar's behavior that piqued her curiosity and imagination more than anything else (more than his tenderness, his pleasant conversation, his interesting pallor and bandaged arm) was his failure to declare himself. She could not help recognizing that he liked her very much; it was likely that he too, with his intelligence and experience, had noticed the special attention she was giving him: why then had she still not seen him at her feet, why had she still not heard his confession? What held him back? Was it shyness, inseparable from true love, or pride, or the flirtatiousness of a wily skirt chaser? It was a puzzle to her. Having thoroughly considered the matter, she decided that shyness was the sole cause of his silence, and she resolved to encourage him by more attention and – if circumstances so demanded – perhaps even by tenderness. She was setting the stage for the most unexpected denouement and impatiently awaited the moment of romantic explanation. A secret, of whatever kind it might be, is always hard for a female heart to bear. Her maneuvers achieved the desired effect: at least Burmin fell into such reveries and his dark eyes came to rest on Maria Gavrilovna with such ardency that the decisive moment seemed to be near. The neighbors talked about the wedding as a matter already settled, and the good Praskovia Petrovna rejoiced over her daughter's having at last found a worthy suitor.

One day the old lady was sitting in the living room playing solitaire when Burmin came in and immediately asked after Maria Gavrilovna.

"She is in the garden," answered the old lady. "Go and join her; I'll wait for you here."

Burmin went out, and the old lady made the sign of the cross, saying to herself: God willing the matter will be settled today!

Burmin found Maria Gavrilovna by the pond, under a willow tree, with a book in her hands and in a white dress – a veritable heroine out of a novel. After the initial exchange of questions, Maria Gavrilovna deliberately failed to keep up the conversation, thereby heightening the mutual embarrassment from which the only escape was a sudden and decisive declaration. And indeed Burmin, feeling the awkwardness of his situation, announced that he had long been seeking an opportunity to open his heart to her, and requested a moment's attention. Maria Gavrilovna closed her book and cast her eyes down as a sign of consent.

"I love you," said Burmin. "I love you passionately." Maria Gavrilovna blushed and lowered her head even further. "It has been imprudent of me to indulge in the enchanting habit of seeing you and listening to you daily . . ."

Maria Gavrilovna remembered St. Preux's first letter. "It is now too late to struggle against my fate; your memory, your dear incomparable image, will remain both the torment and the joy of my life; but I must still perform my painful duty of revealing a horrible secret to you and placing an insurmountable barrier between us."

"It has always been there," interrupted Maria Gavrilovna intensely; "I could never be your wife ..."

"I know," he answered softly, "I know you loved at one time, but death and three years of grieving ... Dear, kind Maria Gavrilovna, don't try to deprive me of my last solace, the thought that you would have agreed to make me happy, if ... Keep silent, for heaven's sake, keep silent. You are lacerating my heart. Yes, I know, I sense, that you would have been mine, but I am the most unhappy creature ... I am married!"

Maria Gavrilovna looked at him in astonishment.

"I am married," continued Burmin. "I have been married for close to four years and I don't know who my wife is, where she is, and whether I am ever to meet her!"

"What are you saying?" exclaimed Maria Gavrilovna. "How strange this is! But continue; I'll tell you afterwards ... please continue."

"At the beginning of 1812," related Burmin, "I was hurrying to Vilno, where my regiment was stationed. Late one evening I came to a post station and was about to have fresh horses harnessed when a terrific blizzard blew up; both the stationmaster and the drivers advised me to stay until it passed over. I followed their advice, but an inexplicable restlessness took hold of me; it was almost as if somebody was pressing me forward. Although the blizzard had not abated, I could not wait any longer: I had the horses harnessed again and rode off straight into the storm. The driver took it into his head to go on the ice of a river, which was supposed to shorten our route by three versts. The banks were piled high with snow, and the driver missed the point where one could get back on the road; we ended up in an unfamiliar place. The storm was not letting up; I saw a faint light and ordered the driver to head for it. We entered a village; the light came from the wooden church. The church was open; several sleighs stood behind the fence; people were going up and down the porch.

" 'Here! Here!' shouted several voices. I told the driver to drive up to them.

" 'For God's sake, where have you been?' somebody said to me. 'Your bride has fainted, the priest doesn't know what to do; we were just about ready to go back home. Get out quickly.'

"I jumped out of the sleigh without a word and entered the church, which was dimly lit by two or three candles. A girl was sitting on a bench in a dark corner of the church; another one was rubbing her temples.

" 'Thank God,' said the second one, 'you have at last arrived. You've nearly killed the young mistress.'

"The old priest came up to me with the question, 'Do you wish me to begin?'

" 'Yes, do, Father, by all means do,' I answered absently.

"They lifted up the girl. She seemed quite pretty to me . . . Inexplicable, unexcusable recklessness . . . I stood by her before the lectern; the priest was in a hurry; the three men and the maid supported the bride and were busy only with her. We were married.

" 'Kiss each other,' we were told.

"My wife turned her pale face toward me. I wanted to kiss her . . . She shrieked, 'Oh, that's not him! It's not him,' and collapsed unconscious.

"The witnesses fixed their frightened eyes on me. I turned around, left the church without the slightest hindrance, flung myself into the sleigh and yelled out 'Go!'

"Good heavens!" exclaimed Maria Gavrilovna, "and you don't know what's become of your poor wife?"

"No, I don't," answered Burmin. "I don't know the name of the village where I was married, I don't remember which post station I had been coming from. At the time I attached so little importance to my wicked prank that, since I left the church, I fell asleep and didn't wake up until the morning, when we were already at the third station. The orderly who was with me then died later in the war, and therefore I have no hope of finding her on whom I played such a cruel joke and who is now so cruelly avenged."

"Oh my God, oh my God," said Maria Gavrilovna, seizing his hand, "so it was you? And you don't recognize me?"

Burmin blanched and threw himself at her feet . . .

1830

MIKHAIL LERMONTOV

THE FATALIST

Translated by Vladimir and Dmitri Nabokov

I ONCE happened to spend two weeks at a Cossack settlement on our left flank. An infantry battalion was also stationed there and officers used to assemble at each other's quarters in turn, and play cards in the evening.

On one occasion, having tired of boston and thrown the cards under the table, we sat on for a very long time at Major S—'s place. The talk, contrary to custom, was entertaining. We discussed the fact that the Moslem belief in a man's fate being written in heaven finds also among us Christians many adherents; each related various unusual occurrences in proof or refutation.

"All this does not prove anything, gentlemen," said the elderly major. "I take it, none of you witnessed the strange cases with which you corroborate your opinions?"

"None, of course," said several, "but we heard it from reliable people. . .."

"It is all humbug!" said someone. "Where are those reliable people who have seen the scroll where the hour of our death is assigned? And if predestination actually exists, why then are we given free will and reason, and why must we account for our actions?"

At this moment, an officer who had been sitting in a corner of the room got up and, slowly coming up to the table, surveyed all present with a calm and solemn gaze. He was of Serbian origin, as was apparent from his name.

Lieutenant Vulich's looks corresponded perfectly to his

nature. A tall stature, a swarthy complexion, black hair, black piercing eyes, a large but regular nose, characteristic of his nation, and a sad chill smile perpetually wandering on his lips – all this seemed to blend in such a way as to endow him with the air of a special being, incapable of sharing thoughts and passions with those whom fate had given him for companions.

He was brave, spoke little but trenchantly; confided in none the secrets of his soul or of his family; drank almost no wine; never courted the Cossack girls (whose charm is hard to imagine for those who have never seen them). It was said, however, that the colonel's wife was not indifferent to his expressive eyes; but he would get seriously annoyed when one hinted at it.

There was only one passion of which he made no secret – the gaming passion. Once seated at the green table, he forgot everything, and usually lost; but continuous bad luck only served to exasperate his obstinacy. It was rumoured that, one night, while on active duty, he dealt out the cards at stuss on his pillow; he was having formidable luck. All of a sudden, shots were heard, the alarm was sounded, there was a general scamper for weapons. "Set your stake for the whole bank," cried Vulich, without rising, to one of the keenest punters. "All right, I set it upon a seven," answered the other, as he rushed off. Despite the general confusion, Vulich went on dealing all alone, and the seven came up for the punter.

When he reached the front line, the firing there was already intensive. Vulic paid no attention either to the bullets or the swords of the Chechens: he was in search of his fortunate punter. "The seven turned up on your side," he shouted on seeing him at last in the firing line, which was beginning to force the enemy out of the forest, and, on coming closer, took out his purse and his wallet and handed them to the lucky gamester, despite the latter's protest that this was not an appropriate place for payment. Upon acquitting himself of this unpleasant duty, he dashed forward, carrying the soldiers with him, and most coolly kept exchanging shots with the Chechens to the end of the engagement.

When Lieutenant Vulich approached the table, everybody fell silent, expecting some eccentric stunt from him.

"Gentlemen!" he said (his voice was quiet though a tone below his usual pitch). "Gentlemen, what is the use of empty arguments? You want proofs? I offer you to try out on me whether a man may dispose of his life at will or a fateful minute is assigned to each of us in advance ... Who is willing?"

"Not I, not I," came from every side. "What an odd fellow! Who would think of such a thing! ..."

"I offer you a wager," I said in jest.

"What kind of wager?"

"I affirm that there is no predestination," I said, pouring on to the table a score of gold coins – all there was in my pocket.

"I accept," answered Vulich in a toneless voice. "Major, you will be umpire. Here are fifteen gold pieces. The other five you owe me, and you would do me a favour by adding them to the rest."

"All right," said the major, "but I don't understand, what is it all about? How are you going to settle the argument?"

Vulich without a word walked into the major's bedroom: we followed him. He went to the wall where there hung some weapons, and among pistols of various calibre, he, at random, took one down from its nail. We still failed to understand, but when he cocked it and poured powder into the pan, several officers, with involuntary exclamations, seized him by the arms.

"What do you want to do? Look here, this is madness!" they cried to him.

"Gentlemen," he said slowly, freeing his arms, "who is willing to pay twenty gold pieces for me?"

All were silent and stepped aside.

Vulich went to the other room and sat down at the table: we all followed him there. With a sign he invited us to take seats around him. He was obeyed in silence: at that moment, he had acquired some mysterious power over us. I looked fixedly into his eyes, but he countered my probing glance with a calm and steady gaze, and his pale lips smiled; but despite his coolness, I seemed to decipher the imprint of death upon his pale face. I had observed – and many a seasoned warrior had confirmed this observation of mine – that often the face of a man who is to die within a few hours bears the strange imprint of his imminent fate, so that an experienced eye can hardly mistake it.

"Tonight you will die," I said to him. He turned to me quickly, but answered slowly and calmly.

"Maybe yes, maybe no . . ." Then, addressing himself to the major, he asked: "Is there a ball in the pistol?" The major, in his confusion, could not remember properly.

"Oh come, Vulich," somebody exclaimed, "surely it's loaded if it was hanging at the head of the bed. Stop fooling!"

"A foolish joke!" another joined in.

"I'll bet you fifty roubles to five that the pistol is not loaded!" cried a third.

New bets were made.

I became bored with this long procedure. "Listen," I said, "either shoot yourself or hang the pistol back in its place and let's go home to bed."

"That's right," many exclaimed, "let's go back to bed."

"Gentlemen, please stay where you are!" said Vulich applying the muzzle of the pistol to his forehead.

Everybody sat petrified.

"Mr Pechorin," he added, "take a card and throw it up into the air."

I took from the table what I vividly remember turned out to be the ace of hearts and threw it upwards. Everyone held his breath; all eyes, expressing fear and a kind of vague curiosity, switched back and forth from the pistol to the fateful ace which quivered in the air and slowly came down. The moment it touched the table, Vulich pulled the trigger . . . the pistol snapped!

"Thank God!" many cried. "It was not loaded . . ."

"Let's take a look, anyway," said Vulich. He cocked the pistol again, took aim at a cap that was hanging above the window. A shot resounded – smoke filled the room. When it dispersed, the cap was taken down. It had been shot clean through the middle, and the bullet had lodged deep in the wall.

For some three minutes, no one was able to utter a word. With perfect composure, Vulich transferred my gold pieces into his purse.

A discussion arose as to why the pistol had missed fire the first time. Some maintained that the pan must have been clogged; others said in a whisper that at first the powder must have been damp and that afterwards Vulich added some fresh powder; but I affirmed that this last supposition was wrong because I had never taken my eyes off the pistol.

"You're a lucky gambler!" I said to Vulich.

"For the first time in my life," he answered, smiling complacently. "This is better than faro or stuss."

"But then, it's a bit more dangerous."

"Bye-the-bye, have you begun to believe in pre-destination?"

"I believe in it, but I cannot understand now why it seemed to me that you must certainly die tonight."

This very man, who only a moment before had calmly aimed a pistol at his own forehead, now suddenly flushed and looked flustered.

"Well, enough of this!" he said, rising up. "Our bet has been settled, and I think your remarks are out of place now." He took his cap and left. This appeared odd to me – and not without reason.

Soon after, everyone went home – commenting variously upon Vulich's vagaries, and probably, in unison, calling me an egoist for having made a bet against a man who was going to shoot himself, as if without me he would not be able to find a convenient occasion! . . .

I was walking home along the empty alleys of the settlement. The moon, full and red, like the glow of a conflagration, began to appear from behind the uneven line of roofs; the stars shone calmly upon the dark-blue vault, and it amused me to recall that, once upon a time, there were sages who thought that the heavenly bodies took part in our trivial conflicts for some piece of land or some imaginary rights. And what happened? These lampads, lit, in the opinion of those sages, merely to illumine their battles and festivals, were burning as brightly as ever, while their passions and hopes had long been extinguished with them, like a small fire lit on the edge of the forest by a carefree wayfarer! But on the other hand, what strength of will they derived from the certitude that the entire sky with its countless inhabitants was looking upon them with mute but permanent sympathy! Whereas we, their miserable descendants, who roam the earth without convictions or pride, without rapture or fear

36

(except for that instinctive dread that compresses our hearts at the thought of the inevitable end), we are no longer capable of great sacrifice, neither for the good of mankind, nor even for our own happiness, because we know its impossibility, and pass with indifference from doubt to doubt, just as our ancestors rushed from one delusion to another. But we, however, do not have either their hopes or even that indefinite, albeit real, rapture that the soul encounters in any struggle with men or with fate.

And many other, similar, thoughts passed through my mind. I did not detain them, since I do not care to concentrate on any abstract thought; and, indeed, what does it lead to? In my early youth, I was a dreamer; I liked to fondle images, gloomy or iridescent by turn, that my restless and avid imagination pictured to me. But what was left me of it? Nothing but weariness, as from a night battle with a phantom, and a vague memory full of regrets. In this vain struggle, I exhausted the ardency of soul and the endurance of will, indispensable for real life. I entered that life after having already lived it through in my mind, and I became bored and disgusted, like one who would read a poor imitation of a book that he has long known.

The event of the evening had made a rather deep impression upon me and had irritated my nerves. I do not know for certain if I now believe in predestination or not, but that night I firmly believed in it: the proof was overwhelming, and despite my laughing at our ancestors and their obliging astrology, I had involuntarily slipped into their tracks. But I stopped myself in time on this dangerous path; and as I have, for rule, never to reject anything decisively, nor trust blindly in anything, I brushed metaphysics aside and began to look under my feet. Such a precaution proved much to the point: I very nearly fell, having stumbled over something fat and

37

soft, but apparently inanimate. Down I bent. The moon now shone right upon the road – and what did I see? Before me lay a pig, slashed in two by a sword. Hardly had I time to inspect it, when I heard the sound of footfalls. Two Cossacks came running out of a lane; one of them came up to me and asked if I had not seen a drunken Cossack chasing a pig. I informed them that I had not encountered the Cossack, and pointed to the unfortunate victim of his frenzied valour.

"The rascal!" said the second Cossack. "Every time he drinks his fill of *chihir'*, there he goes cutting up everything that comes his way. Let's go after him, Eremeich; he must be tied, or else . . ."

They went off; I continued my way with more caution and, at length, reached my quarters safely.

I was living at the house of an old Cossack sergeant, whom I liked for his kindly disposition, and especially for his pretty young daughter, Nastya.

As was her custom, she was waiting for me at the wicket, wrapped up in her fur coat. The moon illumined her sweet lips, now blue with the cold of the night. On seeing it was I, she smiled; but I had other things on my mind. "Good night, Nastya!" I said, as I went by. She was on the point of answering something, but only sighed.

I closed the door of my room, lit a candle and threw myself on my bed; however, sleep made me wait for it longer than usual. The east was already beginning to pale when I fell asleep, but apparently it was written in heaven that I was not to get my fill of sleep that night. At four in the morning, two fists began to beat against my window. I jumped up: what was the matter? "Get up, get dressed!" shouted several voices. I dressed quickly and went out. "Do you know what's hap-pened?" said, with one voice, the three officers who had come to fetch me. They were as pale as death.

"What?"

"Vulich has been killed."

I was stupefied.

"Yes, killed," they continued. "Let's hurry."

"Where to?"

"You'll find out on the way."

Off we went. They told me all that had happened with an admixture of various remarks regarding the strange predestination which had saved him from inevitable death, half an hour before his death. Vulich had been walking alone in a dark street. The drunken Cossack, who had hacked up the pig, happened to pitch into him, and would, perhaps, have gone on without taking notice of him, had not Vulich stopped short and said: "Whom are you looking for, man?" "You!" answered the Cossack, striking him with his sword, and cutting him in two, from the shoulder almost down to the heart. The two Cossacks who had met me and who were on the lookout for the murderer, came along; they picked up the wounded officer, but he was already breathing his last and said only three words: "He was right!" I alone understood the obscure meaning of these words: they referred to me. I had unwittingly foretold the poor fellow's fate; my intuition had not betrayed me; I had really read upon his altered face, the imprint of his imminent end.

The assassin had locked himself up in an empty hut on the outskirts of the settlement: we proceeded thither. A great many women ran, wailing, in the same direction. Here and there, some belated Cossack rushed out into the street fastening on his dagger, and passed us at a run. The commotion was terrible.

When we finally got there, we saw a crowd surrounding the hut: its doors and shutters were locked from within. Officers and Cossacks were eagerly discussing the situation;

39

women were wailing, lamenting and keening. Among them I noticed at once the striking face of an old woman which expressed frantic despair. She sat on a thick log, her elbows propped on her knees and her hands supporting her head: it was the murderer's mother. Now and then her lips moved . . . Was it a prayer they whispered or a curse?

Meanwhile, some decision had to be taken, and the criminal seized. No one, however, ventured to be the first to take the plunge.

I walked up to the window and looked through a chink in the shutter. White-faced, he lay on the floor, holding a pistol in his right hand; a bloodstained sword lay beside him. His expressive eyes rolled dreadfully; at times he would start and clutch at his head as if vaguely recollecting the events of the night. I did not read strong determination in this restless gaze and asked the major why he did not order the Cossacks to break down the door and rush in, because it would be better to do it now than later when he would have fully regained his senses.

At this point an old Cossack captain went up to the door and called him by his name: the man responded.

"You've done wrong, friend Efimych," said the captain. "There's no way out except to submit."

"I will not submit!" replied the Cossack.

"Have fear of the Lord! Think, you're not a godless Chechen, but a decent Christian. Well, if sin has led you astray, there is nothing to be done; one can't avoid one's fate."

"I will not submit!" fiercely cried the Cossack, and one could hear the click of a cocked pistol.

"Hey, my good woman," said the captain to the old woman, "talk a bit to your son, maybe he'll listen to you . . . All this only angers God. And look, the gentlemen have been waiting for two hours now."

The old woman looked at him fixedly and shook her head.

"Vasily Petrovich," said the captain, going up to the major, "he will not surrender – I know him; and if we break the door open, he will kill many of our men. Hadn't you better give the order to shoot him? There is a wide crack in the shutter."

At that moment, an odd thought flashed through my mind. It occurred to me to test my fate as Vulich had.

"Wait," I said to the major, "I shall take him alive." Telling the captain to start a conversation with him and, having stationed three Cossacks at the door, ready to break it in and rush to my assistance at a given signal, I walked around the hut and went close to the fateful window. My heart beat violently.

"Hey you, cursed heathen!" the captain was yelling, "are you laughing at us? Or do you think we shall not be able to subdue you?" He began to knock on the door with all his might. My eye against the chink, I watched the movements of the Cossack who did not expect an attack from this side. Suddenly, I wrenched off the shutter and flung myself through the window, headfirst. A shot sounded above my very ear, a bullet tore off one of my epaulets; but the smoke that filled the room prevented my adversary from finding his sword which lay beside him. I seized him by the arms; the Cossacks burst in, and three minutes had not passed before the criminal was bound and removed under guard. The people dispersed. The officers kept congratulating me – and indeed, there was reason enough.

After all this, how, it would seem, can one escape becoming a fatalist? But then, how can a man know for certain whether or not he is really convinced of anything? And how often we mistake, for conviction, the deceit of our senses or an error of reasoning? I like to have doubts, about

41

everything: this inclination of the mind does not impinge upon resoluteness of character. On the contrary, as far as I am concerned, I always advance with greater courage when I do not know what awaits me. For nothing worse than death can ever occur; and from death there is no escape!

After my return to the fort, I related to Maksim Maksimych all that had happened to me and what I had witnessed, and I desired to know his opinion regarding predestination. At first, he did not understand the word but I explained it to him as best I could; and then he said significantly shaking his head:

"Yes, sir! this is, of course, a rather tricky matter! . . . However, those Asiatic pistol cocks often miss fire if they are not properly oiled or if you do not press hard enough with the finger. I must say, I also do not like Circassian rifles. Somehow, they don't seem to be suitable for the likes of us: the butt is so small you have to be careful not to get your nose burnt . . . But then, those swords they have – ah, they're really something!"

Then he added after some thought:

"Yes, I'm sorry for the poor fellow . . . Why the devil did he talk to a drunk at night! . . . However, this must have been what was assigned to him at his birth!"

Nothing more could I get out of him: he does not care, generally, for metaphysical discussions.

1840

NIKOLAI GOGOL

THE OVERCOAT

Translated by Richard Pevear and Larissa Volokhonsky

IN THE DEPARTMENT of . . . but it would be better not to say in which department. There is nothing more irascible than all these departments, regiments, offices – in short, all this officialdom. Nowadays every private individual considers the whole of society insulted in his person. They say a petition came quite recently from some police chief, I don't remember of what town, in which he states clearly that the government's decrees are perishing and his own sacred name is decidedly being taken in vain. And as proof he attached to his petition a most enormous tome of some novelistic work in which a police chief appears on every tenth page, in some places even in a totally drunken state. And so, to avoid any unpleasantness, it would be better to call the department in question *a certain department*. And so, *in a certain department there served a certain clerk*; a not very remarkable clerk, one might say – short, somewhat pockmarked, somewhat red-haired, even with a somewhat nearsighted look, slightly bald in front, with wrinkles on both cheeks and a complexion that is known as hemorrhoidal . . . No help for it! the Petersburg climate is to blame. As for his rank (for with us rank must be announced first of all), he was what is called an eternal titular councillor, at whom, as is known, all sorts of writers have abundantly sneered and jeered, having the praiseworthy custom of exerting themselves against those who can't bite. The clerk's last name was Bashmachkin. From the name itself one can already see that it once came from *bashmak*, or "shoe"; but when, at what time, and in what way it came from *bashmak* – none of that is known. His father, his grandfather, even his brother in law, and absolutely all the Bashmachkins, went around in boots, merely having them resoled three times a year. His name was Akaky Akaki-evich. The reader will perhaps find that somewhat strange and far-fetched, but he can be assured that it was not fetched at all, but that such circumstances occurred of themselves as made it quite impossible to give him any other name, and here is precisely how it came about.

Akaky Akakievich was born, if memory serves me, during the night of the twenty-third of March. His late mother, a clerk's widow and a very good woman, decided, as was fitting, to have the baby baptized. The mother was still lying in bed opposite the door, and to her right stood the god-father, a most excellent man, Ivan Ivanovich Yeroshkin, who served as a chief clerk in the Senate, and the godmother, the wife of a police officer, a woman of rare virtue, Anna Semyonovna Belobriushkova. The new mother was offered a choice of any of three names, whichever she wished to choose: Mokky, Sossy, or to name the baby after the martyr Khozdazat. "No," thought the late woman, "what sort of names are those?" To please her, they opened the calendar to another place; again three names came out: Trifily, Dula, and Varakhasy. "What a punishment," the old woman said. "Such names, really, I've never heard the like. If only it were Varadat or Varukh, not Trifily and Varakhasy." They turned another page: out came Pavsikakhy and Vakhtisy. "Well, I see now," the old woman said, "it's evidently his fate. If so, better let him be named after his father. His father was Akaky, so let the son also be Akaky." Thus it was that Akaky Akakievich came about. As the child was being baptized, he cried and made such a face as if he anticipated that he would be a

46

titular councillor. And so, that is how it all came about. We have told it so that the reader could see for himself that it happened entirely from necessity and that to give him any other name was quite impossible.

When and at what time he entered the department and who appointed him, no one could recall. However many directors and other superiors came and went, he was always to be seen in one and the same place, in the same position, in the same capacity, as the same copying clerk, so that after a while they became convinced that he must simply have been born into the world ready-made, in a uniform, and with a balding head. In the department he was shown no respect at all. The caretakers not only did not rise from their places when he passed, but did not even look at him, as if a mere fly had flown through the reception room. His superiors treated him somehow with cold despotism. Some chief clerk's assistant simply shoved papers under his nose without even saying "Copy them," or "Here's a nice, interesting little case," or something pleasant, as is customary in well-bred offices. And he took them, looking only at the papers, without regarding the one who put them there or whether he had the right to do so. He took them and immediately settled down to copying them. The young clerks poked fun at him and cracked jokes, to the extent that office wit allowed; told right in front of him various stories they had made up about him, about his landlady, a seventy-year-old crone, saying that she beat him, asking when their wedding was to be, dumping torn-up paper over his head and calling it snow. But not one word of response came from Akaky Akakievich, as if no one was there; it did not even affect the work he did: amidst all this pestering, he made not a single error in his copy. Only when the joke was really unbearable, when they jostled his arm, interfering with what he was doing, would he say, "Let me be. Why do you offend me?" And there was something strange in the words and in the voice in which they were uttered. Something sounded in it so conducive to pity that one recently appointed young man who, following the example of the others, had first allowed himself to make fun of him, suddenly stopped as if transfixed, and from then on everything seemed changed before him and acquired a different look. Some unnatural power pushed him away from his comrades, whose acquaintance he had made thinking them decent, well-mannered men. And long afterwards, in moments of the greatest merriment, there would rise before him the figure of the little clerk with the balding brow, uttering his penetrating words: "Let me be. Why do you offend me?" – and in these penetrating words rang other words: "I am your brother." And the poor young man would bury his face in his hands, and many a time in his life he shuddered to see how much inhumanity there is in man, how much savage coarseness is concealed in refined, cultivated manners, and God! even in a man the world regards as noble and honorable . . .

It would hardly be possible to find a man who lived so much in his work. It is not enough to say he served zealously – no, he served with love. There, in that copying, he saw some varied and pleasant world of his own. Delight showed in his face; certain letters were his favorites, and when he came to one of them, he was beside himself: he chuckled and winked and helped out with his lips, so that it seemed one could read on his face every letter his pen traced. If his zeal had been rewarded correspondingly, he might, to his own amazement, have gone as far as state councillor; yet his reward, as his witty comrades put it, was a feather in his hat and hemorrhoids where he sat. However, it was impossible to say he went entirely unnoticed. One director, being a kindly man and wishing to reward him for long service, ordered that he be given something more important than the usual copying – namely, he was told to change an already existing document into a letter to another institution; the matter consisted merely in changing the heading and changing some verbs from first to third person. This was such a task for him that he got all in a sweat, rubbed his forehead, and finally said, "No, better let me copy something." After that he was left copying forever. Outside this copying nothing seemed to exist for him. He gave no thought to his clothes at all: his uniform was not green but of some mealy orange. The collar he wore was narrow, low, so that though his neck was not long, it looked extraordinarily long protruding from this collar, as with those head-wagging plaster kittens that foreign peddlers carry about by the dozen on their heads. And there was always something stuck to his uniform: a wisp of straw or a bit of thread; moreover, he had a special knack, as he walked in the street, of getting under a window at the precise moment when some sort of trash was being thrown out of it, and, as a result, he was eternally carrying around melon or watermelon rinds and other such rubbish on his hat. Not once in his life did he ever pay attention to what was going on or happening every day in the street, which, as is known, his young fellow clerk always looks at, his pert gaze so keen that he even notices when someone on the other side of the street has the footstrap of his trousers come undone – which always provokes a sly smile on his face.

But Akaky Akakievich, even if he looked at something, saw in everything his own neat lines, written in an even hand, and only when a horse's muzzle, coming out of nowhere, placed itself on his shoulder and blew real wind from its nostrils onto his cheek – only then would he notice that he was not in the middle of a line, but rather in the middle of the

49

street. Coming home, he would sit down straight away at the table, hastily slurp up his cabbage soup and eat a piece of beef with onions, without ever noticing their taste, and he would eat it all with flies and whatever else God sent him at the time. Noticing that his stomach was full, he would get up from the table, take out a bottle of ink, and copy documents he had brought home. If there chanced to be none, he made copies especially for his own pleasure, particularly if the document was distinguished not by the beauty of its style but by its being addressed to some new or important person.

Even in those hours when the gray Petersburg sky fades completely and all clerical folk have eaten their fill and finished dinner, each as he could, according to his salary and his personal fancy – when all have rested after the departmental scratching of pens, the rushing about seeing to their own and other people's needful occupations, and all that irrepressible man heaps voluntarily on himself even more than is necessary – when clerks hasten to give the remaining time to pleasure: the more ambitious rushing to the theater; another going out to devote it to gazing at silly hats; another to a party, to spend it paying compliments to some pretty girl, the star of a small clerical circle; still another, and this happens most often, simply going to his own kind, to some fourth or third floor, two small rooms with a front hall and a kitchen, with some claim to fashion, a lamp or other object that cost great sacrifices, the giving up of dinners, outings – in short, even at that time when all clerks disperse to their friends' small apartments to play cutthroat whist, sipping tea from glasses, with one-kopeck rusks, puffing smoke through long chibouks, repeating while the cards are being dealt some gossip blown over from high society, something a Russian man can never give up under any circumstances, or even, when there is nothing to talk about, retelling the eternal joke about the commandant who was brought word that the horse of Falconet's monument had had its tail docked – in short, even when everything strives for diversion – Akaky Akakievich did not give himself up to any diversion. No one could say he had ever been seen at any party. When he had written his fill, he would go to bed, smiling beforehand at the thought of the next day: What would God send him to copy tomorrow? So flowed the peaceful life of this man who, with a salary of four hundred, was able to content himself with his lot, and so it might have flowed on into extreme old age, had it not been for the various calamities strewn along the path of life, not only of titular, but even of privy, actual, court, and other councillors, even of those who neither give counsel nor take any themselves.

There exists in Petersburg a powerful enemy of all who earn a salary of four hundred roubles or thereabouts. This enemy is none other than our northern frost, though, incidentally, people say it is very healthful. Toward nine o'clock in the morning, precisely the hour when the streets are covered with people going to their offices, it starts dealing such strong and sharp flicks to all noses indiscriminately that the poor clerks decidedly do not know where to put them. At that time, when even those who occupy high positions have an ache in their foreheads from the cold and tears come to their eyes, poor titular councillors are sometimes defenseless. The whole of salvation consists in running as quickly as possible, in your skimpy overcoat, across five or six streets and then standing in the porter's lodge, stamping your feet good and hard, thereby thawing out all your job-performing gifts and abilities, which had become frozen on the way. Akaky Akakievich had for a certain time begun to feel that he was somehow getting it especially in the back and shoulder, though he tried to run across his allotted space as quickly as possible. He thought finally that the sin might perhaps lie with his overcoat. Examining it well at home, he discovered that in two or three places – namely, on the back and shoulders – it had become just like burlap; the broadcloth was so worn out that it was threadbare, and the lining had fallen to pieces. It should be known that Akaky Akakievich's overcoat also served as an object of mockery for the clerks; they even deprived it of the noble name of overcoat and called it a housecoat. Indeed, it was somehow strangely constituted: its collar diminished more and more each year, for it went to mend other parts. The mending did not testify to any skill in the tailor, and the results were in fact crude and unsightly. Seeing what the situation was, Akaky Akakievich decided that the overcoat had to be taken to Petrovich the tailor, who lived somewhere on a fourth floor, up a back entrance, and who, in spite of his blind eye and the pockmarks all over his face, performed the mending of clerkly and all other trousers and tailcoats quite successfully – to be sure, when he was sober and not entertaining any other projects in his head. Of this tailor, of course, not much should be said, but since there exists a rule that the character of every person in a story be well delineated, there's no help for it, let us have Petrovich here as well. In the beginning he was simply called Grigory and was some squire's serf; he began to be called Petrovich when he was freed and started drinking rather heavily on feast days – first on great feasts, and then on all church feasts indiscriminately, wherever a little cross appeared on the calendar. In this respect he was true to the customs of his forebears and, in arguing with his wife, used to call her a worldly woman and a German. Now that we've mentioned the wife, we ought to say a couple of words about her as well; but, unfortunately, not much is known about her, except that Petrovich had a wife, and that she even wore a bonnet, not a kerchief; but it seems she could not boast of her beauty; at least, when meeting her, only guardsmen looked under her bonnet, winking their mustaches and emitting some special noise.

Climbing the stairway leading to Petrovich, which, to do it justice, was all dressed with water and swill, and redolent throughout of that spiritous smell that makes the eyes smart and is inevitably present in all back stairways of Petersburg houses – climbing the stairway, Akaky Akakievich was thinking about how much Petrovich would ask, and mentally decided not to pay more than two roubles. The door was open, because the mistress of the house, while cooking fish, had filled the kitchen with so much smoke that even the cockroaches themselves could no longer be seen. Akaky Akakievich passed through the kitchen, unnoticed even by the mistress herself, and finally, went into the room, where he saw Petrovich sitting on a wide, unpainted wooden table, his legs tucked under him like a Turkish pasha's. His feet, after the custom of tailors sitting over their work, were bare. The eye was struck first of all by his big toe, very familiar to Akaky Akakievich, with a somehow disfigured nail, thick and strong as tortoise shell. From Petrovich's neck hung a skein of silk and thread, and on his knees lay some rag. He had already spent three minutes trying to put a thread through the eye of a needle and missing, and therefore he was very angry with the darkness and even with the thread itself, grumbling under his breath, "Won't go through, the barbarian! Get the better of me, you rascal!" Akaky Akakievich was upset that he had come precisely at a moment when Petrovich was angry: he liked dealing with Petrovich when the latter was already a bit under the influence, or, as his wife used to put it, "got himself tight on rotgut, the one-eyed devil." In that condition, Petrovich usually gave in and agreed very willingly, and even bowed and thanked him each time. Later, it's true, his wife would come, lamenting that her husband had been drunk and had asked too little; but a ten-kopeck piece would be added, and the deal was in the hat. Now, however, Petrovich seemed to be in a sober state, and therefore tough, intractable, and liable to demand devil knows what price. Akaky Akakievich grasped that fact and was, as they say, about to backtrack, but the thing was already under way. Petrovich squinted at him very intently with his only eye, and Akaky Akakievich involuntarily said:

"Good day, Petrovich!"

"Good day to you, sir," said Petrovich, and cocked his eye at Akaky Akakievich's hands, trying to see what sort of booty he was bringing.

"I've come to you, Petrovich, sort of . . ."

It should be known that Akaky Akakievich expressed himself mostly with prepositions, adverbs, and finally, such particles as have decidedly no meaning. If the matter was very difficult, he even had the habit of not finishing the phrase at all, so that very often he would begin his speech with the words "That, really, is altogether sort of . . ." after which would come nothing, and he himself would forget it, thinking everything had been said.

"What's this?" said Petrovich, at the same time giving his uniform a thorough inspection with his only eye, beginning with the collar, then the sleeves, back, skirts, and buttonholes – all of which was quite familiar to him, since it was his own handiwork. Such is the custom among tailors: it's the first thing they do when they meet someone.

"And I've come, Petrovich, sort of . . . this overcoat, the broadcloth . . . you see, in all other places it's quite strong, it got a bit dusty and so it seems as if it's old, but it's new, only in one place it's a bit sort of . . . on the back, and here on one shoulder it's a bit worn, and on this shoulder a little bit – you see, that's all. Not much work . . ."

Petrovich took the housecoat, laid it out on the table first, examined it for a long time, shook his head, and reached his hand out to the windowsill to get his round snuffbox with the portrait of some general on it – which one is not known, because the place where the face was had been poked through by a finger and then pasted over with a rectangular piece of paper. Having taken a pinch, Petrovich stretched the house-coat on his hands and examined it against the light and again shook his head. Then he turned it inside out and shook his head once more, once more opened the lid with the general pasted over with paper, and, having filled his nose with snuff, closed the box, put it away, and finally said:

"No, impossible to fix it – bad wardrobe."

At these words, Akaky Akakievich's heart missed a beat.

"Why impossible, Petrovich?" he said, almost in a child's pleading voice. "It's only a bit worn on the shoulders – surely you have some little scraps . . ."

"Little scraps might be found, we might find some little scraps," said Petrovich, "but it's impossible to sew them on – the stuff's quite rotten, touch it with a needle and it falls apart."

"Falls apart, and you patch it over."

"But there's nothing to put a patch on, nothing for it to hold to, it's too worn out. They pass it off as broadcloth, but the wind blows and it flies to pieces."

"Well, you can make it hold. Otherwise, really, it's sort of . . . !"

"No," Petrovich said resolutely, "it's impossible to do any-thing. The stuff's no good. You'd better make yourself foot cloths out of it when the winter cold comes, because socks don't keep you warm. It's Germans invented them so as to earn more money for themselves." (Petrovich liked needling the Germans on occasion.) "And it appears you'll have to have a new overcoat made."

At the word "new" all went dim in Akaky Akakievich's eyes, and everything in the room became tangled before him. The only thing he saw clearly was the general with paper pasted over his face who was on the lid of Petrovich's snuffbox.

"How's that – new?" he said, still as if in sleep. "I have no money for that."

"Yes, new," Petrovich said with barbaric calm.

"Well, if it must be a new one, what would it, sort of . . ."

"You mean, how much would it cost?"

"Yes."

"Three times fifty and then some would have to go into it," Petrovich said and pressed his lips together meaningfully. He very much liked strong effects, liked somehow to confound one completely all of a sudden and then glance sideways at the face the confounded one pulls at such words.

"A hundred and fifty roubles for an overcoat?" poor Akaky Akakievich cried out – cried out, perhaps, for the first time in all his born days, for he was always distinguished by the softness of his voice.

"Yes, sir," said Petrovich, "depending also on the overcoat. If we put a marten on the collar, plus a hood with silk lining, it may come to two hundred."

"Please, Petrovich," Akaky Akakievich said in a pleading voice, not hearing and not trying to hear all Petrovich's words and effects, "fix it somehow, so that it can serve a while longer at least."

"Ah, no, that'll be work gone for naught and money

wasted," said Petrovich, and after these words Akaky Akakievich left, totally annihilated.

And Petrovich, on his departure, stood for a long time, his lips pressed together meaningfully, without going back to work, feeling pleased that he had not lowered himself or betrayed the art of tailoring.

When he went outside, Akaky Akakievich was as if in a dream. "So it's that, that's what it is," he said to himself. "I really didn't think it would come out sort of . . ." and then, after some silence, he added, "So that's how it is! that's what finally comes out! and I really never would have supposed it would be so." Following that, a long silence again ensued, after which he said, "So that's it! Such an, indeed, altogether unexpected, sort of . . . it's altogether . . . such a circumstance!" Having said this, instead of going home, he went in the entirely opposite direction, without suspecting it himself. On the way, a chimney sweep brushed against him with his whole dirty flank, blackening his whole shoulder; a full hat-load of lime poured down on him from the top of a house under construction. He did not notice any of it, and only later, when he ran into an on-duty policeman who, having set aside his halberd, was shaking snuff from his snuff bottle onto his callused fist, only then did he recover his senses slightly, and that only because the policeman said, "What're you doing, barging into my mug! Don't you have enough sidewalk?" This made him look around and turn back home. Only here did he begin to collect his thoughts, see his situation clearly for what it was, and start talking to himself, not in snatches now but sensibly and frankly, as with a reasonable friend with whom one could discuss the most heartfelt and intimate things. "Ah, no," said Akaky Akakievich, "it's impossible to talk with Petrovich now: now he's sort of . . . his wife must somehow have given him a beating. I'll do better to come to him on Sunday morning: he'll be cockeyed and sleepy after Saturday night, and he'll need the hair of the dog, and his wife won't give him any money, and just then I'll sort of . . . ten kopecks in his hand, he'll be more tractable then, and then the overcoat sort of . . ." So Akaky Akakievich reasoned with himself, encouraged himself and waited for the next Sunday, when, seeing from afar Petrovich's wife leave the house for somewhere, he went straight to him. Petrovich was indeed badly cockeyed after Saturday, could hardly hold his head up, and was quite sleepy; but for all that, as soon as he learned what it was about, it was as if the devil gave him a nudge. "Impossible," he said, "be so good as to order a new one." Here Akaky Akakievich gave him a ten-kopeck piece. "Thank you, sir, I'll fortify myself a bit for your health," said Petrovich, "but concerning the overcoat, please don't trouble yourself – it's no good for anything good. I'll make you a new overcoat, I'll do it up famously, that I will."

Akaky Akakievich tried to mention mending again, but Petrovich did not listen to the end and said, "I'll make you a new one without fail, please count on me for that, I'll do my best. It may even be in today's fashion, the collar fastened by little silver clasps with appliqué."

Here Akaky Akakievich saw that he could not get around a new overcoat, and his spirits wilted completely. How, indeed, with what, with what money to make it? Of course, he could count partly on his future holiday bonus, but that money had been placed and distributed long ago. He needed to get new trousers, to pay an old debt to the shoemaker for putting new vamps on his old boot tops, and he had to order three shirts from the seamstress and a couple of pairs of that item of underwear which it is indecent to mention in print

– in short, absolutely all the money was to be spent; and even if the director was so gracious as to allot him a forty-five- or fifty-rouble bonus, instead of forty, all the same only a trifle would be left, which in the overcoat capital would be like a drop in the ocean. Though he knew, of course, that Petrovich had a trick of suddenly asking devil knows how incongruously high a price, so that his own wife sometimes could not keep herself from exclaiming, "Have you lost your mind, fool that you are! One day he takes a job for nothing, and now the evil one gets him to ask more than he's worth himself." Though he knew, of course, that Petrovich would agree to do it for eighty roubles – even so, where to get the eighty roubles? Now, it might be possible to find half, half could be produced; maybe even a little more; but where to get the other half? . . . But first the reader should learn where the one half would come from. Akaky Akakievich was in the habit of setting aside a half kopeck for every rouble he spent, putting it into a little box with a lock and key and a small hole cut in the lid for dropping money through. At the end of every half year he inspected the accumulated sum of copper and exchanged it for small silver. Thus he continued for a long time, and in this way, over the course of several years, he turned out to have saved a total of more than forty roubles. And so, one half was in hand; but where to get the other half? Where to get the other forty roubles? Akaky Akakievich thought and thought and decided that he would have to cut down his usual expenses, at least for a year; to abolish the drinking of tea in the evening, to burn no candles in the evening, and if there was a need to do something, to go to the landlady's room and work by her candle; to make the lightest and most careful steps possible when walking in the street, over cobbles and pavements, almost on tiptoe, thereby avoiding the rapid wearing out of soles; to send his linen to the laundry as seldom as possible, and to prevent soiling it by taking it off each time on coming home, remaining in a half-cotton dressing gown, a very old one, spared even by time itself. Truth to tell, it was a bit difficult for him at first to get used to such limitations, but later it somehow became a habit and went better; he even accustomed himself to going entirely without food in the evenings; but instead he was nourished spiritually, bearing in his thoughts the eternal idea of the future overcoat. From then on it was as if his very existence became somehow fuller, as if he were married, as if some other person were there with him, as if he were not alone but some pleasant life's companion had agreed to walk down the path of life with him – and this companion was none other than that same overcoat with its cotton-wool quilting, with its sturdy lining that knew no wear. He became somehow livelier, even firmer of character, like a man who has defined and set a goal for himself. Doubt, indecision – in short, all hesitant and uncertain features – disappeared of themselves from his face and actions. Fire occasionally showed in his eyes, the most bold and valiant thoughts even flashed in his head: Might he not indeed put a marten on the collar? These reflections led him nearly to distraction. Once, as he was copying a paper, he even nearly made a mistake, so that he cried "Oh!" almost aloud and crossed himself. In the course of each month, he stopped at least once to see Petrovich, to talk about the overcoat, where it was best to buy broadcloth, and of what color, and at what price, and he would return home somewhat preoccupied yet always pleased, thinking that the time would finally come when all this would be bought and the overcoat would be made. Things went even more quickly than he expected. Contrary to all expectations, the director allotted Akaky Akakievich not forty or forty-five but a whole sixty roubles;

whether he sensed that Akaky Akakievich needed an overcoat, or it happened that way of itself, in any case he acquired
on account of it an extra twenty roubles. This circumstance
speeded the course of things. Another two or three months
of going a bit hungry – and Akaky Akakievich had, indeed,
about eighty roubles. His heart, generally quite calm, began
to throb. The very next day he went shopping with Petrovich. They bought very good broadcloth – and no wonder,
because they had begun thinking about it six months before
and had hardly ever let a month go by without stopping at
a shop and inquiring about prices; and Petrovich himself said
that better broadcloth did not exist. For the lining they chose
chintz, but of such good, sturdy quality that, according to
Petrovich, it was even better than silk and looked more
attractive and glossy. They did not buy a marten, because it
was indeed expensive; but instead they chose a cat, the best
they could find in the shop, a cat which from afar could
always be taken for a marten. Petrovich fussed with the overcoat for a whole two weeks, because there was a lot of quilting
to do; otherwise it would have been ready sooner. For his
work, Petrovich took twelve roubles – it simply couldn't have
been less: decidedly everything was sewn with silk, in small
double seams, and afterwards Petrovich went along each
seam with his own teeth, imprinting it with various designs.
It was . . . it's hard to say precisely which day, but it was probably the most festive day in Akaky Akakievich's life, when
Petrovich finally brought the overcoat. He brought it in the
morning, just before it was time to go to the office. At no
other time could the overcoat have come so appropriately,
because very bitter frosts were already setting in and, it
seemed, were threatening to get still worse. Petrovich came
with the overcoat as befits a good tailor. His face acquired a
more important expression than Akaky Akakievich had ever

seen before. It seemed he felt in full measure that he had done no small thing and had suddenly revealed in himself the abyss that separates tailors who only put in linings and do repairs from those who sew new things. He took the overcoat out of the handkerchief in which he had brought it; the handkerchief was fresh from the laundry, and he proceeded to fold it and put it in his pocket for further use. Having taken out the overcoat, he looked very proud and, holding it in both hands, threw it deftly around Akaky Akakievich's shoulders; then he pulled it down and straightened the back with his hands; then he draped it over Akaky Akakievich unbuttoned. Akaky Akakievich, being a man of a certain age, wanted to try the sleeves; Petrovich helped him on with the sleeves – it turned out that with the sleeves it was also good. In short, it appeared that the overcoat was just right and fitted perfectly. Petrovich did not miss the chance of saying that it was only because he lived without a shingle, on a small street, and, besides, had known Akaky Akakievich for a long time, that he was asking so little; that on Nevsky Prospect he would pay seventy-five roubles for the work alone. Akaky Akakievich did not want to discuss it with Petrovich, and besides was afraid of all those mighty sums with which Petrovich liked to blow smoke. He paid him, thanked him, and left for the office at once in the new overcoat. Petrovich followed him out and, standing in the street, went on for a long time looking at the overcoat in the distance, then went purposely to the side, so as to make a detour down a crooked lane, run back out to the street ahead of him, and thus look at his overcoat from the other direction – that is, straight in the face. Meanwhile, Akaky Akakievich walked on in the most festive disposition of all his feelings. At each instant of every minute he felt that there was a new overcoat on his shoulders, and several times he even smiled from inner satisfaction. In fact, there were two profits: one that it was warm, the other that it was good. He did not notice the road at all and suddenly found himself at the office; in the porter's lodge he took the overcoat off, looked it all over, and entrusted it to the porter's special care. In some unknown way everyone in the department suddenly learned that Akaky Akakievich had a new overcoat and that the housecoat no longer existed. Everyone immediately ran out to the porter's lodge to look at Akaky Akakievich's new overcoat. They began to congratulate him, to cheer him, so that at first he only smiled, but then even became embarrassed. And when everyone accosted him and began saying that they should drink to the new overcoat, and that he should at least throw a party for them all, Akaky Akakievich was completely at a loss, did not know what to do, how to reply, or how to excuse himself from it. After several minutes, blushing all over, he began assuring them quite simple-heartedly that it was not a new overcoat at all, that it was just so, that it was an old overcoat. Finally one of the clerks, even some sort of assistant to the chief clerk, probably in order to show that he was by no means a proud man and even kept company with subordinates, said, "So be it, I'll throw a party instead of Akaky Akakievich and invite everyone tonight for tea: today also happens to be my name day." Naturally, the clerks straight away congratulated the chief clerk's assistant and willingly accepted the invitation. Akaky Akakievich tried to begin excusing himself, but everyone started to say that it was impolite, that it was simply a shame and a disgrace, and it was quite impossible for him not to accept. Afterwards, however, he was pleased when he remembered that he would thus even have occasion to take a stroll that evening in his new overcoat. For Akaky Akakievich the whole of that day was like the greatest festive holiday. He came home in the happiest state of mind, took off his overcoat and hung it carefully on the wall, having once more admired the broad-cloth and the lining, and then he purposely took out for comparison his former housecoat, completely fallen to pieces. He looked at it and even laughed himself: so far was the difference! And for a long time afterwards, over dinner, he kept smiling whenever he happened to think of the condition of his housecoat. He dined cheerfully and wrote nothing after dinner, no documents, but just played a bit of the Sybarite in his bed until it turned dark. Then, without tarrying, he got dressed, put on his overcoat, and left.

Precisely where the clerk who had invited him lived, we unfortunately cannot say: our memory is beginning to fail us badly, and whatever there is in Petersburg, all those houses and streets, has so mixed and merged together in our head that it is very hard to get anything out of it in a decent fashion. Be that as it may, it is at least certain that the clerk lived in a better part of town – meaning not very near to Akaky Akakievich. Akaky Akakievich had first to pass through some deserted, sparsely lit streets, but as he approached the clerk's home, the streets became livelier, more populous, and better lit. Pedestrians flashed by more frequently, ladies began to appear, beautifully dressed, some of the men wore beaver collars, there were fewer cabbies with their wooden-grill sleds studded with gilded nails – on the contrary, coachmen kept passing in raspberry-colored velvet hats, with lacquered sleds and bearskin rugs, or carriages with decorated boxes flew down the street, their wheels shrieking over the snow. Akaky Akakievich looked at it all as at something new. It was several years since he had gone out in the evening. He stopped curiously before a lighted shop window to look at a picture that portrayed some beautiful woman taking off her shoe and thus baring her whole leg, not a bad leg at all; and behind her back, from another room, some man stuck his head out, with side-whiskers and a handsome imperial under his lip. Akaky Akakievich shook his head and chuckled, and then went on his way. Why did he chuckle? Was it because he had encountered something totally unfamiliar, of which everyone nevertheless still preserves some sort of intuition; or had he thought, like many other clerks, as follows: "Well, these Frenchmen! what can you say, if they want something sort of... it's really sort of..." But maybe he didn't think even that – it's really impossible to get inside a man's soul and learn all he thinks.

At last he reached the house where the chief clerk's assistant lived. The chief clerk's assistant lived in grand style: the stairway was lighted, the apartment was on the second floor. Entering the front hall, Akaky Akakievich saw whole rows of galoshes on the floor. Among them, in the middle of the room, a samovar stood hissing and letting out clouds of steam. On the walls hung overcoats and cloaks, some among them even with beaver collars or velvet lapels. Behind the walls, noise and talk could be heard, which suddenly became clear and loud as the door opened and a lackey came out with a tray laden with empty glasses, a pitcher of cream, and a basket of rusks. It was evident that the clerks had gathered long ago and had already finished their first glass of tea. Akaky Akakievich, having hung up his overcoat himself, went into the room, and before him simultaneously flashed candles, clerks, pipes, and card tables, while his hearing was struck vaguely by a rush of conversation arising on all sides and the noise of chairs being moved. He stopped quite awkwardly in the middle of the room, looking about and trying to think what to do. But he was already noticed, greeted with cries, and everyone went at once to the front hall and again examined his overcoat. Akaky Akakievich was somewhat embarrassed, yet being a pure-hearted man, he could not help rejoicing to see how everyone praised his overcoat. After that, naturally, everyone dropped both him and his overcoat and turned, as usual, to the tables set up for whist. All of this – the noise, the talk, the crowd of people – all of it was somehow strange to Akaky Akakievich. He simply did not know what to do, where to put his hands and feet, or his whole self; he finally sat down with the players, looked at the cards, looked into the face of one or another, and in a short while began to yawn, feeling himself bored, the more so as it was long past the time when he customarily went to bed. He tried to take leave of the host, but the host would not let him go, saying that they absolutely had to drink a glass of champagne to the new coat. An hour later a supper was served which consisted of mixed salad, cold veal, pâté, sweet pastry, and champagne. Akaky Akakievich was forced to drink two glasses, after which he felt that the room had become merrier, yet he was unable to forget that it was already midnight and long since time to go home. So that the host should not somehow decide to detain him, he quietly left the room, went to the front hall to find his overcoat, which he saw, not without regret, lying on the floor, shook it, cleaned every feather off it, put it over his shoulders, went downstairs and outside. Outside it was still light. Some small-goods shops, those permanent clubs for servants and various others, were open; those that were closed still showed a stream of light the whole length of the door chink, indicating that they were not yet devoid of company and that the housemaids and servants were probably finishing their talks and discussions, while their masters were thrown into utter perplexity as to their whereabouts. Akaky Akakievich walked along in a merry state of mind, and even suddenly ran, for some unknown reason, after some lady who passed by like

66

lightning, every part of whose body was filled with extra-ordinary movement. However, he stopped straight away and again walked very slowly, as before, marveling to himself at this sprightliness of unknown origin. Soon there stretched before him those deserted streets which even in the daytime are none too cheerful, much less in the evening. Now they had become still more desolate and solitary: street lamps flashed less often – evidently the supply of oil was smaller; there were wooden houses, fences; not a soul anywhere; only snow glittered in the streets, and sleepy low hovels with closed shutters blackened mournfully. He approached a place where the street was intersected by an endless square that looked like a terrible desert, with houses barely visible on the other side.

Far away, God knows where, a light flashed in some sentry box that seemed to be standing at the edge of the world. Here Akaky Akakievich's merriment somehow diminished consid-erably. He entered the square not without some inadvertent fear, as if his heart had a foreboding of something bad. He looked behind him and to the sides: just like a sea all around him. "No, better not to look," he thought and walked with closed eyes, and when he opened them to see how far the end of the square was, he suddenly saw before him, almost in front of his nose, some mustached people, precisely what sort he could not even make out. His eyes grew dim, his heart pounded in his chest. "That overcoat's mine!" one of them said in a thundering voice, seizing him by the collar. Akaky Akakievich was about to shout "Help!" when the other one put a fist the size of a clerk's head right to his mouth and said, "Just try shouting!" Akaky Akakievich felt only that his overcoat was taken off him, he was given a kick with a knee and fell face down in the snow, and then felt no more. After a few minutes, he came to his senses and got to his feet, but

67

no one was there. He felt it was cold in the field and the overcoat was gone; he began to shout, but his voice seemed never to reach the ends of the square. In desperation, shouting constantly, he started running across the square, straight to the sentry box, beside which stood an on-duty policeman, leaning on his halberd, watching with apparent curiosity, desirous of knowing why the devil a man was running toward him from far away and shouting. Akaky Akakievich, running up to him, began shouting in a breathless voice that he had been asleep, not on watch, and had not seen how a man was being robbed. The policeman replied that he had seen nothing; that he had seen him being stopped by two men in the middle of the square but had thought they were his friends; and that, instead of denouncing him for no reason, he should go to the inspector tomorrow and the inspector would find out who took the overcoat. Akaky Akakievich came running home in complete disorder: the hair that still grew in small quantities on his temples and the back of his head was completely disheveled; his side, chest, and trousers were covered with snow. The old woman, his landlady, hearing a terrible knocking at the door, hastily jumped out of bed and ran with one shoe on to open it, holding her nightgown to her breast out of modesty; but when she opened the door she stepped back, seeing what state Akaky Akakievich was in. When he told her what was the matter, she clasped her hands and said he must go straight to the superintendent, that the inspector would cheat him, make promises and then lead him by the nose; and that it was best to go to the superintendent, that he was a man of her acquaintance, because Anna, the Finnish woman who used to work for her as a cook, had now got herself hired at the superintendent's as a nanny, and that she often saw him herself as he drove past their house, and that he also came to

68

church every Sunday, prayed, and at the same time looked cheerfully at everyone, and therefore was by all tokens a good man. Having listened to this decision, Akaky Akakievich plodded sadly to his room, and how he spent the night we will leave to the judgment of those capable of entering at least somewhat into another man's predicament.

Early in the morning he went to the superintendent but was told that he was asleep; he came at ten and again was told: asleep; he came at eleven o'clock and was told that the superintendent was not at home; at lunchtime the scriveners in the front room refused to let him in and insisted on knowing what his business was, what necessity had brought him there, and what had happened. So that finally, for once in his life, Akaky Akakievich decided to show some character and said flatly that he had to see the superintendent himself, in person, that they dared not refuse to admit him, that he had come from his department on official business, and that he would make a complaint about them and they would see. The scriveners did not dare to say anything against that, and one of them sent to call the superintendent. The superintendent took the story about the theft of the overcoat somehow extremely strangely. Instead of paying attention to the main point of the case, he began to question Akaky Akakievich – why was he coming home so late, and had he not stopped and spent some time in some indecent house? – so that Akaky Akakievich was completely embarrassed and left him not knowing whether the case of his overcoat would take its proper course or not. He did not go to the office all that day (the only time in his life). The next day he arrived all pale and in his old housecoat, which now looked still more lamentable. Though some of the clerks did not miss their chance to laugh at Akaky Akakievich even then, still the story of the theft of the overcoat moved many. They decided straight away to take up a collection for him, but they collected a mere trifle, because the clerks had already spent a lot, having subscribed to a portrait of the director and to some book, at the suggestion of the section chief, who was a friend of the author – and so, the sum turned out to be quite trifling. One of them, moved by compassion, decided at least to help Akaky Akakievich with good advice, telling him not to go to the police because, though it might happen that a policeman, wishing to gain the approval of his superior, would somehow find the overcoat, still the overcoat would remain with the police unless he could present legal proofs that it belonged to him; and the best thing would be to address a certain *important person*, so that the *important person*, by writing and referring to the proper quarters, could get things done more successfully. No help for it, Akaky Akakievich decided to go to the *important person*. What precisely the post of the *important person* was, and in what it consisted, remains unknown. It should be realized that this *certain important person* had become an important person only recently, and till then had been an unimportant person. However, his position even now was not considered important in comparison with other, still more important ones. But there will always be found a circle of people for whom something unimportant in the eyes of others is already important. He tried, however, to increase his importance by many other means – namely he introduced the custom of lower clerks meeting him on the stairs when he came to the office; of no one daring to come to him directly, but everything going in the strictest order: a collegiate registrar should report to a provincial secretary, a provincial secretary to a titular or whatever else, and in this fashion the case should reach him. Thus everything in holy Russia is infected with imitation, and each one mimics and apes his superior. It is even said that some titular councillor, when he was made chief of some separate little chancellery at once partitioned off a special room for himself, called it his "office room," and by the door placed some sort of ushers with red collars and galloons, who held the door handle and opened it for each visitor, though the "office room" could barely contain an ordinary writing desk. The ways and habits of the *important person* were imposing and majestic, but of no great complexity. The chief principle of his system was strictness. "Strictness, strictness, and – strictness," he used to say, and with the last word usually looked very importantly into the face of the person he was addressing. Though, incidentally, there was no reason for any of it, because the dozen or so clerks who constituted the entire administrative machinery of the office were properly filled with fear even without that; seeing him from far off, they set their work aside and waited, standing at attention, until their superior passed through the room. His usual conversation with subordinates rang with strictness and consisted almost entirely of three phrases: "How dare you? Do you know with whom you are speaking? Do you realize who is standing before you?" However, he was a kind man at heart, good to his comrades, obliging, but the rank of general had completely bewildered him. On receiving the rank of general, he had somehow become confused, thrown off, and did not know how to behave at all. When he happened to be with his equals, he was as a man ought to be, a very decent man, in many respects even not a stupid man; but as soon as he happened to be in the company of men at least one rank beneath him, he was simply as bad as could be: he kept silent, and his position was pitiable, especially since he himself felt that he could be spending his time incomparably better. In his eyes there could sometimes be seen a strong desire to join in some interesting conversation and circle, but he was stopped by the thought: Would it not be excessive on his part, would it not be familiar, would he not be descending beneath his importance? On account of such reasoning, he remained eternally in the same silent state, only uttering some monosyllabic sounds from time to time, and in this way he acquired the title of a most boring person. It was to this *important person* that our Akaky Akakievich came, and came at a most unfavorable moment, very inopportune for himself, though very opportune for the important person.

The important person was in his office and was talking away very, very merrily with a recently arrived old acquaintance and childhood friend, whom he had not seen for several years. Just then it was announced to him that a certain Bashmachkin was there. "Who's that?" he asked curtly. "Some clerk," came the reply. "Ah! he can wait, now isn't a good time," said the important man. Here it should be said that the important man was stretching it a bit: the time was good, he had long since discussed everything with his friend and their conversation had long since been interspersed with lengthy silences, while they patted each other lightly on the thigh, saying: "So there, Ivan Abramovich!" "So it is, Stepan Varlamovich!" But, for all that, he nevertheless told the clerk to wait, in order to show his friend, a man who had not been in the service and had been living for a long time on his country estate, what lengths of time clerks spent waiting in his anteroom. At last, having talked, or, rather, been silent his fill, and having smoked a cigar in an easy chair with a reclining back, at last he suddenly recollected, as it were, and said to his secretary, who stood in the doorway with papers for a report, "Ah, yes, it seems there's a clerk standing there. Tell him he may come in." Seeing Akaky Akakievich's humble look and his old uniform, he turned to him suddenly and said, "What can I do for you?" in a voice abrupt and firm, which he had purposely studied beforehand in his room, alone and in front of a mirror, a week prior to receiving his present post and the rank of general. Akaky Akakievich, who had been feeling the appropriate timidity for a good while already, became somewhat flustered and explained as well as he could, so far as the freedom of his tongue permitted, adding the words "sort of" even more often than at other times, that the overcoat was perfectly new and he had been robbed in a brutal fashion, and that he was addressing him so that through his intercession, as it were, he could sort of write to the gentleman police superintendent or someone else and find the overcoat. For some reason, the general took this to be familiar treatment.

"What, my dear sir?" he continued curtly. "Do you not know the order? What are you doing here? Do you not know how cases are conducted? You ought to have filed a petition about it in the chancellery; it would pass to the chief clerk, to the section chief, then be conveyed to my secretary, and my secretary would deliver it to me . . ."

"But, Your Excellency," said Akaky Akakievich, trying to collect the handful of presence of mind he had and feeling at the same time that he was sweating terribly, "I made so bold as to trouble you, Your Excellency, because secretaries are, sort of . . . unreliable folk . . ."

"What, what, what?" said the important person. "Where did you pick up such a spirit? Where did you pick up such ideas? What is this rebelliousness spreading among the young against their chiefs and higher-ups!"

The important person seemed not to notice that Akaky Akakievich was already pushing fifty. And so, even if he might be called a young man, it was only relatively – that is, in relation to someone who was seventy years old.

"Do you know to whom you are saying this? Do you realize who is standing before you? Do you realize that? Do you realize, I ask you?"

Here he stamped his foot, raising his voice to such a forceful note that even someone other than Akaky Akakievich would have been frightened by it. Akaky Akakievich was simply stricken, he swayed, shook all over, and was quite unable to stand: if the caretakers had not come running at once to support him, he would have dropped to the floor. He was carried out almost motionless. And the important person, pleased that the effect had even surpassed his expectations, and thoroughly delighted by the thought that his word could even make a man faint, gave his friend a sidelong glance to find out how he had taken it all, and saw, not without satisfaction, that his friend was in a most uncertain state and was even, for his own part, beginning to feel frightened himself.

How he went down the stairs, how he got outside, nothing of that could Akaky Akakievich remember. He could not feel his legs or arms. Never in his life had he been given such a bad roasting by a general, and not his own general at that. He walked, his mouth gaping, through the blizzard that whistled down the streets, blowing him off the sidewalk; the wind, as always in Petersburg, blasted him from all four sides out of every alley. He instantly caught a quinsy and he reached home unable to utter a word; he was all swollen and took to his bed. So strong at times is the effect of a proper roasting! The next day he was found to be in a high fever. Owing to the generous assistance of the Petersburg climate, the illness developed more quickly than might have been expected, and when the doctor came, after feeling his pulse, he found nothing else to do but prescribe a poultice, only so as not to leave the sick man without the beneficent aid of medical science;

74

but he nevertheless declared straight off that within a day and a half it would inevitably be kaput for him. After which he turned to the landlady and said, "And you, dearie, don't waste any time, order him a pine coffin at once, because an oak one will be too expensive for him." Whether Akaky Akakievich heard these fatal words spoken, and, if he heard them, whether they made a tremendous effect on him, whether he regretted his wretched life – none of this is known, because he was in fever and delirium the whole time. Visions, one stranger than another, kept coming to him: first he saw Petrovich and ordered him to make an overcoat with some sort of snares for thieves, whom he kept imagining under the bed, and he even called the landlady every other minute to get one thief out from under his blanket; then he asked why his old housecoat was hanging before him, since he had a new overcoat; then he imagined that he was stand-ing before the general, listening to the proper roasting, and kept murmuring, "I'm sorry, Your Excellency!" – then, finally, he even blasphemed, uttering the most dreadful words, so that his old landlady even crossed herself, never having heard anything like it from him, the more so as these words immediately followed the words "Your Excellency." After that he talked complete gibberish, so that it was impos-sible to understand anything; one could only see that his dis-orderly words and thoughts turned around one and the same overcoat. At last poor Akaky Akakievich gave up the ghost. Neither his room nor his belongings were sealed, because, first, there were no heirs, and, second, there was very little inheritance left – namely, a bunch of goose quills, a stack of white official paper, three pairs of socks, two or three buttons torn off of trousers, and the housecoat already familiar to the reader. To whom all this went, God knows: that, I confess, did not even interest the narrator of this story. Akaky

Akakievich was taken away and buried. And Petersburg was left without Akaky Akakievich, as if he had never been there. Vanished and gone was the being, protected by no one, dear to no one, interesting to no one, who had not even attracted the attention of a naturalist – who does not fail to stick a pin through a common fly and examine it under a microscope; a being who humbly endured office mockery and went to his grave for no particular reason, but for whom, all the same, though at the very end of his life, there had flashed a bright visitor in the form of an overcoat, animating for an instant his poor life, and upon whom disaster then fell as unbearably as it falls upon the kings and rulers of this world . . . Several days after his death, a caretaker was sent to his apartment from the office with an order for him to appear immediately – the chief demanded it. But the caretaker had to return with nothing, reporting that the clerk could come no more, and to the question "Why?" expressed himself with the words: "It's just that he's already dead, buried three days ago . . ." Thus they learned at the office about the death of Akaky Akakievich, and by the next day a new clerk was sitting in his place, a much taller one, who wrote his letters not in a straight hand but much more obliquely and slantwise.

But who could imagine that this was not yet all for Akaky Akakievich, that he was fated to live noisily for a few days after his death, as if in reward for his entirely unnoticed life? Yet so it happened, and our poor story unexpectedly acquires a fantastic ending. The rumor suddenly spread through Petersburg that around the Kalinkin Bridge and far further a dead man had begun to appear at night in the form of a clerk searching for some stolen overcoat and, under the pretext of this stolen overcoat, pulling from all shoulders, regardless of rank or title, various overcoats: with cat, with beaver, with cotton quilting, raccoon, fox, bearskin coats –

76

in short, every sort of pelt and hide people have thought up for covering their own. One of the clerks from the office saw the dead man with his own eyes and recognized him at once as Akaky Akakievich; this instilled such fear in him, however, that he ran away as fast as his legs would carry him and thus could not take a good look, but only saw from far off how the man shook his finger at him. From all sides came ceaseless complaints that the backs and shoulders – oh, not only of titular, but even of privy councillors themselves, were completely subject to chills on account of this nocturnal tearing off of overcoats. An order was issued for the police to catch the dead man at all costs, dead or alive, and punish him in the harshest manner, as an example to others, and in this they nearly succeeded. Namely, a neighborhood policeman on duty had already quite seized the dead man by the collar in Kiriushkin Lane, catching him red-handed in an attempt to pull a frieze overcoat off some retired musician who had whistled on a flute in his day. Having seized him by the collar, he shouted and summoned his two colleagues, whom he charged with holding him while he went to his boot just for a moment to pull out his snuffbox, so as to give temporary refreshment to his nose, frostbitten six times in his life. But the snuff must have been of a kind that even a dead man couldn't stand. The policeman had no sooner closed his right nostril with his finger, while drawing in half a handful with the left, than the dead man sneezed so hard that he completely bespattered the eyes of all three of them. While they tried to rub them with their fists, the dead man vanished without a trace, so that they did not even know whether or not they had indeed laid hands on him. After that, on-duty policemen got so afraid of dead men that they grew wary of seizing living ones and only shouted from far off: "Hey, you, on your way!" and the dead clerk began to appear even beyond the Kalinkin Bridge, instilling no little fear in all timorous people.

We, however, have completely abandoned the *certain important person*, who in fact all but caused the fantastic turn taken by this, incidentally perfectly true, story. First of all, justice demands that we say of this *certain important person* that, soon after the departure of the poor, roasted-to-ashes Akaky Akakievich, he felt something akin to regret. He was no stranger to compassion: his heart was open to many good impulses, though his rank often prevented their manifestation. As soon as his out-of-town friend left his office, he even fell to thinking about poor Akaky Akakievich. And after that, almost every day he pictured to himself the pale Akaky Akakievich, unable to endure his superior's roasting. He was so troubled by the thought of him that a week later he even decided to send a clerk to him, to find out about him and whether he might indeed somehow help him; and when he was informed that Akaky Akakievich had died unexpectedly of a fever, he was even struck, felt remorse of conscience, and was in low spirits the whole day. Wishing to divert himself somehow and forget the unpleasant impression, he went for the evening to one of his friends, where he found a sizable company, and, best of all, everyone there was of nearly the same rank, so that he felt no constraint whatsoever. This had a surprising effect on his state of mind. He grew expansive, became pleasant in conversation, amiable – in short, he spent the evening very pleasantly. At supper he drank two glasses of champagne – an agent known to have a good effect with regard to gaiety. The champagne disposed him toward various extravagances; to wit: he decided not to go home yet, but to stop and see a lady of his acquaintance, Karolina Ivanovna, a lady of German origin, it seems, toward whom he felt perfectly friendly relations. It should be said that the important person was a man no longer young, a good husband, a respectable father of a family. Two sons, one of whom already served in the chancellery, and a comely sixteen-year-old daughter with a slightly upturned but pretty little nose, came every day to kiss his hand, saying, "*Bonjour, papa.*" His wife, still a fresh woman and not at all bad looking, first gave him her hand to kiss and then, turning it over, kissed his hand. Yet the important person, perfectly satisfied, incidentally, with domestic family tendernesses, found it suitable to have a lady for friendly relations in another part of the city. This lady friend was no whit better or younger than his wife; but there exist such riddles in the world, and it is not our business to judge of them. And so, the important person went downstairs, got into his sleigh, and said to the driver, "To Karolina Ivanovna's," and, himself wrapped quite luxuriantly in a warm overcoat, remained in that pleasant state than which no better could be invented for a Russian man, when you are not thinking of anything and yet thoughts come into your head by themselves, each more pleasant than the last, without even causing you the trouble of chasing after and finding them. Filled with satisfaction, he kept recalling all the gay moments of that evening, all his words that had made the small circle laugh; he even repeated many of them in a half whisper and found them as funny as before, and therefore it was no wonder that he himself chuckled heartily. Occasionally, however, a gusty wind interfered with him, suddenly bursting from God knows where and for no apparent reason, cutting at his face, throwing lumps of snow into it, hoisting the collar of his coat like a sail, or suddenly, with supernatural force, throwing it over his head, thereby causing him the eternal trouble of extricating himself from it. Suddenly the important person felt someone seize him quite firmly by the collar. Turning

79

around, he noticed a short man in an old, worn-out uniform, in whom, not without horror, he recognized Akaky Akakievich. The clerk's face was pale as snow and looked exactly like a dead man's. But the important person's horror exceeded all bounds when he saw the dead man's mouth twist and, with the horrible breath of the tomb, utter the following words: "Ah! here you are at last! At last I've sort of got you by the collar! It's your overcoat I need! You didn't solicit about mine, and roasted me besides – now give me yours!" The poor *important person* nearly died. However full of character he was in the chancellery and generally before subordinates, and though at a mere glance at his manly appearance and figure everyone said, "Oh, what character!" – here, like a great many of those who are powerful in appearance, he felt such fear that he even became apprehensive, not without reason, of some morbid fit. He quickly threw the overcoat off his shoulders and shouted to the driver in a voice not his own, "Home at top speed!" The driver, hearing a voice that was usually employed at decisive moments and even accompanied by something much more effective, drew his head between his shoulders just in case, swung his knout, and shot off like an arrow. In a little over six minutes the important person was already at the door of his house. Pale, frightened, and minus his overcoat, he came to his own place instead of Karolina Ivanovna's, plodded to his room somehow or other, and spent the night in great disorder, so that the next morning over tea his daughter told him directly, "You're very pale today, papa." But papa was silent – not a word to anyone about what had happened to him, or where he had been, or where he had wanted to go.

This incident made a strong impression on him. He even began to say "How dare you, do you realize who is before you?" far less often to his subordinates; and if he did say it, it was not without first listening to what the matter was. But still more remarkable was that thereafter the appearances of the dead clerk ceased altogether: evidently the general's overcoat fitted him perfectly; at least there was no more talk about anyone having his overcoat torn off. However, many active and concerned people refused to calm down and kept saying that the dead clerk still appeared in the more remote parts of the city. And, indeed, one policeman in Kolomna saw with his own eyes a phantom appear from behind a house; but, being somewhat weak by nature, so that once an ordinary adult pig rushing out of someone's private house had knocked him down, to the great amusement of the coachmen standing around, for which jeering he extorted a half kopeck from each of them to buy snuff – so, being weak, he did not dare to stop it, but just followed it in the darkness, until the phantom suddenly turned around, stopped, and asked, "What do you want?" and shook such a fist at him as is not to be found even among the living. The policeman said, "Nothing," and at once turned to go back. The phantom, however, was much taller now, had an enormous mustache, and, apparently making its way toward the Obukhov Bridge, vanished completely into the darkness of the night.

1842

LEO TOLSTOY

THE SNOW STORM

Translated by Louise and Aylmer Maude

I

HAVING drunk tea towards seven o'clock in the evening, I left a station, the name of which I have forgotten, though I know it was somewhere in the district of the Don Cossack Army near Novocherkássk. It was already dark when, having wrapped myself in my fur coat, I took my seat under the apron beside Alëshka in the sledge. Near the post-station it seemed mild and calm. Though no snow was falling, not a star was visible overhead and the sky looked extremely low and black, in contrast to the clean snowy plain spread out before us.

We had hardly passed the dark shapes of the windmills, one of which clumsily turned its large sails, and left the settlement behind us, when I noticed that the road had become heavier and deeper in snow, that the wind blew more fiercely on the left, tossing the horses' tails and manes sideways, and that it kept carrying away the snow stirred up by the hoofs and sledge-runners. The sound of the bell began to die down, and through some opening in my sleeve a stream of cold air forced its way behind my back, and I recalled the station-master's advice, not to start for fear of going astray all night and being frozen on the road.

"Shan't we be losing our way?" I said to the driver, and not receiving an answer I put my question more definitely: "I say, driver, do you think we shall reach the next station without losing our way?"

"God only knows," he answered without turning his head. "Just see how the snow drifts along the ground! Nothing of the road to be seen. O Lord!"

"Yes, but you'd better tell me whether you expect to get me to the next station or not?" I insisted. "Shall we get there?"

"We ought to manage it," said the driver, and went on to add something the wind prevented my hearing.

I did not feel inclined to turn back, but the idea of straying about all night in the frost and snow storm on the perfectly bare steppe which made up that part of the Don Army district was also far from pleasant. Moreover, though I could not see my driver very well in the dark, I did not much like the look of him and he did not inspire me with confidence. He sat exactly in the middle of his seat with his legs in, instead of to one side; he was too big, he spoke lazily, his cap, not like those usually worn by drivers, was too big and flopped from side to side; besides, he did not urge the horses on properly, but held the reins in both hands, like a footman who had taken the coachman's place on the box. But my chief reason for not believing in him was because he had a kerchief tied over his ears. In a word he did not please me, and that solemn stooping back of his looming in front of me seemed to bode no good.

"In my opinion we'd better turn back," remarked Alëshka. "There's no sense in getting lost!"

"O Lord! Just look how the snow is driving, nothing of the road to be seen, and it's closing my eyes right up ... O Lord!" muttered the driver.

We had not been going a quarter of an hour before the driver handed the reins to Alëshka, clumsily liberated his legs, and making the snow crunch with his big boots went to look for the track.

"What is it? Where are you going? Are we off the road?"

I asked. But the driver did not answer and, turning his face away from the wind which was beating into his eyes, walked away from the sledge.

"Well, is there a road?" I asked when he returned.

"No, there's nothing," he answered with sudden impatience and irritation, as if I were to blame that he had strayed off the track, and having slowly thrust his big legs again into the front of the sledge he began arranging the reins with his frozen gloves.

"What are we to do?" I asked when we had started again.

"What are we to do? We'll drive where God sends us."

And though we were quite evidently not following a road, we went on at the same slow trot, now through dry snow five inches deep, and now over brittle crusts of frozen snow.

Though it was cold, the snow on my fur collar melted very quickly; the drift along the ground grew worse and worse, and a few dry flakes began to fall from above.

It was plain that we were going heaven knows where, for having driven for another quarter of an hour we had not seen a single verst-post.

"Well, what do you think?" I asked the driver again. "Shall we get to the station?"

"What station? We shall get back, if we give the horses their head they will take us there, but hardly to the next station – we might just perish."

"Well then, let us go back," I said. "And really . . ."

"Then I am to turn back?" said the driver.

"Yes, yes, turn back!"

The driver gave the horses the reins. They began to run faster, and though I did not notice that we were turning, I felt the wind blowing from a different quarter, and we soon saw the windmills appearing through the snow. The driver cheered up and began to talk.

"The other day the return sledges from the other station spent the whole night in a snow storm among haystacks and did not get in till the morning. Lucky that they got among those stacks, else they'd have all been frozen, it was so cold. As it is one of them had his feet frozen, and was at death's door for three weeks with them."

"But it's not cold now, and it seems calmer," I said. "We might perhaps go on?"

"It's warm enough, that's true, but the snow is drifting. Now that we have it at our back it seems easier, but the snow is driving strongly. I might go if it were on courier-duty or something of the kind, but not of my own free will. It's no joke if a passenger gets frozen. How am I to answer for your honour afterwards?"

II

JUST then we heard behind us the bells of several tróykas* which were rapidly overtaking us.

"It's the courier's bell," said my driver. "There's no other like it in the district."

And in fact the bell of the front tróyka, the sound of which was already clearly borne to us by the wind, was exceedingly fine: clear, sonorous, deep, and slightly quivering. As I learnt afterwards it had been chosen by men who made a hobby of tróyka bells. There were three bells – a large one in the middle with what is called a *crimson* tone, and two small ones tuned to a third and a fifth. The ringing of that third and of the quivering fifth echoing in the air was extraordinarily

---

* A tróyka is a three-horse sledge, or, more correctly, a team of three horses.

effective and strangely beautiful in that silent and deserted steppe.

"The post is going," said my driver, when the first of the three tróykas overtook us. "How is the road? Is it usable?" he called out to the driver of the last sledge, but the man only shouted at his horses and did not reply.

The sound of the bells was quickly lost in the wind as soon as the post sledges had passed us.

I suppose my driver felt ashamed.

"Well, let us try it again, sir!" he said to me. "Others have made their way through and their tracks will be fresh."

I agreed, and we turned again, facing the wind and struggling forward through the deep snow. I kept my eyes on the side of the road so as not to lose the track left by the tróykas. For some two versts the track was plainly visible, then only a slight unevenness where the runners had gone, and soon I was quite unable to tell whether it was a track or only a layer of driven snow. My eyes were dimmed by looking at the snow monotonously receding under the runners, and I began to look ahead. We saw the third verst-post, but were quite unable to find a fourth. As before we drove against the wind, and with the wind, and to the right and to the left, and at last we came to such a pass that the driver said we must have turned off to the right, I said we had gone to the left, and Alëshka was sure we had turned right back. Again we stopped several times and the driver disengaged his big feet and climbed out to look for the road, but all in vain. I too once went to see whether something I caught a glimpse of was not the road, but hardly had I taken some six steps with difficulty against the wind before I became convinced that similar layers of snow lay everywhere, and that I had seen the road only in my imagination. When I could no longer see the sledge I cried out: "Driver! Alëshka!" but I felt how the wind caught my voice straight from my mouth and bore it instantly to a distance. I went to where the sledge had been — but it was not there; I went to the right, it was not there either. I am ashamed to remember in what a loud, piercing, and even rather despairing voice I again shouted "Driver!" and there he was within two steps of me. His black figure, with the little whip and enormous cap pushed to one side, suddenly loomed up before me. He led me to the sledge.

"Thank the Lord, it's still warm," he said, "if the frost seized us it would be terrible ... O Lord!"

"Give the horses their head: let them take us back," I said, having seated myself in the sledge. "They will take us back, driver, eh?"

"They ought to."

He let go of the reins, struck the harness-pad of the middle horse with the whip, and we again moved on somewhere. We had travelled on for about half an hour when suddenly ahead of us we recognized the connoisseur's bell and the other two, but this time they were coming towards us. There were the same three tróykas, which having delivered the mail were now returning to the station with relay horses attached. The courier's tróyka with its big horses and musical bells ran quickly in front, with one driver on the driver's seat shouting vigorously. Two drivers were sitting in the middle of each of the empty sledges that followed, and one could hear their loud and merry voices. One of them was smoking a pipe, and the spark that flared up in the wind showed part of his face.

Looking at them I felt ashamed that I had been afraid to go on, and my driver probably shared the same feeling, for we both said at once: "Let us follow them!"

III

MY DRIVER, before the third tróyka had passed, began turning so clumsily that his shafts hit the horses attached behind it. They all three shied, broke their strap, and galloped aside.

"You cross-eyed devil! Can't you see when you're turning into someone, you devil?" one of the drivers seated in the last sledge – a short old man, as far as I could judge by his voice and figure – began to curse in hoarse, quivering tones, and quickly jumping out of the sledge he ran after the horses, still continuing his coarse and harsh abuse of my driver.

But the horses did not stop. The driver followed them, and in a moment both he and they were lost in the white mist of driving snow.

"Vasí-i-li! Bring along the dun horse! I can't catch them without," came his voice.

One of the other drivers, a very tall man, got out of his sledge, silently unfastened his three horses, climbed on one of them by its breeching, and disappeared at a clumsy gallop in the direction of the first driver.

We and the other two tróykas started after the courier's tróyka, which with its bell ringing went along at full trot though there was no road.

"Catch them! Not likely!" said my driver of the one who had run after the horses. "If a horse won't come to other horses, that shows it's bewitched and will take you somewhere you'll never return from."

From the time he began following the others my driver seemed more cheerful and talkative, a fact of which I naturally took advantage, as I did not yet feel sleepy. I began asking where he came from, and why, and who he was, and it turned out that like myself he was from Túla province, a serf from Kirpíchnoe village, that they were short of land there and had had bad harvests since the cholera year. He was one of two brothers in the family, the third having gone as a soldier; that they had not enough grain to last till Christmas, and had to live on outside earnings. His youngest brother was head of the house, being married, while he himself was a widower. An *artél** of drivers came from their village to these parts every year. Though he had not driven before, he had taken the job to help his brother, and lived, thank God, quite well, earning a hundred and twenty assignation rubles a year, of which he sent a hundred home to the family; and that life would be quite good "if only the couriers were not such beasts, and the people hereabouts not so abusive".

"Now why did that driver scold me so? O Lord! Did I set his horses loose on purpose? Do I mean harm to anybody? And why did he go galloping after them? They'd have come back of themselves, and now he'll only tire out the horses and get lost himself," said the God-fearing peasant.

"And what is that black thing there?" I asked, noticing several dark objects in front of us.

"Why, a train of carts. That's pleasant driving!" he went on, when we had come abreast of the huge mat-covered wagons on wheels, following one another. "Look, you can't see a single soul – they're all asleep. Wise horses know of themselves . . . you can't make them miss the way anyhow . . . We've driven that way on contract work ourselves," he added, "so we know."

It really was strange to see those huge wagons covered with snow from their matted tops to their very wheels, and moving along all alone. Only in the front corner of the wagon did the matting, covered two inches thick with snow, lift a

* An *artél* was a voluntary association of workers, which had a manager, contracted as a unit, and divided its earnings among its members.

bit and a cap appear for a moment from under it as our bells tinkled past. The large piebald horse, stretching its neck and straining its back, went evenly along the completely snow-hidden road, monotonously shaking its shaggy head under the whitened harness-bow, and pricking one snow-covered ear when we overtook it.

When we had gone on for another half-hour the driver again turned to me.

"What d'you think, sir, are we going right?"

"I don't know," I answered.

"At first the wind came that way, and now we are going right under the wind. No, we are not going where we ought, we are going astray again," he said quite calmly.

One saw that, though he was inclined to be a coward, yet "death itself is pleasant in company" as the saying is, and he had become quite tranquil now that there were several of us and he no longer had to lead and be responsible. He made remarks on the blunders of the driver in front with the greatest coolness, as if it were none of his business. And in fact I noticed that we sometimes saw the front tróyka on the left and sometimes on the right; it even seemed to me that we were going round in a very small circle. However, that might be an optical illusion, like the impression that the leading tróyka was sometimes going uphill, and then along a slope, or downhill, whereas I knew that the steppe was perfectly level.

After we had gone on again for some time, I saw a long way off, on the very horizon as it seemed to me, a long, dark, moving stripe; and a moment later it became clear that it was the same train of wagons we had passed before. The snow was still covering their creaking wheels, some of which did not even turn any longer, the men were still asleep as before under the matting, and the piebald horse in front blew out its nostrils as before, sniffed at the road, and pricked its ears.

"There, we've turned and turned and come back to the same wagons!" exclaimed my driver in a dissatisfied voice. "The courier's horses are good ones, that's why he's driving them so recklessly, but ours will stop altogether if we go on like this all night."

He cleared his throat.

"Let us turn back, sir, before we get into trouble!"

"No! Why? We shall get somewhere."

"Where shall we get to? We shall spend the night in the steppe. How it is blowing! . . . O Lord!"

Though I was surprised that the driver of the front tróyka, having evidently lost the road and the direction, went on at a fast trot without looking for the road, and cheerfully shouting, I did not want to lag behind them.

"Follow them!" I said.

My driver obeyed, whipping up his horses more reluctantly than before, and did not turn to talk to me any more.

IV

THE STORM grew more and more violent, and the snow fell dry and fine. I thought it was beginning to freeze: my cheeks and nose felt colder than before, and streams of cold air made their way more frequently under my fur coat, so that I had to wrap it closer around me. Sometimes the sledge bumped on the bare ice-glazed ground from which the wind had swept the snow. As I had already travelled more than five hundred versts without stopping anywhere for the night, I involuntarily kept closing my eyes and dozing off, although I was much interested to know how our wandering would end. Once when I opened my eyes I was struck for a moment by what seemed to me a bright light falling on the white plain; the horizon had widened considerably, the lowering black sky had suddenly vanished, and on all sides slanting white streaks of falling snow could be seen. The outlines of the front tróykas were more distinct, and as I looked up it seemed for a minute as though the clouds had dispersed, and that only the falling snow veiled the sky. While I was dozing the moon had risen and was casting its cold bright light through the tenuous clouds and the falling snow. The only things I saw clearly were my sledge, the horses, my driver, and the three tróykas in front of us: the courier's sledge in which a driver still sat, as before, driving at a fast trot; the second, in which two drivers having laid down the reins and made a shelter for themselves out of a coat sat smoking their pipes all the time, as could be seen by the sparks that flew from them; and the third in which no one was visible, as probably the driver was lying asleep in the body of the sledge. The driver of the first tróyka, however, at the time I awoke, occasionally stopped his horses and sought for the road. As soon as we stopped the howling of the wind sounded louder and the vast quantity of snow borne through the air became more apparent. In the snow-shrouded moonlight I could see the driver's short figure probing the snow in front of him with the handle of his whip, moving backwards and forwards in the white dimness, again returning to his sledge and jumping sideways onto his seat, and again amid the monotonous whistling of the wind I heard his dexterous, resonant cries urging on the horses, and the ringing of the bells. Whenever the driver of the front tróyka got out to search for some sign of a road or haystacks, there came from the second tróyka the bold, self-confident voice of one of the drivers shouting to him:

"Hey, Ignáshka, you've borne quite to the left! Bear to the right, facing the wind!" Or: "What are you twisting about for, quite uselessly? Follow the snow, see how the drifts lie, and we'll come out just right." Or: "Take to the right, to the right, mate! See, there's something black – it must be a post." Or: "What are you straying about for? Unhitch the piebald and let him run in front, he'll lead you right out onto the road. That would be better."

But the man who was giving this advice not only did not unhitch one of his own side-horses or get out to look for the road, but did not show his nose from under his sheltering coat, and when Ignáshka, the leader, shouted in reply to one of his counsels that he should take on the lead himself if he knew which way to go, the advice-giver replied that if he were driving the courier's tróyka he would take the lead and take us right onto the road. "But our horses won't take the lead in a snow storm!" he shouted – "they're not that kind of horses!"

"Then don't bother me!" Ignáshka replied, whistling cheerfully to his horses.

The other driver in the second sledge did not speak to Ignáshka at all and in general took no part in the matter, though he was not asleep, as I concluded from his pipe being always alight, and because, whenever we stopped, I heard the even and continuous sound of his voice. He was telling a folk tale. Only once, when Ignáshka stopped for the sixth or seventh time, he apparently grew vexed at being interrupted during the pleasure of his drive, and shouted to him:

"Hullo, why have you stopped again? Just look, he wants to find the road! He's been told there's a snow storm! The surveyor himself couldn't find the road now. You should drive on as long as the horses will go, and then maybe we shan't freeze to death ... Go on, do!"

"I daresay! Didn't a postillion freeze to death last year?" my driver remarked.

The driver of the third sledge did not wake up all the time. Once when we had stopped the advice-giver shouted:

"Philip! Hullo, Philip!" and receiving no reply remarked: "Hasn't he frozen, perhaps? ... Go and have a look, Ignáshka."

Ignáshka, who found time for everything, walked up to the sledge and began to shake the sleeping man.

"Just see what half a bottle of vodka has done! Talk about freezing!" he said, shaking him.

The sleeper grunted something and cursed.

"He's alive, all right," said Ignáshka, and ran forward again. We drove on, and so fast that the little off-side sorrel of my tróyka, which my driver continually touched with the whip near his tail, now and then broke into an awkward little gallop.

V

IT WAS I think already near midnight when the little old man and Vasíli, who had gone after the runaway horses, rode up to us. They had managed to catch the horses and to find and overtake us; but how they had managed to do this in the thick blinding snow storm amid the bare steppe will always remain a mystery to me. The old man, swinging his elbows and legs, was riding the shaft-horse at a trot (the two side-horses were attached to its collar: one dare not let horses loose in a snow storm). When he came abreast of us he again began to scold my driver.

"Look at the cross-eyed devil, really ..."

97

"Eh, Uncle Mítrich!" the folk-tale teller in the second sledge called out: "Are you alive? Get in here with us."

But the old man did not reply and continued his abuse. When he thought he had said enough he rode up to the second sledge.

"Have you caught them all?" someone in it asked.

"What do you think?"

His small figure threw itself forward on the back of the trotting horse, then jumped down on the snow, and without stopping he ran after the sledge and tumbled in, his legs sticking out over its side. The tall Vasíli silently took his old place in the front sledge beside Ignáshka, and the two began to look for the road together.

"How the old man nags ... Lord God!" muttered my driver.

For a long time after that we drove on without stopping over the white waste, in the cold, pellucid, and quivering light of the snow storm. I would open my eyes and the same clumsy snow-covered cap and back would be jolting before me: the same low shaft-bow, under which, between the taut leather reins and always at the same distance from me, the head of our shaft-horse kept bobbing with its black mane blown to one side by the wind. Looking across its back I could see the same little piebald off-horse on the right, with its tail tied up short, and the swingletree which sometimes knocked against the front of the sledge. I would look down – there was the same scurrying snow through which our runners were cutting, and which the wind resolutely bore away to one side. In front, always at the same distance away, glided the first tróyka, while to right and left everything glimmered white and dim. Vainly did my eye look for any new object: neither post, nor haystack, nor fence was to be seen. Everywhere all was white and fluctuating: now the horizon seemed

98

immeasurably distant, now it closed in on all sides to within two paces of me; suddenly a high white wall would seem to rise up on the right and run beside the sledge, then it would suddenly vanish and rise again in front, only to glide on farther and farther away and again disappear. When I looked up it would seem lighter for a moment, as if I might see the stars through the haze, but the stars would run away higher and higher from my sight and only the snow would be visible, falling past my eyes onto my face and the collar of my fur cloak. The sky everywhere remained equally light, equally white, monotonous, colourless, and constantly shifting. The wind seemed to be changing: now it blew in my face and the snow plastered my eyes, now it blew from one side and annoyingly tossed the fur-collar of my cloak against my head and mockingly flapped my face with it; now it howled through some opening. I heard the soft incessant crunching of the hoofs and the runners on the snow; and the clang of the bells dying down when we drove through deep drifts. Only now and then, when we drove against the snow and glided over bare frozen ground, did Ignáshka's energetic whistling and the sonorous sound of the bell with its accompanying bare fifth reach me, and give sudden relief to the dismal character of the desert; and then again the bells would sound monotonous, playing always with insufferable precision the same tune, which I involuntarily imagined I was hearing. One of my feet began to feel the frost, and when I turned to wrap myself up better, the snow that had settled on my collar and cap shifted down my neck and made me shiver, but on the whole I still felt warm in my fur cloak, and drowsiness overcame me.

VI

RECOLLECTIONS and pictures of the distant past super-seded one another with increasing rapidity in my imagination.

"That advice-giver who is always calling out from the second sledge – what sort of fellow can he be?" I thought. Probably red-haired, thick-set, and with short legs, like Theodore Filípych, our old butler." And I saw the staircase of our big house and five domestic serfs with heavy steps bringing a piano from the wing on slings made of towels, and Theodore Filípych with the sleeves of his nankeen coat turned up, holding one of the pedals, running forward, lifting a latch, pulling here at the slings, pushing there, crawling between people's legs, getting into everybody's way, and shouting incessantly in an anxious voice:

"Lean it against yourselves, you there in front, you in front! That's the way – the tail end up, up, up! Turn into the door! That's the way."

"Just let us do it, Theodore Filípych! We can manage it alone," timidly remarks the gardener, pressed against the banisters quite red with straining, and with great effort holding up one corner of the grand piano.

But Theodore Filípych will not be quiet.

"What does it mean?" I reflect. "Does he think he is useful or necessary for the work in hand, or is he simply glad God has given him this self-confident persuasive eloquence, and enjoys dispensing it? That must be it." And then somehow I see the lake, and tired domestic serfs up to their knees in the water dragging a fishing-net, and again Theodore Filípych with a watering-pot, shouting at everybody as he runs up and down on the bank, now and then approaching the brink to empty out some turbid water and to take up fresh, while holding back the golden carp with his hand. But now it is a July noon. I am going some-where over the freshly-mown grass in the garden; under the burning, vertical rays of the sun; I am still very young, and I feel a lack of something and a desire to fill that lack. I go to my favourite place by the lake, between the briar-rose bed and the birch avenue, and lie down to sleep. I remember the feeling with which, lying down, I looked across between the prickly red stems of the rose trees at the dark, dry, crumbly earth, and at the bright blue mirror of the lake. It is a feeling of naïve self-satisfaction and melancholy. Every-thing around me is beautiful, and that beauty affects me so powerfully that it seems to me that I myself am good, and the one thing that vexes me is that nobody is there to admire me. It is hot. I try to sleep so as to console myself, but the flies, the unendurable flies, give me no peace here either: they gather round me and, with a kind of dull persistence, hard as cherry-stones, jump from my forehead onto my hands. A bee buzzes not far from me in the blazing sunlight; yellow-winged butterflies fly from one blade of grass to another as if exhausted by the heat. I look up: it hurts my eyes – the sun glitters too brightly through the light foliage of the curly birch tree whose branches sway softly high above me, and it seems hotter than ever. I cover my face with my handkerchief: it feels stifling, and the flies seem to stick to my hands which begin to perspire. In the very centre of the wild rose bush sparrows begin to bustle about. One of them hops to the ground about two feet from me, energetically pretends to peck at the ground a couple of times, flies back into the bush, rustling the twigs, and chirping merrily flies away. Another also hops down, jerks his little tail, looks about him, chirps, and flies off quick as an arrow after the first one. From the lake comes a sound of beetles* beating the wet linen, and the sound re-echoes and is borne down along the lake. Sounds of laughter and the voices and splashing of bathers are heard. A gust of wind rustles the crowns of the birch trees, still far from me, now it comes nearer and I hear it stir the grass, and now the leaves of the wild roses begin to flutter, pressed against their stems, and at last a fresh stream of air reaches me, lifting a corner of my handkerchief and tickling my moist face. Through the gap where the corner of the kerchief was lifted a fly comes in and flutters with fright close to my moist mouth. A dry twig presses against my back. No, I can't lie still: I had better go and have a bathe. But just then, close to the rose bush, I hear hurried steps and a woman's frightened voice:

"O God! How could such a thing happen! And none of the men are here!"

"What is it? What is it?" running out into the sunshine I ask a woman serf who hurries past me groaning. She only looks round, waves her arms, and runs on. But here comes seventy-year-old Matrëna hurrying to the lake, holding down with one hand the kerchief which is slipping off her head, and hopping and dragging one of her feet in its worsted stocking. Two little girls come running up hand in hand, and a ten-year-old boy, wearing his father's coat and clutching the homespun skirt of one of the girls, keeps close behind them.

"What has happened?" I ask them.

"A peasant is drowning."

"Where?"

"In the lake."

"Who is he? One of ours?"

"No, a stranger."

* The women take their clothes to rinse in lakes or streams, where they beat them with wooden beetles.

102

Iván the coachman, dragging his heavy boots through the newly-mown grass, and the fat clerk Jacob, all out of breath, run to the pond and I after them.

I remember the feeling which said to me: "There you are, plunge in and pull out the peasant and save him, and everyone will admire you," which was exactly what I wanted.

"Where is he? Where?" I ask the throng of domestic serfs gathered on the bank.

"Out there, in the very deepest part near the other bank, almost at the boathouse," says the washerwoman, hanging the wet linen on her wooden yoke. "I look, and see him dive; he just comes up and is gone, then comes up again and calls out: 'I'm drowning, help!' and goes down again, and nothing but bubbles come up. Then I see that the man is drowning, so I give a yell: 'Folk! A peasant's drowning!'"

And lifting the yoke to her shoulder the laundress waddles sideways along the path away from the lake.

"Oh gracious, what a business!" says Jacob Ivánov, the office clerk, in a despairing tone. "What a bother there'll be with the rural court. We'll never get through with it!"

A peasant carrying a scythe pushes his way through the throng of women, children, and old men who have gathered on the farther shore, and hanging his scythe on the branch of a willow slowly begins to take off his boots.

"Where? Where did he go down?" I keep asking, wishing to rush there and do something extraordinary.

But they point to the smooth surface of the lake which is occasionally rippled by the passing breeze. I do not understand how he came to drown; the water is just as smooth, lovely, and calm above him, shining golden in the midday sun, and it seems that I can do nothing and can astonish no one, especially as I am a very poor swimmer and the peasant is already pulling his shirt over his head and ready to plunge in. Everybody looks at him hopefully and with bated breath, but after going in up to his shoulders he slowly turns back and puts his shirt on again he cannot swim.

People still come running and the thing grows and grows; the women cling to one another, but nobody does anything to help. Those who have just come give advice, and sigh, and their faces express fear and despair; but of those who have been there awhile, some, tired with standing, sit down on the grass, while some go away. Old Matrëna asks her daughter whether she shut the oven door, and the boy who is wearing his father's coat diligently throws small stones into the water.

But now Theodore Filípych's dog Tresórka, barking and looking back in perplexity, comes running down the hill, and then Theodore himself, running downhill and shouting, appears from behind the briar-rose bushes:

"What are you standing there for?" he cries, taking off his coat as he runs, "A man drowning, and they stand there! . . . Get me a rope!"

Everybody looks at Theodore Filípych with hope and fear as, leaning his hand on the shoulder of an obliging domestic serf, he prises off his right boot with the toe of the left.

"Over there, where the people are, a little to the right of the willow, Theodore Filípych, just there!" someone says to him.

"I know," he replies, and knitting his brows, in response, no doubt, to the signs of shame among the crowd of women, he pulls off his shirt, removes the cross from his neck and hands it to the gardener's boy who stands obsequiously before him, and then, stepping energetically over the cut grass, approaches the lake.

Tresórka, perplexed by the quickness of his master's movements, has stopped near the crowd and with a smack of his lips eats a few blades of grass near the bank, then looks at his master intently and with a joyful yelp suddenly plunges with him into the water. For a moment nothing can be seen but foam and spray, which even reaches to us; but now Theodore Filípych, gracefully swinging his arms and rhythmically raising and lowering his back, swims briskly with long strokes to the opposite shore. Tresórka, having swallowed some water, returns hurriedly, shakes himself near the throng, and rubs his back on the grass. Just as Theodore Filípych reaches the opposite shore two coachmen come running up to the willow with a fishing-net wrapped round a pole. Theodore Filípych for some unknown reason lifts his arms, dives down once and then a second and a third time, on each occasion squirting a jet of water from his mouth, and gracefully tosses back his hair without answering the questions that are hurled at him from all sides. At last he comes out onto the bank, and as far as I can see only gives instructions as to spreading out the net. The net is drawn in, but there is nothing in it except ooze with a few small carp entangled in it. While the net is being lowered again I go round to that side.

The only sounds to be heard are Theodore Filípych's voice giving orders, the plashing of the wet rope on the water, and sighs of terror. The wet rope attached to the right side of the net, more and more covered by grass, comes farther and farther out of the water.

"Now then, pull together, harder, all together!" shouts Theodore Filípych.

The floats appear dripping with water.

"There is something coming, mates. It pulls heavy!" some one calls out.

Now the net – in which two or three little carp are struggling – is dragged to the bank, wetting and pressing down the grass. And in the extended wings of the net, through a thin swaying layer of turbid water, something white comes in sight. Amid dead silence an impressive, though not loud, gasp of horror passes through the crowd.

"Pull harder, onto the land!" comes Theodore Filípych's resolute voice, and the drowned body is dragged out to the willow over the stubble of burdock and thistle.

And now I see my good old aunt in her silk dress, with her face ready to burst into tears. I see her lilac sunshade with its fringe, which seems somehow incongruous in this scene of death, so terrible in its simplicity. I recall the disappointment her face expressed because arnica could be of no use, and I also recall the painful feeling of annoyance I experienced when, with the naïve egotism of love, she said: "Come away my dear. Oh, how dreadful it is! And you always go bathing and swimming by yourself."

I remember how bright and hot the sun was as it baked the powdery earth underfoot; how it sparkled and mirrored in the lake; how the plump carp plashed near the banks and shoals of little fish rippled the water in the middle; how a hawk hovering high in the air circled over the ducklings, which quacking and splashing had come swimming out through the reeds into the middle of the lake; how curling white thunder-clouds gathered on the horizon; how the mud drawn out onto the bank by the net gradually receded; and how as I crossed the dike I again heard the blows of the beetles re-echoing over the lake.

But that beetle sounds as if two beetles were beating together in thirds, and that sound torments and worries me, the more so because I know that this beetle is a bell, and that Theodore Filípych will not make it stop. Then that beetle, like an instrument of torture, presses my foot which is freezing, and I fall asleep.

I am awakened, as it seems to me, by our galloping very fast and by two voices calling out quite close to me:

"I say, Ignát! Eh, Ignát!" my driver is saying. "You take my passenger. You have to go on anyhow, but what's the use of my goading my horses uselessly? You take him!"

Ignát's voice quite close to me replies:

"Where's the pleasure of making myself responsible for the passenger? . . . Will you stand me a bottle?"

"Oh, come, a bottle . . . say half a bottle."

"Half a bottle, indeed!" shouts another voice. "Wear out the horses for half a bottle!"

I open my eyes. Before them still flickers the same intolerable swaying snow, the same drivers and horses, but now we are abreast of another sledge. My driver has overtaken Ignát, and we drive side by side for some time. Though the voice from the other sledge advises him not to accept less than a bottle, Ignát suddenly reins in his tróyka.

"Well, shift over. So be it! It's your luck. You'll stand half a bottle when we return to-morrow. Is there much luggage?"

My driver jumps out into the snow with unusual alacrity for him, bows to me, and begs me to change over into Ignát's sledge. I am quite willing to, but evidently the God-fearing peasant is so pleased that he has to pour out his gratitude and delight to someone. He bows and thanks me, Alëshka, and Ignát.

"There now, the Lord be praised! What was it like . . . O Lord! We have been driving half the night and don't know where we are going. He'll get you there, dear sir, but my horses are quite worn out."

And he shifts my things with increased zeal.

While my things were being transferred I went with the wind, which almost lifted me off my feet, to the second sledge. That sledge, especially outside the coat which had been arranged over the two men's heads to shelter them from the wind, was more than six inches deep in snow, but behind the coat it was quiet and comfortable. The old man still lay with his legs sticking out, and the story-teller was still going on with his tale.

"Well, when the general comes to Mary in prison, in the King's name, you know, Mary at once says to him: 'General, I don't need you and can't love you, and so, you see, you are not my lover, but my lover is the prince himself . . .'"

"And just then . . ." he went on, but seeing me he stopped for a moment and began filling his pipe.

"Well, sir, have you come to listen to the tale?" asked the other whom I called the advice-giver.

"Yes, you're well off here, quite jolly," I said.

"Why not? It whiles away the time, anyhow it keeps one from thinking."

"And do you know where we are now?"

This question did not seem to please the drivers.

"Who can make out where we are? Maybe we've driven into the Kulmýk country," answered the advice-giver.

"Then what are we going to do?" I asked.

"What can we do? We'll go on, and maybe we'll get somewhere," he said in a dissatisfied tone.

"But suppose we don't get anywhere, and the horses stick in the snow – what then?"

"What then? Why, nothing."

"But we might freeze."

"Of course we might, because one can't even see any haystacks: we have got right among the Kulmýks. The chief thing is to watch the snow."

"And you seem afraid of getting frozen, sir," remarked the old man in a shaky voice.

Though he seemed to be chaffing me, it was evident that he was chilled to his very bones.

"Yes, it is getting very cold," I said.

"Eh, sir, you should do as I do, take a run now and then, that will warm you up."

"Yes, the chief thing is to have a run behind the sledge," said the advice-giver.

VII

"WE'RE READY, your honour!" shouted Alëshka from the front sledge.

The storm was so violent that, though I bent almost double and clutched the skirts of my cloak with both hands, I was hardly able to walk the few steps that separated me from the sledge, over the drifting snow which the wind swept from under my feet. My former driver was already kneeling in the middle of his empty sledge, but when he saw me going he took off his big cap (whereupon the wind lifted his hair furiously) and asked for a tip. Evidently he did not expect me to give him one, for my refusal did not grieve him in the least. He thanked me anyway, put his cap on again, and said: "God keep you, sir ..." and jerking his reins and clicking his tongue, turned away from us. Then Ignát swayed his whole back and shouted to the horses, and the sound of the snow crunching under their hoofs, the cries, and the bells, replaced the howling of the wind which had been peculiarly noticeable while we stood still.

For a quarter of an hour after my transfer I kept awake and amused myself watching my new driver and his horses. Ignát sat like a mettlesome fellow, continually rising in his seat, flourishing over the horses the arm from which his whip was hung, shouting, beating one foot against the other, and bending forward to adjust the breeching of the shaft-horse, which kept slipping to the right. He was not tall, but seemed to be well built. Over his sheepskin he wore a large, loose cloak without a girdle, the collar of which was turned down so that his neck was bare. He wore not felt but leather boots, and a small cap which he kept taking off and putting straight. His ears were only protected by his hair. In all his movements one was aware not only of energy, but even more, as it seemed to me, of a desire to arouse that energy in himself. And the farther we went the more often he straightened himself out, rose in his seat, beat his feet together, and addressed himself to Alëshka and me. It seemed to me that he was afraid of losing courage. And there was good reason for it: though the horses were good the road grew heavier and heavier at every step, and it was plain that they were running less willingly: it was already necessary to touch them up with the whip, and the shaft-horse, a good, big, shaggy animal, stumbled more than once though immediately, as if frightened, it jerked forward again and tossed its shaggy head almost as high as the bell hanging from the bow above it. The right off-horse, which I could not help watching, with a long leather tassel to its breeching which shook and jerked on its off side, noticeably let its traces slacken and required the whip, but from habit as a good and even mettlesome horse seemed vexed at its own weakness, and angrily lowered and tossed its head at the reins. It was terrible to realize that the snow storm and the frost were increasing, the horses growing weaker, the road becoming worse, and that we did not at all know where we were or where we were going – or whether we should reach a station or even a shelter of any sort; it seemed strange and ridiculous to hear the bells ringing so easily and cheerfully, and Ignát shouting as lustily and pleasantly as if we were out for a drive along a village street on a frosty noon during a Twelfth Night holiday – and it was stranger still that we were always driving and driving fast somewhere from where we were. Ignát began to sing some song in a horrid falsetto, but so loud and with such intervals, during which he whistled, that it seemed ridiculous to be afraid while one heard him.

"Hey there, what are you splitting your throat for, Ignát?" came the advice-giver's voice. "Stop a minute!"

"What?"

"Sto-o-op!"

Ignát stopped. Again all became silent, and the wind howled and whined, and the whirling snow fell still more thickly into the sledge. The advice-giver came up to us.

"Well, what now?"

"What now? Where are we going?"

"Who can tell?"

"Are your feet freezing, that you knock them together so?"

"Quite numb!"

"You should go over there: look, where there's something glimmering. It must be a Kulmýk camp. It would warm your feet too."

"All right. Hold the reins ... here you are."

And Ignát ran in the direction indicated.

"You always have to go about a bit and look, then you find the way, or else what's the good of driving about like a fool?" the advice-giver said to me. "See how the horses are steaming."

All the time Ignát was gone – and that lasted so long that I even began to fear he might have lost his way – the advice-giver kept telling me in a self-confident and calm tone how one should behave in a snow storm, that it was best to unharness a horse and let it go, and as God is holy, it would be sure to lead one out and how it is sometimes possible to find the way by the stars, and that had he been driving in front we should long ago have reached the station.

"Well, is there anything?" he asked Ignát when the latter came back, stepping with difficulty knee-deep through the snow.

"There is, there is a camp of some sort," replied Ignát, gasping for breath, "but I can't tell what it is. We must have strayed right into the Prológov estate. We must bear off to the left."

"What's he jabbering about? It's our camp that's behind the Cossack village," rejoined the advice-giver.

"I tell you it's not!"

"Well, I've had a look too, and I know: that's what it is, and if it isn't, then it's Tamýshevsk. Anyhow we must bear to the right, and then we'll come right out to the big bridge at the eighth verst."

"I tell you it's nothing of the sort. Haven't I looked?" said Ignát with annoyance.

"Eh, mate, and you call yourself a driver!"

"Yes, a driver! ... Go and look for yourself."

"Why should I go? I know without going."

Ignát had evidently grown angry: he jumped into the sledge without replying and drove on.

"How numb my legs have got! I can't warm them up," said he to Alëshka, knocking his feet together oftener and oftener, and scooping up and emptying out the snow that had got into his boot-legs.

I felt dreadfully sleepy.

VIII

"CAN IT BE THAT I am freezing to death?" I thought, half asleep. "They say it always begins with drowsiness. It would be better to drown than to freeze – let them drag me out with

112

a net; but it does not matter much whether I freeze or drown if only that stick, or whatever it is, would not prod me in the back and I could forget myself!"

I did so for a few seconds.

"But how will all this end?" I suddenly asked myself, opening my eyes for a moment and peering into the white expanse before me. "How will it all end? If we don't find any haystacks and the horses stop, as they seem likely to do soon, we shall all freeze to death." I confess that, though I was a little afraid, the desire that something extraordinary, something rather tragic, should happen to us, was stronger in me than that fear. It seemed to me that it would not be bad if towards morning the horses brought us of their own accord, half-frozen, to some far-off unknown village, or if some of us were even to perish of the cold. Fancies of this kind presented themselves to me with extraordinary clearness and rapidity. The horses stop, the snow drifts higher and higher, and now nothing is seen of the horses but their ears and the bows above their heads, but suddenly Ignát appears above us with his tróyka, and drives past. We entreat him, we shout that he should take us, but the wind carries our voices away – we have no voices left. Ignát grins, shouts to his horses, whistles, and disappears into some deep, snow-covered ravine. The little old man jumps astride a horse, flourishes his elbows and tries to gallop away, but cannot stir from the spot; my former driver with the big cap rushes at him, drags him to the ground and tramples him into the snow. "You're a wizard!" he shouts. "You're a scold! We shall all be lost together!" But the old man breaks through the heap of snow with his head; and now he is not so much an old man as a hare, and leaps away from us. All the dogs bound after him. The advice-giver, who is Theodore Filípych, tells us all to sit round in a circle, that if the snow covers us it will be all right – we shall be warm that way. And really we are warm and cosy, only I want a drink. I fetch out my lunch-basket, and treat everybody to rum and sugar, and enjoy a drink myself. The storyteller spins a tale about the rainbow, and now there is a ceiling of snow and a rainbow above us. "Now let us each make himself a room in the snow and let us go to sleep!" I say. The snow is soft and warm, like fur. I make myself a room and want to enter it, but Theodore Filípych, who has seen the money in my lunch-basket, says: "Stop! Give me your money – you have to die anyway!" And he grabs me by the leg. I hand over the money and only ask him to let me go; but they won't believe it is all the money I have, and want to kill me. I seize the old man's hand and begin to kiss it with inexpressible pleasure: his hand is tender and sweet. At first he snatches it from me, but afterwards lets me have it, and even caresses me with his other hand. Then Theodore Filípych comes near and threatens me. I run away into my room: it is, however, no longer a room but a long white corridor, and someone is holding my legs. I wrench myself free. My clothes and part of my skin remain in the hands of the man who was holding me, but I only feel cold and ashamed – all the more ashamed because my aunt with her parasol and homoeopathic medicine-chest under her arm is coming towards me arm-in-arm with the drowned man. They are laughing and do not understand the signs I make to them. I throw myself into the sledge, my feet trail behind me in the snow, but the old man rushes after me flapping his elbows. He is already near, but I hear two church bells ringing in front of me, and know that I shall be saved when I get to them. The church bells sound nearer and nearer; but the little old man has caught up with me and falls with his stomach on my face, so that I can scarcely hear the bells. I again grasp his hand and begin to kiss it, but the little old man is

114

no longer the little old man, he is the man who was drowned
... and he shouts: "Ignát, stop! There are the Akhmétkins'
stacks, I think! Go and have a look at them!" This is too terrible. No, I had better wake up ...

I open my eyes. The wind has thrown the flap of Alëshka's
cloak over my face, my knee is uncovered, we are going over
the bare frozen road, and the bells with their quivering third
can be distinctly heard.

I look to see the haystacks, but now that my eyes are open
I see no stacks, but a house with a balcony and the crenellated
wall of a fortress. I am not interested enough to scrutinize
this house and fortress: I am chiefly anxious to see the white
corridor along which I ran, to hear the sound of the church
bells, and to kiss the little old man's hand. I close my eyes
again and fall asleep.

IX

I SLEPT soundly, but heard the ringing of the bells all the
time. They appeared to me in my dream now in the guise of
a dog that barked and attacked me, now of an organ in which
I was one of the pipes, and now of some French verses I was
composing. Sometimes those bells seemed to be an instrument of torture which kept squeezing my right heel. I felt
that so strongly that I woke up and opened my eyes, rubbing
my foot. It was getting frost-bitten. The night was still light,
misty, and white. The same motion was still shaking me and
the sledge; the same Ignát sat sideways, knocking his feet
together; the same off-horse with outstretched neck ran at a
trot over the deep snow without lifting its feet much, while
the tassel on the breeching bobbed and flapped against its
belly. The head of the shaft-horse with its flying mane

stooped and rose rhythmically as it alternately drew the reins tight and loosened them. But all this was covered with snow even more than before. The snow whirled about in front, at the side it covered the horses' legs knee-deep, and the runners of the sledge, while it fell from above on our collars and caps. The wind blew now from the right, now from the left, playing with Ignát's collar, the skirt of his cloak, the mane of the side-horse, and howling between the shafts and above the bow over the shaft-horse's head.

It was growing terribly cold, and hardly had I put my head out of my coat-collar before the frosty, crisp, whirling snow covered my eyelashes, got into my nose and mouth, and penetrated behind my neck. When I looked round, everything was white, light and snowy, there was nothing to be seen but the dull light and the snow. I became seriously frightened. Alëshka was asleep at my feet at the bottom of the sledge, his whole back covered by a thick layer of snow. Ignát did not lose courage: he kept pulling at the reins, shouting, and clapping his feet together. The bell went on ringing just as wonderfully. The horses snorted a little, but ran more slowly and stumbled more and more often. Ignát again leaped up, waved his mitten, and again began singing in his strained falsetto. Before finishing the song he stopped the tróyka, threw down the reins on the front of the sledge, and got out. The wind howled furiously; the snow poured on the skirts of our cloaks as out of a scoop. I turned round: the third tróyka was not to be seen (it had lagged behind somewhere). Near the second sledge, in the snowy mist, I saw the little old man jumping from foot to foot. Ignát went some three steps from the sledge, and sitting down in the snow undid his girdle and pulled off his boots.

"What are you doing?" I asked.

"I must change, or my feet will be quite frozen," he replied, and went on with what he was doing.

It was too cold to keep my neck out of my collar to watch what he was doing. I sat up straight, looking at the off-horse, which with one leg wearily stretched out, painfully whisked its tail that was tied in a knot and covered with snow. The thump Ignát gave the sledge as he jumped onto his seat roused me.

"Where are we now?" I asked. "Shall we get anywhere – say by daybreak?"

"Don't worry, we'll get you there," he replied. "Now that I have changed, my feet are much warmer."

And he drove on, the bell began to ring, the sledge swayed again, and the wind whistled under the runners. We again started to swim over the limitless sea of snow.

X

I FELL soundly asleep. When Alëshka woke me up by pushing me with his foot, and I opened my eyes, it was already morning. It seemed even colder than in the night. No more snow was falling from above, but a stiff dry wind continued to sweep the powdery snow across the plain, and especially under the hoofs of the horses and the runners of the sledge. In the east, to our right, the sky was heavy and of a dark bluish colour, but bright orange oblique streaks were growing more and more defined in it. Overhead, through flying white clouds as yet scarcely tinged, gleamed the pale blue of the sky; on the left, bright, light clouds were drifting. Everywhere, as far as eye could see, deep snow lay over the plain in sharply defined layers. Here and there could be seen greyish mounds, over which fine, crisp, powdery snow swept steadily. No track either of sledge, man, or beast could be seen. The outlines and colour of the driver's back and of the horses were clearly and sharply visible even on the white background. The rim of Ignát's dark-blue cap, his collar, his hair, and even his boots were white. The sledge was completely covered with snow. The right side and forelock of the grey shaft-horse were thick with snow, the legs of the off-horse on my side were covered with it up to the knee, and its curly sweating flank was covered and frozen to a rough surface. The tassel still bobbed up and down in tune to any rhythm you liked to imagine, and the off-horse itself kept running in the same way, only the sunken, heaving belly and drooping ears showing how exhausted she was. The one novel object that attracted my attention was a verst-post from which the snow was falling to the ground, and near which to the right the snow was swept into a mound by the wind, which still kept raging and throwing the crisp snow from side to side. I was very much surprised that we had travelled all night, twelve hours, with the same horses, without knowing where, and had arrived after all. Our bell seemed to tinkle yet more cheerfully. Ignát kept wrapping his cloak around him and shouting; the horses behind us snorted, and the bells of the little old man's and the advice-giver's tróyka tinkled, but the driver who had been asleep had certainly strayed from us in the steppe. After going another half-mile we came across the fresh, only partly obliterated, traces of a three-horsed sledge, and here and there pink spots of blood, probably from a horse that had overreached itself.

"That's Philip. Fancy his being ahead of us!" said Ignát.

But here by the roadside a lonely little house with a signboard was seen in the midst of the snow, which covered it almost to the top of the windows and to the roof. Near the inn stood a tróyka of grey horses, their coats curly with sweat, their legs outstretched and their heads drooping wearily. At the door there was a shovel and the snow had been cleared away, but the howling wind continued to sweep and whirl snow off the roof.

At the sound of our bells, a tall, ruddy-faced, red-haired peasant came out with a glass of vodka in his hand, and shouted something. Ignát turned to me and asked permission to stop. Then for the first time I fairly saw his face.

XI

HIS FACE was not swarthy and lean with a straight nose, as I had expected judging by his hair and figure. It was a round, jolly, very snub-nosed face, with a large mouth and bright light-blue eyes. His cheeks and neck were red, as if rubbed with a flannel; his eyebrows, his long eyelashes, and the down that smoothly covered the bottom of his face, were plastered with snow and were quite white. We were only half a mile from our station and we stopped.

"Only be quick about it!" I said.

"Just one moment," replied Ignát, springing down and walking over to Philip.

"Let's have it, brother," he said, taking the mitten from his right hand and throwing it down with his whip on the snow, and tossing back his head he emptied at a gulp the glass that was handed to him.

The innkeeper, probably a discharged Cossack, came out with a half-bottle in his hand.

"Who shall I serve?" said he.

Tall Vasíli, a thin, brown-haired peasant, with a goatee beard, and the advice-giver, a stout, light-haired man with a thick beard framing his red face, came forward and also drank a glass each. The little old man too went over to the drinkers, but was not served, and he went back to his horses, which were fastened behind the sledge, and began stroking one of them on the back and croup.

The little old man's appearance was just what I had imagined it to be: small, thin, with a wrinkled livid face, a scanty beard, sharp little nose, and worn yellow teeth. He had a new driver's cap on, but his coat was shabby, worn, smeared with tar, torn on one shoulder, had holes in the skirt, and did not cover his knees and the homespun trousers which were tucked into his huge felt boots. He himself was bent double, puckered up, his face and knees trembled, and he tramped about near the sledge evidently trying to get warm.

"Come, Mítrich, you should have a glass; you'd get fine and warm," said the advice-giver.

Mítrich's face twitched. He adjusted the harness of one of his horses, straightened the bow above its head, and came over to me.

"Well, sir," he said, taking the cap off his grey head and bending low, "we have been wandering about together all night, looking for the road: won't you give me enough for a small glass? Really sir, your honour! I haven't anything to get warm on," he added with an ingratiating smile.

I gave him a quarter-ruble.* The innkeeper brought out a small glass of vodka and handed it to the old man. He took off his mitten, together with the whip that hung on it, and put out his small, dark, rough, and rather livid hand towards the glass; but his thumb refused to obey him, as though it did not belong to him. He was unable to hold the glass and dropped it on the snow, spilling the vodka.

* At that time about sixpence.

All the drivers burst out laughing.

"See how frozen Mítrich is, he can't even hold the vodka."

But Mítrich was greatly grieved at having spilt the vodka.

However, they filled another glass for him and poured it into his mouth. He became cheerful in a moment, ran into the inn, lit his pipe, showed his worn yellow teeth, and began to swear at every word he spoke. Having drained the last glass, the drivers returned to their tróykas and we started again.

The snow kept growing whiter and brighter so that it hurt one's eyes to look at it. The orange-tinted reddish streaks rose higher and higher, and growing brighter and brighter spread upwards over the sky; even the red disk of the sun became visible on the horizon through the blue-grey clouds; the sky grew more brilliant and of a deeper blue. On the road near the settlement the sledge tracks were clear, distinct, and yellowish, and here and there we were jolted by cradle-holes in the road; one could feel a pleasant lightness and freshness in the tense, frosty air.

My tróyka went very fast. The head of the shaft-horse, and its neck with its mane fluttering around the bow, swayed swiftly from side to side almost in one place under the special bell, the tongue of which no longer struck the sides but scraped against them. The good off-horses tugged together at the frozen and twisted traces, and sprang energetically, while the tassel bobbed from right under the horse's belly to the breeching. Now and then an off-horse would stumble from the beaten track into the snowdrift, throwing up the snow into one's eyes as it briskly got out again. Ignát shouted in his merry tenor; the dry frosty snow squeaked under the runners; behind us two little bells were ringing resonantly and festively, and I could hear the tipsy shouting of the drivers. I looked back. The grey shaggy off-horses, with their necks outstretched and breathing evenly, their bits awry, were leaping over the snow. Philip, flourishing his whip, was adjusting his cap; the little old man, with his legs hanging out, lay in the middle of the sledge, as before.

Two minutes later my sledge scraped over the boards before the clean-swept entrance of the station house, and Ignát turned to me his snow-covered merry face, smelling of frost.

"We've got you here after all, sir!" he said.

1856

IVAN TURGENEV

THE LIVE RELIC

Translated by Charles and Natasha Hepburn

Motherland of long-suffering –
Land of the Russian people!

F. TYUTCHEV

THE French proverb has it that a dry fisherman and a wet hunter make a sorry sight. Never having been addicted to fishing, I am no judge of a fisherman's feelings in fine clear weather and of the extent to which, in a downpour, the satisfaction afforded him by a good catch offsets the unpleasantness of getting wet. But, for the hunter, rain is a real disaster. A disaster of this kind befell Ermolai and myself on one of our excursions after blackcock in the district of Belevo. From daybreak the rain had not stopped. We had done everything possible to escape it. We had put rubber capes practically over our heads, we had stood under trees to avoid the drops. Our waterproof capes, besides hindering us from shooting, had let the water through in the most shameless manner; and, as for the trees – true, at first there seemed to be no drops, but then the water accumulated in the leaves suddenly burst through; every branch poured down on us like a rain-pipe, a cold stream found its way under the cravat and ran down the spinal column . . . That was the last straw, as Ermolai put it. "No, Pyotr Petrovich," he exclaimed at last, "we can't go on like this! . . . We can't shoot to-day. The dogs' noses are washed-out, the guns are misfiring . . . Phew! It's too much!"

"What shall we do?" I asked.

"I'll tell you what. We'll go to Alexeyevka. You may not know it it's a little farm, belonging to your mother; eight versts from here. We'll spend the night there, and tomorrow ..."

"We'll come back here?"

"No, not here ... I know some places beyond Alexeyevka much better than here for blackcock."

I did not think fit to inquire of my trusty companion why he had not conducted me straight to these places, and the same day we reached my mother's farm, the existence of which I confess I had not suspected until then. Beside the farm we found a little pavilion, very decrepit, but uninhabited and therefore clean; in it I passed a fairly peaceful night.

The next day I woke up very early. The sun had just risen; there was not a cloud in the sky; the whole scene sparkled brightly with a double brilliance: the brilliance of the early morning rays, and of the previous day's downpour.

While my dog-cart was being harnessed, I went for a stroll in a small garden, once an orchard, now run wild, which surrounded the pavilion on all sides with its lush, scented growth. Oh, how good it was in the open air, under the clear sky, in which larks were trilling, and from which their sweet voices fell in silver beads! They had certainly carried off dewdrops on their wings, and their songs seemed drenched in dew. I took off my cap and joyously breathed in with all my lungs ... On the slope of a shallow ravine, beside a fence, I saw a bee-garden; a narrow path led towards it, winding like a snake between unbroken walls of weed and nettle, above which towered, planted heaven knows how, the pointed stalks of dark-green hemp.

I went along the path, and came to the bee-garden. Beside it stood a little wattle shed, the place where the hives were put

126

in winter. I looked in through the half-open door: it was dark, quite dry; there was a smell of mint and balm. In a corner there was an arrangement of trestles and on them, covered in a blanket, a sort of small figure ... I was going away ...

"Master, I say, master! Pyotr Petrovich!" came a voice, weak, slow and husky, like the rustling of sedge in a marsh.

I stopped.

"Pyotr Petrovich! Come closer, please!" repeated the voice. It issued from the corner where I had noticed the trestles.

I came closer – and stood stock-still from amazement. Before me lay a live human being, but what on earth ...?

A head completely dried up, all one colour, the colour of bronze, nothing more nor less than an ancient icon; a nose as thin as the blade of a knife; lips almost invisible – only the pale glimmer of teeth and eyes and, winding out from under a handkerchief on the brow, a few thin strands of yellow hair. Beside the chin, on the fold of the blanket, slowly twisting their twig-like fingers, moved two tiny hands of the same bronze colour. I looked closer: the face was far from ugly, it was beautiful even – but strange and frightening. And all the more frightening because on it, on its metallic cheeks, I could see – forcing ... forcing its way, but unable to spread across – a smile.

"Don't you know me, master?" whispered the voice again; it seemed an exhalation from the hardly-moving lips. "But how could you know me! – I'm Lukerya ... D'you remember, I used to lead the country dances, at your mother's, at Spasskoye ... d'you remember, I used to lead the singing, too?"

"Lukerya!" I exclaimed. "Is it you? Is it possible?"

"Yes, master, it is. I'm Lukerya."

I didn't know what to say, and gazed as if dumbfounded at that dark, motionless face, with its bright, death-like eyes fixed upon me! Was it possible? This mummy – Lukerya, the greatest beauty of all our household – tall, plump, pink and white full of laughter and dancing and song! Lukerya, clever Lukerya, who was courted by all our young swains, for whom I too had sighed in secret, I – a lad of sixteen years!

"For goodness' sake, Lukerya," I said at last, "what's happened to you?"

"Oh, I've had terrible trouble! But you mustn't be put off, master, you mustn't look down on me for my bad luck – sit down over there on the cask – nearer, or you won't be able to hear me ... you see what a fine voice I've got! ... Well, I *am* glad to see you! How did you come to turn up at Alexeyevka like this?"

Lukerya spoke very quietly and faintly, but without faltering.

"Ermolai, the hunter, brought me here. But tell me ..."

"Tell you about my trouble? – Very well, master. It happened some time ago now, six or seven years back. I had just been betrothed to Vasily Polyakov – d'you remember him, a fine-looking chap, with curly hair – he was serving as butler at your mother's? You had left the country by then and gone to Moscow to study. Vasily and I loved each other very much; he was never out of my thoughts. It was in the spring. Well, one night ... It was not long before dawn ... and I couldn't sleep: a nightingale in the garden was singing so wonderfully sweet! ... I couldn't stay still, I got up and went out to the porch to listen to him. He went flowing, flowing on ... and suddenly it seemed to me that someone with Vasily's voice was calling me, quietly-like: 'Lusha!' I looked round, half-asleep, you know – slipped, fell right off the floor of the porch and went flying down, thump, on the ground! And it didn't seem as though I'd hurt myself badly, because I got up at once and went back to my room. Only it felt as if inside

128

me – in my belly – something had torn ... Let me get my breath ... just a minute, master."

Lukerya paused and I looked at her in bewilderment. What bewildered me particularly was that she told her story almost gaily, without groans or sighs, never complaining or asking for sympathy.

"From then on," continued Lukerya, "I started fading and withering away; a blackness came over me, it got hard for me to walk, and then – I couldn't even use my legs; neither stand nor sit: I'd just lie the whole time. And I didn't want to eat or drink; I got thinner and thinner. From the kindness of her heart your mother showed me to the doctors and sent me to hospital. But I got no relief from it. Not a single doctor could even say what my illness was. They did everything they could think of to me: they burnt my back with red-hot iron, they sat me down in broken ice – all no good. At length I grew all stiff, like a board ... So the mistress decided that there was nothing more to be done to cure me, and as it isn't possible to keep a cripple in the manor house ... well, they sent me over here – because here I have relations. And here I live, as you see."

Lukerya paused again and again, made an effort to smile.

"But it's a terrible plight to be in!" I exclaimed ... and, not knowing what to add, I asked: "And what about Vasily Polyakov?"

It was a very stupid question.

Lukerya turned her eyes away.

"What about Polyakov? He moped and moped, and married someone else – a girl from Glinnoye. D'you know Glinnoye? Not far from us. Her name was Agrafena. He loved me very much ... but he was young, you see ... there was no reason why he should stay a bachelor. And what sort of a sweetheart could I be to him now? He found himself a good

129

wife ... they've got children. He lives on a neighbouring estate, in the agent's office; your mother let him go with a passport, and, praise be to God, he's very happy."

"And so you just lie and lie?" I asked again.

"Yes, master, I have lain like this for more than six years. In summer I lie here in this wattle hut, but when it gets cold they'll move me inside the bath-house. And there I lie."

"But who looks after you? Who keeps an eye on you?"

"Oh, there are good folk here, too. They don't leave me to myself. And I don't take much looking after. As for food, I don't eat anything, and as for water – here it is in the mug: there's a supply of clear spring water always standing there. I can reach the mug myself: one of my hands still works. There's a girl here, an orphan; now and again she looks in on me, bless her. She was here just now ... didn't you meet her? Pretty, she is, and fair-skinned. She brings me flowers; I'm very fond of them, of flowers. There are no garden flowers here ... there were, but they've died out. But wild flowers are good, too, they smell even better than garden ones. Take the lily of the valley ... What could be sweeter?"

"Aren't you bored, aren't you restless, my poor Lukerya?"

"What can I do? I don't want to lie to you – it was very sad at first; but then I got used to it, I grew patient – I came not to mind; there are some people who are even worse off."

"In what way?"

"Some people haven't even anywhere to go! And some are blind or deaf! But I, praise be to God, I can see beautifully and I can hear everything, everything. If a mole burrows underground – even so, I hear him. And I can smell every smell, even the faintest there are! If buckwheat blossoms in the field, or lime in the garden – you needn't tell me: I'm always the first to know. So long as only a breath of wind comes from there. No, why anger God? – there are many worse off than I. For example, someone who's well can sin very easily; but even sin itself has left me. The other day Father Alexei, the priest, came to give me communion, and said: 'I need not confess you: how can you sin in your condition?' And I answered him: 'But what about sin in thought, Father?' 'Well,' he says and laughs, 'that's not a big sin.' And even in this sin of thought I couldn't be much of a sinner," continued Lukerya, "because I've taught myself not to think and, more important still, not to remember. Time passes quicker like that."

I was, I confess, surprised. "You're quite alone all the time, Lukerya; then how can you prevent thoughts coming into your head? Or do you sleep all the time?"

"Oh, no, master! I can't always sleep. Although I have no big pains, it nags me here, inside me, and in my bones, too; it doesn't let me sleep as I ought to. No . . . I just lie by myself, I lie and lie – and I don't think; I feel that I'm alive and breathing – and that all of me is here. I look and I listen. The bees in the garden will buzz and bumble away; the pigeon will sit on the roof and start cooing; the mother-hen will look in with her chickens to pick up the crumbs; or else a sparrow will fly in, or a butterfly – I enjoy it so much. The year before last some swallows even built a nest over there in the corner and hatched a family. How funny it was! One of them would fly in, drop into the nest, feed the chicks and away. You'd look again, and the other would already be there inside. Sometimes they wouldn't fly in, but just swoop past the open door. And at once the chicks – how they'd squeak and open their beaks! . . . I thought they'd come the next year, too, but they say that some sportsman hereabouts shot them with his gun. What good can it have done him? A whole swallow is no bigger than a beetle. How cruel you are, you sporting gentlemen!"

"I don't shoot swallows," I hastened to observe.

"Then, once," began Lukerya again, "I had a great joke! A hare ran in, really he did! The hounds were after him, but he came lolloping straight in at the door! ... He sat right close to me – sat for quite a while – kept moving his nose and twitching his whiskers – a regular officer! And how he looked at me. He must have understood that he'd nothing to fear from me. At last he got up, hop-hop to the door, looked round from the threshold – what a one he was! Such a funny one!"

Lukerya looked up at me ... as if to say, isn't it amusing? To please her, I laughed. She bit her dried-up lips.

"Well, in winter, of course, I'm worse off, because it's dark; it would be a pity to light a candle, and what for? Although I know my letters and was always fond of reading, what is there to read? There are no books here at all, and, even if there were, how am I going to hold one? Father Alexei brought me a calendar to occupy my mind; then he saw that it was no good, and he went and took it away again. But even when it's dark, there's always something to hear; a cricket chirrups, or somewhere a mouse starts scratching. Then, too, the best plan is not to think!

"Or else I say prayers," continued Lukerya after a short rest. "Only I don't know many of them, these prayers. And why should I go and bother the Lord God? What can I ask Him for? He knows better than I do what I need. He has sent me a cross – it means He must love me. That's how we are told to understand it. I say 'Our Father' and 'Mother of God' and the prayer for all that suffer – and then I just go on lying again without a thought in my head. And I don't mind!"

Two minutes passed. I didn't break the silence and didn't stir on the narrow little cask which served me for a seat. The cruel, stony immobility of the unfortunate living creature lying before me communicated itself to me, too: I, too, was as if benumbed.

"Listen, Lukerya," I began at length. "Listen, I'm going to suggest something to you. Would you like me to arrange for them to take you to hospital, a good hospital in town? Who knows, perhaps they could still cure you? In any case you won't be alone ..."

Lukerya just moved her eyebrows. "Oh, no, master," she said in a worried whisper, "don't move me to hospital, don't touch me. I'll only get more suffering out of it. What's the use of treating me now! ... Why, once a doctor came here: he wanted to look at me. I said to him: 'Don't bother me, for the Lord Christ's sake.' What was the good of asking him! He started turning me over, moved my arms and legs, bent them about; he said: 'I'm doing this for science's sake; you see, I'm in the service of science! and you,' he said, 'can't resist me, because for my troubles I've had an Order given me, and I try my best for fools like you.' He pulled me about, and pulled me about, he told me the name of my illness – a learned sort of name – and with that he went away. And for a whole week afterwards all my bones ached. You say I'm alone, always alone. No, not always. I get visitors. I'm quiet – not in anyone's way. Peasant-girls will come to me and gossip: a pilgrim-woman will look in and start telling of Jerusalem and Kiev and the holy cities. And it's not as if I was frightened to be alone. I'm even better off, I promise you ... Master, don't touch me, don't take me to hospital ... Thank you, you're kind, but don't touch me, my dear."

"Well, as you like, Lukerya. I just thought that, for your own good ..."

"I know, master, that it was for my own good, but, master, dear master, who can help anyone else? Who can get inside someone else's soul? Let everyone help himself! You won't believe me – but sometimes I lie alone like this . . . and it's as if there was no one in the whole world but me. I'm the only one alive! And it seems to me, it sort of dawns on me . . . ideas come to me – and such strange ones!"

"What are they about, Lukerya, these ideas of yours?"

"That, master, I can't tell you either: you'd never make it out. And I forget them afterwards. It will come, like a little cloud, it will burst, it will be all fresh and good, but what it was – you'll never understand! Only it seems to me that if there were people near me, none of this would happen, and I'd feel nothing except my own unhappiness."

Lukerya sighed painfully. Her chest was doing its work no better than the rest of her body.

"I can see by looking at you, master," she began again, "that you feel very sorry for me. But don't feel too sorry, don't indeed! Listen, I'll tell you something: even now, sometimes, I . . . well, you remember how gay I used to be in my time? Such a lively one! . . . Well, do you know what? Even now I sing songs."

"Songs? . . . You?"

"Yes, songs, old songs, round songs, carols, songs of all sorts! You see, I used to know many of them and I've not forgotten. Only I don't sing dance songs. As I am now, there wouldn't be any point."

"So you sing them . . . to yourself?"

"To myself, and aloud. I can't sing loudly, but loud enough to understand. I told you about the girl who comes to see me. An orphan, so she's an understanding sort. Well, I've taught her; she's already caught four songs from me. Don't you believe it? Wait, now I'm going to . . ."

Lukerya collected her strength . . . The thought that this half-dead creature was getting ready to sing horrified me in spite of myself. But, before I could say a word, there trembled in my ears a drawn-out, scarcely audible, but pure and true note . . . and after it followed another, then another. Lukerya was singing "In the meadows". She sang with no play of expression on her petrified face; even her eyes were fixed. But so touchingly did her poor, forced little voice sound, wavering like a wisp of smoke; so hard did she strive to pour out her whole soul . . . It was no longer horror that I felt: an indescribable pity gripped my heart.

"Oh, I can't!" she said suddenly. "I haven't the strength . . . I've been so pleased to see you."

She closed her eyes.

I put my hand on her tiny, cold fingers . . . She looked up at me – and her dark eyelids, trimmed with golden lashes, like those of an ancient statue, closed again. After a moment they glittered in the twilight . . . A tear had moistened them.

I sat there motionless as before.

"Just look at me!" said Lukerya suddenly, with unexpected force and, opening her eyes wide, tried to wipe the tears from them. "Oughtn't I to be ashamed? What do I want? This hasn't happened to me for a long time . . . not since the day when Vasily Polyakov was here last spring. As long as he was sitting talking to me – I didn't mind – but when he went away – I fairly cried away to myself! Where did it all come from? . . . But tears cost nothing to girls like us. Master," added Lukerya, "I expect you've got a handkerchief . . . Don't be put off, wipe my eyes."

I hastened to carry out her wish, and left her the handkerchief. At first she refused it . . . "What do I want with such a present?" she said. The handkerchief was very plain, but clean and white. Then she seized it in her weak fingers and did not loosen them again. I had grown used to the darkness in which we both were, and could make out her features clearly, could even discern a faint ruddiness, showing through the bronze of her face, could descry in that face, or so at least I thought, the traces of her former beauty,

"You asked me, master," began Lukerya again, "if I sleep. I certainly don't sleep much, but every time, I dream – good dreams! I never dream about myself as ill: I'm always well and young, in my dreams ... The only pity is that I wake up – and I want to have a good stretch – but it's as if I was all in chains. Once I had such a marvellous dream! Would you like me to tell you? Well, listen. I was standing in a field and all round was rye, so tall, and ripe like gold! ... And with me there was a red dog, fierce, very fierce – trying all the time to bite me. And in my hands I had a sickle, not just an ordinary sickle, but absolutely like the moon, when it's like a sickle. And with this moon I had to cut down the rye, every stalk of it. Only I was very tired from the heat, and the moon dazzled me, and laziness came over me; and around me corn-flowers were growing, such big ones! and they all had their heads turned towards me, and I thought: I'll pick these corn-flowers, Vasya promised to come – so I'll make a garland for myself first ... I've still got time for reaping. I began to pick the cornflowers, but they melted between my fingers, and melted, and there was nothing I could do! So I couldn't make my garland. But then I heard someone coming towards me, quite near, and calling: 'Lusha! ... Lusha! ...' Oh, I thought, what a shame – I haven't finished! Never mind, I'll put this moon on my head instead of the cornflowers. I put on the moon, just like a head-dress, and at once I seemed to be all aglow. I lit up the whole field around. I looked, and over the very tops of the ears of rye comes sweeping quickly towards me, not Vasya, but Christ himself! And how I knew that it was Christ, I can't say – He was not as He is in pictures – yet it was Him! Beardless, tall, young and in white, but with a golden belt – and He stretches out His hand to me. 'Never fear,' He says, 'my well-adorned bride, but follow Me; you will lead the dances in My Heavenly Kingdom and play the music of Paradise.' And how I clung to His hand! – my dog at once went for my legs ... But away we whirled! He was ahead ... His wings spread out over all the sky, long, like a seagull's – and I went after Him! And the dog had to stay behind. It was only then that I understood that this dog was my illness, and that there would be no place for it in the kingdom of heaven."

Lukerya was silent for a minute.

"And then I had another dream," she began again – "or perhaps this one was a vision ... I don't know. It seemed to me that I was alone in this cabin and that my dead parents came to me – my father and mother – and bowed low to me, but said nothing. And I asked them: 'Why are you bowing to me, father and mother?' 'Why,' they said, 'because you're suffering so much in this world that you've not only lightened your own soul's burden, but you've taken a heavy weight off us as well, and it's got much easier for us in the other world. You've already finished with your own sins; now you're overcoming ours.' And, so saying, my parents bowed to me again – and I could see them no longer: the walls were all I could see. I wondered very much afterwards what it was that had come over me. I even told the priest in confession. But he thinks that it couldn't have been a vision, because visions come only to those of the priestly calling.

"Then I had another dream," Lukerya went on. "I was sitting by a high-road, under a willow-tree, holding a peeled stick, with a bundle on my shoulder and my head wrapped in a kerchief – a regular pilgrim-woman! And I had to go somewhere far, far away, on a pilgrimage. And pilgrims kept on going past me; quietly they'd go, as if against their will, always the same way: they had sad faces, all very much like one another. And I saw, winding her way amongst them, a woman a head taller than the others, wearing a strange dress, not like ours in Russia. And her face was strange, too, a stern, fasting sort of face, and all the others seemed to keep away from her; and suddenly she turned – and came straight for me. She stopped and looked at me; her eyes were like a falcon's, yellow, big, and oh, so bright. And I asked her: 'Who are you?' and she said to me: 'I am your death.' I ought to have been afraid, but on the contrary I was glad, so glad, I crossed myself! And this woman, my death, said to me: 'I'm sorry for you, Lukerya, but I can't take you with me. – Goodbye!' Lord! how sad I was then! . . . 'Take me,' I said, 'mother, dearest one, take me!' And my death turned round to me, began to talk to me . . . I understood that she was telling me my hour, but darkly, as if in riddles . . . 'After St. Peter's,' she said . . . With that I woke up . . . That's the sort of strange dreams I have!"

Lukerya looked up . . . reflected . . .

"Only my trouble is this: it happens that a whole week goes by and I don't go to sleep once. Last year a lady drove by, saw me, and gave me a bottle with some medicine against sleeplessness; she told me to take ten drops at a time. It helped me a great deal and I slept. Only now the bottle has been finished long ago . . . D'you know what medicine that was, and how to get it?"

The passing lady had clearly given Lukerya opium. I promised to get her just such a bottle, and again could not refrain from admiring her patience aloud.

"Eh, master!" she rejoined. "What are you saying? What is this patience of mine? Simeon on the Pillar really did have great patience: he stood on his pillar for thirty years! And another martyr ordered himself to be buried in the ground up to his chest and the ants ate his face. And once, someone who had read many books told me that there was a certain country, and this country had been conquered by the heathen, and they tortured or put to death all the people in it; and try as the people of the country might, they couldn't free themselves. And then there appeared among those people a saintly virgin: she took a great sword, she put on herself clothes weighing seventy pounds, went out against the heathen and drove them all out beyond the sea. And only after she had driven them out, she said to them: 'Now burn me, because such was my promise, to die by fire for my people.' And the heathen took her and burnt her, and her people have been free ever since! There was a great deed for you! and what have I done?"

I marvelled to myself at this far-flung version of the Joan of Arc legend, and, after a pause, I asked Lukerya how old she was.

"Twenty-eight ... or twenty-nine ... less than thirty. But why count them, the years? I'll tell you something more ..."

Lukerya suddenly coughed dully and groaned.

"You're talking a great deal," I remarked to her. "It can do you harm."

"True," she whispered, in a hardly audible voice, "it's the end of our talk, but no matter. Now, when you go away, I shall have all the silence I want. At least, I have got a lot off my mind ..."

I started saying good-bye to her, repeated my promise to send her the medicine, and asked her to think carefully once more and tell me whether there was nothing she needed.

"I need nothing; I'm absolutely content, praise be to God," she pronounced, with extreme effort, but also with emotion. "May God grant health to everyone! And you, mas-ter, please speak to your mother – the peasants here are poor

139

– if she would only bring down their rent, just a little! They haven't enough land, they make nothing out of it! ... They would pray to God for you , but I need nothing, I'm absolutely content."

I gave Lukerya my word to carry out her request, and was already making for the door when she called me back.

"D'you remember, master," she said, with a wonderful brightening of her eyes and lips, "what hair I had? D'you remember – right down to my knees! For a long time I couldn't make up my mind ... Such hair it was! ... But how could I comb it! In my condition! So I cut it off ... yes ... Well, good-bye, master! I can't say more ..."

The same day, before setting out to shoot, I had a talk about Lukerya with the local constable. I learnt from him that in the village she was called "the Live Relic", also that she caused no trouble; there was not a grumble to be heard from her, not a complaint. "She asks nothing for herself, on the contrary she's grateful for everything; she's as quiet as quiet can be, that I must say. She's been smitten by God," so the constable concluded, "for her sins, no doubt; but we don't go into that. As for condemning her, for example, no, we certainly don't condemn her. Let her be!"

A few weeks later I heard that Lukerya was dead. Death had come for her after all ... and "after St. Peter's". The story went that on the day of her death she kept hearing the sound of bells, although it is more than five versts from Alexeyevka to the church, and it was on a weekday. Besides, Lukerya said that the sound came, not from church, but "from above". Probably she did not venture to say – from heaven.

1874

FYODOR DOSTOYEVSKY

THE DREAM OF A
RIDICULOUS MAN

Translated by Richard Pevear and Larissa Volokhonsky

I

I AM A RIDICULOUS man. They call me mad now. That would be a step up in rank, if I did not still remain as ridiculous to them as before. But now I'm no longer angry, now they are all dear to me, and even when they laugh at me – then, too, they are even somehow especially dear to me. I would laugh with them – not really at myself, but for love of them – if it weren't so sad for me to look at them. Sad because they don't know the truth, and I do know the truth. Ah, how hard it is to be the only one who knows the truth! But they won't understand that. No, they won't understand it.

Before, it caused me great anguish that I seemed ridiculous. Not seemed, but was. I was always ridiculous, and I know it, maybe right from birth. Maybe from the age of seven I already knew I was ridiculous. Then I went to school, then to the university, and what – the more I studied, the more I learned that I was ridiculous. So that for me, all my university education existed ultimately as if only to prove and explain to me, the deeper I went into it, that I was ridiculous. And as with learning, so with life. Every passing year the same consciousness grew and strengthened in me that my appearancc was in all respects ridiculous. I was ridiculed by everyone and always. But none of them knew or suspected that if there was one man on earth who was more aware than anyone else of my ridiculousness, it was I myself, and this was the most vexing thing for me, that they didn't know it, but here I myself was to blame: I was always so proud that I would never confess it to anyone for anything. This pride grew in me over the years, and if it had so happened that I allowed myself to confess to anyone at all that I was ridiculous, I think that same evening I'd have blown my head off with a revolver. Oh, how I suffered in my youth over being unable to help myself and suddenly somehow confessing it to my comrades. But once I reached early manhood, I became a bit calmer for some reason, though with every passing year I learned more and more about my terrible quality. Precisely for some reason, because to this day I cannot determine why. Maybe because a dreadful anguish was growing in my soul over one circumstance which was infinitely higher than the whole of me: namely – the conviction was overtaking me that everywhere in the world it *made no difference*. I had had a presentiment of this for a very long time, but the full conviction came during the last year somehow suddenly. I suddenly felt that it would *make no difference* to me whether the world existed or there was nothing anywhere. I began to feel and know with my whole being that *with me there was nothing*. At first I kept thinking that instead there had been a lot before, but then I realized that there had been nothing before either, it only seemed so for some reason. Little by little I became convinced that there would never be anything. Then I suddenly stopped being angry with people and began almost not to notice them. Indeed, this was manifest even in the smallest trifles: it would happen, for instance, that I'd walk down the street and bump into people. It wasn't really because I was lost in thought: what could I have been thinking about, I had completely ceased to think then: it made no difference to me. And it would have been fine if I had resolved questions – oh, I never resolved a single one, and there were so many! But it began to *make no difference* to me, and the questions all went away.

And then, after that, I learned the truth. I learned the truth last November, precisely on the third of November, and since that time I remember my every moment. It was a gloomy evening, as gloomy as could be. I was returning home then, between ten and eleven o'clock, and I remember I precisely thought that there could not be a gloomier time. Even in the physical respect. Rain had poured down all day, and it was the coldest and gloomiest rain, even some sort of menacing rain, I remember that, with an obvious hostility to people, and now, between ten and eleven, it suddenly stopped, and a terrible dampness set in, damper and colder than when it was raining, and a sort of steam rose from everything, from every stone in the street and from every alleyway, if you looked far into its depths from the street. I suddenly imagined that if the gaslights went out everywhere, it would be more cheerful, and that with the gaslights it was sadder for the heart, because they threw light on it all. I'd had almost no dinner that day, and had spent since early evening sitting at some engineer's, with two more friends sitting there as well. I kept silent, and they seemed to be sick of me. They talked about something provocative and suddenly even grew excited. But it made no difference to them, I could see that, and they got excited just so. I suddenly told them that: "Gentlemen," I said, "it makes no difference to you." They weren't offended, but they all started laughing at me. It was because I said it without any reproach and simply because it made no difference to me. And they could see that it made no difference to me, and found that amusing.

When I thought in the street about the gaslights, I looked up at the sky. The sky was terribly dark, but one could clearly make out the torn clouds and the bottomless black spots between them. Suddenly in one of these spots I noticed a little star and began gazing at it intently. Because this little star gave me an idea I resolved to kill myself that night. I had firmly resolved on it two months earlier, and, poor as I was, had bought an excellent revolver and loaded it that same day. But two months had passed and it was still lying in the drawer; but it made so little difference to me that I wished finally to seize a moment when it was less so – why, I didn't know. And thus, during those two months, returning home each night, I thought I was going to shoot myself. I kept waiting for the moment. And so now this little star gave me the idea, and I resolved that it would be that night *without fail*. And why the star gave me the idea – I don't know.

And so, as I was looking at the sky, this girl suddenly seized me by the elbow. The street was empty, and almost no one was about. Far off a coachman was sleeping in his droshky. The girl was about eight years old, in a kerchief and just a little dress, all wet, but I especially remembered her wet, torn shoes, and remember them now. They especially flashed before my eyes. She suddenly started pulling me by the elbow and calling out. She didn't cry, but somehow abruptly shouted some words, which she was unable to pronounce properly because she was chilled and shivering all over. She was terrified by something and shouted desperately: "Mama! Mama!" I turned my face to her, but did not say a word and went on walking, but she was running and pulling at me, and in her voice there was the sound which in very frightened children indicates despair. I know that sound. Though she did not speak all the words out, I understood that her mother was dying somewhere, or something had happened with them there, and she had run out to call someone, to find something so as to help her mother. But I did not go with her, and, on the contrary, suddenly had the idea of chasing

146

her away. First I told her to go and find a policeman. But she suddenly pressed her hands together and, sobbing, choking, kept running beside me and wouldn't leave me. It was then that I stamped my feet at her and shouted. She only cried out: "Mister! Mister! . . ." but suddenly she dropped me and ran headlong across the street: some other passerby appeared there, and she apparently rushed from me to him.

I went up to my fifth floor. I live in a rented room, a furnished one. It's a poor and small room, with a half-round garret window. I have an oilcloth sofa, a table with books on it, two chairs, and an armchair, as old as can be, but a Voltaire one. I sat down, lighted a candle, and began to think. Next door, in another room, behind a partition, there was bedlam. It had been going on for two days. A retired captain lived there, and he had guests – some six scurvy fellows, drinking vodka and playing blackjack with used cards. The previous night they'd had a fight, and I know that two of them had pulled each other's hair for a long time. The landlady wanted to lodge a complaint, but she's terribly afraid of the captain. The only other tenants in our furnished rooms are a small, thin lady, an army wife and out-of-towner, with three small children who had already fallen ill in our rooms. She and her children are afraid of the captain to the point of fainting, and spend whole nights trembling and crossing themselves, and the smallest child had some sort of fit from fear. This captain, I know for certain, sometimes stops passersby on Nevsky Prospect and begs money from them. They won't take him into any kind of service, yet, strangely (this is what I've been driving at), in the whole month that he had been living with us, the captain had never aroused any vexation in me. Of course, I avoided making his acquaintance from the very start, and he himself got bored with me from the first, yet no matter how they shouted

147

behind their partition, and however many they were – it never made any difference to me. I sit the whole night and don't really hear them, so far do I forget about them. I don't sleep at night until dawn, and that for a year now. I sit all night at the table in the armchair and do nothing. I read books only during the day. I sit and don't even think, just so, some thoughts wander about and I let them go. A whole candle burns down overnight. I quietly sat down at the table, took out the revolver, and placed it in front of me. As I placed it there, I remember asking myself: "Is it so?" and answering myself quite affirmatively: "It is." Meaning I would shoot myself. I knew that I would shoot myself that night for certain, but how long I would stay sitting at the table before then – that I did not know. And of course I would have shot myself if it hadn't been for that girl.

II

YOU SEE: though it made no difference to me, I did still feel pain, for instance. If someone hit me, I would feel pain. The same in the moral respect: if something very pitiful happened, I would feel pity, just as when it still made a difference to me in life. And I felt pity that night: I certainly would have helped a child. Why then, had I not helped the little girl? From an idea that had come along then: as she was pulling and calling to me, a question suddenly arose before me, and I couldn't resolve it. The question was an idle one, but I got angry. I got angry owing to the conclusion that, if I had already resolved to kill myself that night, it followed that now more than ever everything in the world should make no difference to me. Why, then, did I suddenly feel that it did make a difference, and that I pitied the girl? I remember that

I pitied her very much; even to the point of some strange pain, even quite incredible in my situation. Really, I'm unable to express the fleeting feeling I had then any better, but the feeling continued at home as well, when I had already settled at my table, and I was extremely vexed, as I hadn't been for a long time. Reasoning flowed from reasoning. It seemed clear that, if I was a man and not yet a zero, then, as long as I did not turn into a zero, I was alive and consequently could suffer, be angry, and feel shame for my actions. Good. But if I was going to kill myself in two hours, for instance, then what was the girl to me and what did I care then about shame or anything in the world? I turned into a zero, an absolute zero. And could it be that the awareness that I would presently cease to exist *altogether*, and that therefore nothing would exist, could not have the slightest influence either on my feeling of pity for the girl, or upon the feeling of shame after the meanness I had committed? And I had stamped and shouted at the unfortunate child in a savage voice precisely because, "you see, not only do I feel no pity, but even if I commit some inhuman meanness, I can do so now, because in two hours everything will be extinguished." Do you believe this was why I shouted? I'm now almost convinced of it. It seemed clear that life and the world were now as if dependent on me. One might even say that the world was now as if made for me alone: I'd shoot myself and there would be no more world, at least for me. Not to mention that maybe there would indeed be nothing for anyone after me, and that as soon as my consciousness was extinguished, the whole world would be extinguished at once, like a phantom, like a mere accessory of my consciousness, it would be done away with, for maybe all this world and all these people were – just myself alone. I remember that, sitting and reasoning, I turned all these new questions, which

149

came crowding one after another, even in quite a different direction and invented something quite new. For instance, there suddenly came to me a strange consideration, that if I had once lived on the moon or on Mars, and had committed some most shameful and dishonorable act there, such as can only be imagined, and had been abused and dishonored for it as one can only perhaps feel and imagine in a dream, a nightmare, and if, ending up later on earth, I continued to preserve an awareness of what I had done on the other planet, and knew at the same time that I would never ever return there, then, looking from the earth to the moon – would it *make any difference* to me, or not? Would I feel shame for that act, or not? The questions were idle and superfluous, since the revolver was already lying in front of me, and I knew with my whole being that *this* was certain to be, but they excited me, and I was getting furious. It was as if I couldn't die now without first resolving something. In short, this girl saved me, because with the questions I postponed the shot. Meanwhile, everything was also quieting down at the captain's: they had ended their card game and were settling down to sleep, grumbling and lazily finishing their squabbles. It was then that I suddenly fell asleep, something that had never happened to me before, at the table, in the armchair. I fell asleep quite imperceptibly to myself. Dreams, as is known, are extremely strange: one thing is pictured with the most terrible clarity, with a jeweler's thoroughness in the finish of its details, and over other things you skip as if without noticing them at all – for instance, over space and time. Dreams apparently proceed not from reason but from desire, not from the head but from the heart, and yet what clever things my reason has sometimes performed in sleep! And yet quite inconceivable things happen with it in sleep. My brother, for instance, died five years ago. Sometimes I see him in my dreams: he takes part in my doings, we are both very interested, and yet I remember and am fully aware, throughout the whole dream, that my brother is dead and buried. Why, then, am I not surprised that, though he is dead, he is still here by me and busy with me? Why does my reason fully admit all this? But enough. I'll get down to my dream. Yes, I had this dream then, my dream of the third of November! They tease me now that it was just a dream. But does it make any difference whether it was a dream or not, if this dream proclaimed the Truth to me? For if you once knew the truth and saw it, then you know that it is the truth and there is and can be no other, whether you're asleep or alive. So let it be a dream, let it be, but this life, which you extol so much, I wanted to extinguish by suicide, while my dream, my dream – oh, it proclaimed to me a new, great, renewed, strong life!

Listen.

III

I SAID THAT I fell asleep imperceptibly and even as if while continuing to reason about the same matters. Suddenly I dreamed that I took the revolver and, sitting there, aimed it straight at my heart – my heart, not my head; though I had resolved earlier to shoot myself in the head, and precisely in the right temple. Having aimed it at my chest, I waited for a second or two, and my candle, the table, and the wall facing me suddenly started moving and heaving. I hastily fired.

In dreams you sometimes fall from a height, or are stabbed, or beaten, but you never feel pain except when you are somehow really hurt in bed, then you do feel pain and it almost always wakes you up. So it was in my dream: I felt no pain, but I imagined that, as I fired, everything shook inside me and everything suddenly went out, and it became terribly black around me. I became as if blind and dumb, and now I'm lying on something hard, stretched out on my back, I don't see anything and can't make the slightest movement. Around me there is walking and shouting, there is the captain's bass and the landlady's shrieking – and suddenly another break, and now I'm being carried in a closed coffin. And I feel the coffin heave and I start reasoning about that, when suddenly for the first time I'm struck by the idea that I'm dead, quite dead, I know this and do not doubt it, I can't see, I can't move, yet I feel and reason. But I quickly come to terms with it and, as is usual in dreams, accept the reality without arguing.

And now they bury me in the ground. Everyone leaves, I'm alone, completely alone. I can't move. Always before, whenever I actually imagined to myself how I would be buried in the grave, my only association with the grave proper was the feeling of dampness and cold. So now, too, I felt that I was very cold, especially the tips of my toes, but I didn't feel anything else.

I lay there and, strangely – didn't expect anything, accepting without argument that a dead man has nothing to expect. But it was damp. I don't know how much time passed – an hour, or a few days, or many days. But then suddenly a drop of water that had seeped through the lid of the coffin fell on my closed left eye, another followed it in a minute, then a third a minute later, and so on and so on, with a minute's interval. A deep indignation suddenly blazed up in my heart, and suddenly I felt physical pain in it. "It's my wound," I thought, "it's my shot, there's a bullet there . . ." The drop kept dripping, each minute and straight onto my closed eye. And I suddenly called out, not in a voice, for I was motionless, but with my whole being, to the master of all that was coming to pass with me.

"Whoever you are, if you're there, and if there exists anything more reasonable than what is coming to pass now, allow it to be here, too. And if you are taking revenge on me for my unreasonable suicide by the ugliness and absurdity of my subsequent existence, know, then, that no matter what torment befalls me, it will never equal the contempt I am silently going to feel, even if the torment were to last millions of years! . . ."

I called out and fell silent. For almost a whole minute the deep silence lasted, and one more drop even fell, but I knew, boundlessly and inviolably, I knew and believed that everything was certain to change presently. And then suddenly my grave gaped wide. That is, I don't know whether it was opened and dug up, but I was taken by some dark being unknown to me, and we found ourselves in space. I suddenly could see again: it was deep night, and never, never has there been such darkness! We were rushing through space far from earth. I did not ask the one carrying me about anything, I waited and was proud. I assured myself that I was not afraid and swooned with delight at the thought that I was not afraid. I don't remember how long we rushed like that, and cannot imagine it: everything was happening as it always does in dreams, when you leap over space and time and over the laws of being and reason, and pause only on the points of the heart's reverie. I remember that I suddenly saw a little star in the darkness. "Is that Sirius?" I asked, suddenly unable to restrain myself, for I did not want to ask about anything. "No, it is the very star you saw between the clouds, as you were returning home," the being who was carrying me replied. I knew that it had as if a human countenance. Strangely, I did not like this being, I even felt a deep revulsion. I had expected complete nonexistence and with that had shot myself in the heart. And here I am in the hands of a being – not a human one, of course – but who *is*, who exists: "Ah, so there is life beyond the grave!" I thought with the strange light-mindedness of dreams, but the essence of my heart remained with me in all its depth: "And if I must *be* again," I thought, "and live again according to someone's ineluctable will, I don't want to be defeated and humiliated!" "You know I'm afraid of you, and you despise me for it," I said suddenly to my companion, unable to hold back the humiliating question, which contained a confession, and feeling my humiliation like the prick of a needle in my heart. He did not answer my question, but I suddenly felt that I was not despised or laughed at, and not even pitied, and that our journey had an unknown and mysterious purpose which concerned me alone. Fear was growing in my heart. Something was being communicated to me, mutely but tormentingly, from my silent companion, and was as if penetrating me. We were rushing through dark and unknown spaces. I had long ceased to see constellations familiar to the eye. I knew that in the heavenly spaces there were stars whose light reached the earth only after thousands or millions of years. Maybe we were already flying through those spaces. I awaited something in a terrible anguish that wrung my heart. And suddenly the call of some highly familiar feeling shook me: I suddenly saw our sun! I knew it could not be *our* sun, which had generated *our* earth, and that we were at an infinite distance from our sun, but for some reason I recognized, with my whole being, that it was absolutely the same as our sun, its replica and double. The call of a sweet feeling sounded delightfully in my soul: the native power of light, the same light that gave birth to me, echoed in my heart and resurrected it, and I felt life, the former life, for the first time after my grave.

"But if this is the sun, if this is absolutely the same as our sun," I cried out, "then where is the earth?" And my companion pointed to the little star that shone in the darkness with an emerald brilliance. We were rushing straight toward her.

"And are such replicas really possible in the universe, is that really the law of nature? . . . And if that is the earth there, is it really the same as our earth . . . absolutely the same, unfortunate, poor, but dear and eternally beloved, giving birth to the same tormenting love for herself even in her most ungrateful children? . . ." I cried out, shaking with irrepressible, rapturous love for that former native earth I had abandoned. The image of the poor little girl whom I had offended flashed before me.

"You will see all," my companion replied, and some sadness sounded in his words. But we were quickly approaching the planet. It was growing before my eyes, I could already make out the ocean, the outlines of Europe, and suddenly a strange feeling of some great, holy jealousy blazed up in my heart: "How can there be such a replica, and what for? I love, I can love, only the earth I left, where the stains of my blood were left, when I, the ungrateful one, extinguished my life with a shot in the heart. But never, never did I cease to love that earth, and even on that night, as I was parting from her, I perhaps loved her more tormentingly than ever before. Is there suffering on this new earth? On our earth we can love truly only with suffering and through suffering! We're unable to love otherwise and we know no other love. I want suffering, in order to love. I want, I thirst, to kiss, this very minute, pouring out tears, that one earth alone which I left, and I do not want, I do not accept life on any other! . . ."

But my companion had already left me. Suddenly, as if quite imperceptibly, I came to stand on this other earth, in the bright light of a sunny day, lovely as paradise. I was standing, it seems, on one of those islands which on our earth make up the Greek archipelago, or somewhere on the coast of the mainland adjacent to that archipelago. Oh, everything was exactly as with us, but seemed everywhere to radiate some festivity and a great, holy, and finally attained triumph. The gentle emerald sea splashed softly against the shores and kissed them with love – plain, visible, almost conscious. Tall, beautiful trees stood in all the luxury of their flowering, and their numberless leaves, I was convinced, greeted me with their soft, gentle sound, as if uttering words of love. The grass glittered with bright, fragrant flowers. Flocks of birds flew about in the air and, fearless of me, landed on my shoulders and arms, joyfully beating me with their dear, fluttering wings. And finally I got to see and know the people of that happy earth. They came to me themselves, they surrounded me, kissed me. Children of the sun, children of their sun – oh, how beautiful they were! Never on our earth have I seen such beauty in man. Maybe only in our children, in their first years, can one find a remote, though faint, glimmer of that beauty. The eyes of these happy people shone with clear brightness. Their faces radiated reason and a sort of consciousness fulfilled to the point of serenity, yet they were mirthful faces; a childlike joy sounded in the words and voices of these people. Oh, at once, with the first glance at their faces, I understood everything, everything! This was the earth undefiled by the fall, the people who lived on it had not sinned, they lived in the same paradise in which, according to the legends of all mankind, our fallen forefathers lived, with the only difference that the whole earth here was everywhere one and the same paradise. These people, laughing joyfully, crowded around me and caressed me; they took me with them and each of them wished to set me at ease. Oh, they didn't ask me about anything, but it seemed to me as if they already knew everything, and wished quickly to drive the torment from my face.

IV

YOU SEE, once again: well, let it be only a dream! But the feeling of love from these innocent and beautiful people remained in me ever after, and I feel that their love pours upon me from there even now. I saw them myself, I knew them and was convinced, I loved them, I suffered for them afterward. Oh, I at once understood, even then, that in many ways I would never understand them; to me, a modern Russian progressive and vile Petersburger, it seemed insoluble, for instance, that they, while knowing so much, did not have our science. But I soon realized that their knowledge was fulfilled and nourished by different insights than on our earth, and that their aspirations were also quite different. They did not wish for anything and were at peace, they did not aspire to a knowlege of life, as we do, because their life was fulfilled. But their knowledge was deeper and loftier than our science; for our science seeks to explain what life is, it aspires to comprehend it, in order to teach others to live; but they knew how to live even without science, and I understood that, but I could not understand their knowledge. They pointed out their trees to me, and I could not understand the extent of the love with which they looked at them: as if they were talking with creatures of their own kind. And you know, perhaps I wouldn't be mistaken if I said that they did talk to them! Yes, they had found their language, and I'm convinced that the trees understood them. They looked at the whole of nature in the same way – at the animals, who lived in peace with them, did not attack them, and loved them, won over by their love. They pointed out the stars to me and talked of them with me about something I couldn't understand, but I'm convinced that they had some contact, as it were, with the heavenly stars, not just in thought, but in some living way. Oh, these people did not even try to make me understand them, they loved me even without that, but on the other hand I knew that they would also never understand me, and therefore I hardly ever spoke to them about our earth, I only kissed before them that earth on which they lived and wordlessly adored them, and they saw it and allowed me to adore them without being ashamed of my adoring them, because they loved much themselves. They did not suffer for me when sometimes, in tears, I kissed their feet, joyfully knowing at heart with what force of love they would respond to me. At times I asked myself in astonishment: how could they manage, all this while, not to insult a man such as I, and never once provoke in a man such as I any feeling of jealousy or envy? Many times I asked myself how I, a braggart and a liar, could manage not to speak to them about my knowledge – of which they, of course, had no notion – not to wish to astonish them with it, if only out of love for them? They were frisky and gay as children. They wandered through their beautiful groves and forests, they sang their beautiful songs, they ate their light food – fruit from their trees, honey from their forests, and milk from the animals who loved them. For their food and clothing they labored little and but lightly. There was love among them, and children were born, but I never observed in them any impulses of that *cruel* sensuality that overtakes almost everyone on our earth, each and every one, and is the only source of almost all the sins of our mankind. They rejoiced in the children they had as new partakers of their bliss. Among them there was no quarreling or jealousy, they did not even understand what it meant. Their children were everyone's children, because they all constituted one family. They had almost no illnesses, though there was death, but their old people died quietly, as if falling asleep, surrounded by those bidding them farewell, blessing them, smiling at them, and receiving bright parting smiles themselves. I saw no sorrow or tears at that, there was only love increased as if to the point of rapture, but a rapture that was calm, fulfilled, contemplative. One might think they were in touch with their dead even after their death and that the earthly union between them was not interrupted by death. They barely understood me when I asked them about eternal life, but they were apparently so convinced of it unconsciously that it did not constitute a question for them. They had no temples, but they had some essential, living, and constant union with the Entirety of the universe; they had no faith, but instead had a firm knowledge that when their earthly joy was fulfilled to the limits of earthly nature, there would then come for them, both for the living and for the dead, a still greater expansion of their contact with the Entirety of the universe. They waited for this moment with joy, but without haste, without suffering over it, but as if already having it in the presages of their hearts, which they conveyed to one another. In the evenings, before going to sleep, they liked to sing in balanced, harmonious choruses. In these songs they expressed all the feelings that the departing day had given them, praised it, and bade it farewell. They praised nature, the earth, the sea, the forest. They liked to compose songs about each other and praised each other like children; these were the most simple songs, but they flowed from the heart and penetrated hearts. And not in songs only, but it seemed they spent their whole life only in admiring each other. It was a sort of mutual being-in-love, total, universal. And some of their songs, solemn and rapturous, I hardly understood at all. While I understood the words, I was never able to penetrate their full meaning. It remained as if inaccessible to my mind, yet my heart was as if unconsciously pervaded by it more and more. I often told them that I had long ago had a presentiment of all this, that all this joy and glory had already spoken to me on our earth in an anguished call, sometimes reaching the point of unbearable sorrow; that I had had a presentiment of them all and of their glory in the dreams of my heart and the reveries of my mind, that I had often been unable, on our earth, to watch the setting sun without tears … That my hatred of the people of our earth always contained anguish: why am I unable to hate them without loving them, why am I unable not to forgive them, and why is there anguish in my love for them: why am I unable to love them without hating them? They listened to me, and I saw that they could not imagine what I was talking about, but I did not regret talking to them about it: I knew they understood all the intensity of my anguish for those whom I had abandoned. Yes, when they looked at me with their dear eyes pervaded by love, when I felt that in their presence my heart, too, became as innocent and truthful as theirs, I did not regret not understanding them. The feeling of the fullness of life took my breath away, and I silently worshipped them.

Oh, everyone laughs in my face now and assures me that even in dreams one cannot see such details as I'm now telling, that in my dream I saw or felt only a certain sensation generated by my own heart in delirium, and that I invented the details when I woke up. And when I disclosed to them that perhaps it was actually so – God, what laughter they threw in my face, what fun they had at my expense! Oh, yes, of course, I was overcome just by the sensation of that dream, and it alone survived in the bloody wound of my heart: yet the real images and forms of my dream, that is, those that I actually saw at the time of my dreaming, were fulfilled so harmoniously, they were so enchanting and beautiful, and so true, that having awakened, I was, of course, unable to embody them in our weak words, so that they must have been as if effaced in my mind, and therefore, indeed, perhaps I myself unconsciously was forced to invent the details afterward; and of course distorted them, especially with my so passionate desire to hurry and tell them at least somehow. And yet how can I not believe that it all really was? And was, perhaps, a thousand times better, brighter, and more joyful than I'm telling? Let it be a dream, still it all could not but be. You know, I'll tell you a secret: perhaps it wasn't a dream at all! For here a certain thing happened, something so terribly true that it couldn't have been imagined in a dream. Let my dream have been generated by my heart, but was my heart alone capable of generating the terrible truth that happened to me afterward? How could I myself invent or imagine it in my heart? Can it be that my paltry heart and capricious, insignificant mind were able to rise to such a revelation of the truth! Oh, judge for youselves: I've concealed it so far, but now I'll finish telling this truth as well. The thing was that I . . . corrupted them all!

V

YES, YES, it ended with me corrupting them all! How it could have happened I don't know, but I remember it clearly. The dream flew through thousands of years and left in me just a sense of the whole. I know only that the cause of the fall was I. Like a foul trichina, like an atom of plague infecting whole countries, so I infected that whole happy and previously sinless earth with myself. They learned to lie and began to love the lie and knew the beauty of the lie. Oh, maybe it started *innocently*, with a joke, with coquetry, with amorous play, maybe, indeed, with an atom, but this atom of lie penetrated their hearts, and they liked it. Then sensuality was quickly born, sensuality generated jealousy, and jealousy – cruelty ... Oh, I don't know, I don't remember, but soon, very soon, the first blood was shed; they were astonished and horrified, and began to part, to separate. Alliances appeared, but against each other now. Rebukes, reproaches began. They knew shame, and shame was made into a virtue. The notion of honor was born, and each alliance raised its own banner. They began tormenting animals, and the animals withdrew from them into the forests and became their enemies. There began the struggle for separation, for isolation, for the personal, for mine and yours. They started speaking different languages. They knew sorrow and came to love sorrow, they thirsted for suffering and said that truth is attained only through suffering. Then science appeared among them. When they became wicked, they began to talk of brotherhood and humaneness and understood these ideas. When they became criminal, they invented justice and prescribed whole codices for themselves in order to maintain it, and to ensure the codices they set up the guillotine. They just barely remembered what they had lost, and did not even want to believe that they had once been innocent and happy. They even laughed at the possibility of the former happiness and called it a dream. They couldn't even imagine it in forms and images, but – strange and wonderful thing – having lost all belief in their former happiness, having called it a fairy tale, they wished so much to be innocent and happy again, once more, that they fell down before their hearts' desires like children, they deified their desire, they built temples and started praying to their own idea, their own "desire," all the while fully believing in its unrealizability and unfeasibility, but adoring it in tears and worshipping it. And yet, if it had so happened that they could have returned to that innocent and happy condition which they had lost, or if someone had suddenly shown it to them again and asked them: did they want to go back to it? – they would certainly have refused. They used to answer me: "Granted we're deceitful, wicked, and unjust, we *know* that and weep for it, and we torment ourselves over it, and torture and punish ourselves perhaps even more than that merciful judge who will judge us and whose name we do not know. But we have science, and through it we shall again find the truth, but we shall now accept it consciously, knowledge is higher than feelings, the consciousness of life is higher than life. Science will give us wisdom, wisdom will discover laws, and knowledge of the laws of happiness is higher than happiness." That's what they used to say, and after such words each of them loved himself more than anyone else, and they couldn't have done otherwise. Each of them became so jealous of his own person that he tried as hard as he could to humiliate and belittle it in others, and gave his life to that. Slavery appeared, even voluntary slavery: the weak willingly submitted to the strong, only so as to help them crush those still weaker than themselves. Righteous men appeared, who came to these people in tears and spoke to them of their pride, their lack of measure and harmony, their loss of shame. They were derided or stoned. Holy blood was spilled on the thresholds of temples. On the other hand, people began to appear who started inventing ways for everyone to unite so that each of them, without ceasing to love himself more than anyone else, would at the same time not hinder others, and thus live all together in a harmonious society, as it were. Whole wars arose because of this idea. At the same time, the warring sides all firmly believed that science, wisdom, and the sense of self-preservation would finally force men to unite in harmonious and reasonable society, and therefore, to speed things up meanwhile, the "wise" tried quickly to exterminate all the "unwise," who did not understand their idea, so that they would not hinder its triumph. But the sense of self-preservation quickly began to weaken, proud men and sensualists appeared who directly demanded everything or nothing. To acquire everything, they resorted to evildoing, and if that did not succeed – to suicide. Religions appeared with a cult of nonbeing and self-destruction for the sake of eternal peace in nothingness. Finally, these people grew weary in meaningless toil, and suffering appeared on their faces, and these people proclaimed that suffering is beauty, for only in suffering is there thought. They sang suffering in their songs. I walked among them, wringing my hands, and wept over them, but I loved them perhaps still more than before, when there was as yet no suffering on their faces and they were innocent and so beautiful. I loved their defiled earth still more than when it had been a paradise, only because grief had appeared on it. Alas, I had always loved grief and sorrow, but only for myself, for myself, while over them I wept, pitying them. I stretched out my arms to them, in despair accusing, cursing, and despising myself. I told them that I, I alone, had done it all; that it was I who had brought them depravity, infection, and the lie! I beseeched them to crucify me on a cross, I taught them how to make a cross. I couldn't, I hadn't the strength to kill myself, but I wanted to take the suffering from them, I longed for suffering, I longed to shed my blood to the last drop in this suffering. But they just laughed at me and in the end began to consider me some sort of holy fool. They vindicated me, they said they had received only what they themselves had wanted, and that everything could not but be as it was. Finally, they announced to me that I was becoming dangerous for them and that they would put me in a madhouse if I didn't keep quiet. Here sorrow entered my soul with such force that my heart was wrung, and I felt I was going to die, and here ... well, here I woke up.

It was already morning, that is, not light yet, but it was about six o'clock. I came to my senses in the same armchair, my candle had burned all the way down, everyone was asleep at the captain's, and around me was a silence rare in our apartment. First of all, I jumped up extremely surprised; nothing like that had ever happened to me, even down to trifling little details: for instance, never before had I fallen asleep in my armchair like that. Here suddenly, while I was standing and coming to my senses – suddenly my revolver flashed before me, ready, loaded – but I instantly pushed it away from me! Oh, life, life now! I lifted up my arms and called out to the eternal truth; did not call out, but wept; rapture, boundless rapture, elevated my whole being. Yes, life and – preaching! I decided on preaching that same moment, and, of course, for the rest of my life! I'm going out to preach, I want to preach – what? The truth, for I saw it, saw it with my own eyes, saw all its glory!

And so, since then I've been preaching! What's more – I love those who laugh at me more than all the rest. Why that's so I don't know and can't explain, but let it be so. They say I'm already getting confused now, that is, if I'm already so confused now, how will it be later? The veritable truth: I'm getting confused now, and maybe it will be worse later. And of course I'm going to get confused a few times before I discover how to preach, that is, in what words and in what deeds, because it's very hard to do. I see it clear as day even now, but listen: is there anyone who doesn't get confused? And yet everyone goes toward one and the same thing, at least everyone strives for one and the same thing, from the sage to the last robber, only by different paths. This is an old truth, but what is new here is this: I cannot get very confused. Because I saw the truth, I saw and I know that people can be beautiful and happy without losing the ability to live on earth. I will not and cannot believe that evil is the normal condition of people. And they all laugh merely at this belief of mine. But how can I not believe: I saw the truth – it's not that my mind invented it, but I saw it, I saw it, and its *living image* filled my soul for all time. I saw it in such fulfilled wholeness that I cannot believe it is impossible for people to have it. And so, how could I get confused? I'll wander off, of course, even several times, and will maybe even speak in other people's words, but not for long: the living image of what I saw will always be with me and will always correct and direct me. Oh, I'm hale, I'm fresh, I'm going, going, even if it's for a thousand years. You know, I even wanted to conceal, at first, that I corrupted them all, but that was a mistake – already the first mistake! But truth whispered to me that I was *lying*, and guarded and directed me. But how to set up paradise – I don't know, because I'm unable to put it into words. After my dream, I lost words. At least all the main words, the most necessary ones. But so be it: I'll go and I'll keep talking, tirelessly, because after all I saw it with my own eyes, though I can't recount what I saw. But that is what the scoffers don't understand: "He had a dream," they say, "a delirium, a hallucination." Eh! As if that's so clever? And how proud they are! A dream? what is a dream? And is our life not a dream? I'll say more: let it never, let it never come true, and let there be no paradise (that I can understand!) – well, but I will preach all the same. And yet it's so simple: in one day, *in one hour* – it could all be set up at once! The main thing is – love others as yourself, that's the main thing, and it's everything, there's no need for anything else at all: it will immediately be discovered how to set things up. And yet this is merely an old truth, repeated and read a billion times, but still it has never taken root! "The consciousness of life is higher than life, the knowledge of the laws of happiness is higher than happiness" – that is what must be fought! And I will. If only everyone wants it, everything can be set up at once.

And I found that little girl . . . And I'll go! I'll go!

1877

ANASTASIYA MIROVICH

ELSA

Translated by Catriona Kelly

"SILENCE," said the pastor, closing his bible. "If even the words of our divine Saviour cannot express poor Elsa's condition, what may human language say of her?"

Elsa's mother went on weeping; her tears came in such floods that she could not wipe them away. They poured from her eyes like floods from a great salty sea – oh yes! a salty sea!

"Elsa," she said to her daughter, "what time is it?"

"Cock-crow," Elsa replied.

So they sat, the three of them, in the dark of the night, and it did not enter anyone's head that it was time they were in bed.

"Elsa, my child," said the pastor, "tell us what happened to you."

The girl shook back her thick hair and laid her arms on the table. She began tracing her finger over the pattern on the tablecloth, and telling them what had happened. It was the third time already that night she had told them; had ten thousand nights been stretched end to end, they would have spent each one in the same way.

"We left in the early morning to search for waste land where we might bury those we had killed. They were all Saxon Guards; they were all wearing blue uniforms with gold braid. When one of them was dying he cursed me, saying I should give birth to vipers, not children. We hid our knives far away; we covered all the traces of our crime."

"Elsa, my child," said the pastor with a sigh, "did you not think of us whilst you were murdering them?"

"No," she replied. "On the way back some people asked us if we knew anything about the murder of three sentries next to the prison. We said that we did not. The wind throbbed in our ears, the pavements trembled under our feet. When we reached town, someone had already been falsely accused of the murder. My friends were overjoyed, and made haste to leave town, saying it was dangerous to remain. They packed their suitcases and ate cheese sandwiches, staring at the clock all the time so they could be sure not to miss their train. The man we had freed when we killed the Saxon Guards kept kissing me on the hands and the neck; he was muttering as though he were delirious, 'I knew that you would follow me on everywhere. You abandoned your father and mother for my sake. You were not afraid to become a murderess. – See,' he said, turning to his comrades, 'here is a woman who knows how to love!' I fastened his bags; I could find no words to say."

"They have gone away," said the pastor, "gone away down the Rhein. But you are still here."

"You have been alone since ten o'clock," her mother observed.

"I began to tidy the room, but nothing would take away the smell of blood, it would not stop clinging to me. I kissed my crucifix and went to bed."

"So Christ was with you after all," the pastor said.

"I no longer understand him."

"You will understand him in time," her mother said with conviction.

Dull patches of red showed on Elsa's cheeks; she was dry-eyed and staring fixedly.

"Amen," said the pastor.

172

"Amen," said Elsa.

But still they stayed where they were; dawn found them at the table, and the pale morning sun gave Elsa's flushed cheeks a desperate caress.

That was not how it ended.

The man who had been unjustly executed came back to earth, put on the clothes that he had been wearing, and went to find Elsa. He had something to say to her; for many years he searched for her tirelessly.

Late one night he came up to the house and looked through the lighted window; he saw Elsa sitting at the table and tracing the pattern on the cloth with her finger, and her parents staring at her in silence.

He knocked, and was let into the house. The pastor was on the point of saying "Amen" when the door opened, and in came the man.

"Elsa, I greet you," he said. "I shall be with you always."

And all three crossed themselves, obedient to the will of God.

1902

ANTON CHEKHOV

THE BISHOP

Translated by Richard Pevear and Larissa Volokhonsky

I

ON THE EVE OF Palm Sunday the vigil was going on in the Old Petrovsky Convent. It was almost ten o'clock when they began to hand out the pussywillows, the lights were dim, the wicks were sooty, everything was as if in a mist. In the twilight of the church, the crowd heaved like the sea, and to Bishop Pyotr, who had been unwell for three days, it seemed that all the faces – old and young, men's and women's – were alike, that everyone who came up to get a branch had the same expression in their eyes. The doors could not be seen in the mist, the crowd kept moving, and it looked as if there was and would be no end to it. A women's choir was singing, a nun was reading the canon.

How hot it was, how stifling! How long the vigil was! Bishop Pyotr was tired. His breathing was labored, short, dry, his shoulders ached with fatigue, his legs trembled. And it was unpleasantly disturbing that some holy fool cried out now and then from the gallery. Besides, the bishop suddenly imagined, as if in sleep or delirium, that his own mother, Marya Timofeevna, whom he had not seen for nine years, or else an old woman resembling his mother, came up to him in the crowd, and, receiving a branch from him, stepped away, all the while gazing happily at him, with a kind, joyful smile, until she mingled with the crowd again. And for some reason tears poured down his face. His soul was at peace, all was well, yet he gazed fixedly at the choir on the left, where they were reading, where not a single person could be made out in the evening darkness – and wept. Tears glistened on his face, his beard. Then someone else began to weep near him, then someone else further away, then another and another, and the church was gradually filled with quiet weeping. But in a short while, some five minutes, the convent choir began to sing, there was no more weeping, everything was as before.

The service was soon over. As the bishop was getting into his carriage to go home, the whole moonlit garden was filled with merry, beautiful ringing of the expensive, heavy bells. The white walls, the white crosses on the graves, the white birches and black shadows, and the distant moon in the sky, which stood directly over the convent, now seemed to live their own special life, incomprehensible, yet close to mankind. April was just beginning, and after the warm spring day it turned cooler, slightly frosty, and a breath of spring could be felt in the soft, cold air. The road from the convent to town was sandy, they had to go at a walking pace; and on both sides of the carriage, in the bright, still moonlight, pilgrims trudged over the sand. And everyone was silent, deep in thought, everything around was welcoming, young, so near – the trees, the sky, even the moon – and one wanted to think it would always be so.

At last the carriage drove into town and rolled down the main street. The shops were closed, except that of the merchant Yerakin, the millionaire, where they were trying out electric lighting, which was flickering badly, and people crowded around. Then came wide, dark streets, one after another, deserted, then the high road outside town, the fields, the smell of pines. And suddenly there rose up before his eyes a white, crenellated wall, and behind it a tall bell tower, all flooded with light, and beside it five big, shining, golden domes – this was St. Pankraty's Monastery, where Bishop Pyotr lived. And here, too, high above the monastery hung the quiet, pensive moon. The carriage drove through the gate, creaking over the sand, here and there the black figures of monks flashed in the moonlight, footsteps were heard on the flagstones . . .

"Your mother came while you were away, Your Grace," the cell attendant reported, when the bishop came to his quarters.

"Mama? When did she come?"

"Before the vigil. She first asked where you were, and then went to the convent."

"That means it was her I saw in church! Oh, Lord!"

And the bishop laughed with joy.

"She asked me to tell Your Grace," the attendant went on, "that she will come tomorrow. There's a girl with her, probably a granddaughter. They're staying at Ovsyannikov's inn."

"What time is it now?"

"Just after eleven."

"Ah, how vexing!"

The bishop sat for a while in the drawing room, pondering and as if not believing it was so late. His arms and legs ached, there was a pain in the back of his head. He felt hot and uncomfortable. Having rested, he went to his bedroom and there, too, sat for a while, still thinking about his mother. He heard the attendant leave and Father Sisoy, a hieromonk, cough on the other side of the wall. The monastery clock struck the quarter hour.

The bishop changed his clothes and began to read the prayers before going to sleep. He read these old, long-familiar prayers attentively, and at the same time thought about his mother. She had nine children and around forty

179

grandchildren. Once she had lived with her husband, a deacon, in a poor village, lived there for a long time, from the age of seventeen to the age of sixty. The bishop remembered her from early childhood, almost from when he was three – and how he loved her! Sweet, dear, unforgettable childhood! Why does this forever gone, irretrievable time, why does it seem brighter, more festive and rich, than it was in reality? When he had been sick as a child or a youth, how tender and sensitive his mother had been! And now his prayers were mixed with memories that burned ever brighter, like flames, and the prayers did not interfere with his thoughts of his mother.

When he finished praying, he undressed and lay down, and at once, as soon as it was dark around him, he pictured his late father, his mother, his native village Lesopolye ... Wheels creaking, sheep bleating, church bells ringing on bright summer mornings, gypsies under the windows – oh, how sweet to think of it! He remembered the priest of Lesopolye, Father Simeon, meek, placid, good-natured; he was skinny and short himself, but his son, a seminarian, was of enormous height and spoke in a furious bass; once he got angry with the cook and yelled at her: "Ah, you Iehudiel's ass!" and Father Simeon, who heard it, did not say a word and was only ashamed because he could not remember where in holy scripture there was mention of such an ass. After him the priest in Lesopolye was Father Demyan, who was a heavy drinker and was sometimes drunk to the point of seeing a green serpent, and he was even nicknamed "Demyan the Serpent-seer." The schoolmaster in Lesopolye was Matvei Nikolaich, a former seminarian, a kind man, not stupid, but also a drunkard; he never beat his students, but for some reason always had a bundle of birch switches hanging on the wall with a perfectly meaningless Latin inscription under it

– *Betula kinderbalsamica secuta*. He had a shaggy black dog that he called Syntax.

And the bishop laughed. Five miles from Lesopolye was the village of Obnino, with its wonder-working icon. In summer the icon was carried in procession to all the neighboring villages, and bells rang the whole day, now in one village, now in another, and to the bishop it had seemed then that the air was vibrant with joy, and he (he was then called Pavlusha) had followed after the icon, hatless, barefoot, with naïve faith, with a naïve smile, infinitely happy. In Obnino, he now recalled, there were always many people, and the priest there, Father Alexei, in order to manage the proskomedia, made his deaf nephew Ilarion read the lists "for the living" and "for the dead" sent in with the prosphoras; Ilarion read them, getting five or ten kopecks every once in a while for a liturgy, and only when he was gray and bald, when life had passed, did he suddenly notice written on one slip: "What a fool you are, Ilarion!" At least till the age of fifteen, Pavlusha remained undeveloped and a poor student, so that they even wanted to take him from theological school and send him to work in a shop; once, when he went to the Obnino post office for letters, he looked at the clerks for a long time and then said: "Allow me to ask, how do you receive your salary – monthly or daily?"

The bishop crossed himself and turned over on the other side, in order to sleep and not think anymore.

"My mother has come . . ." he remembered and laughed.

The moon looked in the window, the floor was lit up, and shadows lay on it. A cricket called. In the next room, on the other side of the wall, Father Sisoy snored, and something lonely, orphaned, even vagrant could be heard in his old man's snoring. Sisoy had once been the steward of the diocesan bishop, and now he was called "the former father steward"; he was seventy years old, lived in the monastery ten miles from town, also lived in town, or wherever he happened to be. Three days ago he had come to St. Pankraty's Monastery, and the bishop had let him stay with him, in order to talk with him somehow in leisure moments about various things, local ways . . .

At half past one the bell rang for matins. He heard Father Sisoy cough, grumble something in a displeased voice, then get up and walk barefoot through the rooms.

"Father Sisoy!" the bishop called.

Sisoy went to his room and shortly afterwards appeared, wearing boots now and holding a candle; over his underclothes he had a cassock, on his head an old, faded skullcap.

"I can't sleep," said the bishop, sitting up. "I must be unwell. And what it is, I don't know. A fever!"

"You must've caught cold, Your Grace. You should be rubbed with tallow."

Sisoy stood for a while and yawned: "O Lord, forgive me, a sinner."

"At Yerakin's today they burned electricity," he said. "I doan like it!"

Father Sisoy was old, lean, bent, always displeased with something, and his eyes were angry, protruding, like a crayfish's.

"Doan like it!" he said, going out. "Doan like it, God help 'em all!"

II

THE NEXT DAY, Palm Sunday, the bishop served the liturgy in the town cathedral, then visited the diocesan bishop, visited a certain very sick old general's widow and finally went home. Between one and two o'clock he had dinner with two dear guests: his old mother and his niece Katya, a girl of about eight. All through dinner the spring sun looked through the window from outside, shining merrily on the white tablecloth and in Katya's red hair. Through the double windows one could hear the noise of rooks in the garden and the singing of starlings.

"It's nine years since we saw each other," the old woman said, "but yesterday in the convent, when I looked at you – Lord! You haven't changed a bit, only you've lost weight, and your beard has grown longer. Ah, Queen of Heaven, Holy Mother! And yesterday during the vigil, nobody could help themselves, everybody wept. Looking at you, I suddenly wept, too – though why, I don't know. It's God's holy will!"

And, in spite of the tenderness with which she said it, she was clearly embarrassed, as if she did not know whether to address him formally or informally, to laugh or not, and seemed to feel more like a deacon's widow than his mother. But Katya gazed without blinking at her uncle, the bishop, as if trying to figure out what sort of man he was. Her hair rose from under the comb and velvet ribbon and stood out like a halo, her nose was turned up, her eyes were sly. Before sitting down to dinner she had broken a tea glass, and now her grandmother, as she talked, kept moving glasses and cups away from her. The bishop listened to his mother and remembered how, many years ago, she used to take him and his brothers and sisters to visit relatives whom she considered wealthy; she was solicitous for her children then, and for her grandchildren now, and so she had brought Katya . . .

"Your sister Varenka has four children," she told him. "Katya here is the oldest, and, God knows what was the cause of it, but my son-in-law, Father Ivan, took sick and died three

183

days before the Dormition. And my Varenka is now fit to go begging through the world."

"And how is Nikanor?" the bishop asked about his oldest brother.

"All right, thank God. He's all right, and able to get by, Lord be blessed. Only there's one thing: his son Nikolasha, my grandson, didn't want to follow the clerical line, but went to the university to become a doctor. He thinks it's better, but who knows! It's God's holy will."

"Nikolasha cuts up dead people," said Katya, and she spilled water in her lap.

"Sit still, child," the grandmother remarked calmly and took the glass from her. "Pray when you eat."

"We haven't seen each other for so long!" the bishop said and tenderly stroked his mother's shoulder and arm. "I missed you when I was abroad, mama, I missed you terribly."

"I thank you."

"I used to sit by the open window in the evening, alone as could be, they'd start playing music, and homesickness would suddenly come over me, and I thought I'd give anything to go home, to see you . . ."

His mother smiled, brightened up, but at once made a serious face and said:

"I thank you."

His mood changed somehow suddenly. He looked at his mother and could not understand where she got that timid, deferential expression in her face and voice, or why it was there, and he did not recognize her. He felt sad, vexed. Besides, his head ached just as yesterday, he had bad pain in his legs, the fish seemed insipid, tasteless, and he was thirsty all the time . . .

After dinner two rich ladies, landowners, came and spent

an hour and a half sitting silently with long faces; the archimandrite, taciturn and slightly deaf, came on business. Then the bells rang for vespers, the sun set behind the woods, and the day was gone. Returning from church, the bishop hastily said his prayers, went to bed, and covered himself warmly.

The memory of the fish he had eaten at dinner was unpleasant. The moonlight disturbed him, and then he heard talking. In a neighboring room, probably the drawing room, Father Sisoy was discussing politics:

"The Japanese are at war now. They're fighting. The Japanese, my dear, are the same as the Montenegrins, the same tribe. They were both under the Turkish yoke."

And then came the voice of Marya Timofeevna:

"So we said our prayers and had tea, and so then we went to see Father Yegor in Novokhatnoe, which is ..."

And it was "we had tea" or "we drank a glass" time and again, as if all she ever did in her life was drink tea. The bishop slowly, listlessly remembered the seminary, the theological academy. For three years he had taught Greek at the seminary, by which time he could no longer read without glasses; then he was tonsured a monk and was made a school inspector. Then he defended his thesis. When he was thirty-two, they made him rector of the seminary, he was consecrated archimandrite, and life then was so easy, pleasant, it seemed so very long that he could see no end to it. Then he fell ill, lost weight, nearly went blind, and on his doctors' advice had to abandon everything and go abroad.

"And what then?" Sisoy asked in the neighboring room.

"And then we had tea ..." answered Marya Timofeevna.

"Father, your beard is green!" Katya suddenly said in surprise and laughed.

The bishop recalled that the gray-haired Father Sisoy's beard did indeed have a green tinge, and he laughed.

"Lord God, what a punishment the girl is!" Sisoy said loudly, getting angry. "Spoiled as they come! Sit still!"

The bishop remembered the white church, perfectly new, in which he served when he lived abroad, remembered the sound of the warm sea. His apartment consisted of five rooms, high-ceilinged and bright, there was a new desk in the study, a library. He read a lot, wrote often. And he remembered how homesick he was, how a blind beggar woman sang of love and played the guitar outside his window every day, and each time he listened to her, for some reason he thought of the past. Eight years passed and he was recalled to Russia, and now he was installed as an auxiliary bishop, and the past had all withdrawn somewhere into the distance, the mist, as if it had been a dream . . .

Father Sisoy came into his bedroom with a candle.

"Well," he was surprised, "you're already asleep, Your Grace?"

"Why not?"

"But it's early, ten o'clock, or not even that. I bought a candle today, I wanted to rub you with tallow."

"I have a fever . . ." said the bishop, and he sat up. "In fact, I do need something. My head doesn't feel right . . ."

Sisoy removed his shirt and began to rub his chest and back with candle tallow.

"There . . . there . . ." he said. "Lord Jesus Christ . . . There. Today I went to town, visited – what's his name? – the archpriest Sidonsky . . . Had tea with him . . . I doan like him! Lord Jesus Christ . . . There . . . Doan like him at all!"

THE DIOCESAN BISHOP, old, very fat, was suffering from rheumatism or gout and had not left his bed for a month. Bishop Pyotr went to see him almost every day and received petitioners in his stead. And now when he was unwell, he was struck by the emptiness, the pettiness of all that people asked about and wept about; he was angered by their back-wardness, their timidity; and the mass of all these petty and unnecessary things oppressed him, and it seemed to him that he now understood the diocesan bishop, who once, when he was young, had written *Lessons on Freedom of Will*, but now seemed totally immersed in trifles, had forgotten everything, and did not think of God. The bishop must have grown unaccustomed to Russian life while abroad, and it was not easy for him; he found the people coarse, the women peti-tioners boring and stupid, the seminarians and their teachers uncultivated, sometimes savage. And the papers, incoming and outgoing, numbering in the tens of thousands, and what papers! Rural deans throughout the diocese gave the priests, young and old, and even their wives and children, marks for behavior, A's and B's, and sometimes also C's, and it was necessary to talk, read, and write serious papers about all that. And he decidedly did not have a single free moment, his soul trembled all day, and Bishop Pyotr found peace only when he was in church.

He also could not get used to the fear which, without wishing it, he aroused in people, despite his quiet, modest nature. All the people of the province, when he looked at them, seemed to him small, frightened, guilty. In his pres-ence they all grew timid, even old archpriests, they all "plopped down" at his feet, and recently a woman petitioner, the elderly wife of a village priest, had been unable to utter a single word from fear, and so had gone away with nothing. And he, who in his sermons never dared to speak badly of people, never reproached them, because he felt pity for them, lost his temper with petitioners, became angry, flung their petitions to the floor. In all the time he had been there, not a single person had spoken to him sincerely, simply, humanly; even his old mother seemed not the same, not the same at all! And why, one asked, did she talk incessantly and laugh so much with Sisoy, while with him, her son, she was serious, usually silent, bashful, which did not become her at all? The only person who behaved freely in his presence and said whatever he liked was old Sisoy, who had been around bishops all his life and had outlived eleven of them. And that was why he felt at ease with him, though he was unquestionably a difficult, fussy man.

On Tuesday after the liturgy the bishop was at the diocesan bishop's house and received petitioners there, became upset, angry, then went home. He was still unwell and felt like going to bed; but he had no sooner come home than he was informed that Yerakin, a young merchant, a donor, had come on very important business. He had to be received. Yerakin stayed for about an hour, talked very loudly, almost shouted, and it was difficult to understand what he said.

"God grant that!" he said, going out. "Most unfailingly! Depending on the circumstances, Your Episcopal Grace! I wish that!"

After him came an abbess from a distant convent. And when she left, the bells rang for vespers, and he had to go to church.

In the evening the monks sang harmoniously, inspiredly, the office was celebrated by a young hieromonk with a black beard; and the bishop, listening to the verses about the Bridegroom who cometh at midnight and about the chamber that is adorned, felt, not repentance for his sins, not sorrow, but inner peace, silence, and was carried in his thoughts into the distant past, into his childhood and youth, when they had also sung about the Bridegroom and the chamber, and now that past appeared alive, beautiful, joyful, as it probably never had been. And perhaps in the other world, in the other life, we shall remember the distant past, our life here, with the same feeling. Who knows! The bishop sat in the sanctuary, it was dark there. Tears flowed down his face. He was thinking that here he had achieved everything possible for a man in his position, he had faith, and yet not everything was clear, something was still lacking, he did not want to die; and it still seemed that there was some most important thing which he did not have, of which he had once vaguely dreamed, and in the present he was stirred by the same hope for the future that he had had in childhood, and in the academy, and abroad.

"They're singing so well today!" he thought, listening to the choir. "So well!"

IV

ON THURSDAY HE served the liturgy in the cathedral, and there was the washing of feet. When the church service ended and people were going home, it was sunny, warm, cheerful, the water ran noisily in the ditches, and from the fields outside town came the ceaseless singing of larks, tender, calling all to peace. The trees were awake and smiled amiably, and over them, God knows how far, went the fathomless, boundless blue sky.

On coming home, Bishop Pyotr had tea, then changed his clothes, went to bed, and told his cell attendant to close the window blinds. The bedroom became dark. What weariness, though, what pain in his legs and back, a heavy, cold pain, and what a ringing in his ears! He lay without sleeping for a long time, as it now seemed to him, for a very long time, and it was some trifle that kept him from sleeping, that flickered in his brain as soon as his eyes closed. As on the previous day, voices, the clink of glasses and teaspoons came through the wall from neighboring rooms . . . Marya Timofeevna, merry and bantering, was telling Father Sisoy something, and he responded sullenly, in a displeased voice: "Oh, them! Hah! What else!" And again the bishop felt vexed and then hurt that the old woman behaved in an ordinary and simple way with strangers, but with him, her son, was timid, spoke rarely, and did not say what she wanted to say, and even, as it had seemed to him all those days, kept looking for an excuse to stand up, because she was embarrassed to sit in his presence. And his father? If he were alive, he would probably be unable to utter a single word before him . . .

Something fell on the floor in the next room and smashed; it must have been Katya dropping a cup or a saucer, because Father Sisoy suddenly spat and said angrily:

"The girl's a sheer punishment, Lord, forgive me, a sinner! There's never enough with her!"

Then it became quiet, only sounds from outside reached him. And when the bishop opened his eyes, he saw Katya in his room, standing motionless and looking at him. Her red hair, as usual, rose from behind her comb like a halo.

"It's you, Katya?" he asked. "Who keeps opening and closing the door downstairs?"

"I don't hear it," Katya said and listened.

"There, somebody just passed by."

"It's in your stomach, uncle!"

He laughed and patted her head.

"So you say cousin Nikolasha cuts up dead people?" he asked after a pause.

"Yes. He's studying."

"Is he kind?"

"Kind enough. Only he drinks a lot of vodka."

"And what illness did your father die of?"

"Papa was weak and very, very thin, and suddenly – in his throat. I got sick then and so did my brother Fedya, all in the throat. Papa died, and we got well."

Her chin trembled and tears welled up in her eyes and rolled slowly down her cheeks.

"Your Grace," she said in a high little voice, now crying bitterly, "mama and all of us were left in such misery . . . Give us a little money . . . Be so kind . . . dear uncle! . . ."

He, too, became tearful and for a long time was too upset to utter a word, then he patted her head, touched her shoulder, and said:

"Very well, very well, child. The bright resurrection of Christ will come, and then we'll talk . . . I'll help you . . . I will . . ."

Quietly, timidly, his mother came in and crossed herself before the icons. Noticing that he was not asleep, she asked:

"Would you like some soup?"

"No, thank you . . ." he replied. "I don't want any."

"You don't look well . . . seems to me. But then how could you not get sick! On your feet the whole day, the whole day – my God, it's painful even to look at you. Well, Easter's not far off, God grant you'll be able to rest, then we can talk, and I won't bother you with my talk now. Let's go, Katechka, let His Grace sleep."

And he remembered how, a long, long time ago, when he

was still a boy, she had spoken with a rural dean in just the same jokingly deferential tone . . . Only by her extraordinarily kind eyes and the timid, worried glance she cast at him as she left the room, could one see that she was his mother. He closed his eyes and it seemed he slept, but twice he heard the clock strike and Father Sisoy cough on the other side of the wall. His mother came in once more and gazed at him timidly for a moment. Someone drove up to the porch in a coach or a carriage, judging by the sound. Suddenly there came a knock, the bang of a door: the attendant came into his bedroom.

"Your Grace!" he called.

"What?"

"The horses are ready, it's time to go to the Lord's Passion."

"What time is it?"

"A quarter past seven."

He dressed and drove to the cathedral. He had to stand motionless in the middle of the church through all twelve Gospel readings, and the first Gospel, the longest, the most beautiful, he read himself. A vigorous, healthy mood came over him. The first Gospel – "Now is the Son of Man glorified" – he knew by heart; and as he read, he raised his eyes from time to time and saw on both sides a whole sea of lights, heard the sizzle of candles, but, as in previous years, he was unable to see the people, and it seemed to him that they were the same people as in his childhood and youth, that they would be the same every year, but for how long – God only knew.

His father had been a deacon, his grandfather a priest, his great-grandfather a deacon, and all his ancestry, perhaps since the time when Russia embraced Christianity, had belonged to the clergy, and the love for church services, the clergy, the ringing of bells, was innate in him, deep, ineradicable; in church, especially when he celebrated the office himself, he felt active, vigorous, happy. And so he did now. Only when the eighth Gospel had been read, he felt that his voice had weakened, even his coughing had become inaudible, his head ached badly, and he was troubled by a fear that he was about to fall down. And indeed his legs had gone quite numb, so that he gradually ceased to feel them, and it was incomprehensible to him how and on what he was standing, and why he did not fall down ...

When the service ended, it was a quarter to twelve. Returning home, the bishop undressed at once and lay down, without even saying his prayers. He was unable to speak, and it seemed to him that he would now be unable to stand. As he pulled the blanket over him, he suddenly had a longing to be abroad, an unbearable longing! He thought he would give his life only not to see those pathetic, cheap blinds, the low ceilings, not to breathe that oppressive monastery smell. If there had been just one person to whom he could talk, unburden his soul!

For a long time he heard someone's footsteps in the next room and could not remember who it was. At last the door opened and Sisoy came in, holding a candle and a teacup.

"In bed already, Your Grace?" he asked. "And I've come because I want to rub you with vodka and vinegar. If you rub it in well, it can be of great benefit. Lord Jesus Christ ... There ... There ... And I've just been to our monastery ... I doan like it! I'll leave here tomorrow, Your Grace, I want no more of it. Lord Jesus Christ ... There ..."

Sisoy was unable to stay long in one place, and it seemed to him that he had been living in St. Pankraty's Monastery for a whole year by then. And, above all, listening to him, it was hard to understand where his home was, whether he

loved anyone or anything, whether he believed in God ...
He did not understand himself why he was a monk, and he
did not think about it, and the time of his tonsuring had
long been erased from his memory; it looked as if he had
simply been born a monk.

"I'll leave tomorrow. God bless the lot of them!"

"I'd like to talk with you ... I never can get around to it,"
the bishop said softly, forcing himself. "I don't know anyone
or anything here."

"So be it, if you like I'll stay till Sunday, but no longer.
I want none of it! Pah!"

"What sort of bishop am I?" the bishop went on softly. "I
should be a village priest, a deacon ... or a simple monk ...
All this oppresses me, oppresses me ..."

"What? Lord Jesus Christ ... There ... Well, go to sleep,
Your Grace! ... No point! Forget it! Good night!"

The bishop did not sleep all night. And in the morning,
around eight o'clock, he began to have intestinal bleeding.
The cell attendant became frightened and ran first to the
archimandrite, then for the monastery doctor, Ivan Andre-
ich, who lived in town. The doctor, a stout old man with a
long gray beard, examined the bishop for a long time, and
kept shaking his head and scowling, then said:

"You know, Your Grace, you've got typhoid fever."

Within an hour the bishop became very thin from the
bleeding, pale, pinched, his face shrank, his eyes were now
big, he looked older, smaller, and it seemed to him that he
was thinner, weaker, more insignificant than anyone, that all
that had once been had gone somewhere very far away and
would no longer repeat itself, would not be continued.

"How good!" he thought. "How good!"

His old mother came. Seeing his shrunken face and big
eyes, she became frightened, fell on her knees by his bed, and

started kissing his face, shoulders, hands. And to her, too, it seemed that he was thinner, weaker, and more insignificant than anyone, and she no longer remembered that he was a bishop, and she kissed him like a child very near and dear to her.

"Pavlusha, my darling," she said, "my dear one! ... My little son! ... What makes you like this? Pavlusha, answer me!"

Katya, pale, stern, stood nearby and did not understand what was the matter with her uncle, why there was such suffering on her grandmother's face, why she was saying such touching, sad words. And he could no longer say a word, he understood nothing, and imagined that he was now a simple, ordinary man, walking briskly, merrily across the fields, tapping his stick, and over him was the broad sky, flooded with sunlight, and he was free as a bird and could go wherever he liked!

"My little son, Pavlusha, answer me!" said the old woman. "What's the matter with you? My dear one!"

"Don't trouble His Grace," Sisoy said crossly, passing through the room. "Let him sleep ... there's no point ... forget it! ..."

Three doctors came, held a consultation, then left. The day was long, unbelievably long, then night came and lasted a very, very long time, and towards morning on Saturday the cell attendant went up to the old woman, who was lying on a sofa in the drawing room, and asked her to go to the bedroom: the bishop had bid the world farewell.

The next day was Easter. There were forty-two churches and six monasteries in the town; a resounding, joyful ringing of bells hung over the town from morning till evening, never silent, stirring up the spring air; the birds sang, the sun shone brightly. It was noisy on the big market square, swings were swinging, barrel organs playing, accordions shrieked, drunken voices shouted. In the afternoon people went driving about the main streets in short, all was cheerful, all was well, just as it had been the year before, and as it would also be, in all probability, the year after.

A month later a new auxiliary bishop was appointed, and no one thought of Bishop Pyotr anymore. Soon he was completely forgotten. And only the old woman, the mother of the deceased, who now lives with her deacon son-in-law in a forsaken little provincial town, when she went out before evening to meet her cow, and got together by the pasture with other women, would begin telling them about her children and grandchildren, and how she once had a son who was a bishop, and she said it timidly, afraid they would not believe her . . .

And indeed not everyone believed her.

1902

IVAN BUNIN

THE GENTLEMAN FROM
SAN FRANCISCO

Translated by S. S. Koteliansky, D. H. Lawrence
and Leonard Woolf

"Woe to thee, Babylon, that mighty city!"
Apocalypse

THE GENTLEMAN from San Francisco – nobody either in Capri or Naples ever remembered his name – was setting out with his wife and daughter for the Old World, to spend there two years of pleasure.

He was fully convinced of his right to rest, to enjoy long and comfortable travels, and so forth. Because, in the first place he was rich, and in the second place, notwithstanding his fifty-eight years, he was just starting to live. Up to the present he had not lived, but only existed; quite well, it is true, yet with all his hopes on the future. He had worked incessantly – and the Chinamen whom he employed by the thousand in his factories knew what that meant. Now at last he realized that a great deal had been accomplished, and that he had almost reached the level of those whom he had taken as his ideals, so he made up his mind to pause for a breathing space. Men of his class usually began their enjoyments with a trip to Europe, India, Egypt. He decided to do the same. He wished naturally to reward himself in the first place for all his years of toil, but he was quite glad that his wife and daughter should also share in his pleasures. True, his wife was not distinguished by any marked susceptibilities, but then elderly American women are all passionate travellers. As for his daughter, a girl no longer young and somewhat delicate,

199

travel was really necessary for her: apart from the question of health, do not happy meetings often take place in the course of travel? One may find one's self sitting next to a multimillionaire at table, or examining frescoes side by side with him.

The itinerary planned by the Gentleman of San Francisco was extensive. In December and January he hoped to enjoy the sun of southern Italy, the monuments of antiquity, the tarantella, the serenades of vagrant minstrels, and, finally, that which men of his age are most susceptible to, the love of quite young Neapolitan girls, even when the love is not altogether disinterestedly given. Carnival he thought of spending in Nice, in Monte Carlo, where at that season gathers the most select society, the precise society on which depend all the blessings of civilization – the fashion in evening dress, the stability of thrones, the declaration of wars, the prosperity of hotels; where some devote themselves passionately to automobile and boat races, others to roulette, others to what is called flirtation, and others to the shooting of pigeons which beautifully soar from their traps over emerald lawns, against a background of forget-me-not sea, instantly to fall, hitting the ground in little white heaps. The beginning of March he wished to devote to Florence, Passion Week in Rome, to hear the music of the Miserere; his plans also included Venice, Paris, bull-fights in Seville, bathing in the British Isles; then Athens, Constantinople, Egypt, even Japan ... certainly on his way home. ... And everything at the outset went splendidly.

It was the end of November. Practically all the way to Gibraltar the voyage passed in icy darkness, varied by storms of wet snow. Yet the ship travelled well, even without much rolling. The passengers on board were many, and all people of some importance. The boat, the famous *Atlantis*, resembled

a most expensive European hotel with all modern equip-
ments: a night refreshment bar, Turkish baths, a newspaper
printed on board; so that the days aboard the liner passed in
the most select manner. The passengers rose early, to the
sound of bugles sounding shrilly through the corridors in
that grey twilit hour, when day was breaking slowly and sullenly over the grey-green, watery desert, which rolled heavily
in the fog. Clad in their flannel pyjamas, the gentlemen took
coffee, chocolate, or cocoa, then seated themselves in marble
baths, did exercises, thereby whetting their appetite and their
sense of well-being, made their toilet for the day, and proceeded to breakfast. Till eleven o'clock they were supposed
to stroll cheerfully on deck, breathing the cold freshness of
the ocean; or they played table-tennis or other games, that
they might have an appetite for their eleven o'clock refreshment of sandwiches and bouillon; after which they read their
newspaper with pleasure, and calmly awaited luncheon –
which was a still more varied and nourishing meal than
breakfast. The two hours which followed luncheon were
devoted to rest. All the decks were crowded with lounge
chairs on which lay passengers wrapped in plaids, looking at
the mist-heavy sky or the foamy hillocks which flashed
behind the bows, and dozing sweetly. Till five o'clock, when,
refreshed and lively, they were treated to strong, fragrant tea
and sweet cakes. At seven bugle-calls announced a dinner of
nine courses. And now the Gentleman from San Francisco,
rubbing his hands in a rising flush of vital forces, hastened
to his state cabin to dress.

In the evening, the tiers of the *Atlantis* yawned in the
darkness as with innumerable fiery eyes, and a multitude of
servants in the kitchens, sculleries, wine-cellars, worked with
a special frenzy. The ocean heaving beyond was terrible, but
no one thought of it, firmly believing in the captain's power

over it. The captain was a ginger-haired man of monstrous size and weight, apparently always torpid, who looked in his uniform with broad gold stripes very like a huge idol, and who rarely emerged from his mysterious chambers to show himself to the passengers. Every minute the siren howled from the bows with hellish moroseness, and screamed with fury, but few diners heard it – it was drowned by the sounds of an excellent string band, exquisitely and untiringly playing in the huge two-tiered hall that was decorated with marble and covered with velvet carpets, flooded with feasts of light from crystal chandeliers and gilded girandoles, and crowded with ladies in bare shoulders and jewels, with men in dinner-jackets, elegant waiters and respectful maîtres d'hôtel, one of whom, he who took the wine-orders only, wore a chain round his neck like a lord mayor. Dinner-jacket and perfect linen made the Gentleman from San Francisco look much younger. Dry, of small stature, badly built but strongly made, polished to a glow and in due measure animated, he sat in the golden-pearly radiance of this palace, with a bottle of amber Johannisberg at his hand, and glasses, large and small, of delicate crystal, and a curly bunch of fresh hyacinths. There was something Mongolian in his yellowish face with its trimmed silvery moustache, large teeth blazing with gold, and strong bald head blazing like old ivory. Richly dressed, but in keeping with her age, sat his wife, a big, broad, quiet woman. Intricately, but lightly and transparently dressed, with an innocent immodesty, sat his daughter, tall, slim, her magnificent hair splendidly done, her breath fragrant with violet cachous, and the tenderest little rosy moles showing near her lip and between her bare, slightly powdered shoulder blades. The dinner lasted two whole hours, to be followed by dancing in the ball-room, whence the men, including, of course, the Gentleman from San

Francisco, proceeded to the bar; there, with their feet cocked up on the tables, they settled the destinies of nations in the course of their political and stock-exchange conversations, smoking meanwhile Havana cigars and drinking liqueurs till they were crimson in the face, waited on all the while by negroes in red jackets with eyes like peeled, hard-boiled eggs. Outside, the ocean heaved in black mountains; the snowstorm hissed furiously in the clogged cordage; the steamer trembled in every fibre as she surmounted these watery hills and struggled with the storm, ploughing through the moving masses which every now and then reared in front of her, foam-crested. The siren, choked by the fog, groaned in mortal anguish. The watchmen in the look-out towers froze with cold, and went mad with their super-human straining of attention. As the gloomy and sultry depths of the inferno, as the ninth circle, was the submerged womb of the steamer, where gigantic furnaces roared and dully giggled, devouring with their red-hot maws mountains of coal cast hoarsely in by men naked to the waist, bathed in their own corrosive dirty sweat, and lurid with the purple-red reflection of flame. But in the refreshment bar men jauntily put their feet up on the tables, showing their patent-leather pumps, and sipped cognac or other liqueurs, and swam in waves of fragrant smoke as they chatted in well-bred manner. In the dancing hall light and warmth and joy were poured over everything; couples turned in the waltz or writhed in the tango, while the music insistently, shamelessly, delightfully, with sadness entreated for one, only one thing, one and the same thing all the time. Amongst this resplendent crowd was an ambassador, a little dry modest old man; a great millionaire, clean-shaven, tall, of an indefinite age, looking like a prelate in his old-fashioned dress-coat; also a famous Spanish author, and an international beauty already the least bit faded, of unenviable reputation; finally an exquisite loving couple, whom everybody watched curiously because of their uncon- cealed happiness. He danced only with her, and sang, with great skill, only to her accompaniment, and everything about them seemed so charming! – and only the captain knew that this couple had been engaged by the steamship company to play at love for a good salary, and that they had been sailing for a long time, now on one liner, now on another.

At Gibraltar the sun gladdened them all: it was like early spring. A new passenger appeared on board, arousing general interest. He was a hereditary prince of a certain Asiatic state, travelling incognito: a small man, as if all made of wood, though his movements were alert; broad-faced, in gold- rimmed glasses, a little unpleasant because of his large black moustache which was sparse and transparent like that of a corpse; but on the whole inoffensive, simple, modest. In the Mediterranean they met once more the breath of winter. Waves, large and florid as the tail of a peacock, waves with snow-white crests heaved under the impulse of the tramont- ane wind, and came merrily, madly rushing towards the ship, in the bright lustre of a perfectly clear sky. The next day the sky began to pale, the horizon grew dim, land was approaching: Ischia, Capri could be seen through the glasses, then Naples herself, looking like pieces of sugar strewn at the foot of some dove-coloured mass; whilst beyond, vague and deadly white with snow, a range of distant mountains. The decks were crowded. Many ladies and gentlemen were put- ting on light fur-trimmed coats. Noiseless Chinese servant boys, bandy-legged, with pitch-black plaits hanging down to their heels, and with girlish thick eyebrows, unobtrusively came and went, carrying up the stairways plaids, canes, valises, hand-bags of crocodile leather, and never speaking above a whisper. The daughter of the Gentleman from San

Francisco stood side by side with the prince, who, by a happy circumstance, had been introduced to her the previous evening. She had the air of one looking fixedly into the distance towards something which he was pointing out to her, and which he was explaining hurriedly, in a low voice. Owing to his size, he looked amongst the rest like a boy. Altogether he was not handsome, rather queer, with his spectacles, bowler hat, and English coat, and then the hair of his sparse moustache just like horse-hair, and the swarthy, thin skin of his face seeming stretched over his features and slightly varnished. But the girl listened to him, and was so excited that she did not know what he was saying. Her heart beat with incomprehensible rapture because of him, because he was standing next to her and talking to her, to her alone. Everything, everything about him was so unusual – his dry hands, his clean skin under which flowed ancient, royal blood, even his plain, but somehow particularly tidy European dress; everything was invested with an indefinable glamour, with all that was calculated to enthrall a young woman. The Gentleman from San Francisco, wearing for his part a silk hat and grey spats over patent-leather shoes, kept eyeing the famous beauty who stood near him, a tall, wonderful figure, blonde, with her eyes painted according to the latest Parisian fashion, holding on a silver chain a tiny, cringing, hairless little dog, to which she was addressing herself all the time. And the daughter, feeling some vague embarrassment, tried not to notice her father.

Like all Americans, he was very liberal with his money when travelling. And like all of them, he believed in the full sincerity and good-will of those who brought his food and drinks, served him from morn till night, anticipated his smallest desire, watched over his cleanliness and rest, carried his things, called the porters, conveyed his trunks to the hotels. So it was everywhere, so it was during the voyage, so it ought to be in Naples. Naples grew and drew nearer. The brass band, shining with the brass of their instruments, had already assembled on deck. Suddenly they deafened everybody with the strains of their triumphant rag-time. The giant captain appeared in full uniform on the bridge, and like a benign pagan idol waved his hands to the passengers in a gesture of welcome. And to the Gentleman from San Francisco, as well as to every other passenger, it seemed as if for him alone was thundered forth that rag-time march, so greatly beloved by proud America; for him alone the captain's hand waved, welcoming him on his safe arrival. Then, when at last the *Atlantis* entered port and veered her many-tiered mass against the quay that was crowded with expectant people, when the gangways began their rattling – ah, then what a lot of porters and their assistants in caps with golden galloons, what a lot of all sorts of commissionaires, whistling boys, and sturdy ragamuffins with packs of postcards in their hands rushed to meet the Gentleman from San Francisco with offers of their services! With what amiable contempt he grinned at those ragamuffins as he walked to the automobile of the very same hotel at which the prince would probably put up, and calmly muttered between his teeth, now in English, now in Italian – "Go away! Via!"

Life at Naples started immediately in the set routine. Early in the morning, breakfast in a gloomy dining-room with a draughty damp wind blowing in from the windows that opened on to a little stony garden: a cloudy, unpromising day, and a crowd of guides at the doors of the vestibule. Then the first smiles of a warm, pinky-coloured sun, and from the high, overhanging balcony a view of Vesuvius, bathed to the feet in the radiant vapours of the morning sky, while beyond, over the silvery-pearly ripple of the bay, the subtle outline of

Capri upon the horizon! Then nearer, tiny donkeys running in two-wheeled buggies away below on the sticky embankment, and detachments of tiny soldiers marching off with cheerful and defiant music.

After this a walk to the taxi-stand, and a slow drive along crowded, narrow, damp corridors of streets, between high, many-windowed houses. Visits to deadly-clean museums, smoothly and pleasantly lighted, but monotonously, as if from the reflection of snow. Or visits to churches, cold, smelling of wax, and always the same thing: a majestic portal, curtained with a heavy leather curtain: inside, a huge emptiness, silence, lonely little flames of clustered candles ruddying the depths of the interior on some altar decorated with ribbon: a forlorn old woman amid dark benches, slippery gravestones under one's feet, and somebody's infallibly famous "Descent from the Cross." Luncheon at one o'clock on San Martino, where quite a number of the very selectest people gather about midday, and where once the daughter of the Gentleman from San Francisco almost became ill with joy, fancying she saw the prince sitting in the hall, although she knew from the newspapers that he had gone to Rome for a time. At five o'clock, tea in the hotel, in the smart salon where it was so warm, with the deep carpets and blazing fires. After which the thought of dinner – and again the powerful commanding voice of the gong heard over all the floors, and again strings of bare-shouldered ladies rustling with their silks on the staircases and reflecting themselves in the mirrors, again the wide-flung, hospitable, palatial dining-room, the red jackets of musicians on the platform, the black flock of waiters around the maître d'hôtel, who with extraordinary skill was pouring out a thick, roseate soup into soup-plates. The dinners, as usual, were the crowning event of the day. Every one dressed as if for a wedding, and so abundant were the dishes, the wines, the table-waters, sweetmeats, and fruit, that at about eleven o'clock in the evening the chamber-maids would take to every room rubber hot-water bottles, to warm the stomachs of those who had dined.

None the less, December of that year was not a success for Naples. The porters and secretaries were abashed if spoken to about the weather, only guiltily lifting their shoulders and murmuring that they could not possibly remember such a season; although this was not the first year they had had to make such murmurs, or to hint that "everywhere something terrible is happening." ... Unprecedented rains and storms on the Riviera, snow in Athens, Etna also piled with snow and glowing red at night; tourists fleeing from the cold of Palermo. ... The morning sun daily deceived the Neapolitans. The sky invariably grew grey towards midday, and fine rain began to fall, falling thicker and colder. The palms of the hotel approach glistened like wet tin; the city seemed peculiarly dirty and narrow, the museums excessively dull; the cigar-ends of the fat cab-men, whose rubber rain-capes flapped like wings in the wind, seemed insufferably stinking, the energetic cracking of whips over the ears of thin-necked horses sounded altogether false, and the clack of the shoes of the signorini who cleaned the tram-lines quite horrible, while the women, walking through the mud, with their black heads uncovered in the rain, seemed disgustingly short-legged: not to mention the stench and dampness of foul fish which drifted from the quay where the sea was foaming. The gentleman and lady from San Francisco began to bicker in the mornings; their daughter went about pale and head-achey, and then roused up again, went into raptures over everything, and was lovely, charming. Charming were those tender, complicated feelings which had been aroused in her by the meeting with the plain little man in whose veins ran such special blood. But after all, does it matter what awakens a maiden soul – whether it is money, fame, or noble birth?. . . Everybody declared that in Sorrento, or in Capri, it was quite different. There it was warmer, sunnier, the lemon-trees were in bloom, the morals were purer, the wine unadulterated. So behold, the family from San Francisco decided to go with all their trunks to Capri, after which they would return and settle down in Sorrento: when they had seen Capri, trodden the stones where stood Tiberius' palaces, visited the famous caves of the Blue Grotto, and listened to the pipers from Abruzzi, who wander about the isle during the month of the Nativity, singing the praises of the Virgin.

On the day of departure – a very memorable day for the family from San Francisco – the sun did not come out even in the morning. A heavy fog hid Vesuvius to the base, and came greying low over the leaden heave of the sea, whose waters were concealed from the eye at a distance of half a mile. Capri was completely invisible, as if it had never existed on earth. The little steamer that was making for the island tossed so violently from side to side that the family from San Francisco lay like stones on the sofas in the miserable saloon of the tiny boat, their feet wrapped in plaids, and their eyes closed. The lady, as she thought, suffered worst of all, and several times was overcome with sickness. It seemed to her that she was dying. But the stewardess who came to and fro with the basin, the stewardess who had been for years, day in, day out, through heat and cold, tossing on these waves, and who was still indefatigable, even kind to every one – she only smiled. The younger lady from San Francisco was deathly pale, and held in her teeth a slice of lemon. Now not even the thought of meeting the prince at Sorrento, where he was due to arrive by Christmas, could gladden her. The gentleman lay flat on his back, in a broad overcoat and a flat cap, and did not loosen his jaws throughout the voyage. His face grew dark, his moustache white, his head ached furiously. For the last few days, owing to the bad weather, he had been drinking heavily, and had more than once admired the "tableaux vivants." The rain whipped on the rattling window-panes, under which water dripped on to the sofas, the wind beat the masts with a howl, and at moments, aided by an onrushing wave, laid the little steamer right on its side, whereupon something would roll noisily away below. At the stopping places, Castellamare, Sorrento, things were a little better. But even the ship heaved frightfully, and the coast with all its precipices, gardens, pines, pink and white hotels, and hazy, curly green mountains swooped past the window, up and down, as it were on swings. The boats bumped against the side of the ship, the sailors and passengers shouted lustily, and somewhere a child, as if crushed to death, choked itself with screaming. The damp wind blew through the doors, and outside on the sea, from a reeling boat which showed the flag of the Hotel Royal, a fellow with guttural French exaggeration yelled unceasingly: "Rrroy-al! Hotel Rrroy-al!" intending to lure passengers aboard his craft. Then the Gentleman from San Francisco, feeling, as he ought to have felt, quite an old man, thought with anguish and spite of all these "Royals," "Splendids," "Excelsiors," and of these greedy, good-for-nothing, garlic-stinking fellows called Italians. Once, during a halt, on opening his eyes and rising from the sofa he saw under the rocky cliff-curtain of the coast a heap of such miserable stone hovels, all musty and mouldy, stuck on top of one another by the very water, among the boats, and the rags of all sorts, tin cans and brown fishing-nets, and, remembering that this was the very Italy he had come to enjoy, he was seized with despair. . . . At last, in the twilight, the black mass of the island began to loom nearer, looking as if it were bored through at the base with little red lights. The wind grew softer, warmer, more sweet-smelling. Over the tamed waves, undulating like black oil, there came flowing golden boa-constrictors of light from the lanterns of the harbour. ... Then suddenly the anchor rumbled and fell with a splash into the water. Furious cries of the boatmen shouting against one another came from all directions. And relief was felt at once. The electric light of the cabin shone brighter, and a desire to eat, drink, smoke, move once more made itself felt. ... Ten minutes later the family from San Francisco disembarked into a large boat; in a quarter of an hour they had stepped on to the stones of the quay, and were soon seated in the bright little car of the funicular railway. With a buzz they were ascending the slope, past the stakes of the vineyards and wet, sturdy orange-trees, here and there protected by straw screens, past the thick glossy foliage and the brilliancy of orange fruits. ... Sweetly smells the earth in Italy after rain, and each of her islands has its own peculiar aroma.

The island of Capri was damp and dark that evening. For the moment, however, it had revived, and was lighted up here and there as usual at the hour of the steamer's arrival. At the top of the ascent, on the little piazza by the funicular station stood the crowd of those whose duty it was to receive with propriety the luggage of the Gentleman from San Francisco. There were other arrivals too, but none worthy of notice: a few Russians who had settled in Capri, untidy and absent-minded owing to their bookish thoughts, spectacled, bearded, half-buried in the upturned collars of their thick woollen overcoats. Then a group of long-legged, long-necked, round-headed German youths in Tirolese costumes, with knapsacks over their shoulders, needing no assistance, feeling everywhere at home and always economical in tips.

The Gentleman from San Francisco, who kept quietly apart from both groups, was marked out at once. He and his ladies were hastily assisted from the car, men ran in front to show them the way, and they set off on foot, surrounded by urchins and by the sturdy Capri women who carry on their heads the luggage of decent travellers. Across the piazza, that looked like an opera scene in the light of the electric globe that swung aloft in the damp wind, clacked the wooden pattens of the women-porters. The gang of urchins began to whistle to the Gentleman from San Francisco, and to turn somersaults around him, whilst he, as if on the stage, marched among them towards a mediæval archway and under huddled houses, behind which led a little echoing lane, past tufts of palm-trees showing above the flat roofs to the left, and under the stars in the dark blue sky, upwards towards the shining entrance of the hotel. ... And again it seemed as if purely in honour of the guests from San Francisco the damp little town on the rocky little island of the Mediterranean had revived from its evening stupor, that their arrival alone had made the hotel proprietor so happy and hearty, and that for them had been waiting the Chinese gong which sent its howlings through all the house the moment they crossed the doorstep.

The sight of the proprietor, a superbly elegant young man with a polite and exquisite bow, startled for a moment the Gentleman from San Francisco. In the first flash, he remembered that amid the chaos of images which had possessed him the previous night in his sleep, he had seen that very man, to a T the same man, in the same full-skirted frock-coat and with the same glossy, perfectly smoothed hair. Startled, he hesitated for a second. But long, long ago he had lost the last mustard-seed of any mystical feeling he might ever have had, and his surprise at once faded. He told the curious coincidence of dream and reality jestingly to his wife and daughter, as they passed along the hotel corridor. And only his daughter glanced at him with a little alarm. Her heart suddenly contracted with home-sickness, with such a violent feeling of loneliness in this dark, foreign island, that she nearly wept. As usual, however, she did not mention her feelings to her father.

Reuss XVII., a high personage who had spent three whole weeks on Capri, had just left, and the visitors were installed in the suite of rooms that he had occupied. To them was assigned the most beautiful and expert chambermaid, a Belgian with a thin, firmly corseted figure, and a starched cap in the shape of a tiny indented crown. The most experienced and distinguished-looking footman was placed at their service, a coal-black, fiery-eyed Sicilian, and also the smartest waiter, the small, stout Luigi, a tremendous buffoon, who had seen a good deal of life. In a minute or two a gentle tap was heard at the door of the Gentleman from San Francisco, and there stood the maître d'hôtel, a Frenchman, who had come to ask if the guests would take dinner, and to report, in case of answer in the affirmative – of which, however, he had small doubt – that this evening there were Mediterranean lobsters, roast beef, asparagus, pheasants, etc., etc. The floor was still rocking under the feet of the Gentleman from San Francisco, so rolled about had he been on that wretched, grubby Italian steamer. Yet with his own hands, calmly, though clumsily from lack of experience, he closed the window which had banged at the entrance of the maître d'hôtel, shutting out the drifting smell of distant kitchens and of wet flowers in the garden. Then he turned and replied with unhurried distinctness, that they would take dinner, that their table must be far from the door, in the very centre of the dining-room, that they would have local wine and champagne, moderately dry and slightly cooled. To all of which the maître d'hôtel gave assent in the most varied intonations, which conveyed that there was not and could not be the faintest question of the justness of the desires of the Gentleman from San Francisco, and that everything should be exactly as he wished. At the end he inclined his head and politely inquired:

"Is that all, sir?"

On receiving a lingering "Yes," he added that Carmela and Giuseppe, famous all over Italy and "to all the world of tourists," were going to dance the tarantella that evening in the hall.

"I have seen picture-postcards of her," said the Gentleman from San Francisco, in a voice expressive of nothing. "And is Giuseppe her husband?"

"Her cousin, sir," replied the maître d'hôtel.

The Gentleman from San Francisco was silent for a while, thinking of something, but saying nothing; then he dismissed the man with a nod of the head. After which he began to make preparations as if for his wedding. He turned on all the electric lights, and filled the mirrors with brilliance and reflection of furniture and open trunks. He began to shave and wash, ringing the bell every minute, and down the corridor raced and crossed the impatient ringings from the rooms of his wife and daughter. Luigi, with the nimbleness peculiar to certain stout people, making grimaces of horror which brought tears of laughter to the eyes of chambermaids dashing past with marble-white pails, turned a cart-wheel to the gentleman's door, and tapping with his knuckles, in a voice of sham timidity and respectfulness reduced to idiocy, asked:

"Ha suonato, Signore?"

From behind the door, a slow, grating, offensively polite voice:

"Yes, come in."

What were the feelings, what were the thoughts of the Gentleman from San Francisco on that evening so significant to him? He felt nothing exceptional, since unfortunately everything on this earth is too simple in appearance. Even had he felt something imminent in his soul, all the same he would have reasoned that, whatever it might be, it could not take place immediately. Besides, as with all who have just experienced sea-sickness, he was very hungry, and looked forward with delight to the first spoonful of soup, the first mouthful of wine. So he performed the customary business of dressing in a state of excitement which left no room for reflection.

Having shaved, washed, and dexterously arranged several artificial teeth, standing in front of the mirror, he moistened his silver-mounted brushes and plastered the remains of his thick pearly hair on his swarthy yellow skull. He drew on to his strong old body, with its abdomen protuberant from excessive good living, his cream-coloured silk underwear, put black silk socks and patent-leather slippers on his flat-footed feet. He put sleeve-links in the shining cuffs of his snow-white shirt, and bending forward so that his shirt front bulged out, he arranged his trousers that were pulled up high by his silk braces, and began to torture himself, putting his collar-stud through the stiff collar. The floor was still rocking beneath him, the tips of his fingers hurt, the stud at moments pinched the flabby skin in the recess under his Adam's apple, but he persisted, and at last, with eyes all strained and face dove-blue from the over-tight collar that enclosed his throat, he finished the business and sat down exhausted in front of the pier glass, which reflected the whole of him, and repeated him in all the other mirrors.

"It is awful!" he muttered, dropping his strong, bald head, but without trying to understand or to know what was awful. Then, with habitual careful attention examining his gouty-jointed short fingers and large, convex, almond-shaped finger-nails, he repeated: "It is awful. . . ."

As if from a pagan temple shrilly resounded the second gong through the hotel. The Gentleman from San Francisco got up hastily, pulled his shirt-collar still tighter with his tie, and his abdomen tighter with his open waistcoat, settled his cuffs and again examined himself in the mirror. . . . "That Carmela, swarthy, with her enticing eyes, looking like a mulatto in her dazzling-coloured dress, chiefly orange, she must be an extraordinary dancer – " he was thinking. So, cheerfully leaving his room and walking on the carpet to his wife's room, he called to ask if they were nearly ready.

"In five minutes, Dad," came the gay voice of the girl from behind the door. "I'm arranging my hair."

"Right-o!" said the Gentleman from San Francisco.

Imagining to himself her long hair hanging to the floor, he slowly walked along the corridors and staircases covered with red carpet, downstairs, looking for the reading-room. The servants he encountered on the way pressed close to the wall, and he walked past as if not noticing them. An old lady, late for dinner, already stooping with age, with milk-white hair and yet decolletée in her pale grey silk dress, hurried at top speed, funnily, henlike, and he easily overtook her. By the glass-door of the dining-room, wherein the guests had already started the meal, he stopped before a little table heaped with boxes of cigars and cigarettes, and taking a large Manilla, threw three liras on the table. After which he passed along the winter terrace, and glanced through an open window. From the darkness came a waft of soft air, and there loomed the top of an old palm-tree that spread its boughs over the stars, looking like a giant, bringing down the far-off smooth quivering of the sea. ... In the reading-room, cosy with the shaded reading-lamps, a grey, untidy German, looking rather like Ibsen in his round silver-rimmed spectacles and with mad astonished eyes, stood rustling the newspapers. After coldly eyeing him, the Gentleman from San Francisco seated himself in a deep leather armchair in a corner, by a lamp with a green shade, put on his pince-nez, and, with a stretch of his neck because of the tightness of his shirt-collar, obliterated himself behind a newspaper. He glanced over the headlines, read a few sentences about the never-ending Balkan war, then with a habitual movement turned over the page of the newspaper – when suddenly the lines blazed up before him in a glassy sheen, his neck swelled, his eyes bulged, and the pince-nez came flying off his nose. ... He lunged forward, wanted to breathe – and rattled wildly. His lower jaw dropped, and his mouth shone with gold fillings. His head fell swaying on his shoulder, his shirt-front bulged out basket-like, and all his body, writhing, with heels scraping up the carpet, slid down to the floor, struggling desperately with some invisible foe.

If the German had not been in the reading-room, the frightful affair could have been hushed up. Instantly, through obscure passages the Gentleman from San Francisco could have been hurried away to some dark corner, and not a single guest would have discovered what he had been up to. But the German dashed out of the room with a yell, alarming the house and all the diners. Many sprang up from the table, upsetting their chairs, many, pallid, ran towards the reading-room, and in every language it was asked: "What – what's the matter?" None answered intelligibly, nobody understood, for even to-day people are more surprised at death than at anything else, and never want to believe it is true. The proprietor rushed from one guest to another, trying to keep back those who were hastening up, to soothe them with assurances that it was a mere trifle, a fainting-fit that had overcome a certain Gentleman from San Francisco. ... But no one heeded him. Many saw how the porters and waiters were tearing off the tie, waistcoat, and crumpled dress-coat from that same gentleman, even, for some reason or other, pulling off his patent evening-shoes from his black-silk, flat-footed feet. And he was still writhing. He continued to struggle with death, by no means wanting to yield to that which had so unexpectedly and rudely overtaken him. He rolled his head, rattled like one throttled, and turned up the whites of his eyes as if he were drunk. When he had been hastily carried into room No. 43, the smallest, wretchedest, dampest, and coldest room at the end of the bottom corridor, his daughter came running with her hair all loose, her dressing-gown flying open, showing her bosom raised by her corsets: then his wife, large and heavy and completely dressed for dinner, her mouth opened round with terror. But by that time he had already ceased rolling his head.

In a quarter of an hour the hotel settled down somehow or other. But the evening was ruined. The guests, returning to the dining-room, finished their dinner in silence, with a look of injury on their faces, whilst the proprietor went from one to another, shrugging his shoulders in hopeless and natural irritation, feeling himself guilty through no fault of his own, assuring everybody that he perfectly realized "how disagreeable this is," and giving his word that he would take "every possible measure within his power" to remove the trouble. The tarantella had to be cancelled, the superfluous lights were switched off, most of the guests went to the bar, and soon the house became so quiet that the ticking of the clock was heard distinctly in the hall, where the lonely parrot woodenly muttered something as he bustled about in his cage preparatory to going to sleep, and managed to fall asleep at length with his paw absurdly suspended from the little upper perch. . . . The Gentleman from San Francisco lay on a cheap iron bed under coarse blankets on to which fell a dim light from the obscure electric lamp in the ceiling. An ice-bag slid down on his wet, cold forehead; his blue, already lifeless face grew gradually cold; the hoarse bubbling which came from his open mouth, where the gleam of gold still showed, grew weak. The Gentleman from San Francisco rattled no longer; he was no more – something else lay in his place. His wife, his daughter, the doctor, and the servants stood and watched him dully. Suddenly that which they feared and expected happened. The rattling ceased. And slowly, slowly under their eyes a pallor spread over the face of the deceased, his features began to grow thinner, more transparent . . . with a beauty which might have suited him long ago. . . .

Entered the proprietor. "Gia, e morto!" whispered the doctor to him. The proprietor raised his shoulders, as if it were not his affair. The wife, on whose cheeks tears were slowly trickling, approached and timidly asked that the deceased should be taken to his own room.

"Oh no, madame," hastily replied the proprietor, politely, but coldly, and not in English, but in French. He was no longer interested in the trifling sum the guests from San Francisco would leave at his cash desk. "That is absolutely impossible." Adding by way of explanation, that he valued that suite of rooms highly, and that should he accede to madame's request, the news would be known all over Capri and no one would take the suite afterwards.

The young lady, who had glanced at him strangely all the time, now sat down in a chair and sobbed, with her handkerchief to her mouth. The elder lady's tears dried at once, her face flared up. Raising her voice and using her own language she began to insist, unable to believe that the respect for them had gone already. The manager cut her short with polite dignity. "If madame does not like the ways of the hotel, he dare not detain her." And he announced decisively that the corpse must be removed at dawn: the police had already been notified, and an official would arrive presently to attend to the necessary formalities. "Is it possible to get a plain coffin?" madame asked. Unfortunately not! Impossible! And there was no time to make one. It would have to be arranged somehow. Yes, the English soda-water came in large strong boxes – if the divisions were removed.

The whole hotel was asleep. The window of No. 43 was open, on to a corner of the garden where, under a high stone wall ridged with broken glass, grew a battered banana tree. The light was turned off, the door locked, the room deserted. The deceased remained in the darkness, blue stars glanced at him from the black sky, a cricket started to chirp with sad carelessness in the wall. . . . Out in the dimly-lit corridor two chambermaids were seated in a window-sill, mending something. Entered Luigi, in slippers, with a heap of clothes in his hand.

"Pronto?" he asked, in a singing whisper, indicating with his eyes the dreadful door at the end of the corridor. Then giving a slight wave thither with his free hand: "Patenza!" he shouted in a whisper, as though sending off a train. The chambermaids, choking with noiseless laughter, dropped their heads on each other's shoulders.

Tip-toeing, Luigi went to the very door, tapped, and

cocking his head on one side asked respectfully, in a sub-
dued tone:

"Ha suonato, Signore?"

Then contracting his throat and shoving out his jaw, he
answered himself in a grating, drawling, mournful voice,
which seemed to come from behind the door:

"Yes, come in. . . ."

When the dawn grew white at the window of No. 43, and
a damp wind began rustling the tattered fronds of the banana
tree; as the blue sky of morning lifted and unfolded over
Capri, and Monte Solaro, pure and distinct, grew golden,
catching the sun which was rising beyond the far-off blue
mountains of Italy; just as the labourers who were mending
the paths of the islands for the tourists came out for work, a
long box was carried into room No. 43. Soon this box
weighed heavily, and it painfully pressed the knees of the
porter who was carrying it in a one-horse cab down the winding white high-road, between stone walls and vineyards,
down, down the face of Capri to the sea. The driver, a weakly
little fellow with reddened eyes, in a little old jacket with
sleeves too short and bursting boots, kept flogging his wiry
small horse that was decorated in Sicilian fashion, its harness
tinkling with busy little bells and fringed with fringes of scarlet wool, the high saddle-peak gleaming with copper and
tufted with colour, and a yard-long plume nodding from the
pony's cropped head, from between the ears. The cabby had
spent the whole night playing dice in the inn, and was still
under the effects of drink. Silent, he was depressed by his
own debauchery and vice: by the fact that he gambled away
to the last farthing all those copper coins with which his
pockets had yesterday been full, in all four lire, forty cente-
simi. But the morning was fresh. In such air, with the sea all

round, under the morning sky headaches evaporate, and man soon regains his cheerfulness. Moreover, the cabby was cheered by this unexpected fare which he was making out of some Gentleman from San Francisco, who was nodding with his dead head in a box at the back. The little steamer, which lay like a water-beetle on the tender bright blueness which brims the bay of Naples, was already giving the final hoots, and this tooting resounded again cheerily all over the island. Each contour, each ridge, each rock was so clearly visible in every direction, it was as if there were no atmosphere at all. Near the beach the porter in the cab was overtaken by the head porter dashing down in an automobile with the lady and her daughter, both pale, their eyes swollen with the tears of a sleepless night. . . . And in ten minutes the little steamer again churned up the water and made her way back to Sorrento, to Castellamare, bearing away from Capri for ever the family from San Francisco. . . . And peace and tranquillity reigned once more on the island.

On that island two thousand years ago lived a man entangled in his own infamous and strange acts, one whose rule for some reason extended over millions of people, and who, having lost his head through the absurdity of such power, committed deeds which have established him for ever in the memory of mankind; mankind which in the mass now rules the world just as hideously and incomprehensibly as he ruled it then. And men come here from all quarters of the globe to look at the ruins of the stone house where that one man lived, on the brink of one of the steepest cliffs in the island. On this exquisite morning all who had come to Capri for that purpose were still asleep in the hotels, although through the streets already trotted little mouse-coloured donkeys with red saddles, towards the hotel entrances where they would wait patiently until, after a good sleep and a square meal, young and old American men and women, German men and women would emerge and be hoisted up into the saddles, to be followed up the stony paths, yea to the very summit of Monte Tiberio, by old persistent beggar-women of Capri, with sticks in their sinewy hands. Quieted by the fact that the dead old Gentleman from San Francisco, who had intended to be one of the pleasure party but who had only succeeded in frightening the rest with the reminder of death, was now being shipped to Naples, the happy tourists still slept soundly, the island was still quiet, the shops in the little town not yet open. Only fish and greens were being sold in the tiny piazza, only simple folk were present, and amongst them, as usual without occupation, the tall old boatman Lorenzo, thorough debauchee and handsome figure, famous all over Italy, model for many a picture. He had already sold for a trifle two lobsters which he had caught in the night, and which were rustling in the apron of the cook of that very same hotel where the family from San Francisco had spent the night. And now Lorenzo could stand calmly till evening, with a majestic air showing off his rags and gazing round, holding his clay pipe with its long reed mouth-piece in his hand, and letting his scarlet bonnet slip over one ear. For as a matter of fact he received a salary from the little town, from the commune which found it profitable to pay him to stand about and make a picturesque figure – as everybody knows. . . . Down the precipices of Monte Solaro, down the stony little stairs cut in the rock of the old Phœnician road came two Abruzzi mountaineers, descending from Anacapri. One carried a bagpipe under his leather cloak, a large goat skin with two little pipes; the other had a sort of wooden flute. They descended, and the whole land, joyous, was sunny beneath them. They saw the rocky, heaving shoulder of the island, which lay almost entirely at their feet, swimming in the fairy blueness of the water. Shining morning vapours rose over the sea to the east, under a dazzling sun which already burned hot as it rose higher and higher; and there, far off, the dimly cerulean masses of Italy, of her near and far mountains, still wavered blue as if in the world's morning, in a beauty no words can express. ... Halfway down the descent the pipers slackened their pace. Above the road, in a grotto of the rocky face of Monte Solaro stood the Mother of God, the sun full upon her, giving her a splendour of snow-white and blue raiment, and royal crown rusty from all weathers. Meek and merciful, she raised her eyes to heaven, to the eternal and blessed mansions of her thrice-holy Son. The pipers bared their heads, put their pipes to their lips: and there streamed forth naive and meekly joyous praises to the sun, to the morning, to Her, Immaculate, who would intercede for all who suffer in this malicious and lovely world, and to Him, born of Her womb among the caves of Bethlehem, in a lowly shepherd's hut, in the far Judean land. ...

And the body of the dead old man from San Francisco was returning home, to its grave, to the shores of the New World. Having been subjected to many humiliations, much human neglect, after a week's wandering from one warehouse to another, it was carried at last on to the same renowned vessel which so short a time ago, and with such honour, had borne him living to the Old World. But now he was to be hidden far from the knowledge of the voyagers. Closed in a tar-coated coffin, he was lowered deep into the vessel's dark hold. And again, again the ship set out on the long voyage. She passed at night near Capri, and to those who were looking out from the island, sad seemed the lights of the ship slowly hiding themselves in the sea's darkness. But there aboard the liner, in the bright halls shining with lights and marble, gay dancing filled the evening, as usual. . . .

The second evening, and the third evening, still they danced, amid a storm that swept over the ocean, booming like a funeral service, rolling up mountains of mourning darkness silvered with foam. Through the snow the numerous fiery eyes of the ship were hardly visible to the Devil who watched from the rocks of Gibraltar, from the stony gateway of two worlds, peering after the vessel as she disappeared into the night and storm. The Devil was huge as a cliff. But huger still was the liner, many storeyed, many funnelled, created by the presumption of the New Man with the old heart. The blizzard smote the rigging and the funnels, and whitened the ship with snow, but she was enduring, firm, majestic – and horrible. On the topmost deck rose lonely amongst the snowy whirlwind the cosy and dim quarters where lay the heavy master of the ship, he who was like a pagan idol, sunk now in a light, uneasy slumber. Through his sleep he heard the sombre howl and furious screechings of the siren, muffled by the blizzard. But again he reassured himself by the nearness of that which stood behind his wall, and was in the last resort incomprehensible to him: by the large, apparently armoured cabin which was now and then filled with a mysterious rumbling, throbbing, and crackling of blue fires that flared up explosive around the pale face of the telegraphist who, with a metal hoop fixed on his head, was eagerly straining to catch the dim voices of vessels which spoke to him from hundreds of miles away. In the depths, in the under-water womb of the *Atlantis*, steel glimmered and steam wheezed, and huge masses of machinery and thousand-ton boilers dripped with water and oil, as the motion of the ship was steadily cooked in this vast kitchen heated by hellish furnaces from beneath. Here bubbled in their awful concentration the powers which were being transmitted to the keel, down an infinitely long round tunnel lit up and brilliant like a gigantic gun-barrel, along which slowly, with a regularity crushing to the human soul, revolved a gigantic shaft, precisely like a living monster coiling and uncoiling its endless length down the tunnel, sliding on its bed of oil. The middle of the *Atlantis*, the warm, luxurious cabins, dining-rooms, halls, shed light and joy, buzzed with the chatter of an elegant crowd, was fragrant with fresh flowers, and quivered with the sounds of a string orchestra. And again amidst that crowd, amidst the brilliance of lights, silks, diamonds, and bare feminine shoulders, a slim and supple pair of hired lovers painfully writhed and at moments convulsively clashed. A sinfully discreet, pretty girl with lowered lashes and hair innocently dressed, and a tallish young man with black hair looking as if it were glued on, pale with powder, and wearing the most elegant patent-leather shoes and a narrow, long-tailed dress coat, a beau resembling an enormous leech. And no one knew that this couple had long since grown weary of shamly tormenting themselves with their beatific love-tortures, to the sound of bawdy-sad music; nor did any one know of that thing which lay deep, deep below at the very bottom of the dark hold, near the gloomy and sultry bowels of the ship that was so gravely overcoming the darkness, the ocean, the blizzard. . . .

1915

TEFFI

THE QUIET BACKWATER

Translated by Anne Marie Jackson

EVERY SEA, every large river and every stormy lake has its own quiet backwater.

The water there is clear and calm. No reeds rustle, no ripples disturb the smooth surface. Should anything touch this surface – a dragonfly's wing or the long leg of a dancing evening mosquito – now there's an event for you.

If you climb the steep bank and look down, you'll see right away where this quiet backwater begins. It's as if it's been marked off by a ruler.

Out there, beyond this line, waves toss and turn in anguish. They rock from side to side, as if from madness and pain, and suddenly, in a last despairing leap, they throw themselves towards the heavens, only to crash back down into the dark water, leaving the wind to snatch at clumps of wild, helpless foam.

But in the backwater, this side of the sacred line, it is quiet. Instead of waves rising in mutiny and flinging themselves at the heavens, the heavens themselves come down to the backwater, in clear azure and little puffs of cloud in the daytime, and garbed in all the mystery of the stars at night.

The estate is called Kamyshovka.

You can see that it once stood on the very edge of the river. But the river retreated and left behind it, as a forget-me-not, a little blue-eyed lake – a joy to ducks – and masses of stiff reeds growing in the front garden.

The main house is abandoned; the doors and windows are boarded up.

Life lingers on only in the lodge — a cross-eyed, lopsided little building.

Here live a retired laundress and a retired coachman. They are not doing nothing; they are looking after the estate.

In her old age the laundress has sprouted a beard, while the coachman, yielding to her more powerful personality, has turned into such an old woman's blouse that he calls himself Fedorushka.

They live righteously. They speak little, and because both are hard of hearing, both always have their say. If one actually manages to hear the other, they understand only hazily, so they keep to what is near and dear, what they lived through long ago, what they know all about and have already recalled many a time.

Besides the coachman and the laundress there are other souls living on the estate: a cunning mare who thinks only about oats and how she might work less, and a glutton of a cow. There are chickens too, of course, though it's hard to say how many – you can't say there are four, but neither can you say there are five. If you throw them some grain and are careful to say, "Come and get it, God bless!", then four chickens come running. But just you forget that blessing and along comes a fifth. Where it's come from no one knows – and it gobbles up all the seed and bullies the other hens. It's big and grey, and evidently it likes seed that hasn't been blessed.

What a worry it all is! The grain belongs to the master and mistress. Sooner or later the mistress will come and ask, "Who's been pecking at my grain? Four beaks or five?"

How will they answer that?

They are afraid they'll be called to account. It's been a hard winter. They've got through firewood aplenty. Fear sets them thinking: across the river lie piles of state-owned wood ready for the spring floating. They harness the mare, cross the river and bring back a load. When they've used it all up they go back for more. How glorious it is having such fine wood right there on your doorstep. Even the mare, sly though she is, doesn't pretend to be tired. She hauls the wood with pleasure.

And then comes – would you believe it? – a summons from the magistrate.

The magistrate asks, "Why did you steal the wood?"

"What do you mean, 'why'? To heat the stove. We've burnt all our own wood already. When her ladyship comes, she'll give us what for."

The magistrate could have been worse. He doesn't shout at them – but he does tell them to put the wood back. Why did he have to be so stingy? Yes, he'd brought them nothing but trouble.

And how had he found out, this magistrate? They hadn't seen anyone when they were fetching the wood. Apparently it was the tracks from their sled – going across the river to the piles of wood and back to their door again.

Tracks? Weren't people cunning nowadays? The things they could figure out!

It's a warm day. Four red hens are pecking at scattered, properly blessed crusts of bread.

The table has been brought out onto the porch for tea. There's company today. The coachman's kinswoman has come from the village – his grandniece, a girl called Marfa. It's Marfa's name day and she has come here to celebrate.

She's a large girl, white, big-boned and slack-jawed. Her name-day dress is of such an intolerably bright pink that it even verges on blue. The day is clear and golden – the grass is young and garish green, the sky's the bluest of blues, and the yellow flowers in the grass are like little suns – but before the girl's dress they all seem dim and faded.

The old laundress looks at the dress. She squints and screws up her eyes. She feels that the girl's bearing lacks dignity.

"Why do you keep fidgeting?" the old woman grumbles. "Where's your manners? It's your name day, your patron saint is looking down at you from on high, but you – you're like a heifer with your tail swishing this way and that."

"What's that, Granny Pelageya?" the girl asks in surprise. "I haven't wiggled a finger since I sat down."

The old woman screws up her eyes at the bright, bright dress and can't understand what's the matter, what can be making her eyes so cloudy.

"Why don't you go and fetch the samovar?"

Along comes the old coachman. His face is anxious, his brows knitted together – evidently he has been having to deal with the cunning mare.

"She's eaten all the oats again. No matter how much you give her, she cleans up every last grain. The cunning creature! She's got more tricks than many a man. She could outwit more than a few of us, I tell you. I'll be in for it when the mistress comes."

"Yes, you'll be in for it all right," echoes the laundress. "Look! Her stores are nearly all gone! But it's her own fault. How does she expect me to feed a man – a peasant – all winter long? You think it's cheap feeding a peasant? Give him a potato and he wants butter too. Give him porridge and he's got to have broth as well. Is a peasant ever going to try and eat less? All he cares about is stuffing his belly."

The coachman nods sympathetically and even heaves a sigh, although he does half sense that the "peasant" in question might be himself. But that's the way things are. Deep in his soul he feels a certain awe before this peasant nature of his.

"Yes, peasants are peasants. Is a peasant going to try and eat less?"

Then the slack-jawed girl brought out a samovar with green stains down its side.

"Come and have yourselves some tea!" she said.

The old woman began blinking and screwing up her eyes again.

"Who's that you're talking to? Who is it you're calling to the table?"

"Why, you, Granny. And you, Grandpa."

"Then that's what you should say. There was a woman who called everyone to dinner with the words: 'Come and sit yourselves down.' But she didn't say, 'Let the baptized souls come and sit themselves down.' So anyone who felt like it came to dinner: they crawled out from on top of the stove, from behind the stove, from the sleeping shelf, from the bench and from under the bench, all the unseen and unheard, all the unknown and undreamt of. Great big eyes peering, great big teeth clacking. 'You called us,' they said. 'Now feed us.' But what could she do? She could hardly feed such a crowd."

"What happened? What did they all do?" asked the girl, goggle-eyed.

"What do you think?"

"What?"

"Well, they did what they do."

"What did they do?"

"They all did what they had to do."

"But what was it they had to do, Granny?"

"Ask too many questions – there's no knowing who'll answer."

The girl hunched herself up in fright and looked away to one side.

"Why do you keep fidgeting?" The old woman was squinting at the girl's bright pink skirt. "And you the name-day girl! Your name day is your saint's feast day – it's a holy day. The name day of the bee is the day of Saints Zosima and Savvaty. The bee may be a simple, humble creature – but all the same, on her name day she doesn't buzz, she doesn't sting. She just settles on a little flower and thinks about her guardian angel."

"We pay our respects to the mare on the day of Saints Frolus and Laurus," said the coachman, blowing on the tea he had poured out into his chipped saucer.

"The Feast of the Annunciation is the bird's name day. She doesn't weave her nest or peck for grain. She sings, but only softly and respectfully."

"On Saint Vlas's Day we pay our respects to the cattle," said the coachman, still trying to get a word in.

"And the Feast of the Holy Spirit is the earth's name day. On this day no one dares to trouble the earth. No one burrows or digs or picks flowers – none of that is allowed. Burying the dead is not allowed. It's a great sin to insult the earth on her name day. The beasts understand this too – and on the Day of the Holy Spirit no beast will scratch the earth with a claw, or stamp it with a hoof, or strike it with a paw. It's a great sin. Every beast knows about feast days. The glow-worm celebrates on St. John the Baptist's Day. He blows on his little flames and prays to his angel. Then it's Saint Aquilina's Day – the name day of red berries – that's when your strawberries and raspberries and currants and brambles and cranberries and cowberries and all the other little forest berries celebrate their name day. On Saint Aquilina's Day there's not a wolf, fox or hare will lay a paw on a red berry. Even the bear's afraid: why would he want to make trouble for himself? He doesn't take a single step until he's sniffed around and made sure he won't be trampling on any berries."

The girl seemed frightened again. She was looking away to one side, tucking her flat feet under her pink skirt. Snuffling and sighing.

The coachman also wanted to have his say.

He might not know many things. He had been in the army. A long time ago. They had had to push back the enemy. Then they had had to push on somewhere else. And somewhere else. Where? Who knows? No one can remember everything.

"Three years I was away. Then I came back home. 'Hello, Fedorushka,' says the wife, and the youngsters, too. And there in the corner, I see a cradle. And in the cradle a nursling. All right, I think, if it's a nursling it's a nursling. The next day I ask my eldest, 'Who's that there in the cradle?' 'That,' she says, 'is a little 'un.' All right, if it's a little 'un then it's a little 'un. The day after that I ask my eldest, 'So, where'd you get this little 'un?' 'Grandma,' she says, 'brought it.' Well, if it was Grandma then it was Grandma. The child began to grow. I heard him being called Petka. All right then, Petka. He grew big. And last year Petka's son got married. But I never did find out where this Petka came from. And now? Well, I doubt anyone can remember any more."

"I can't remember," murmured the old woman. "I can't remember the cow's name day. It's vexing not to know. I've grown old and forgetful. And it's a sin to hurt someone's feelings."

They shut the gate behind the pink girl. The day was over. It was time to go to sleep.

It had been a difficult day. You can't fall asleep straight away after a day like that. After guests have been round you always sleep poorly. The tea, and the talk, and the finery, and all the fuss.

"So when is the cow's name day? Unless you know, you might say an unkind word to her on her name day – and that's a sin. But the cow can't say anything. She'll keep her mouth shut. While up on high an angel will begin to weep ..."

It's hard being old! Hard!

Beyond the window the night is a deep blue. It calls something to mind – but just what, it is impossible to remember.

Softly rustle the reeds forgotten by the river.

The river has gone away; it has left the reeds behind.

1916

MIKHAIL BULGAKOV

THE ADVENTURES
OF CHICHIKOV

*A Poem in Ten Items with a Prologue
and an Epilogue*

Translated by Carl R. Proffer

"Hold it, hold it, you idiot!" Chichikov shouted to Selifan.

"Why I'll give you a taste of my sword!" shouted a courier with yard-long moustachioes, galloping straight at them. "Can't you see this is a government carriage, the devil flog your soul!"

PROLOGUE

A BIZARRE DREAM ... It was as if a joker-satan had opened the doors to the kingdom of shades – over the entrance to which an inextinguishable lamp inscribed "Dead Souls" flickers. The kingdom of the dead started to stir, and an endless line filed out of it.

Manilov in a thick bear-fur coat, Nozdryov in someone else's carriage, Derzhimorda on a fire-wagon, Selifan, Petrushka, Fetinya ...

And last of all *he* set off – Pavel Ivanovich Chichikov in his celebrated chaise.

And the whole band headed into Soviet Rus, and then astonishing events occurred there. And what sort they were – the following items show ...

SWITCHING FROM HIS chaise to a car in Moscow, and flying through Moscow gullies in it, Chichikov scolded Gogol violently.

"May blisters as big as haystacks bubble under his eyes, the son of a devil! He's befouled and polluted my reputation so badly there's no place I can show my nose. If anyone finds out that I'm Chichikov, they'll naturally toss me to the devil's mother in two shakes! And it's still all right if they just toss me and I don't end up sitting in Lubyanka, God forbid. And it's all Gogol's doing, may he and all his kith and kin ..."

And meditating thus, he drove in through the gates of that same inn out of which he had driven one hundred years ago.

Absolutely everything in it was as before: the cockroaches peeped out of the cracks, and it was as if there were even more of them – but there were a few small changes too. Thus, for example, in place of the sign "Inn" hung a placard with the inscription "Dormitory No. Such-and-such," and, it goes without saying, the grime and filth was such as Gogol could not even have fantasized.

"A room!"

"Your order!"

But not for a second was the brilliant Pavel Ivanovich nonplussed.

"The manager!"

"Wham!" the manager is an old acquaintance: old Bald Pimen who one time ran "The Shark," and who had now opened a café on Tverskoy Boulevard – in the Russian style with German trimmings: orgeats, balsams, and of course, prostitutes. The guest and manager exchanged kisses, susurrated back and forth, and in a wink the matter was closed without any order. Pavel Ivanovich had a makeshift snack of leftovers and flew off to arrange for work.

II

HE APPEARED EVERYWHERE and enchanted everyone with his bows slightly to the side and the colossal erudition which had always distinguished him.

"Fill out the questionnaire."

They gave Pavel Ivanovich a questionnaire a yard long, containing one hundred of the trickiest questions: where are you from, where have you been, and why? . . .

Pavel Ivanovich had not been sitting there for more than five minutes before he had filled every bit of space on the questionnaire. But his hand was trembling as he handed it in.

"Well," he thought, "now they'll read what a treasure I am, and . . ."

And absolutely nothing happened.

In the first place, no one read the questionnaire; in the second place, it fell into the hands of the lady registrar who handled it as usual: she processed it as an outgoing instead of incoming document and then immediately stuck it somewhere, so that the questionnaire vanished as if into the waters of the sea.

Chichikov grinned and went to work.

III

AND FROM THEN on everything got easier and easier. First of all, Chichikov looked around, and saw that wherever he spat, his old buddies were there, holding positions. He flew into an office where, he heard, rations were issued, and he hears:

"I know you, you skinflint, you'd take a live cat, skin it and give it out as a ration! But you just give me a side of mutton and some oatmeal. Because even if you sugarcoat it I won't put that toad you call a ration in my mouth, and I won't take your putrid herring either!"

He looks – there's Sobakevich.

As soon as he arrived, Sobakevich made it his first duty to demand a ration. And by God he got it! Ate it and asked for seconds. Got them. Not enough! Then they dished out a second meal for him; they'd first given him a single one – now a shock-worker's ration. Not enough! They gave him some sort of reserve amount. He bolted that and demanded more. And he made a scandal about demanding it. He cursed them all as "Judases," said that scoundrel sits on scoundrel and persecutes scoundrel and that there is only one decent man, the clerk, and he's a pig, if you tell the truth!

They gave him an academician's ration.

No sooner did Chichikov see how Sobakevich handled the rations than he instantly finagled things for himself too. But, of course, he surpassed Sobakevich. He got rations for himself, for his nonexistent wife and baby, for Selifan, for Petrushka, for that same old guy about whom Betrishchev had told, for his old mother who was not in this world. And academician's portions for all. So that they started delivering the groceries to him by truck.

And having settled the food problem thus, he headed for other offices to find a position.

Once as he was flying along Kuznetsky in his car, he met Nozdryov. The latter made it his first duty to report that he had already sold the watch and chain. And indeed, he had neither watch nor chain on him. But Nozdryov did not despair. He told how he had made out at a lottery when he had won a half pound of vegetable oil, lamp glass, and soles for children's shoes, but how he had had no luck after that, and how he, dammit, had reported his six hundred million rubles to the government. He told how he had proposed that VNESHTORG [Foreign Trade Ministry] send a shipment of genuine Caucasian daggers abroad. And they did. And he would have made millions on it if it were not for the damned English, who had noticed the inscription "Made by Savely Sibiryakov" and rejected them all as defective. He dragged Chichikov to his hotel room and plied him with amazing cognac supposedly brought from France, in which, however, full-strength moonshine could be tasted. And, in the end, his cock-and-bull stories got to the point where he started maintaining he had been issued eight hundred yards of textiles, a baby-blue automobile with gold trim, and an order for living space in a building with columns.

When his brother-in-law Mizhuev expressed some doubt, he swore at him, calling him not a Sofron, but simply a bastard.

In a word, he bored Chichikov so much that he did not know how to get out fast enough.

But Nozdryov's stories gave him the idea of going into export trade himself.

IV

AND SO HE DID. Again he filled out a questionnaire and went to work and showed himself in all his glory. He shipped sheep across the border in double sheepskins with Brabant lace underneath; he smuggled in jewels inside wheels, shafts, ears, and the devil only knows what sort of places.

And in the shortest period he turned up with about five hundred oranges capital.

But he did not rest there – he submitted an application to the proper place expressing a desire to take a lease on a certain enterprise, and he used extraordinary colors to paint up a picture of the profits the government would have from it.

At the government office mouths simply gaped open – the profit was indeed colossal. They asked to be shown the enterprise. If you please. On Tverskoy Boulevard right opposite the Strastnoy Monastery, across the street – it is called "Pampas on Tverboul." They sent an inquiry to the proper place: "Is there any such thing there?" They were answered: "There is, and it's known to all Moscow." "Fine."

"Turn in a technical estimate."

Chichikov already has the estimate in his shirt.

They gave him the lease.

Then, without wasting any time, Chichikov flew off to the proper place.

"An advance, please."

"Present an authorization in triplicate with the required signatures and seals."

Two hours had not passed before he presented the authorization too. All in order. As many seals as stars in the sky. And the signatures all right there.

"Signing for the manager – Neuvazhai-Korito, for the secretary – Kuvshinnoe Rilo, for the chairman of the Tariff Estimate Commission – Elizavet Vorobey."

"Right. Here's your order."

The cashier just gurgled when he saw the total.

Chichikov signed the receipt and carted away the banknotes in three carriages.

And then off to another office:

"A loan, my merchandise as collateral."

"Show the merchandise."

"By all means. Your agent, please."

"Get the agent!"

Tfu! The agent is an acquaintance too – Rotozei Emelyan.

Chichikov picks him up and takes him away. He takes him to the first cellar they come to – and points to it. Emelyan sees an enormous quantity of goods lying there.

"M-yes . . . And it's all yours?"

"All mine."

"Well," says Emelyan, "then I congratulate you. You're not a millionaire – you're even a trillionaire!"

And Nozdryov, who at this point had caught up with him, poured oil on the fire.

"See that," he says, "see that car with the boots in it, driving through that gate? Well, those are his boots too."

And then he got carried away, dragged Emelyan to the street and pointed.

"See those stores? Well, those are all his stores. Everything on that side of the street – it's all his. And the ones on this side – they're his too. See the trolley? His. The streetlights? . . . His. See? See?"

And he spins him in all directions.

So that Emelyan begged: "I believe it! I see . . . Just let my soul rest."

They went back to the office.

There they are asked, "Well?"

Emelyan just waved his arm.

"It's . . ." he says, "it's indescribable!"

"Well, if it's indescribable – give him $n + 1$ billion."

V

AFTER THAT CHICHIKOV'S career developed in a dizzying fashion. What he was up to is beyond the mind's powers to comprehend. He founded a trust to pour iron from sawdust, and got a loan on that too. He became a shareholder in a huge cooperative, and he fed all Moscow on sausage made from already dead animals. Having heard that in Moscow "everything had been settled" now, the landowner Korobochka expressed a desire to acquire some real estate; Chichikov formed a company with Zamukhryshkin and Uteshitelny and sold her the Manège, the exposition hall opposite the university. He signed a contract for the electrification of the city – which is so big you can't get out of it even if you gallop for three years – and making contact with the former mayor, he set up some sort of wood fence, put in landmarkers so that it would appear some planning was going on, and as for the money dispensed for electrification, he wrote that it had been stolen by the gangs of Captain Kopeikin. In a word, he worked miracles.

And soon the rumor that Chichikov was a trillionaire was being trumpeted all over Moscow. Government organizations began to rush pell-mell to get him as a specialist. Chichikov had already rented a five-room apartment for five billion; Chichikov was already lunching and supping at the "Empire."

VI

BUT SUDDENLY THE crash came.

Chichikov was ruined by Nozdryov, as Gogol had correctly predicted, and he was finished off by Korobochka.

Without any desire to do him dirty, but simply because he was drunk, Nozdryov babbled something in passing about sawdust and about Chichikov taking a lease on a nonexistent enterprise, and concluded all of this with words to the effect that Chichikov was a swindler and that he would have him shot.

The public fell to thinking, and the winged rumor took off like a spark.

And at this point, idiot Korobochka pushed into a government office to make inquiries about whether she could open a bakery in the Manège. Vainly they kept assuring her that the Manège was a government building, and that it was impossible to buy or open anything in it – but the stupid old crone understood none of it.

But the rumors about Chichikov kept getting worse and worse. People began to wonder what sort of bird this Chichikov was and where he was from. Slanderous tales got started, one more ominous and monstrous than the next. Uneasiness entered the hearts of all. Telephones started to jangle, conferences began ... The Commission on Construction with the Commission on Inspection, the Commission on Inspection with ZHILOTDEL, ZHILOTDEL with NARKOMZDRAV, NARKOMZDRAV with GLAVKUST-PROM, GLAVKUSTPROM with NARKOMPROS, NARK-OMPROS with PROLETKULT, etc.

They rushed to Nozdryov. That, of course, was stupid. They all knew that Nozdryov was a liar, that not a word Nozdryov said could be believed. But they summoned Nozdryov and he answered every item in order.

He announced that Chichikov had in fact leased a nonexistent enterprise, and that he, Nozdryov, saw no reason why he shouldn't have since everyone does it. To the question, was Chichikov a White Guard spy, he answered that he was a spy and that not long ago they had even wanted to shoot him, but that for some reason he had not been shot. To the question, is Chichikov a forger of counterfeit banknotes, he answered that he was a forger and even told an anecdote about Chichikov's extraordinary skill, how when he had learned that the government wanted to put out new notes Chichikov had rented an apartment in Marina Grove and issued from there 18 billion rubles' worth of fake notes, and, to top it off, this was two days before the real ones came out, and when they had raided the apartment and sealed it shut, in one night Chichikov mixed the fake banknotes with real ones so that afterward the devil himself couldn't tell which were fake and which genuine. To the question, was it true that Chichikov was exchanging his billions for diamonds so that he could escape abroad, Nozdryov answered that it was true, and that he himself was helping him and taking part in the deal, and that if it weren't for him, nothing would come of it.

After Nozdryov's stories everyone was overwhelmed by the most complete depression. They see there's no possibility of finding out what Chichikov is. And it is unknown how all this would have ended if it had not been for one person in this company. True, like all the others he had never had a copy of Gogol in his hands, but he commanded a small dose of common sense.

So he exclaimed, "You know what Chichikov is?"

And when they all thundered, in chorus, "Who?"

He said in a sepulchral voice: "A swindler."

VII

ONLY AT THIS point did the light dawn on everyone. They

rushed to look for the questionnaire. Nowhere to be found. As an incoming document. No sign of it. In the filing cabinet – not a sign. To the registrar. "How should I know? Ask Ivan Grigorych."

To Ivan Grigorych. "Where is it?"

"It's none of my business. Ask the secretary, etc., etc."

And suddenly, unexpectedly, in a wastepaper basket – there it is.

They started reading and froze.

"First name? Pavel. Patronymic? Ivanovich. Surname? Chichikov. Social Status? Gogol character. Occupation before the Revolution? Purchase of dead souls. Draft Status? Neither fish, nor fowl – nor the devil knows what. Party Affiliation? Sympathizer [but with whom – unknown]. Have you ever been arrested? A wavy zigzag. Home Address? Turn into the courtyard, the third floor on the right, ask the field-officer's wife, Podtochina, in the information office, she knows. Personal signature? A splotch!!"

They read and turned to stone.

They yelled to Instructor Bobchinsky, "Get going over to Tverskoy Boulevard to the enterprise he leased, and the yard where his merchandise is, maybe something will turn up there!"

Bobchinsky returns. Round eyes.

"An extraordinary event!"

"Well?!"

"There ain't no enterprise at all there. He gave the address of the Pushkin Monument. And the goods aren't his, they're the ARA's."

Here they all howled, "Holy Saints! So that's the kind of goose he is! And we gave him billions!! Now, it turns out we've got to nab him!"

And they started trying.

VIII

A FINGER PRESSED a button,

"A courier."

The door opened and Petrushka presented himself. He had left Chichikov a long time ago and become a courier for a government office.

"Take this package immediately and be on your way immediately."

Petrushka said, "Yes, sir."

He immediately took the package, immediately got on his way, and immediately lost it.

They called Selifan at the garage.

"A car. On the double."

"Medjutly."

Selifan shook himself, covered the motor with a pair of warm pants, put on his jacket, hopped into the seat, whistled, honked, and flew off.

What Russian does not love a swift ride?

Selifan loved it too, and therefore at the entrance to Lubyanka he was forced to choose between a trolley car and a plate-glass store window. In a brief instant of time Selifan chose the latter, swerved away from the trolley, and like a whirlwind, screaming "Help!" drove through the store window.

Here even Tentetnikov, who was in charge of all the Selifans and Petrushkas, lost his patience.

Fire them both and send them pig farming!

They fired him. Sent him to the Employment Bureau. From there these orders were made: Plyushkin's Proshka was to replace Petrushka, Grigory Try-To-Get-There-But-You-Won't to replace Selifan. And meanwhile things were boiling along!

250

"The authorization for the advance!"

"Here, if you please."

"Ask Neuvazhai-Korito here."

This turned out to be impossible. Some two months before Neuvazhai had been purged from the Party, and then he purged himself from Moscow immediately after that, since there was absolutely nothing more for him to do there.

"Kuvshinnoe Rilo?"

He went off somewhere into the sticks to advise a GUBOTDEL.

Then they took up Elizavet Vorobey. No such fellow. True, there is a typist named Elizavet, but not Vorobey. There is Vorobey who is an assistant to the deputy of the junior clerk of the Deputy Manager of some subsection, but his first name is not Elizavet.

They got hold of the typist.

"It's you?!"

"Nothing of the sort! Why me? Here Elizavet ends with a hard sign, and I surely don't have a hard sign on my name. Quite the contrary . . ."

And she breaks into tears. They leave her in peace.

But meanwhile, as they were fussing around with Vorobey, the lawyer Samosvistov let Chichikov know on the side that a big fuss had begun over the matter, and naturally, all trace of Chichikov disappeared.

And in vain they raced by car to the address he had given: when they turned to the right, there was no information office there at all, of course; but there was a cheap public dining hall which had been abandoned and ruined long ago. And the cleaning woman Fetinya came out to them and said there weren't nobody there.

Next door, it's true, turning to the left, they did find an information office – but there was no field-officer's wife

251

sitting there, only some Podstega, Sidorovna, and it goes without saying, she was ignorant not only of Chichikov's address but even of her own.

IX

THEN DESPAIR FELL over them all. The case had gotten so mixed-up that even the devil couldn't have found anything to his taste in it. The nonexistent lease got confused with the sawdust, Brabant lace with electrification, Korobochka's purchase with diamonds. Nozdryov was still stuck to the case, both the sympathizer Rotozei Emelyan and the non-Party member Antoshka the Thief turned out to be involved, and some sort of Panama hat with Sobakevich's ration cards in it was discovered. And the whole province was off on the light fantastic!

Samosvistov worked without rest, and stirred into the general stew some wanderings connected to trunks, and a case of falsified expense accounts for government trips (this alone turned out to implicate up to 50,000 people), etc., etc.

In a word, the devil only knows what had got started. And both those from under whose noses the billions had been requisitioned, and those who had to find it were rushing around in terror, and there was only one indisputable fact confronting them: "The billions were here and have vanished."

Finally, some Uncle Mityay got up and said, "Well, fellows ... Obviously we can't get around appointing an investigative commission."

X

AND RIGHT AT that point (something you'll never see in a dream), I emerged like some *deus ex machina* and said,

"Let me handle it."

They were astonished.

"But ... you ... know how to?"

And I said, "Put your minds at ease."

They vacillated, then in red ink: "Assigned."

Here I got started (I've never had such a nice dream in my life!).

Thirty-five thousand motorcyclists swept up to me from all sides.

"Do you need something?"

And I say to them, "I don't need anything. Don't interrupt your work. I'll manage by myself. Single-handedly."

I sucked in my breath and barked so loudly that the windows rattled.

"Get me Lyapkin-Tyapkin! On the double! On the telephone!"

"Then it's impossible to get him ... The telephone's broken."

"Oh! Broken! The cord's torn loose? So that it doesn't dangle there for nothing, hang the one who's making the report to me with it!"

Lord! What had begun!

"Please, sir ... What are you doing, sir ... This ... he, he ... this instant ... Hey! Repairmen! The cord! Fix it immediately!"

In two shakes they fixed it and gave it to me.

And I tore ahead.

"Tyapkin? The Bastard! Lyapkin? Arrest the scoundrel! Give me the lists! What? Not ready? Have them ready in five minutes or you'll find yourself on the lists of dead souls! Who's *that*? Manilov's wife is the registrar? Boot her out! Ulinka Deiiishcheva is the typist? Boot her out! Sobakevich? Arrest him! That good-for-nothing Murzofeykin works for you? Shuller Uteshitelny? Arrest them! And the one who gave them the jobs too! Take him! And him! And this one! Out with Fetinya! Send the poet Tryapichkin, Selifan, and Petrushka to the accounting office! Nozdryov to the cellar! ... This minute! This second!! Who signed the authorization? Get him in here, the scoundrel!! Even if he's on the bottom of the sea!"

Thunder rumbled through hell ...

"A devil's flown down on us! Where'd they get one like that?"

And I say, "Get me Chichikov!"

"I'm ... I'm ... impossible to find him. He's hiding ..."

"Oh, hiding? Marvelous! Then you'll go to jail for him."

"Plea ..."

"Shut up!!"

"This minute ... This ... Hold on just a second. They're looking, sir."

And in two instants they found him.

And in vain Chichikov crawled at my feet and tore his hair and coat and assured me that he had a disabled mother.

"Mother?!" I thundered, "Mother? ... Where are the billions? Where is the people's money?! Thief!! Cut the bastard open! He's got the diamonds in his stomach!"

They slit him open. There they were.

"All of it?"

"All, sir."

"A rock around his neck and down an ice hole with him!"

And it got quiet and all clear.

And I said on the telephone, "All clear."

So they answer me, "Thanks. Ask anything you want."

Thus I jumped around the telephone. And I almost poured into the telephone all of those estimated expenditures which had been tormenting me for a long time.

"Pants ... A pound of sugar ... A twenty-five watt bulb ..."

But I suddenly remembered that a decent writer should be unselfish, I relented and muttered into the receiver, "Nothing but Gogol's works in a binding like the edition of his works I recently sold at the market."

And ... pow! I have a gold-embossed Gogol on my desk!

I was so glad to have Nikolai Vasilievich – who had often comforted me on bleak, sleepless nights – that I bellowed, "Hurrah!"

And ...

EPILOGUE

... OF COURSE, I woke up. And nothing – no Chichikov, no Nozdryov, and, most important, no Gogol.

"Oh, ho, ho," I thought to myself and started to get dressed, and again life went parading before me in its quotidian way.

1922

OSIP MANDELSTAM

MUSIC IN PAVLOVSK

Translated by Clarence Brown

I REMEMBER well the remote and desolate years of Russia, the decade of the nineties, slowly slipping past in their unhealthy tranquillity and deep provincialism – a quiet backwater: the last refuge of a dying age. At morning tea there would be talk about Dreyfus, there were the names of Colonels Esterhazy and Picquart, vague disputes about some "Kreutzer Sonata" and, behind the high podium of the glass railroad station in Pavlovsk, the change of conductors, which seemed to me a change of dynasties. Immobile newsboys on the corners, without cries, without movements, awkwardly rooted to the sidewalk – narrow droshkies with a little collapsible seat for a third passenger – and, all in all, I picture the nineties in my mind in scenes scattered apart but inwardly bound together by the quiet misery and the painful, doomed provincialism of the life that was dying.

The ladies' wide bouffant sleeves, luxuriously puffed-up at the shoulders and pulled tight at the elbows, and their wasp waists; the moustaches, imperials, carefully trimmed beards; men's faces and haircuts such as one could find now only in the portrait gallery of some run-down barbershop where there are pictures of the "Capoul cut" and the "coq."

What, in a word, were the nineties? Ladies' bouffant sleeves and music in Pavlovsk: the balloons of the ladies' sleeves and all the rest revolve around the glass railroad station in Pavlovsk, and Galkin, the conductor, stands at the center of the world.

259

In the middle of the nineties all Petersburg streamed into Pavlovsk as into some Elysium. Locomotive whistles and railroad bells mingled with the patriotic cacophony of the *1812 Overture*, and a peculiar smell filled the huge station where Tchaikovsky and Rubinstein reigned. The humid air from the mouldy parks, the odor of the decaying hotbeds and hothouse roses – this was blended with the heavy exhalations from the buffet, the acrid smoke of cigars, a burning smell from somewhere in the station, and the cosmetics of the crowd of many thousands.

As it turned out, we became "winter people" in Pavlovsk, that is, we lived the year round in our *dacha* in that old ladies' town, that Russian demi-Versailles, the city of court lackeys, widows of high officials, redheaded policemen, consumptive pedagogues (it was thought more salubrious to live in Pavlovsk) and grafters who had raked together enough money for a detached villa. O, those years – when Figner was losing his voice and the double caricature of him passed around from hand to hand: on one side he was singing and on the other stopping up his ears. When carefully bound volumes of *The Field*, *Universal Virgin Soil*, and the *Foreign Literature Herald*, crushing book stands and card tables beneath their weight, were to constitute for a long time to come the basis of the libraries of the petty bourgeoisie.

There are nowadays no encyclopedias of science and technology like those bound monsters. But the *Universal Panoramas* and *Virgin Soils* were true fonts of knowledge of the world. I loved the "miscellany" about ostrich eggs, two-headed calves, and festivals in Bombay and Calcutta, and especially the pictures, the huge, full-page pictures: Malayan swimmers bound to boards and skimming through waves the size of a three-storied house; the mysterious experiment of a M. Fouqué: a metal sphere with an enormous pendulum

skimming around it in the midst of a throng of serious gentlemen wearing neckties and pointed beards. I have a feeling
that the grownups read the same thing as I, that is, mainly
the supplements, the immense, burgeoning literature of the
supplements to *The Field* and the rest. Our interests were, in
general, identical, and at the age of seven or eight I was fully
abreast of the century. More and more often I heard the
expression *fin de siècle*, the end of the century, repeated with
frivolous hauteur and with a sort of coquettish melancholy.
It was as if, having acquitted Dreyfus and settled accounts
with Devil's Island, that strange century had lost all meaning.

It is my impression that the men were exclusively absorbed
day and night by the Dreyfus affair, while the women – that
is, the ladies with the bouffant sleeves – hired and fired the
servants, an activity that provided inexhaustible food for
lively and delightful conversations.

On Nevskij Prospekt in the building of the Roman Cath-
olic Church of St. Catherine there lived a respectable little
old man named père Lagrange. One of the functions of His
Reverence was to recommend poor young French girls who
were seeking positions as governesses in respectable houses.
Ladies came to consult père Lagrange straight from the
Gostinyj Dvor with their parcels in their hands. He would
come out in his decrepit way, wearing his shabby cassock,
and affectionately banter the children with unctuous Cath-
olic jokes, spiced with French wit. The recommendations of
père Lagrange were taken very seriously.

The famous employment office for cooks, nursemaids,
and governesses on Vladimir Street, to which I was rather
often taken along, resembled a genuine slave market. Those
who were looking for a place were led out in turn. The ladies
sniffed them over and asked to see their references. The
recommendation of some totally unknown lady, especially if

261

it were the wife of a general, was regarded as sufficiently weighty; but it sometimes happened that the creature who had been led out for sale, having carefully examined the buyer, would make a rude noise right in her face and walk away. Then the intermediary in this slave traffic would come running up with apologies and talk about the decline of manners.

Once again I glance back at Pavlovsk and take morning strolls through all the walks and parquets of the station, where over a foot of confetti and serpentin has collected overnight – remnants of the storm which used to be called a "benefit performance." Kerosene lamps were being converted to electricity. The horsecars still ran along the streets of Petersburg behind stumbling nags out of *Don Quixote*. Along Goroxovaja as far as the Alexander Garden one could see the *karetka*, the most ancient form of public vehicle in Petersburg. Only on the Nevskij could one hear the clanging bells of the new express trams, painted yellow rather than the usual dirty wine color, and drawn by enormous, sleek horses.

1925

ISAAC BABEL

DOLGUSHOV'S DEATH

Translated by Peter Constantine

THE VEILS OF battle swept toward the town. At midday, Korotchaev, the disgraced commander of the Fourth Division, who fought alone and rode out seeking death, flew past us in his black Caucasian cloak. As he came galloping by, he shouted over to me, "Our communications have been cut, Radzivillov and Brody are in flames!"

And off he charged – fluttering, black, with eyes of coal.

On the plain, flat as a board, the brigades were regrouping. The sun rolled through the crimson dust. Wounded men sat in ditches, eating. Nurses lay on the grass and sang in hushed voices. Afonka's scouts roamed over the field, looking for dead soldiers and ammunition. Afonka rode by two paces from me and, without turning his head, said, "We got a real kick in the teeth! Big time! They're saying things about our division commander – it looks like he's out. Our fighters don't know what's what!"

The Poles had advanced to the forest about three versts away from us, and set up their machine guns somewhere nearby. Flying bullets whimper and yelp; their lament has reached an unbearable pitch. The bullets plunge into the earth and writhe, quaking with impatience. Vytyagaichenko, the commander of the regiment, snoring in the hot sun, cried out in his sleep and woke up. He mounted his horse and rode over to the lead squadron. His face was creased with red stripes fron his uncomfortable sleep, and his pockets were filled with plums.

"Son of a bitch!" he said angrily, spitting out a plum stone. "A damn waste of time! Timoshka, hoist the flag!"

"Oh, so we're going for it?" Timoshka asked, pulling the flagpole out of the stirrup and unrolling the flag on which a star had been painted, along with something about the Third International.*

"We'll see what happens," Vytyagaichenko said, and suddenly shouted wildly, "Come on, girls, onto your horses! Gather your men, squadron leaders!"

The buglers sounded the alarm. The squadrons lined up in a column. A wounded man crawled out of a ditch and, shading his eyes with his hand, said to Vytyagaichenko, "Taras Grigorevich, I represent the others here. It looks like you're leaving us behind."

"Don't worry, you'll manage to fight them off," Vytyagaichenko muttered, and reared his horse.

"We sort of think we won't be able to fight them off, Taras Grigorevich," the wounded man called after Vytyagaichenko as he rode off.

Vytyagaichenko turned back his horse. "Stop whimpering! Of course I won't leave you!" And he ordered the carts to be harnessed.

At that very moment the whining, high-pitched voice of my friend Afonka Bida burst out, "Let's not set off at full trot, Taras Grigorevich! It's five versts. How are we supposed to hack them down if our horses are worn out? Why the rush? You'll be there in time for the pear pruning on St. Mary's Day!"

* The Third Communist International, 1919–1943, an organization founded in Moscow by delegates of twelve countries to promote Communism worldwide.

"Slow trot!" Vytyagaichenko ordered, without raising his eyes.

The regiment rode off.

"If what they're saying about the division commander is true," Afonka whispered, reining in his horse, "and they're getting rid of him, well then thank you very much – we might as well kill off the cattle and burn down the barn!"

Tears flowed from his eyes. I looked at him in amazement. He spun like a top, held his cap down, wheezed, and then charged off with a loud whoop.

Grishchuk, with his ridiculous *tachanka*,[*] and I stayed behind, rushing back and forth among walls of fire until the evening. Our divisional staff had disappeared. Other units wouldn't take us in. The regiments pushed forward into Brody but were repelled. We rode to the town cemetery. A Polish patrol jumped up from behind the graves, put their rifles to their shoulders, and started firing at us. Grishchuk spun his *tachanka* around. It shrieked with all its four wheels.

"Grishchuk!" I yelled through the whistling and the wind.

"What damn stupidity!" he shouted back morosely.

"We're done for!" I hollered, seized by the exhilaration of disaster. "We're finished!"

"All the trouble our womenfolk go to!" he said even more morosely. "What's the point of all the matchmaking, marrying, and in-laws dancing at weddings?"

A rosy tail lit up in the sky and expired. The Milky Way surfaced from under the stars.

"It makes me want to laugh!" Grishchuk said sadly, and pointed his whip at a man sitting at the side of the road. "It makes me want to laugh that women go to such trouble!"

---

[*] An open carriage or buggy with a machine gun mounted on the back.

The man sitting by the roadside was Dolgushov, one of the telephonists. He stared at us, his legs stretched out in front of him.

"Here, look," Dolgushov said, as we pulled up to him. "I'm finished . . . know what I mean?"

"I know," Grishchuk answered, reining in the horses.

"You'll have to waste a bullet on me," Dolgushov said.

He was sitting propped up against a tree. He lay with his legs splayed far apart, his boots pointing in opposite directions. Without lowering his eyes from me, he carefully lifted his shirt. His stomach was torn open, his intestines spilling to his knees, and we could see his heart beating.

"When the Poles turn up, they'll have fun kicking me around. Here's my papers. Write my mother where, what, why."

"No," I replied, and spurred my horse.

Dolgushov placed his blue palms on the ground and looked at his hands in disbelief.

"Running away?" he muttered, slumping down. "Then run, you bastard!"

Sweat slithered over my body. The machine guns hammered faster and faster with hysterical tenacity. Afonka Bida came galloping toward us, encircled by the halo of the sunset.

"We're kicking their asses!" he shouted merrily. "What're you up to here, fun and games?"

I pointed at Dolgushov and moved my horse to the side.

They spoke a few words, I couldn't hear what they said. Dolgushov held out his papers. Afonka slipped them into his boot and shot Dolgushov in the mouth.

"Afonka," I said, riding up to him with a pitiful smile. "*I* couldn't have done that."

"Get lost, or I'll shoot you!" he said to me, his face turning white. "You spectacled idiots have as much pity for us as a cat has for a mouse!"

And he cocked his trigger.

I rode off slowly, without looking back, a feeling of cold and death in my spine.

"Hey! Hey!" Grishchuk shouted behind me, and grabbed Afonka's hand. "Cut the crap!"

"You damn lackey bastard!" Afonka yelled at Grishchuk. "Wait till I get my hands on him!"

Grishchuk caught up with me at the bend in the road. Afonka was not with him. He had ridden off in the opposite direction.

"Well, there you have it, Grishchuk," I said to him. "Today I lost Afonka, my first real friend."

Grishchuk took out a wrinkled apple from under the cart seat.

"Eat it," he told me, "please, eat it."

1926

MARINA TSVETAEVA

LIFE INSURANCE

.

Translated by Jane A. Taubman

THEY WERE SITTING, peacefully having supper – or perhaps dinner, it's a question of words, for the salad was the
same – and so, fusing Russian supper with French dinner
in a Roman salad, they ate: the father, the mother, and
the son.

"Mama, how plentiful the French are!" said the son
suddenly.

"It's not the French who are plentiful, but the Russians!"
the mother replied heatedly. "And, in general, the word is
usually applied to countries."

"W-h-y-y?" the boy was astounded. "How can a country
be plentiful? It doesn't have hands."

At that second, a knock sounded at the door, and the
mother, who hadn't yet figured out her son's latest linguistic
half-breed, went to open it. There, in the pitch darkness of
the landing, stood someone very tall, hat in hand.

"Excuse me, madam," he said in a youthful voice, "I'm
the inspector . . ."

The mother took a step back, then let him in. The young
man strode at her heels into the kitchen, where he stood –
between the dinner table, the dish table, the gas, the stove,
the sink and the chairs of the diners – as if on the single spot
that was dry from the flood and firm between two abysses:
on one foot, crossing it with the other, the left one.

"Yes?" inquired the mother with her eyebrows, not raising
her eyes, and already seated back at the salad.

"Excuse me for interrupting your dinner, but I am the inspector, and ..."

"Taxes!" she said wordlessly to herself. "But we paid them not long ago, or, perhaps, they've remembered that kidnapped general again and they've begun to take a census of all the Russian emigres?"

"Here's my card," the young man continued, raising it to her eyes and immediately – the way they show children tomorrow's "surprise" just for a minute – retrieving an open booklet with some sort of photograph, perhaps really a good likeness if she'd had a chance to look carefully either at it or at the person proffering it.

"But why doesn't he say *sûreté* and show his badge?" she thought, mentally performing for him the gesture of displaying the badge. "And what's he arresting us for, after all?"

"*Assurance*," his voice rang out above her as if in confirmation.

Hearing at last the fatal word (for she took it for "*sûreté*") she stopped eating and began to wait.

"I'm heading for Nuellement," the voice continued from above, "and I'm inspecting apartments from the standpoint of fire."

("Good Lord!" flashed through her head. "And I have a worn electric cord, all knotted up, which keeps shorting! And what in heaven is Nuellement?")

"You don't seem to understand French?" he inquired, letting those present understand that from the moment of his arrival, in response to everything he had said, they had uttered not only not a single word, but not even a single syllable, so that he could legitimately have asked: "It seems you've lost your power of speech?"

"Oh, no!" exclaimed the mother, wounded to the quick,

and as a result growing more spirited. "We understand per-fectly. But, pardon me, what do you want from us?"

"You're asking what I want from you?" continued the voice with amusement. "I already told you, I'm on my way to Nuellement!"

"He's unemployed!" she thought. "Evidently, he's on his way home to Nuellement and he's checking stoves on the way. I should give him something." And, at last throwing him a glance:

"We're not very rich," she said timidly, "and all our stoves are clean, but nevertheless . . ." and she immediately stopped, for she realized that the face she saw standing over her was handsome, young, ruddy, clean-shaven and scrubbed, not at all an unemployed face – even less that of a stove-repairer – a face below which, as her gaze moved back to her plate, it made out both a new cherry-colored tie and a clean gray suit.

"But this is precisely for the poor," the resident of Nuelle-ment became exuberant. "What do the wealthy need it for? Even if their whole family dies off, it won't ruin their lives. This is precisely for those who are hard up, who live by the sweat of their brow."

"But what exactly is 'this'?" she asked, growing bolder.

"Life insurance – but didn't I say that?" And, with new force: "I'm going around to Nuellement (and suddenly she understood that there was no Nuellement at all, that there was "*annuellement*," the last syllable of which he pronounced "mon") and I'm primarily trying to interest low-income people, those who live by the work of their hands."

(Shifting his eyes to the slender hands of her husband, with their long fingers): "Your husband is an artist?"

"No," forced out the husband.

"No?" he verified with the wife.

"No," confirmed the wife.

"That's curious," he said, pensively, "I was sure he was an artist. I'm primarily going to talk with you, since your husband has the look of someone who doesn't understand French. So, it's important precisely for those who live by the labor of their hands. Imagine you have the misfortune to lose your husband," he said, letting himself go on as if he were speaking not of an obviously present, living and chewing husband, but of some allegorical personage whom she had never laid eyes on and whom for that very reason she had no way of losing, "and you are left alone, with three small children, the youngest still an infant."

"I have no infants," she answered. "The boy you see in front of you is nine."

"But others have them, you can't say that others don't," the inspector corrected her gently (the way they correct a good student who has made a mistake on an exam). "I knew one woman with six small children, and when her husband took a fall at a construction site . . ."

"Oh!" she exclaimed, trembling at this terrible vision. "How awful! Did he fall far?"

"Yes, from the seventh floor," confirmed the inspector, now standing firmly on his other leg. "And I myself gave her the settlement. You don't think she was happy?"

"How awful!" his listener cried a second time, this time with an entirely different meaning. "How awful to be happy about that kind of money!"

"But she had children," the inspector admonished, "Six small children, and she wasn't happy about their father's death, but about their good fortune. And if you, *madame*, were to have the misfortune of losing your husband . . ."

"Listen!" she cried. "This is the second time you've mentioned my husband's death. It's offensive. *We* are not accustomed to speaking this way in front of the living. We're foreigners, I'll even tell you we're Russians and (already *en route* to the other room to get her cigarettes) Russians can't stand to hear such things, Russians can only listen to talk of their own death. Yes!"

"*Madame*," sounded the voice of the young man, already in the corridor, "you've misunderstood me. I didn't at all mean to say that you'd surely lose your husband, I only wanted to say that it could happen to you as it could happen to anyone."

"Now that's the third time you've said it!" the young woman interrupted, already smoking and heading straight at him, herding him back into the kitchen. "And I don't want to hear any more. If this is life insurance, then I declare to you that I don't insure other people's lives."

"But *monsieur* would insure his own."

"Neither our own nor anyone else's – it's not in our blood, and besides, we have no money, we have to move to another apartment and . . ."

"But my proposal is meant just for people who are moving to another apartment. All kinds of accidents can happen during a move: a free-standing wardrobe, for instance, a wardrobe which has been standing for twenty years, a wardrobe with a mirror, you understand me? Suddenly it falls, and . . ."

("How awful!' and she actually closed her eyes. "Our wardrobe, which was given to us precisely because it was so unstable . . .")

"We're not afraid of falling wardrobes," she continued in a firm voice. "We, of course, do everything we can to keep the wardrobe from falling, but when a wardrobe falls – that's fate, you understand? That's the way any Russian will answer you."

"Russians always say 'no'," the young man said pensively,

rocking his knees back and forth. "In Medon (I live in Medon) there's a whole Russian building, where no one speaks French. You knock on the door, and a gentleman or a lady comes out and says: '*nyet*!' Then I go away immediately, because I know that they won't understand me. Yes, it's not often that they understand me as you do, *madame*. So, to return to the insurance . . ."

"Better not!" she exclaimed heatedly. "We have no reason in the world to buy insurance: in the first place, we're terribly poor and won't pay in any case, I warn you, as an honest person. You'll keep coming and you won't get any money; you'll write letters, and we'll never answer them. In the second place, and for us this is the most important, my husband and I are sickened by the thought of getting money for the death of either one of us."

"Does *monsieur* agree with you?" asked the inspector. "He doesn't seem to understand French."

"He understands it perfectly, and he thinks just the way I do." (And so as to smooth things over a bit, to distract him): "Perhaps, when my son grows up and gets married . . . But we're of a different generation, a lyric generation . . ." (and seeing that this time it was he who failed to understand), "We're 'sentimental,' 'superstitious,' 'fatalistic,' you've probably heard that? About the 'Slavic soul'?"

"Yes, I even saw a film about it with my mother. An old Russian general *dans un bonnet d'astrakhan* is getting married in a huge cathedral, and, noticing that his young wife loves a poor officer, he immediately goes off to Siberia alone, throwing him his purse from his sled. My mother even cried . . ." And, after long meditation, "Your sentiments do you honor, and let's hope that your son will give you joy. Does he always have such an appetite?"

("I should ask him to sit down," flashed through her head

for the umpteenth time. "He's a guest, but where can I fit another chair? Or at least offer him a cigarette ...")

"I'm the fifteenth son," continued the inspector in a pensive and totally different voice, as if he were dreaming, "and there were two more after me. I'm twenty-six, and my mother is fifty-two. She's had seventeen children, and two cases of pneumonia, and two operations – in fact, three, because the second time they forgot a piece of sheeting inside her ... And she looks as if she were my sister, and she's just as slender as you. She and I always laugh and joke."

"How marvelous – seventeen!" his listener exclaimed, fervently but without conviction. "Are they all alive?"

"No, I'm the only one left. My last brother – he was thirty-four – was killed last year when his car hit a tree."

"And the others?" she asked hesitantly.

"The others? All died in accidents. They drowned, they fell, others were burned alive (*il y en a qui sont brulés vifs*)."

"Joan of Arc," her son muttered, barely audibly.

"You understand that I can't get married? That possibly I'll do that later, possibly later ... Mother – she simply couldn't take it... Oh, we were raised very strictly, and if even now I dared contradict my father, I'd get a slap in the face, of course, and I'd accept it. My father is sixty-two, he weighs a hundred and five kilos."

"But your parents probably aren't Parisians?"

"Yes, they are – that is, my mother's a Parisian, my father's from Normandy. Take a look at me, I'm not all that small," he kept towering over her. "But of all of us – them – I'm the least successful. The others were giants! But since it's just me who survived, I shouldn't marry – neither marry nor perish in an accident, for if I were to *pass away*, then there'd be three passing away. My mother is about your height and build, but

279

even such mothers have big sons. Oh, you don't know my mother. Every time, no matter how late I come home from work – accidents happen at all hours, of course! – at ten or eleven, at twelve, at one, she gets up and warms up my dinner. Today, in fact, she's meeting me at Issy-les-Moulineaux. How can I get married? I'm twenty-six, and not once, you understand, not once have I gone to the movies without her or gone for a boat ride. *On prend tous ses plaisirs ensemble.* How could I possibly get married?"

"You're a fantastic son!" she exclaimed with all her heart, involuntarily shifting her gaze to her own, as if in query. "God grant you health, and your mother, and your father!"

"Yes, health is essential to me. I can't pass away. Let's hope your son will bring you joy, too. What would you like to be, little boy?"

"*Service militaire*, and then a pilot."

"No, you can't be a pilot. Your mother would have to look into the sky too often, and there are accidents enough on the ground. Now military service, that's something else. It's a good time, the best time, you'll never be so happy again . . . And so, *madame*, I wish you happiness in your son. And excuse me if I have somehow offended your feelings . . . You love your husband, you have a hearth, insurance won't help you, as it does me. Now I understand you . . ."

And, this time grasping the doorknob, towards which he had already stretched his hand – countless times! – without result, he said, with a deep bow:

"Thank you and good-bye."

"You're out of your mind!" exploded the husband, jumping up from the table like a beast. "I'm going to be late because of you!"

"Why didn't you just leave?" she asked, herself sensing the hypocrisy of the question.

"Why? Because the two of you were blocking the door, I was trapped."

"I accidentally ate the whole tomato, forgive me, mama, I was listening so carefully that I ate your share, too." And, putting the spout of the teapot to his lips, "Oh, I'm thirsty! You know, my throat dried out from listening to him talk."

A knock at the door.

"Excuse me, *madame*, I only wanted to add that today I'm taking my mother to the movies ..."

When she had seen off her husband – getting instead of a farewell squeeze of the hand the handle of the door he slammed behind him, and after she had put her son to bed – he fell asleep like a rock – only then, and not even right away, did she come to her senses. The whole episode had the vagueness of a dream, and her heart was beating like that of the worker who fell from the seventh floor. She went over to the table and on the back of the first envelope that came to hand she calculated that at twenty-six he could have been the fifteenth child of a fifty-two-year-old mother only if she had married at fifteen and had her seventeen children one after another, without a break. It does happen ... it's not easy, but it's possible. And it's much more plausible if, for instance, there were three sets of twins (who, of course, perished in pairs: two drowned together, two fell at the same time, two burned to a crisp together. Then there would be fewer deaths, too ...). But, nevertheless, for all seventeen of them, minus only him, to have died in accidents, all so different, and every possible kind of accident ... Taking into account the tone, at once both free-and-easy and official, in which he conveyed the information, as if rattling off a menu by heart ... And when she compared that voice with the one in which he spoke about the mother who was meeting him at Issy-les-Moulineaux ...

What on earth had that been? She didn't know. But even if he had cooked it all up on the spot in a flood of strange inspiration – nevertheless, wasn't it a touching myth about himself, the mother of seventeen children, and the last surviving, insanely devoted son? wasn't it a kind of daydream about a better self, the real self? wasn't it the wail of a real *profession manquée*? The full potential of filiality?

At twenty-six, tall, handsome – and in his own view, not to mention that of the Paris streets – irresistible, for him to tell an unknown woman, who wasn't so old herself, and looked very young indeed in the dark of the corridor, that to this day he gets slapped by his father and takes it willingly. Could this be the daydream of a modern young man?

"Perhaps," she pursued her thought, "I can't swear to it . . . Perhaps there were no seventeen children, perhaps, since they didn't exist, there were no seventeen deaths, and perhaps the father from Normandy, who slapped him in the face – each slap weighing one hundred five kilos! – didn't exist either, perhaps – and, it seems, most likely, and this, evidently, was the key, *there was no father at all*.

But there was a mother.

1934

NINA BERBEROVA

THE BIG CITY

Translated by Marian Schwartz

IT WAS AUTUMN when I arrived in the city. A powerful, insistent wind raced through the streets. I could sense but not see an ocean on three sides of me (the city was on a cape) – over there, in the harbor, among the docks, along with the cruisers and giant freighters. From there the ocean hurled its rain and its hurricanes down upon the city. Shredded skies, heavy morning fogs that lay on the roofs, and people, so many people.

I was staying in a hotel downtown. It was as if I still couldn't get up the nerve to go further uptown, as if I might still be on the verge of going back to where I'd come from. The man on duty had only one arm and wore a great big medal that swung against his chest. It was a medal for saving lives. But whose? I kept wanting to ask him. I had so much to do and worry about right away, though, that I never did get around to asking. What lives? If they were ordinary lives, like mine, then just how did he go about it? But there was never a quiet moment for this question. I was looking for a job. I was looking for a refuge. Money was in short supply and time was flying. The unfamiliar mirage all around me seemed to share nothing whatever in common with my entire life and destiny so far.

There are attics and basements for men like me. I decided to find myself a room first. I walked up and down the side streets of the downtown area for a long time before I saw a paper sign: Room for Rent.

"Why don't you take a whole building?" the janitor asked me, and he led me to the four-story building next door. It was propped up by heavy boards leaning against the façade. "You could live here in peace until summer, but they're razing it then."

I declined, primarily because there wasn't a pane of glass in any of the windows. You could see the cheerful but dirty wallpaper of the second-floor ceiling through the hole in the first, but that could have been patched easily. As I was walking out, I recalled a scrap of a poem:

I'd like to go
Where they hammer nails with violins
And feed the evening fires with flutes. . . .

Which is to say, for a moment I felt like a violin or a flute. It's a good thing no one could tell that I'd started feeling sorry for myself.

The other room, which I found at dusk, was all done up in cretonne – huge green flowers and pink leaves. The material covered the two beds. The short woman, her arms crossed high across her breast as if she were about to burst into song, pointed to one of the two beds and said: "That's where I sleep."

Before she said this she gave me a touching and actually rather humble look.

I bowed and walked out.

Green flowers and pink leaves, the street-level windows, and rain that fell suddenly, straight down, and very hard, not with a dancing, ingratiating slant but rather with a confident sound: I'll strike everything, crush everything. That was what the evening was like for me. "But you cannot, you simply cannot let it get you down," I told myself. "You're a violin, or a flute, or a drum, that fate has been beating on for twenty years. Despair is prohibited. Spitting on the floor is

286

prohibited. What could that stranger ever tell you? Jumping out the window will lead to no good, too. *Pericoloso sporgersi.*"

The next morning I headed uptown.

On the tenth, fifteenth, twentieth floor of huge buildings, right under the roof, they sometimes rent out garret rooms. Cheap. Life goes on downstairs: elevators go up, dogs bark, telephones ring, perfume wafts; people living in warm, spacious apartments play games. But under the roof a corridor runs all the way around the building and looks out at four different streets, and the numbered doors follow closely one after the other: 283, 284, 285, and then, out of the blue, 16, 17, and again, in the almost quiet of the clouds, 77, 78, 79, a landing, a turn, the service elevator descending with someone's trunks, a trash receptacle as big as the Tsar Bell in the Kremlin but without a piece knocked off, a light burning, the corridor ahead a couple of hundred yards long. A fire extinguisher, a hose, a crawl hole to the roof. If you opened it at night, in would rush the starry gloom, the chill of coming nights and days, and that same autumn wind, that same nearby ocean that rings the city, droning, and the rumble of the streets somewhere below, an incessant, fiery rumble.

I paid a week in advance and moved in that evening. I locked the door. I wasn't locking myself in; I was trying to lock the world out. And then another world, many times greater than the first, welled up inside of me, here, within these four walls. This world had an ocean, too, a city, a sky, an endless stream of people walking past me, rain, and wind. Besides these, though, it also had the memory of a journey: the sun, the Italian town where you and I stayed not so long ago, the fragrant shore where toy boats strung with lanterns sailed by in the evening, and the pink steam that hung over a volcano as old as the universe. At first you thought the potted

287

palms in the hotel garden were artificial, but one morning a flower bloomed with a light pop.

All of this was mine, needed and beloved by me alone, alive only inside me. I was trying to lock out what belonged to everyone. That hum and rumble you could hear from far away, but you didn't have to listen to it. I washed up, had a bite of cheese, bread, and an apple, and lay down on the narrow, hard, but clean bed. Suddenly, reflected light began streaming through the uncurtained window – onto me and everything around me.

The red needle of a distant skyscraper was reflected in the sink, and a blue flame fell on the face of my watch. Something orange played with the door lock, and the ceiling suddenly looked as if it had been sliced by a long ray. Something flickered in the corner. I didn't guess right away that these were the buttons on my jacket, which I had dropped on the chair. It was as if an airplane had sailed over me from wall to wall, nearly grazing me with its propeller. A precise raspberry circle ran across the ceiling (a fire truck racing somewhere with its distant clanging). God knows how many times it had already been reflected before flitting in my eyes. A lilac spark lay on my chest for a few moments before shifting to the windowpane and staying there. It felt as if, despite the fact that I had settled on the eighteenth floor, the entire city was running down my shoulders, face, and arms, as if the streets were passing not somewhere below but here, across and through me, and blinking in my eyes with dozens of reflected lights.

I woke up after noon and saw that the room needed painting. I got dressed, went out into the corridor, locked the door, which bore the number 199, and rang for the elevator. It was the service elevator, which was the only one I was allowed to use. A man in a gray livery jacket and frayed trousers greeted me politely. I asked him whether I could go up and down myself without bothering him. He said that was quite impossible, but that if I liked I could use one of the other two elevators at the end of the corridor, where the trash bins were.

"What a large building," I said as we flew down. "There must be twenty entrances."

"Twenty-four entrances," he said, "forty-two elevators, and 3,656 tenants."

"Exactly 3,656?" I exclaimed. This figure reminded me of the flowering palm.

"Exactly," he replied.

Before buying paint and a brush, I spent rather a long time walking around the streets. I had arrived a week before and already was starting to understand a lot and guess even more. The diversity of faces that flashed by astonished me. There was no majority in this city; all the people were unusual. This was what distinguished it from the cities I had seen before. What was even more amazing was that I could not forget for a second that all these millions of women and men – or else their fathers, or their grandfathers – had taken the same journey as I had. So not only was there no majority, but people's pasts were not equal either. There was one more circumstance that surprised me in an odd way, but I'll get back to that later.

I bought paint and a brush, returned to my room, and began painting the gray door a pale green. Immediately, I started to sing. The paint went on evenly and smelled of drying oil. I painted and sang, trying not to splatter the floor or myself. I began to get the feeling that I could live here, that in this room – as one of 3,656 tenants in this building – I was in the right place, and that after the first night spent here something had insinuated itself into me, filled me, laid down with me in bed, and was now pulsing through my veins.

I painted and sang and thought, meanwhile, about how, if you were with me, you would be standing next to me and saying, Isn't there an apron you can put on? You'll smear yourself and ruin your only trousers! And suddenly, as if in revenge for that thought, I let a fairly long drip that reminded me of the shape of a willow leaf fall on my knee.

I rubbed the spot for a long time, but it wouldn't go away. I stopped singing and scratched distractedly at the material, which had worn thin over long years of wear. The spot doubled in size. Now it was huge, dry, and white. And suddenly I remembered seeing painters working by the stairs at the end of the corridor when I was going out in the afternoon for paint. And painters, according to my lights, ought to have turpentine.

"Maybe here the painters have something even better than turpentine," I told myself, as I wiped off the brush and smoothed my hair. By the way, about turpentine. The fact that my first childhood memory is connected with it has left me with a special, though rather unusual, feeling for turpentine all my life.

I was not yet three. One evening I came down with a cold. My mother (quite young and ever cheerful) ran out to the pharmacy and gave me a sweet, tasty medicine. I had to take it every four hours, for my cough. In the night I woke up and saw my mother standing over me, smiling, rosy with sleep, wearing a long white gown trimmed in lace and offering me a spoonful. I swallowed the sweet, tasty stuff, holding it for a second in my mouth preliminarily. Suddenly I saw the vision with the empty spoon in her hand disappear, melt away. She'd fainted. My mother was lying on the floor, unconscious, having realized she had given me not my medicine but the turpentine she had rubbed me down with before bedtime.

They wouldn't let me fall asleep. The doctor loomed over me like a tall tower and interrogated me. Did it burn? Hurt? They had me drink hot milk. "It was very tasty," I said. "Give me more." If I were not afraid of being misunderstood, I would say that this memory of the swallowed turpentine lent a certain cast to my entire life.

Hastily putting myself in order and buttoning my top button, I went out, locked the door, and went to the left, toward the exit: 198, 197 – all the doors were identical. At about 155 the corridor took a turn, and there were 12, 13, 14. And indeed, on the broad landing, where huge, dry mops were stood up on end, two painters, one black and one white, were stroking the wall with broad brushes, and the paint was coming out nice and even, without any bubbles.

"Pardon me," I said. "Could I have a little turpentine? You see I . . . by accident. . . ."

I showed them the spot.

The black man and the white man both looked at me and at the spot and turned away, each continuing to stroke his own corner deftly and evenly.

"Turpentine, please," I repeated.

The black man tugged at his nose.

"Here's the thing, sir," he said, but as if he weren't addressing me. "There's a man living in room 274 who has what you need. At least that's what we've heard. But we don't have any turpentine. Am I telling the truth or what?"

The white man let out a sound that expressed sympathy.

"There's a man living there who sometimes definitely has what you need. Or so we've heard," the black man continued, "and that's why I'm telling you. Go to his room and knock on the door as hard as you can. You'll find your turpentine there, if what we've been told is true. Am I telling the truth or what?"

Once again the white man emitted a sympathetic grunt, and it seemed to me that all this might very well be the truth. I thanked him and continued on. Soon the corridor made another turn; it doubtless ran all the way around the building.

How many times I turned with it I don't remember anymore. I was looking for door 274. Once I thought I'd found it: there was 271, 272, 273, but then it started back with single-digit numbers. I figured at some point I'd reach my own room this way, but when? And what awaited me in the meantime?

The ceiling lights were switched on. From time to time I heard sounds coming from behind doors, first here, then there: water flowing, someone arguing, a sewing machine running, hammering. A child beginning to cry. According to my calculations, at least a quarter of an hour had passed and I was still walking and walking – and then suddenly I came to an impasse, or rather, a staircase that spiraled downward. I took a look, leaning over the railing. And I was drawn down.

What I saw astonished me. It was a covered street complete with stores, offices, lamps, mailboxes, shoeshine men. The only thing it didn't have was automobiles, and the shuffling of feet over the stone slabs reminded me of that little Italian town. But that's beside the point. Now that I'm used to it all, I know that sometimes in the huge buildings of this city, on one of its upper floors, they set up something resembling a street. Now I certainly see nothing strange in the fact that, for the convenience of the people living in the building, a post office has been opened below me, that a tobacconist, a hairdresser, a shoemaker, a pharmacist, and a baker have opened their own establishments. That first time, though, it all seemed to me like a fantastic dream, and for a moment I doubted that I myself had rented a room on the eighteenth rather than the second floor. The ceiling, however, told me that I was not outside but inside the building. A little girl was standing in front of a bookshop window scratching the top of her head. A fat man sprawled out in a chair watched his shoes being shined. The sounds of some song came from a radio store and the smell of pastries from the little blue candy shop.

I didn't walk down that street. I ran. Shops alternated with offices. I noticed a sign for a dentist. There were homes and land for sale – prairies, riverbanks, and lake shores. Here was a domestic employment bureau. Round lamps hung on iron rings, a mailman dashed by, two women jabbering and laughing looked straight at me. And suddenly I came to a spiral staircase. Whether it was the same one I'd come down or a different one I couldn't tell, but I ran up it. I ran up and recognized a familiar series of doors, which I walked by quickly, checking the numbers.

After about twenty minutes I began noticing that I was getting close to the door I was looking for. Now the numbers were going backward: 277, 276, 275. At last! Door 274, no different from the other doors, right in front of me. Except that it was ajar.

Knocking cautiously on the doorjamb, I took a deep breath. No answer was forthcoming. I knocked once more and quietly walked in. The room, twice as big as mine, was piled high with furniture. There was even an armchair on top of the cupboard, which was open wide and spilling out bits of old material, evidently upholstery fabric. Pictures were hung all the way to the ceiling. One showed a ship in full sail over the stormy sea. Old picture frames were stacked in a corner. A marble bust of some Roman stood amid the rubble. The entire right-hand wall was taken up by a broad old sofa upholstered in a Scotch plaid, and on it, calmly, in a comfortable pose, as if he were expecting someone, sat the master of this room, a man nearly sixty. He was smiling. His face was pleasant – once it had been handsome, but the features were flabby now, the eyes bloated. They were big, dark, somewhat sad, but good eyes, intelligent eyes, under heavy dark lids, in a soft and good face. His hair was in disarray and longer than men ordinarily wear it. He had on an old – very old – loose jacket and slippers on his feet. Once again I looked him in the eye and bowed slightly.

"Pardon me," I said, almost not feeling shy, although at that moment my arrival seemed rather odd even to me. "The painters told me – they're working over there – about turpentine. . . . You must be an artist, right? I have this spot here, and I'd like. . . ."

Still smiling calmly and cozily, he took a bottle off a shelf. "People live so amazingly," I thought, "and each in his own way. Especially during the day. At night, all kinds of lights must find their way here, too."

The man moistened a clean rag with turpentine, squatted with a slight crackling of bones, and wiped my knee. The familiar smell tickled my nostrils. The doctor had towered over me. His glasses had gleamed in the dark sky and his beard had raced by like a cloud. "That's very odd," he said angrily and for the umpteenth time he shrugged. And my mother, who had put on some kind of skirt, was leaning on to the wall to keep from falling a second time. I never again saw her seeming so serious. "It's absolutely incomprehensible. The child must be made of pig iron!" I was sitting on the bed and looking at them avidly in hopes of a second spoonful. "My little puss, my chick, my sweetkins! Throw up! My darling!" my mother pleaded. I shook my head. I didn't even understand her murmurings, why she was begging me so in such humiliating fashion.

The man straightened up with more slight crackling. The spot was gone.

"What did the painters tell you?"

"They told me to knock as hard as I could!"

"What fools!"

"But your door was ajar."

"That was their idea of a joke. I never close it. Whenever someone needs to, they come in."

"What about at night?"

"I shut the door at night."

"What does your window look out on? May I take a look?"

While I was making my way over to the window, he said: "Except that I'm not an artist. I'm a framer and upholsterer."

I looked out the window and saw roofs and skyscrapers that were already familiar to me. In the dusk of the gathering night, lights glowed, advertisements flashed, the red needle, my nocturnal raspberry friend, reached into the high and cloudless sky directly in front of me. Above it an airplane with a blue star on its tail flew by, and some word blinked and pulsed well beyond the bridge.

"Take a look through my binoculars," the man said, handing me the heavy old instrument by its strap. "A marvelous view! Over there, between those two smokestacks, sometimes you can see the sea, and a little more to your right you can see the zoo."

I brought the binoculars up to my eyes, twirled one little wheel and then the other. And suddenly a block away, in a lighted window that hung in front of me in the sky, I saw a room and two little boys in it. They were standing at the table, and each one had a knife in his hand. Both had just cut their own arm and were trying to drip blood on the piece of paper that lay in front of them. One of them was wearing a feathered headdress and the other a Mexican mask pushed back on his forehead. I looked higher up. A woman was attempting to open the closed drawer of a high narrow bookcase, trying to find the right key. She was in a dreadful hurry, and in the lefthand corner of the room, I couldn't hear it but I could see very distinctly a record player playing. The record was spinning.

In a neighboring window a body was lying on a sofa, and a dog was circling it mournfully. The sad, elegant, pedigree borzoi shuddered and looked out the window, so that our eyes actually seemed to meet for a moment.

"What kind of binoculars are these?" I said, finally swallowing my saliva. "What on earth is this?"

The man smiled at me trustingly and gently: "This is nothing! There are even better ones. Once I held in my hands a gadget they say a German saw Petersburg through in '42, and then, a year later, the pyramid of Cheops."

I looked again. The boys had signed their names in blood, the dog was looking at me as if it were made of stone, and the record was still turning. A floor lower a drawing class was in session, and lower still two couples were dancing in the semi-darkness. More to the left, where the façade of that distant building ended, through the gap, the harbor lights twinkled on a white steamer that had sailed out to sea. The dark blue water was flooded with violet reflections, black smoke hung perfectly still, and beyond it you could just make out a flat island with a tall radio tower. (Was that the green eye that had spent last night on my shoulder?) The flat island turned muddy, and beyond it was the real and boundless ocean.

I bent over a little, and there, far far away, under the

stripped trees of some park I didn't know, where white, round street lamps shone with hundreds of lights, in the autumn gloom, I saw wild beasts behind the bars of their cages. I saw a guard signal to a tiger to go through a small low door, which it did, and the door dropped. On a sand-sprinkled clearing, a pensive, two-humped camel laid his shaggy little head on the back of another.

A large heavy hand dropped onto my shoulder. I remembered where I was. "Now he's going to ask me to leave," I thought.

"This is a very entertaining activity," said the man, and at close range I now saw his tired, dark brown eyes, and his thin but broad eyebrows tinged with gray. "You can look and look until your eyes go funny. I don't do it anymore. Maybe sometimes at night, when I can't get to sleep, if someone has an uncurtained window."

Could he have seen me yesterday from this window? I thought at that moment. Is that possible? Of course not. That's impossible. We can't see what's going on in our own building.

"Won't you have a seat?"

There was now a chair behind me, a lamp had been turned on, and a glass had appeared in front of me. Our conversation flowed as if we had known each other for a long time, a little bit about everything: beauty and the greatness of this big city, where to look for work, how to use the telephone booth by the elevator, and where to buy bread and milk. A few precious words about insignificant matters. I never knew I liked precious words about insignificant matters, and a quiet voice and big hand pouring me wine, and the attentive expression with which he listened to me. I felt good. I felt untroubled and warm. I told him I was happy to have met him, that he had amazing, unusual, mind-boggling binoculars, that if you really tried, I was sure, even from here, you could see the pyramid of Cheops through them.

And once again I walked over to the window.

The dog was gone. So were the boys. The ship had gone around the island and had probably been sailing at full speed for a while. Certain windows, though, windows that hadn't been there before, were now lit up here and there. I began looking. A ceiling light was burning in a narrow room. There was a table and a chair. And some kind of bucket. A man was sleeping on the bed. There was something familiar about him. No, it just seemed that way.

A woman opened the door slowly and walked in. She stopped, looked, and walked over to the sleeping man. The bucket was full of light green paint and on top of it I had set down my brush. You came up to me and put your hand on my chest, your skinny, ever cool hand, and a moment later you took it away and lowered your eyes to me. You were wearing the same dress you were wearing the day I left. It was too long for you, but there was no time to deal with alterations or to mend it at the collar, where it was coming apart at the seam. A lock of your hair fell on my forehead, you kissed me, you began to cry. You were with me. You were telling me something. It was probably about "us." You were always talking about "us." Not "you," my happiness with you, but "us." It's not when people switch to the familiar form of "you," it's when they switch to "we." "You" can be taken away in parting to the end of the earth, but not "we." It breaks down the moment people part.

"Finish your wine," said the man whose guest I still was. "I'm sure you'll find a job in your field very soon, and in general I can see you are an educated man. You know how to behave in society."

"Forgive me," I said, hastily making my way to the exit.

298

"I've overstayed my welcome, and I came without being introduced and with a request right away. I don't know how to thank you."

"There, you see?" He smiled. "Didn't I say you were a polite, educated man? Stop by any time. You're always welcome. I light the fire on Saturdays and my girlfriend comes over. I'll tell her to bring a lady friend for you. She's a young girl and works as a cashier. We feed the fire with that old harp lying in the corner. I've already sawed it in two."

I stepped out into the corridor. My door turned out to be almost next to his. It was locked, of course, just as I had left it. And inside, of course, there was no light on – when I went out it was still daytime and I'd had no reason to turn it on.

Now I can say something about that observation I made when I went out that afternoon for paint. I realized then that every person brings whatever he can to this big city. One brings the shadow of Elsinor's prince, another the long shadow of the Spanish knight, a third the profile of the immortal Dublin seminarian, a fourth some dream, or thought, or melody, the noonday heat of some treasure, the memory of a snow-drifted grave, the divine grandeur of a mathematical formula, or the strum of guitar strings. All this has dissolved on this cape and formed the life I plan to take part in too from now on. With you, who are not here with me but alive in this air I breathe.

1952

VLADIMIR NABOKOV

THE VANE SISTERS

I

I MIGHT NEVER have heard of Cynthia's death, had I not run, that night, into D., whom I had also lost track of for the last four years or so; and I might never have run into D. had I not got involved in a series of trivial investigations.

The day, a compunctious Sunday after a week of blizzards, had been part jewel, part mud. In the midst of my usual afternoon stroll through the small hilly town attached to the girls' college where I taught French literature, I had stopped to watch a family of brilliant icicles drip-dripping from the eaves of a frame house. So clear-cut were their pointed shadows on the white boards behind them that I was sure the shadows of the falling drops should be visible too. But they were not. The roof jutted too far out, perhaps, or the angle of vision was faulty, or, again, I did not chance to be watching the right icicle when the right drop fell. There was a rhythm, an alternation in the dripping that I found as teasing as a coin trick. It led me to inspect the corners of several house blocks, and this brought me to Kelly Road, and right to the house where D. used to live when he was instructor here. And as I looked up at the eaves of the adjacent garage with its full display of transparent stalactites backed by their blue silhouettes, I was rewarded at last, upon choosing one, by the sight of what might be described as the dot of an exclamation mark leaving its ordinary position to glide down very fast – a jot faster than the thaw-drop it raced. This twinned twinkle was delightful but not completely satisfying; or rather it only sharpened my appetite for other tidbits of light and shade, and I walked on in a state of raw awareness that seemed to transform the whole of my being into one big eyeball rolling in the world's socket.

Through peacocked lashes I saw the dazzling diamond reflection of the low sun on the round back of a parked automobile. To all kinds of things a vivid pictorial sense had been restored by the sponge of the thaw. Water in overlapping festoons flowed down one sloping street and turned gracefully into another. With ever so slight a note of meretricious appeal, narrow passages between buildings revealed treasures of brick and purple. I remarked for the first time the humble fluting – last echoes of grooves on the shafts of columns – ornamenting a garbage can, and I also saw the rippling upon its lid – circles diverging from a fantastically ancient center. Erect, dark-headed shapes of dead snow (left by the blades of a bulldozer last Friday) were lined up like rudimentary penguins along the curbs, above the brilliant vibration of live gutters.

I walked up, and I walked down, and I walked straight into a delicately dying sky, and finally the sequence of observed and observant things brought me, at my usual eating time, to a street so distant from my usual eating place that I decided to try a restaurant which stood on the fringe of the town. Night had fallen without sound or ceremony when I came out again. The lean ghost, the elongated umbra cast by a parking meter upon some damp snow, had a strange ruddy tinge; this I made out to be due to the tawny red light of the restaurant sign above the sidewalk; and it was then – as I loitered there, wondering rather wearily if in the course of my return tramp I might be lucky enough to find the same in neon blue – it was then that a car crunched to a standstill near me and D. got out of it with an exclamation of feigned pleasure.

He was passing, on his way from Albany to Boston, through the town he had dwelt in before, and more than once in my life have I felt that stab of vicarious emotion followed by a rush of personal irritation against travelers who seem to feel nothing at all upon revisiting spots that ought to harass them at every step with wailing and writhing memories. He ushered me back into the bar that I had just left, and after the usual exchange of buoyant platitudes came the inevitable vacuum which he filled with the random words: "Say, I never thought there was anything wrong with Cynthia Vane's heart. My lawyer tells me she died last week."

II

HE WAS STILL young, still brash, still shifty, still married to the gentle, exquisitely pretty woman who had never learned or suspected anything about his disastrous affair with Cynthia's hysterical young sister, who in her turn had known nothing of the interview I had had with Cynthia when she suddenly summoned me to Boston to make me swear I would talk to D. and get him "kicked out" if he did not stop seeing Sybil at once – or did not divorce his wife (whom incidentally she visualized through the prism of Sybil's wild talk as a termagant and a fright). I had cornered him immediately. He had said there was nothing to worry about – had made up his mind, anyway, to give up his college job and move with his wife to Albany, where he would work in his father's firm; and the whole matter, which had threatened to become one of those hopelessly entangled situations that drag on for years, with peripheral sets of well-meaning friends endlessly discussing it in universal secrecy – and even founding, among themselves, new intimacies upon its alien woes – came to an abrupt end.

I remember sitting next day at my raised desk in the large classroom where a midyear examination in French Lit. was being held on the eve of Sybil's suicide. She came in on high heels, with a suitcase, dumped it in a corner where several other bags were stacked, with a single shrug slipped her fur coat off her thin shoulders, folded it on her bag, and with two or three other girls stopped before my desk to ask when I would mail them their grades. It would take me a week, beginning from tomorrow, I said, to read the stuff. I also remember wondering whether D. had already informed her of his decision – and I felt acutely unhappy about my dutiful little student as during 150 minutes my gaze kept reverting to her, so childishly slight in close-fitting gray, and kept observing that carefully waved dark hair, that small, small-flowered hat with a little hyaline veil as worn that season, and under it her small face broken into a cubist pattern by scars due to a skin disease, pathetically masked by a sunlamp tan that hardened her features, whose charm was further impaired by her having painted everything that could be painted, so that the pale gums of her teeth between cherry-red chapped lips and the diluted blue ink of her eyes under darkened lids were the only visible openings into her beauty.

Next day, having arranged the ugly copybooks alphabetically, I plunged into their chaos of scripts and came prematurely to Valevsky and Vane, whose books I had somehow misplaced. The first was dressed up for the occasion in a semblance of legibility, but Sybil's work displayed her usual combination of several demon hands. She had begun in very pale, very hard pencil which had conspicuously embossed the black verso, but had produced little of permanent value on the upper side of the page. Happily the tip soon broke, and Sybil continued in another, darker lead, gradually lapsing into the blurred thickness of what looked almost like charcoal, to which, by sucking the blunt point, she had contributed some traces of lipstick. Her work, although even poorer than I had expected, bore all the signs of a kind of desperate conscientiousness, with underscores, transposes, unnecessary footnotes, as if she were intent upon rounding up things in the most respectable manner possible. Then she had borrowed Mary Valevsky's fountain pen and added: "*Cette examain est finie ainsi que ma vie. Adieu, jeunes filles!* Please, *Monsieur le Professeur*, contact *ma soeur* and tell her that Death was not better than D minus, but definitely better than Life minus D."

I lost no time in ringing up Cynthia, who told me it was all over – had been all over since eight in the morning – and asked me to bring her the note, and when I did, beamed through her tears with proud admiration for the whimsical use ("Just like her!") Sybil had made of an examination in French literature. In no time she "fixed" two highballs, while never parting with Sybil's notebook – by now splashed with soda water and tears – and went on studying the death message, whereupon I was impelled to point out to her the grammatical mistakes in it and to explain the way "girl" is translated in American colleges lest students innocently bandy around the French equivalent of "wench," or worse. These rather tasteless trivialities pleased Cynthia hugely as she rose, with gasps, above the heaving surface of her grief. And then, holding that limp notebook as if it were a kind of passport to a casual Elysium (where pencil points do not snap and a dreamy young beauty with an impeccable complexion winds a lock of her hair on a dreamy forefinger, as she meditates over some celestial test), Cynthia led me upstairs to a chilly little bedroom, just to show me, as if I were the police or a sympathetic Irish neighbor, two empty pill bottles and the tumbled bed from which a tender, inessential body, that D. must have known down to its last velvet detail, had been already removed.

III

IT WAS FOUR or five months after her sister's death that I began seeing Cynthia fairly often. By the time I had come to New York for some vacational research in the Public Library she had also moved to that city, where for some odd reason (in vague connection, I presume, with artistic motives) she had taken what people, immune to gooseflesh, term a "cold water" flat, down in the scale of the city's transverse streets. What attracted me was neither her ways, which I thought repulsively vivacious, nor her looks, which other men thought striking. She had wide-spaced eyes very much like her sister's, of a frank, frightened blue with dark points in a radial arrangement. The interval between her thick black eyebrows was always shiny, and shiny too were the fleshy volutes of her nostrils. The coarse texture of her epiderm looked almost masculine, and, in the stark lamplight of her studio, you could see the pores of her thirty-two-year-old face fairly gaping at you like something in an aquarium. She used cosmetics with as much zest as her little sister had, but with an additional slovenliness that would result in her big front teeth getting some of the rouge. She was handsomely dark, wore a not too tasteless mixture of fairly smart heterogeneous things, and had a so-called good figure; but all of her was curiously frowzy, after a way I obscurely associated with left-wing enthusiasms in politics and "advanced" banalities in art, although, actually, she cared for neither. Her coily hairdo, on a part-and-bun basis, might have looked feral and bizarre had it not been thoroughly domesticated by its own soft unkemptness at the vulnerable nape. Her fingernails were gaudily painted, but badly bitten and not clean. Her lovers were a silent young photographer with a sudden laugh and two older men, brothers, who owned a small printing establishment across the street. I wondered at their tastes whenever I glimpsed, with a secret shudder, the higgledy-piggledy striation of black hairs that showed all along her pale shins through the nylon of her stockings with the scientific distinctness of a preparation flattened under glass; or when I felt, at her every movement, the dullish, stalish, not particularly conspicuous but all-pervading and depressing emanation that her seldom bathed flesh spread from under weary perfumes and creams.

Her father had gambled away the greater part of a comfortable fortune, and her mother's first husband had been of Slav origin, but otherwise Cynthia Vane belonged to a good, respectable family. For aught we know, it may have gone back to kings and soothsayers in the mists of ultimate islands. Transferred to a newer world, to a landscape of doomed, splendid deciduous trees, her ancestry presented, in one of its first phases, a white churchful of farmers against a black thunderhead, and then an imposing array of townsmen engaged in mercantile pursuits, as well as a number of learned men, such as Dr. Jonathan Vane, the gaunt bore (1780–1839), who perished in the conflagration of the steamer *Lexington* to become later an habitué of Cynthia's tilting table. I have always wished to stand genealogy on its head, and here I have an opportunity to do so, for it is the last scion, Cynthia, and Cynthia alone, who will remain of any importance in the Vane dynasty. I am alluding of course to her artistic gift, to her delightful, gay, but not very popular paintings, which the friends of her friends bought at long intervals – and I dearly should like to know where they went after her death, those honest and poetical pictures that illumined her living room – the wonderfully detailed images of metallic things, and my favorite, *Seen Through a Windshield* – a windshield partly covered with rime, with a brilliant trickle (from an imaginary car roof) across its transparent part and, through it all, the sapphire flame of the sky and a green-and-white fir tree.

IV

CYNTHIA HAD A feeling that her dead sister was not altogether pleased with her – had discovered by now that she and I had conspired to break her romance; and so, in order to disarm her shade, Cynthia reverted to a rather primitive type of sacrificial offering (tinged, however, with something of Sybil's humor), and began to send to D.'s business address, at deliberately unfixed dates, such trifles as snapshots of Sybil's tomb in a poor light; cuttings of her own hair which was indistinguishable from Sybil's; a New England sectional map with an inked-in cross, midway between two chaste towns, to mark the spot where D. and Sybil had stopped on October the twenty-third, in broad daylight, at a lenient motel, in a pink and brown forest; and, twice, a stuffed skunk.

Being as a conversationalist more voluble than explicit, she never could describe in full the theory of intervenient auras that she had somehow evolved. Fundamentally there was nothing particularly new about her private creed since it presupposed a fairly conventional hereafter, a silent solarium of immortal souls (spliced with mortal antecedents) whose main recreation consisted of periodical hoverings over the dear quick. The interesting point was a curious practical twist that Cynthia gave to her tame metaphysics. She was sure that her existence was influenced by all sorts of dead friends each of whom took turns in directing her fate much as if she were a stray kitten which a schoolgirl in passing gathers up, and presses to her cheek, and carefully puts down again, near some suburban hedge – to be stroked presently by another transient hand or carried off to a world of doors by some hospitable lady.

For a few hours, or for several days in a row, and sometimes recurrently, in an irregular series, for months or years, anything that happened to Cynthia, after a given person had died, would be, she said, in the manner and mood of that person. The event might be extraordinary, changing the course of one's life; or it might be a string of minute incidents just sufficiently clear to stand out in relief against one's usual day and then shading off into still vaguer trivia as the aura gradually faded. The influence might be good or bad; the main thing was that its source could be identified. It was like walking through a person's soul, she said. I tried to argue that she might not always be able to determine the exact source since not everybody has a recognizable soul; that there are anonymous letters and Christmas presents which anybody might send; that, in fact, what Cynthia called "a usual day" might be itself a weak solution of mixed auras or simply the routine shift of a humdrum guardian angel. And what about God? Did or did not people who would resent any omnipotent dictator on earth look forward to one in heaven? And wars? What a dreadful idea – dead soldiers still fighting with living ones, or phantom armies trying to get at each other through the lives of crippled old men.

But Cynthia was above generalities as she was beyond logic. "Ah, that's Paul," she would say when the soup spitefully boiled over, or: "I guess good Betty Brown is dead" when she won a beautiful and very welcome vacuum cleaner in a charity lottery. And, with Jamesian meanderings that exasperated my French mind, she would go back to a time when Betty and Paul had not yet departed, and tell me of the showers of well-meant, but odd and quite unacceptable, bounties – beginning with an old purse that contained a check for three dollars which she picked up in the street and, of course, returned (to the aforesaid Betty Brown – this is where she first comes in – a decrepit colored woman hardly able to walk), and ending with an insulting proposal from an old beau of hers (this is where Paul comes in) to paint "straight" pictures of his house and family for a reasonable remuneration – all of which followed upon the demise of a certain Mrs. Page, a kindly but petty old party who had pestered her with bits of matter-of-fact advice since Cynthia had been a child.

Sybil's personality, she said, had a rainbow edge as if a little out of focus. She said that had I known Sybil better I would have at once understood how Sybil-like was the aura of minor events which, in spells, had suffused her, Cynthia's, existence after Sybil's suicide. Ever since they had lost their mother they had intended to give up their Boston home and move to New York, where Cynthia's paintings, they thought, would have a chance to be more widely admired; but the old home had clung to them with all its plush tentacles. Dead Sybil, however, had proceeded to separate the house from its view – a thing that affects fatally the sense of home. Right across the narrow street a building project had come into loud, ugly, scaffolded life. A pair of familiar poplars died that spring, turning to blond skeletons. Workmen came and broke up the warm-colored lovely old sidewalk that had a special violet sheen on wet April days and had echoed so memorably to the morning footsteps of museum-bound Mr. Lever, who upon retiring from business at sixty had devoted a full quarter of a century exclusively to the study of snails.

Speaking of old men, one should add that sometimes these posthumous auspices and interventions were in the nature of parody. Cynthia had been on friendly terms with an eccentric librarian called Porlock who in the last years of his dusty life had been engaged in examining old books for miraculous misprints such as the substitution of *l* for the second *h* in the word "hither." Contrary to Cynthia, he cared nothing for the thrill of obscure predictions; all he sought was the freak itself, the chance that mimics choice, the flaw that looks like a flower; and Cynthia, a much more perverse amateur of misshapen or illicitly connected words, puns, logogriphs, and so on, had helped the poor crank to pursue a quest that in the light of the example she cited struck me as statistically insane. Anyway, she said, on the third day after his death she was reading a magazine and had just come across a quotation from an imperishable poem (that she, with other gullible readers, believed to have been really composed in a dream) when it dawned upon her that "Alph" was a prophetic sequence of the initial letters of Anna Livia Plurabelle (another sacred river running through, or rather around, yet another fake dream), while the additional *h* modestly stood, as a private signpost, for the word that had so hypnotized Mr. Porlock. And I wish I could recollect that novel or short story (by some contemporary writer, I believe) in which, unknown to its author, the first letters of the words in its last paragraph formed, as deciphered by Cynthia, a message from his dead mother.

V

I AM SORRY to say that not content with these ingenious fancies Cynthia showed a ridiculous fondness for spiritualism. I refused to accompany her to sittings in which paid mediums took part: I knew too much about that from other sources. I did consent, however, to attend little farces rigged up by Cynthia and her two poker-faced gentlemen friends of the printing shop. They were podgy, polite, and rather eerie old fellows, but I satisfied myself that they possessed considerable wit and culture. We sat down at a light little table, and crackling tremors started almost as soon as we laid our fingertips upon it. I was treated to an assortment of ghosts that rapped out their reports most readily though refusing to elucidate anything that I did not quite catch. Oscar Wilde came in and in rapid garbled French, with the usual anglicisms, obscurely accused Cynthia's dead parents of what appeared in my jottings as "*plagiatisme*." A brisk spirit contributed the unsolicited information that he, John Moore, and his brother Bill had been coal miners in Colorado and had perished in an avalanche at "Crested Beauty" in January 1883. Frederic Myers, an old hand at the game, hammered out a piece of verse (oddly resembling Cynthia's own fugitive productions) which in part reads in my notes:

> *What is this – a conjuror's rabbit,*
> *Or a flawy but genuine gleam –*
> *Which can check the perilous habit*
> *And dispel the dolorous dream?*

Finally, with a great crash and all kinds of shudderings and jiglike movements on the part of the table, Leo Tolstoy visited our little group and, when asked to identify himself by specific traits of terrene habitation, launched upon a complex description of what seemed to be some Russian type of architectural woodwork ("figures on boards – man, horse, cock, man, horse, cock"), all of which was difficult to take down, hard to understand, and impossible to verify.

I attended two or three other sittings which were even sillier but I must confess that I preferred the childish entertainment they afforded and the cider we drank (Podgy and Pudgy were teetotalers) to Cynthia's awful house parties.

She gave them at the Wheelers' nice flat next door – the sort of arrangement dear to her centrifugal nature, but then, of course, her own living room always looked like a dirty old palette. Following a barbaric, unhygienic, and adulterous custom, the guests' coats, still warm on the inside, were carried by quiet, baldish Bob Wheeler into the sanctity of a tidy bedroom and heaped on the conjugal bed. It was also he who poured out the drinks, which passed around by the young photographer while Cynthia and Mrs. Wheeler took care of the canapés.

A late arrival had the impression of lots of loud people unnecessarily grouped within a smoke-blue space between two mirrors gorged with reflections. Because, I suppose, Cynthia wished to be the youngest in the room, the women she used to invite, married or single, were, at the best, in their precarious forties; some of them would bring from their homes, in dark taxis, intact vestiges of good looks, which, however, they lost as the party progressed. It has always amazed me the ability sociable weekend revelers have of finding almost at once, by a purely empiric but very precise method, a common denominator of drunkenness, to which everybody loyally sticks before descending, all together, to the next level. The rich friendliness of the matrons was marked by tomboyish overtones, while the fixed inward look of amiably tight men was like a sacrilegious parody of pregnancy. Although some of the guests were connected in one way or another with the arts, there was no inspired talk, no wreathed, elbow-propped heads, and of course no flute girls. From some vantage point where she had been sitting in a stranded mermaid pose on the pale carpet with one or two younger fellows, Cynthia, her face varnished with a film of beaming sweat, would creep up on her knees, a proffered plate of nuts in one hand, and crisply tap with the other the athletic leg of Cochran or Corcoran, an art dealer, ensconced, on a pearl-gray sofa, between two flushed, happily disintegrating ladies.

At a further stage there would come spurts of more riotous gaiety. Corcoran or Coransky would grab Cynthia or some other wandering woman by the shoulder and lead her into a corner to confront her with a grinning imbroglio of private jokes and rumors, whereupon, with a laugh and a toss of her head, she would break away. And still later there would be flurries of intersexual chumminess, jocular reconciliations, a bare fleshy arm flung around another woman's husband (he standing very upright in the midst of a swaying room), or a sudden rush of flirtatious anger, of clumsy pursuit – and the quiet half-smile of Bob Wheeler picking up glasses that grew like mushrooms in the shade of chairs.

After one last party of that sort, I wrote Cynthia a perfectly harmless and, on the whole, well-meant note, in which I poked a little Latin fun at some of her guests. I also apologized for not having touched her whiskey, saying that as a Frenchman I preferred the grape to the grain. A few days later I met her on the steps of the Public Library, in the broken sun, under a weak cloudburst, opening her amber umbrella, struggling with a couple of armpitted books (of which I relieved her for a moment), *Footfalls on the Boundary of*

Another World by Robert Dale Owen, and something on "Spiritualism and Christianity"; when, suddenly, with no provocation on my part, she blazed out at me with vulgar vehemence, using poisonous words, saying – through pear-shaped drops of sparse rain – that I was a prig and a snob; that I only saw the gestures and disguises of people; that Corcoran had rescued from drowning, in two different oceans, two men – by an irrelevant coincidence both called Corcoran; that romping and screeching Joan Winter had a little girl doomed to grow completely blind in a few months; and that the woman in green with the freckled chest whom I had snubbed in some way or other had written a national best-seller in 1932. Strange Cynthia! I had been told she could be thunderously rude to people whom she liked and respected; one had, however, to draw the line somewhere and since I had by then sufficiently studied her interesting auras and other odds and ids, I decided to stop seeing her altogether.

VI

THE NIGHT D. informed me of Cynthia's death I returned after eleven to the two-story house I shared, in horizontal section, with an emeritus professor's widow. Upon reaching the porch I looked with the apprehension of solitude at the two kinds of darkness in the two rows of windows: the darkness of absence and the darkness of sleep.

I could do something about the first but could not duplicate the second. My bed gave me no sense of safety; its springs only made my nerves bounce. I plunged into Shakespeare's sonnets – and found myself idiotically checking the first letters of the lines to see what sacramental words they might form. I got FATE (LXX), ATOM (CXX), and, twice, TAFT (LXXXVIII, CXXXI). Every now and then I would glance around to see how the objects in my room were behaving. It was strange to think that if bombs began to fall I would feel little more than a gambler's excitement (and a great deal of earthy relief) whereas my heart would burst if a certain suspiciously tense-looking little bottle on yonder shelf moved a fraction of an inch to one side. The silence, too, was suspiciously compact as if deliberately forming a black backdrop for the nerve flash caused by any small sound of unknown origin. All traffic was dead. In vain did I pray for the groan of a truck up Perkins Street. The woman above who used to drive me crazy by the booming thuds occasioned by what seemed monstrous feet of stone (actually, in diurnal life, she was a small dumpy creature resembling a mummified guinea pig) would have earned my blessings had she now trudged to her bathroom. I put out my light and cleared my throat several times so as to be responsible for at least *that* sound. I thumbed a mental ride with a very remote automobile but it dropped me before I had a chance to doze off. Presently a crackle (due, I hoped, to a discarded and crushed sheet of paper opening like a mean, stubborn night flower) started and stopped in the wastepaper basket, and my bed table responded with a little click. It would have been just like Cynthia to put on right then a cheap poltergeist show.

I decided to fight Cynthia. I reviewed in thought the modern era of raps and apparitions, beginning with the knockings of 1848, at the hamlet of Hydesville, New York, and ending with grotesque phenomena at Cambridge, Massachusetts; I evoked the ankle bones and other anatomical castanets of the Fox sisters (as described by the sages of the University of Buffalo); the mysteriously uniform type of delicate adolescent in bleak Epworth or Tedworth, radiating the

318

same disturbances as in old Peru; solemn Victorian orgies with roses falling and accordions floating to the strains of sacred music; professional impostors regurgitating moist cheesecloth; Mr. Duncan, a lady medium's dignified husband, who, when asked if he would submit to a search, excused himself on the ground of soiled underwear; old Alfred Russel Wallace, the naive naturalist, refusing to believe that the white form with bare feet and unperforated earlobes before him, at a private pandemonium in Boston, could be prim Miss Cook whom he had just seen asleep, in her curtained corner, all dressed in black, wearing laced-up boots and earrings; two other investigators, small, puny, but reasonably intelligent and active men, closely clinging with arms and legs about Eusapia, a large, plump elderly female reeking of garlic, who still managed to fool them; and the skeptical and embarrassed magician, instructed by charming young Margery's "control" not to get lost in the bathrobe's lining but to follow up the left stocking until he reached the bare thigh – upon the warm skin of which he felt a "teleplastic" mass that appeared to the touch uncommonly like cold, uncooked liver.

VII

I WAS APPEALING to flesh, and the corruption of flesh, to refute and defeat the possible persistence of discarnate life. Alas, these conjurations only enhanced my fear of Cynthia's phantom. Atavistic peace came with dawn, and when I slipped into sleep the sun through the tawny window shades penetrated a dream that somehow was full of Cynthia.

This was disappointing. Secure in the fortress of daylight, I said to myself that I had expected more. She, a painter of glass-bright minutiae – and now so vague! I lay in bed, thinking my dream over and listening to the sparrows outside: Who knows, if recorded and then run backward, those bird sounds might not become human speech, voiced words, just as the latter become a twitter when reversed? I set myself to reread my dream – backward, diagonally, up, down – trying hard to unravel something Cynthia-like in it, something strange and suggestive that must be there.

I could isolate, consciously, little. Everything seemed blurred, yellow-clouded, yielding nothing tangible. Her inept acrostics, maudlin evasions, theopathies – every recollection formed ripples of mysterious meaning. Everything seemed yellowly blurred, illusive, lost.

1958

ANDREI BITOV

GEGHARD

Translated by Susan Brownsberger

THE GATES

"WHAT HAS HE SEEN?" they would ask, meaning me. My friend would recite the list. Everyone, after hearing it, said firmly and always, "He must go to Geghard." The unanimity was tiresome like a conspiracy. What was Geghard? Where was Geghard? They shrugged. No one tried to explain. You'll see.

To me, Geghard was only a name – an insistent, even a nagging sound. This in itself was a kind of token, as it later turned out.

... The open space of Armenia waved its wings and fluttered, like a butterfly, and then, like a butterfly, suddenly folded them. A bronze lion, with more than the usual resemblance to a cat, turned its head to us and lifted a paw, signifying that we had arrived. (A little later, when I saw the same lion on an ancient wall, I recognized the source of the contemporary professional sculptor's genius.)

The lion stood on a beautiful tall column at the throat of a ravine. As we entered the narrowing throat, we seemed to drive faster and faster, accelerating and corkscrewing inward like water in a whirlpool. Suddenly, folding our wings with quiet ease, we found ourselves in the ravine.

Then and there, satiety ended. A shivering, lucid hunger to see ... The very place was like a temple. In the middle of open space, it was built of open space. Like a temple, it had an entrance (the lion stood at the gates), and only within the gates was the sanctuary revealed, as a sigh and an embarrassed hush.

Here, sight resounded.

A visible sound, extraordinary in its breadth and roundness, was born from the sheer walls of the ravine, where the wind caught like a musician's breath in the mouthpiece of a trumpet and burst out, through the coils of the bell, to wide-open space. We were in a kingdom of no return, although we did not recognize yet that we could never go back, and were therefore unafraid.

For the moment, we breathed rapture – and rapture breathed us. For the moment, it was a frivolous rapture, a tourist's, with no day of reckoning.

At the left rose a choir of cliffs. From the dense, shady, deep sound at the bottom they grew upward in several stages, brightening and thinning, joined by voices ever new, ever higher; the wind-sculpted arrows at the top were like a choir of boys. At the right, like an orchestra shell, the floor of the hollow spiraled downward to a silvery woodwind stream, green leaves lacy as a flute, and the calm, confident brows of the percussion section – the rocks and boulders. The earthly intelligibility of invented instruments, which vanish in the mystery of the human voice like a part in a machine, like a feature in a face, like a plowshare in the earth – the tools of labor, and the object of that labor – all this melted into the chorus of the cliffs. A puff of smoke curled up from the bank of the stream, and dotlike performers swarmed around it: pilgrims broiling shish kebab. An uncommonly red dress among them looked like the first leaf of autumn.

Before us stood a church, harmonious, integral, and no doubt a thousand years old. In this natural temple, the church was like an ancillary structure; it evoked no tingle of awe. Its fresh zinc roof and steeple, and its sturdy walls with their bright rectangles of modern mending, also underscored the impression that it was an outbuilding to the temple. The church was not to blame for this, however, since in all respects it was a masterpiece, and no one – only its natural setting – could have taken that title away from it.

But behind it rose a new choir of cliffs. Nestled at the foot of this vertical sound, the church was but one of the performers of the wondrous music, one of the many and forgotten virtuosi of the past. For what is the performer to the music? A votary, not the creator ...

The roof of this temple was the sky. Just recently, before the gates, the blue of the sky had been a pale, faded covering for an open expanse, but here, delimited by the choir of cliffs, it acquired an extraordinary intensity, deep and close.

"My God!" we exclaimed. We gazed at this frozen music – frozen at its topmost, highest point – and behind us, like wings, we could feel the upflung arms of its conductor and creator. The eternal, only, premier performance. "My God!" we exclaimed, losing our earthly shame at banality, and shedding the banality along with the shame. "They chose the right place!"

THE ASCENT

YES, THIS WAS a temple readied by nature; understandably, it had become the citadel and cloister of early, persecuted Christianity (the Armenians accepted Christianity long before we did, in the fourth century). This place, so unexpected in Armenia, so unlike anything else in it, this place that simply cannot be (but, since it is, can no longer *not* be), was created in the beginning expressly for this purpose, and then waited its hour, unpeopled, until divined by the first believers . . .

But the place, as it turns out, wasn't yet Geghard. That is, it bore the name, of course, but it was Geghard without an accent on the word, it was just Geghard. And, especially, the thousand-year-old church in this spot couldn't be *the* Geghard.

. . . We climbed up to the ancient cave temples at the first level of the cliff, the bottom line of the stave. We walked in. Time disappeared. The narrow, shallow grottoes, with their rough, smoke-blackened walls, recalled a mine face. As a former mining engineer, I even discovered the traces of blast holes. Crude niches for images, small bowls for offerings, a narrow trough to drain blood, the ancient and no longer smeary soot on the roof – and freshly scratched names, the symbols of a new tourist era, and colorful modern rags (prayers for the cure of relatives), and modern wax from melted candles, the stalactites of these caves. What humility and majesty of faith in these destitute stone chambers!* The temple had been created by nature itself, but the caves were its altars. There had been no disturbance of nature's harmony, no meddling, no modernization of the natural temple. Speak a word, and the cliff would respond in a deep voice, as though you had awakened a musical pitch frozen

* These caves are the key to the history of the nation. Armenians were slaughtered as "infidels," yet in fact they were annihilated for their fidelity – to the land, to the language, to Christ. They lost their lives, but not their homeland. If they had followed the natural instinct of self-preservation and given up their faith, less blood might have been shed, but the nation would have dissolved and vanished. For Armenians, the word *Geghard* is more than the name of a holy place, it is also a certain figurative concept – Geghard is the stronghold of the faith. The word is pregnant with meaning.

in the rock. This was a place for prayer; you could never come here in idle curiosity . . .

Squinting shyly, we emerged into the light. We examined the crosses chiseled on the face of the cliff, we ran our hands over them. The ornate Armenian cross! How gradually and beautifully it has acquired its canonical features. Not one cross repeats the lines of another. The proportions change, the round softness disappears, melts away, the crosses become straighter and stricter. But the primary cross is an eight-petaled flower. The petals draw near each other in pairs – a cross with split ends. Did the cross derive from a flower? Or did an artist perhaps liken the symbol to nature and life by first splitting the ends, then spreading them apart to approximate the shape of a flower? No one knows, and there is no one to ask.

We went back down, passed through the gates in the tall church fence – very recent, so extrinsic – and walked toward that strong, harmonious little church with its bucketlike zinc dome. I looked at the church with idle indifference, not really focusing on it. We would be inside in a minute, I thought.

But no, we began to scramble upward again, along a wall where the church grew into the cliff.

"First we go this way," they told me, gently and insistently.

"What's up here?"

"You'll see in a minute."

Oh, that dignified habit of refusing to anticipate my impression with enthusiastic stories! Never once did I have a clear idea where they were taking me, or why; the joys of first encounter were never frittered away in forewarning and preconception. As it turned out, the cave chapels of the first Christians, too, were not *the* Geghard.

The lofty but brief emotion we had felt in the caves did

not match the busy urban jauntiness that still clung to us. We talked loudly, not quite looking at each other. Unconscious of our split mood, however, we merely made an instinctive effort to lower the altitude of our momentary blaze of feeling. Our gaze was distracted by details. A tourist's graffito at an unthinkable height. A man selling photographs of General Andranik. A small-minded placard: "Do Not Litter." A bee garden, so suddenly beautiful and natural on the soil of the monastery. Two workmen puttering about near the hives ... Our emotion was declining, we were feeling better and better. Freed of embarrassment, we became childlike. We turned off the path and went scrambling up the cliff with inappropriate athleticism. Somewhere we had lost our self-possession, and every one of us must have felt somewhat ashamed of our corpulent, winded boyishness. But privately, not together.

And now I think I understand what makes a tourist scratch his name, throw litter, sing songs, and have his picture taken in the most unsuitable places – defile, as it were, the monuments of history and nature. The monument stands high, after all – unbearably, ringingly high! – compared to his ignorant soul. And in that soul, so gauche, untaught, and muffled, it gives rise to an echo, and the echo is a mystery to him. What, if not total disarray in his emotions, could cast him up on a height (physical) so mortally dangerous (physically)? Not just the girl who is waiting down below, after all. (He doesn't climb poles or scale buildings in the city, does he?) I think the sight of true greatness and beauty is as irritating to the unprepared eye as a harsh light or sound. From then on, all reactions are Pavlovian.

Why did the barbarians wreak devastation?

What were we if not spoiled children, in the mature and perfect society of churches and cliffs? ...

As writers, certainly, we might have thought ourselves better prepared for perfect sight? . . . But no. We have tried for so long to tell the truth to the world, and haven't told the truth to ourselves or to each other. And now we don't tell it – not merely because we're hiding it – but because we no longer know it. We didn't scratch our names (perhaps only because we'd already seen them in print), but in our case the same urge took other forms. Our prosaism, I would even say our "novelism," compulsively sought out the lowest, most earthly details, the ones most safely grounded.

Thus, as we climbed up, we saw an old man, a priest, on a second-story balcony of a residence situated opposite the church. He was seated at a table, looking at a book. A girl came and went in the background, waiting on him. The old man sat perfectly motionless, looking at the book (yes, looking at it, not reading it; his eyes, too, seemed to be motionless, although we couldn't see them from a distance). He was strikingly beautiful, with an aquiline profile, a high, pure brow, white curls, youthful skin, gaunt, pale . . . Oh, how poor are words, compared to a beauty canonical, perfect, and ancient! He was not a work of art, not a beautiful illustration, this old man; he was beautiful in the same sublime, ideal, absolute way as Geghard. And as motionless as its thousand-year-old stones. He had sat down to dine and opened a book, but he had been sitting here forever, eternally – or so I would have thought, looking at him – and even the table of food and drink before him could never make him look earthly . . . My friend and I, glancing at each other, realized that we had seen the old man at the same moment and in the same way. "What a face!" I said tritely. "Yes," said my friend, who is a wise man. "I wonder, now: if I were that handsome, led a holy life, and lived long enough to have hair like that – could I have a face like that? Impossible. Never." Again, this was too exalted for us – everything, absolutely everything here was so beautiful, even the people! . . . My friend's friend, who was walking behind us – an interesting poet, I'm told demeaned himself by saying, with an ugly smile, "With that face, the funniest thing would be if he were looking at pornographic pictures." "Dreadful!" I said, with a laugh. "The worst of it is, you may well be right." Let him read what he wishes – but oh, if we can even think such thoughts of him, we'll never have a face like his!

Now we had reached our mysterious goal. A small entrance, carved in the cliff, reminded me of the entrances to the ancient chapels we had just visited. Silently my friends let me pass ahead, and I stepped into the darkness of the cavern . . .

Oh, we were bad little boys!

THE SUMMIT

THIS WAS Geghard . . . I stood in the center, craning my neck. There, high above me, was a small blue circle – that was where the light came from. That was the sky. "*He* began from there . . . through that opening. He chiseled out the temple . . ." my friend told me in a childish whisper. And although I stood far below, I still see this temple in my mind's eye from the top down, the way he must have seen it as he stood there, on the cliff, up above, when there was as yet no temple beneath his feet.

Widening down from the blue round of sky came the bowl of the vault, and when it attained a hemisphere, the dome stopped short, to hang above us in a perfect circle. Tangent to the hemisphere, four columns extended perpendicularly downward, dissolving, when they reached me far

330

below, into the slab on which I stood – and then the dome rested, reposed, on the four columns, which were so graceful and perfect in form that, without expert knowledge, I will not undertake to describe them. From the lower rim of the dome the hollow body of the temple widened to the four sides, from each quarter of the circle, in four rounded petals; out there, in regions far distant from the center, the walls sloped steeply down, projecting the four petals to the base – I was standing on the projection plane. On that plane I recognized, again, the flowerlike Armenian cross.

I was standing at the bottom ... The arcs of the walls extended into the dusk, and the columns rushed upward to become the dome, from whose summit the round blue eye of the sky gazed at me. All this was inside the cliff, all of one integral stone. The forms were so harmonious, unique, absolute – I had never seen such perfection, and will never see it again. The word *genius* is too low to define what I saw.

He ... chiseled it out ... through that opening way up there, from the top down ... this whole temple ... Who was he? He has no name, nor can he ever, although he was one man. God, in this nameless man, removed the excess stone from the cliff, and what remained was the temple. This was a man of *faith*, of a faith like God's. Nothing but faith is capable of creating such a thing. An unbeliever would have been unable, and a fanatic would have broken down. A miracle of human faith – that is Geghard.

There was no reinforcement in the temple, of any kind.

The temple was already in the cliff; he had only to extract the stone from it ... No machines could have done this. Only by hands, only by fingernails could this temple have been scratched out, only one grain of sand at a time. No mistake, no superfluous fracture, could be made in this cliff, because the temple was in it. No blueprint, no calculation, because what was there was *this* temple, these forms and these outlines. He had faith and a single vision, that was all. He did not need to pray, or go to church, or know the word of God – God was in him. He had no blueprint; in his own mind he had vaults so honest and pure that he could transfer them here without error. His mind was the image of the future temple, and the temple was a likeness of God.

Now I'm piecing together the tongue-tied logic of words – I have no other recourse. But at that time I had no words, and couldn't have had, and shouldn't have had – I did not exist. I became like *him*, I now had the same muteness, the same absence of self, the same living faith, because I was contained in his honest and pure mind, in his faith, in his integral and single thought, where no other thought could possibly exist. This was his immortality.

But our imperfect souls couldn't bear this for long. We exchanged glances at last. Then, recalling that as their guest I must be shown everything, my friends left me in the center while they enigmatically dispersed to the sides. Each stopped by a column, and they started to sing. It was an ancient Armenian melody, slow and sorrowful. The echo repeated their voices many times over, the entire cliff responding like a bell. Inside the stone bell, we were the clapper. The polyphony was just as organic and harmonious as the lines of the temple; it could not have been otherwise. Both line and sound obeyed one law here ... Surely our many-branched knowledge implies that we are bereft of a single-unified law? When that law is gone, of course, we have architecture, blueprints, rules, calculations, physics, acoustics, machines – we work like ants, trying to perfect the fragments of the unified whole that we have lost ...

The song was beautiful, but when it was finished we were able to carry our weary, burdened souls out into the world.

... Simply a cliff, quite undisturbed and ordinary. That same church, the body of it so extrinsic and worldly ... But when I raised my eyes and saw those beautiful cliffs stretching upward so severely, freezing there like arrows in the deep blue sky, a choir fallen silent on its topmost note, I was even more struck with wonder at the same magnificent resemblance. Now it had been reversed. Those cliffs were now a likeness of the temple from which I had emerged. The temple was more primordial than nature, and nature had come to resemble it. This whole marvelous place and sky were the image of the creation I had just seen, and indeed, they, too, were a creation.

All things here reflected and echoed each other, affirming the harmony and unity of all existing forms. When we attempted to isolate and identify this unity, our gaze slid up and up, seeking something to stop on as the center of the likeness, and could stop on nothing. We had nowhere else to look but the sky ...

Worship in this temple has never ceased. The candle may be placed on any stone.

ESCAPE

WE CLIMBED UP still higher. More in fear now than in awe, I peered into the sky-blue opening from which *he* had begun ... It was a mute black hole. "This," my friend said, peering over my shoulder into the hole, "is why I come so seldom. I wouldn't have come, if it weren't for you ... How can anyone return from here – go back to the same place, as the same man?" Then, increasingly aware of an empty weariness, we descended a steep, sweeping curve. A Volga stood in the courtyard (it hadn't been there when we climbed up). The driver was tinkering with the engine. Nearby, squatting on his haunches, so that the hem of his black cassock lay on the ground and hid his feet, was the handsome old man we had seen with the book, on the balcony. I saw him up close; I could have touched him. He really did have a splendid face, splendid countenance – we hadn't been imagining things. He had squatted down to examine an automobile spark plug, which he held in front of him with three fingers. His fingers were just as inspired as his face. He was looking at the spark plug in exactly the same way he had looked at the book: just as motionlessly, with the same simple, unworldly, divine grandeur. His eyelids were very slightly lowered, but his pure, marble brow was imperturbable, and as sensitive as an eyelid. Oh, we had been wrong! There was no book, no spark plug! There was nothing anymore.

Down by the stream we glimpsed that same red dress and a curl of blue smoke. A subtle aroma of shish kebab reached us, signifying that hunger, not prayer, was what tormented us. "If only we had a bottle!" the driver said. "We could go down and share in the shish kebab."

How hastily, how willingly the car lurched forward to bear us away from Geghard! As if we had been spat out. No one looked back. When you enter, everything opens up for you, but when you leave, you see only the return road. We glided out from under the lion's paw.

And now, and now, only joys awaited us! We felt better and better, hungrier and hungrier. We stopped and drank water from a stream, we stopped and ate shish kebab and drank vodka, and finally, toward sunset, we reached Garrni. Garrni is the Soviet Union's only pagan temple. The ruins of it. Garrni is splendid.

But here you can eat, drink, dance, sing. It's a pagan temple. We sat on cyclopean rubble, drank *chacha* obtained from the temple watchman, joked (or tried to) with women in a Polish tour group, winked, chortled, guffawed, whooped, hooted ... For some reason we passed ourselves off as an all-star soccer team ... We watched a most amazing sunset, while the ravine below us sank deeper and deeper into darkness.

And at last we were driving back – jolly, boisterous, so happy! – to the city of Erevan, leaving everything behind and taking no note of the transition. Night had already descended; the driver swung the wheel hard as we rounded a bend; moths leaped, a gleam of silver in the headlights; in the back, my friends sang their beautiful songs beautifully, and I was so moved that I almost sang along in my native Armenian tongue. Ahead, the lights of Erevan came in view.

We shook hands and parted.

It was all so simple: the sky had cracked, the earth had split, the ground had quaked, the abyss had opened – just another day lived, so long, see you tomorrow.

1969

LUDMILLA PETRUSHEVSKAYA

IMMORTAL LOVE

Translated by Sally Laird

SO WHAT BECAME of the heroes of our romance? It must be said that after Ivanov's departure everything remained in place, just as it had been before. For life itself doesn't move on just because a single person has moved, any more than the roof caves in on a whole institution, and all the people in it, just because of his departure. So that the fact that the roof had, figuratively speaking, caved in on Lena, and that life had definitely moved on for her, didn't mean anything for anyone else, and the world remained just as it was when Ivanov was there, regardless of the fact that Ivanov had gone, leaving in his wake only a gaping hole.

So Lena was forced to go on working just where Ivanov had left his gaping hole, and where only a week ago Lena herself, as if in jest, had sunk to her knees before Ivanov's desk. She knelt there as if in prayer, her hands clasped and her eyes closed, literally a couple of yards from where Ivanov, seated at his desk, was calmly putting his papers in order and laughing good-naturedly, as if unaware of the condition into which Lena had sunk. Right up to the moment when Ivanov had started tidying his desk she had evidently kept hoping that something would happen, a reprieve of some kind, for it couldn't be over just like that, it couldn't have all come to nothing; and when Ivanov began tidying his desk prior to his departure she fell to her knees as if senseless with grief. She knelt there for ten whole minutes, and for the duration of these ten minutes everyone went about their business as

339

usual, a trifle embarrassed but quite composed; they took it all in their stride, never batting an eyelid, as if over the years they'd seen a good many scenes like this. Everyone took it as a form of hysterical behaviour which merited neither attention nor intervention, nor any indication of belief in the genuine existence of the grief and despair that such hysterical behaviour generally suggests.

And Lena herself knelt there quite calmly, without any noisy demonstrations of feeling; and thus the two or three people present in the room at the time were forced to acknowledge that the only thing left to a person in these circumstances was precisely the right to kneel, and that there was a sweetness in that very act of kneeling.

Finally Ivanov departed, and Lena was left behind, and it was clear as daylight that Lena would go after him, by some means or other and notwithstanding the fact that here in her native city she had obligations towards her mother, her son and her husband.

Lena never discussed her plans for the future with anyone and went on working as usual; she did, however, befriend the librarian, and this was an indication that she planned to escape. For the librarian, Tonya, a sweet and mournful blonde, was herself a wanderer, adventuress and escapee. Just like Lena, Tonya had a home where she lived with her child, a little girl; but from time to time she abdicated her maternal responsibilities, made arrangements at work and, leaving the child in her parents' care, set off for another town to see the man she loved, the object of her desire; and moreover she set off unasked, uninvited, slept at the railway station, hid out on the stairs and so forth, all in the hope of catching a glimpse of her beloved.

Lena made friends with Tonya and spent her lunch hours with her in various snack bars and coffee shops, and after work they'd walk together to the tram stop, afterwards going their separate ways on different trams, Tonya to pick up her daughter from kindergarten, and Lena to her apartment, where her duties towards her mother, her son and her husband awaited her.

As later emerged, however, none of these duties absolutely had to be fulfilled, for in the end Lena left in any case for the town where Ivanov now worked, and returned only many years later, seven years to be precise; returned with her mind bedimmed, full of paranoid fears; returned because her husband, Albert, had brought her home.

Here, however, some clarification is in order concerning the nature of Lena's duties towards her mother, her son and her husband.

It all began with the arrival of Lena's son, to whom Lena gave birth in unbelievable torment, though without uttering a single cry. The child itself had evidently been through similar torments, for it suffered a brain haemorrhage during its birth, and three months afterwards the doctor informed Lena that her little son would never, in all likelihood, be able to speak, let alone walk.

Lena spent a year looking after the child, and then it was time for her to go back to work, and she went back to work, finding a childminder for her son. Her mother was unable to give her any assistance, for she took leave of her senses three months after the boy was born, obviously from despair at the sight of the motionless little creature; although, as the psychiatrist said at the hospital, the cause of madness should be sought within, rather than without; and other, quite insignificant circumstances might just as well have served to trigger her illness; at all events, a trigger there undoubtedly was.

That spring, when Ivanov went away, Lena was preoccupied with purely practical affairs: she had rented a dacha on the edge of town, where her son, by now seven years old, was to live with his minder, herself and Albert. Lena organised the move to the dacha and lived there for two months; but in July of that year she picked herself up, left the dacha and their apartment in town and her friend the escapee Tonya. She left on the pretext that she had enrolled at a college, supposedly departing for no great length of time, but in fact, as it turned out, for seven years.

She did indeed enrol, for the second time in her life, at a college of some kind, and three years later was borne away from the college hostel in an ambulance, which took her to a psychiatric hospital in a state of the blackest spiritual despair, though precisely what circumstances had served in this instance to trigger illness will never now be known.

And now let us see what became of Ivanov. Strangely enough, despite his brilliant start in life, he too sank into gloom and desolation, though not quite so rapidly as Lena.

But things weren't so complicated in Ivanov's case; everything was much simpler and cruder with him, and could be explained solely by his partiality to alcohol. Over the course of the years Ivanov dug his own grave, and in the end, following an almighty row, was relegated to the humblest of posts, humble at least by comparison with his former status; he found himself head of a department consisting of just two persons – the sort of post occupied by someone at the start of his career.

So this was the end of that romance which, to everyone else, had seemed to end with Ivanov's departure – though to this day it isn't clear whether it did in fact end at all.

But now it's the figure of Albert, Lena's husband, that comes, in all his titanic greatness, to tower over the story, Albert who throughout those years bore everything that Lena was unable to bear, indeed bore more; it was he, after all, who, seven years after she had vanished, set off to fetch her, knowing everything there was to know, and brought her home, whether because in some unfathomable way he needed her, or because he felt compassion for her, sitting in her hospital bed in a godforsaken district of some strange city, deprived of absolutely everything except that bed, buried alive in her deep vault as Ivanov was in his.

Strictly speaking it was Lena and Ivanov who experienced that unquenchable, immortal love which turns out, on examination, to be just the unfulfilled, unrealised desire to propagate the species, unrealised for different reasons in different cases, but in this case for the simple reason that Lena had once given birth to a motionless child, and thus had reason to doubt her ability to give birth to healthy children at all. But whatever the case may be, whatever the real reason for Ivanov's abandoning Lena, the fact remains: the instinct to propagate the species remained unfulfilled, and quite possibly that was all there was to it.

And yet in this story, whose every detail has now been clarified, it's Albert who should provoke the greatest astonishment: Albert who after seven years came to fetch home his wife, with whom he'd long since lost all contact. What feelings inspired him to do it? – that's the mystery. You could explain it all in terms of that same immortal love, but not everything can be explained so simply. And so the figure of Albert continues, in its titanic greatness, to tower over the otherwise simple, human story.

1970s

VLADIMIR SOROKIN

START OF THE SEASON

Translated by Sally Laird

AS SERGEI STEPPED out onto the narrow, barely distinguishable path that snaked through the marsh, Kuzma Yegorich stopped him with a warning hand on his shoulder:

"No, Sergei, there's no going through that way."

"Why not?" asked Sergei, turning to him.

Brushing a horse-fly from his face, the huntsman answered in his slow, deliberate way:

"There was a downpour yesterday, turned it into a quagmire. Down there in Panin's Deeps you'll be up to your waist, and I'll be up to my neck. We'd best go round it."

"Through the clearings?"

"No need for that. We'd do a good mile extra that way. No, it's shorter round by the dirt track."

"OK, let's go that way. You know best," said Sergei, turning back.

"That's right," the huntsman chuckled, adjusting the battered old hat that kept sliding over his eyes. "I know this place like the back of my hand. I've been tramping round these parts for well-nigh fifty years."

"I bet you know every tree."

"I do, son, that I do," the huntsman sighed, and strode off in front of Sergei.

The bushes growing by the marsh soon thinned out and were replaced by a young birch wood. It was drier here; the yellowed grass was waist-high and crunched softly underfoot. The huntsman lit a cigarette; a cloud of blue, sweetish smoke drifted behind him as he walked, hunched in his quilted jacket. Sergei reached into his pocket and pulled out an empty pack of *Yava* cigarettes, he crushed it in his hand and tossed it in the grass. A faint breeze rustled the birch leaves and shook the grass-heads. Sergei plucked a blade of grass as he went, stuck it in his mouth and glanced around. A slight mist hung over the marsh behind them; a pair of kites, uttering faint cries, circled in the pinkish-yellow light. When the birch wood came to an end Kuzma Yegorich began to bear rightwards. They crossed a shallow ravine, skirted round a ridge of projecting rock, and entered a spruce grove. Sergei drew the grass-blade from his mouth and aimed it at a fir tree; the blade disappeared among its milky green branches. Now the track broadened out and became more distinct. Adjusting the gun-strap which was slipping from his shoulder, the huntsman turned to Sergei:

"Have you never walked round here?"

"No, Yegorich. I've never been here before."

"We're in the back of beyond here." The huntsman walked alongside him, watching his step.

"Fine spruce. Nice and firm."

"Yes. The spruce here's quite exceptional."

"And the wood's so dense," Sergei muttered, glancing round. "Must be a lot of wood- and hazel-grouse . . ."

"There used to be, that's right. What with the marsh and the berries growing alongside, you could do very well. Since then though, the wood-grouse have died out. I can't make out why. But there are plenty of hazel-grouse. They flock to the bait in droves – keep on flying in. You just have to hit 'em."

"But why have the wood-grouse died out?" Sergei asked.

"That's what I don't know." The huntsman screwed up his eyes and stroked his beard. "I don't know. There's no one

348

much around to kill 'em, we're out in the wilds here. All I know is that wood-grouse are funny birds. Cautious. The black and the hazel-grouse, now – they'll crop up no matter what. Don't mind where they live. But these other ones . . ."

Sergei looked up. The tall firs formed an arch overhead, barely admitting the faint sunlight. Underfoot the ground was soft and dry.

"So there were no other villages here, Yegorich, apart from Korobka?"

The huntsman shook his head:

"What d'you mean, no other villages! There used to be three. Two small ones, farmsteads really, and one with about forty houses."

"And nowadays?"

"Oh, they've all gone elsewhere now. The old folks have died. And the young ones are drawn to the town. So the cottages are all boarded up now. Left to rot."

"Are they far from here?"

"The village is about five miles, the farms are a bit further on."

"I see . . . We should go and have a look."

"Aye, we can do, no reason why not. You can go and see the nettles climbing up through the windows!"

Sergei shook his head and adjusted his gun:

"That's a shame."

"It is, a downright shame. Makes you sick to look at those houses. Such good straight frames, all spruce wood. Lord knows, they should be taken away and used."

"Well, is there no one to do that?"

The huntsman gestured impatiently:

"Ah well . . . no one wants to bother. People've got lazy."

"That's going too far. Look how hard your men were working down at the sawmill today."

349

"You call that hard work?" said Kuzma Yegorich, astonished.

"Why, didn't you think they were working hard?"

The huntsman again made a dismissive gesture:

"That's not the way to work. Was that how we worked before the war? Counting the hours? In those days we were never out of the forest, there were times we'd forget what needed doing at home, my wife, rest her soul, would be scolding away because the hay needed mowing, but there was the counting to do, and the cones, and the planting! You'd be the last to mow when everyone else had long since stored the hay and was sitting drinking tea."

Sergei looked at him, smiling. The huntsman was striding along, his gnarled hands spread out before him.

"What if we were back in war-time? In those days if the muzhiks knew that five miles away there were ten timber frames going to waste – they'd be down there tomorrow to get them. But nowadays they're just left to rot . . . makes you sick to see them . . ."

He fell silent, adjusting his hat.

The spruce began to thin out; rays of sunlight broke through the canopy of needles and fell on the road, slanting past the grey-brown trunks of the trees.

"We turn off here and then we're almost there," said the huntsman, waving his hand.

They turned down a path overgrown with bushes. From somewhere ahead came a burst of noise, a sudden flurry of heavy wings, and several wood-grouse flew out from among the trees. The huntsman stopped and followed them with his eyes:

"There they go. A whole brood . . . so they haven't disappeared . . ." They stood and watched the departing birds.

"What fine birds." Sergei shook his head.

"Yes. By autumn you won't be able to tell the young ones from the old ... What a din they made ..."

Kuzma Yegorich walked cautiously on, scanning the ground, then bent down:

"Look at this, Sergei ..."

Sergei came up to him and squatted down. The earth was strewn with pine needles and dotted with bird droppings; here and there bright yellow flowers could be seen.

"They're still here after all." Kuzma Yegorich smiled and picked up one of the dry, worm-like droppings; he kneaded it and tossed it away. "I hope these ones don't fly off ..."

Sergei nodded sympathetically.

Beyond the woods lay a large meadow, the grass had been mown and three solitary oaks stood in the middle. A huge haystack could be seen on the far side right by the meadow's edge. The huntsman rubbed his head and glanced around:

"Well, we're out of the woods. Now it's just half a mile and we're at the clearings."

Sergei brushed a cobweb from his face:

"So we went round to the right?"

"Ah-ha."

"That was quick. And I wanted to go through the clearings."

The huntsman chuckled:

"It's shorter this way."

Sergei shook his head.

"You know every twist and turn, don't you, Yegorich?"

"I do, I do ..."

They crossed the meadow and entered a dense thicket of mixed soft and hard wood. Kuzma Yegorich moved confidently forward, crunching over the twigs, parting and holding back the supple hazel branches. His grey quilted

351

jacket was soon covered in cobwebs and a dry twig lodged itself in his collar.

"You must get a lot of mushrooms here, do you, Yegor-ich?" Sergei said, following the huntsman.

"Sometimes, it depends."

"What's it been like this summer?"

"Not bad. Marya brought three buckets. We pickled them."

To the left, surrounded by bushes, stood an oak tree that had been struck by lightning. The trunk, split down the middle, looked white in the dusky green light.

"Look what happened to that one," said Sergei, nodding.

"Yes. And it wasn't standing by itself either."

"There's another one over there. I wonder why this one got struck . . ."

"Probably God could see it better."

Sergei laughed.

"Why do you laugh? Once, back in fifty-eight, there were four of us walking across the field after the hay-mowing, all carrying pitchforks and scythes over our shoulders. And there was a woman walking along carrying nothing but an empty porridge pot. And she was the one that got struck by lightning. She didn't have any metal on her and she was shorter than everyone else. So God must've been settling his accounts with her . . ."

"Just chance," Sergei muttered.

"There's no such thing as chance," the huntsman inter-rupted him confidently.

They came to the end of the thicket; a broad clearing, bathed in sunlight, could be seen between the trees.

Kuzma Yegorich turned to Sergei and raised one finger:

"Quietly now. Otherwise he'll hear us and that will be that."

"Which way?" whispered Sergei, taking the gun from his shoulder.

"We've got to get through those bushes over there ..."

The huntsman took his double-barrelled gun from his shoulder, cocked it, and, with the butt under his armpit and the barrel downwards, headed across the clearing. Sergei followed a short way behind. The clearing was very wide. Bushes and ferns had sprouted round the massive stumps, and the tall grass formed a wall across the entire clearing. The huntsman walked carefully round the stumps, stepping across the fallen tree trunks. Sergei tried not to lag behind. In the middle of the clearing a grouse-hen flew out from under the huntsman's feet and flapped heavily away. Kuzma Yegorich uttered a cheerful oath, watched it fly off, and walked on. When they were close to the edge of the clearing, he silently indicated a tall fir. Sergei nodded, put down his gun, took off his rucksack and began to undo it. The huntsman stood with his gun at the ready, watching out and listening intently. Sergei took a rope and a small cassette recorder out of his rucksack. He tied a stone to the end of the rope and, leaning backwards, hurled it high into the tree. The stone tugged the rope across three thick branches and, falling, swung round Sergei's head. Sergei quickly grabbed it, untied the stone and set about attaching the recorder to the rope. When he had finished he pressed the button and pulled the rope's free end. The recorder, bursting into song in Vysotsky's husky voice, climbed rapidly into the air. The higher it climbed, swaying at the end of the taut rope, the louder the sound became, the strained, heart-breaking voice resounding through the quiet autumn woods to the rhythmic strumming of the guitar:

"All's quiet down at the graveyard, so civilised, so nice, and not a single soul in sight, a real paradise!" The recorder disappeared among the branches, fell silent, then again burst out:

"I bo o ought come home brew and come ha a alva, come Rrriga beer and nice salt herring, and off to the loo-oony-bin went to see how my brrrother and the loo-oonies were faring."

Sergei hurriedly wound the rope round the trunk of the fir tree, picked up his gun and, squatting down, shifted the plastic safety-catch with his thumb.

"And the li-i-ife they lead, the loooonies' life, it's the life for which all of us long, whene-e-ever you want you can go-o to slee-eep, whene-e-ever you want sing a song!" – the words sang out from the fir tree.

The huntsman peered intently into the depths of the wood. The recorder finished the song about the loonies and struck up another – about a fellow who failed to shoot. The huntsman and Sergei went on waiting, motionless. Two ducks flew over the clearing. The forest echo scrambled the words, sending them booming back. Sergei shifted to a more comfortable kneeling position.

"The German sni-i-iper finished me o-off, killing the o-one who fa-ailed to shoo-oot!" Vysotsky sang, then fell silent.

From the fir tree came the muffled sound of conversation and then laughter from a sparse audience.

The huntsman leaned farther forward and suddenly waved his hand, pointing to his gun. Vysotsky casually tuned his guitar. Between the trees Sergei made out a stocky figure; he took aim.

"Wait! Wait!" the huntsman whispered frantically, hiding behind a bush. "He's too far off! Let him get closer, if you just wound him he'll get away!"

Sergei licked his dry lips and lowered the gun. Vysotsky struck a resounding chord:

"The curving shore has go-o-one, the oak trees are no mo-o-ore, there's no-o good o-o-ak wood to be had to ma-a-ake our parquet flo-o-or. Two hu-u-ulking oafs, they saw the o-o-oaks, and set to work a-cho-o-oppin', they cut them do-o-own, the lot of them, and ma-a-ade them into co-o-offins."

The stocky figure ran towards the fir tree, crunching over the twigs. Sergei lifted his gun, took aim and, trying to stop his sweaty hands from trembling, fired a quick double. The song issuing from the tree was drowned in the burst of gun-fire. The dark figure fell, then stirred, trying to get up. While Sergei was feverishly re-loading, the huntsman half-rose from behind the bush and delivered two resounding shots.

"Ce-e-ease, ce-e-ease, anguish in my bree-east! That's only the start, now hear the re-e-est!" Vysotsky drawled. Peering through the powdery smoke, Sergei again lifted his gun, but the huntsman waved at him to stop:

"That's enough, no need to shoot at a corpse. Let's go and have a look . . ."

Cautiously they went up, holding their guns at the ready. He lay about thirty metres away, his arms flung out, his face buried in a small anthill. The huntsman reached him first and prodded his side with his boot. The corpse did not stir. Sergei poked his boot at the bloody head. It lolled helplessly to one side, revealing an ear with the lobe joined to the head. Excited ants were crawling over it. Sergei put his gun down next to the corpse and quickly drew a knife from the leather sheath hanging from his belt. The huntsman took the corpse by the arm and turned it over on its back. The face was covered in blood and swarming with sticky ants. The quilted jacket was open and bloody traces of gun-shot were visible on

355

the bare chest. Sergei thrust his knife firmly into the brown nipple, stood up and wiped his sweating brow with the back of his hand. Crimson blood gushed out of the corpse's mouth.

"Fine specimen," the huntsman muttered, smiling, and taking a pen-knife from his pocket, began skilfully to cut the clothes from the corpse. Sergei silently surveyed the dead man.

"The cat in the story is re-e-eally there, he's singing his so-ong and spinning his ya-a-arn ..."

"We should take it down, Sergei," said the huntsman, looking up.

Sergei nodded and walked over to the fir tree.

"This is where he copped it ... made quite a hole ..." the huntsman muttered, baring the corpse's stomach.

Sergei went up to the tree, untied the knot and carefully lowered the recorder.

"That's only the sta-art – now he-ear the rrrest!" Vysotsky managed to sing, then fell silent, cut off by the click of the switch.

Sergei wound in the rope and put it back in his rucksack together with the recorder. The huntsman meanwhile deftly cut off the head; he rolled it aside with his boot and straightened up, breathing heavily:

"Let the blood drain off, then we'll spread him out ..."

Sergei returned and squatted down in front of the corpse:

"Got him so quickly, didn't we, Yegorich, unbelievable, really."

"You got him, and I finished him off!" the huntsman chuckled. "Seems I haven't quite gone blind."

"You were great."

"Straight out of the depths he came too, the little devil."

"Yes, it was an awkward angle."

"But you gave him a good one! Punctured his belly!"

"You must've got him in the head . . ."

"Ah-ha. I tend to aim higher . . . We'd better drag him away from the ants or they'll get stuck all over him . . ."

"Let's pull him under the oak tree . . ."

They took the corpse by the legs and pulled. The head remained lying by the ant heap. The huntsman came back, picked it up by the ear and brought it over to the oak. Blood flowed from the neck of the corpse. Sergei took out a flask of cognac, swallowed a mouthful and passed it to Kuzma Yegorich. The latter wiped his sticky fingers on his trousers, carefully took the flask and drank:

"Strong stuff . . ."

Sergei examined the corpse:

"What a stocky fellow. Look at those powerful shoulders."

The huntsman took another swig and handed back the flask:

"Healthy specimen . . . Alright then; let's gut him . . ."

He quickly ripped open the stomach, cut out the heart and, moving aside the violet intestines, began to cut out the liver:

"He got hit here too . . ."

Sergei smiled and looked up. Almost invisible, a kite hovered over the wood, barely moving its wings.

"We can cook the liver now," Kuzma Yegorich muttered, rummaging in the intestines.

"Good idea," Sergei responded. "Grill it on charcoal."

"Or do it on a skewer. Fresh liver's very nice that way, you know . . ."

"I know," Sergei smiled and again lifted the flask to his lips.

"Well, here's to a fine season, Yegorich."

"Same to you, same to you, Sergei . . ."   1985

TATYANA TOLSTAYA

SWEET SHURA

Translated by Antonina W. Bouis

THE FIRST time Alexandra Ernestovna passed me it was early spring, and she was gilded by the pink Moscow sun. Stockings sagging, shoes shabby, black suit shiny and frayed. But her hat! ... The four seasons – snow balls, lilies of the valley, cherries, and barberries – were entwined on the pale straw platter fastened to the remainder of her hair with a pin *this* big. The cherries dropped down and clicked against each other. She has to be ninety, I thought. But I was off by six years. The sunny air ran down a sunbeam from the roof of the cool old building and then ran back up, up, where we rarely look – where the iron balcony hangs suspended in the uninhabited heights, where there is a steep roof, a delicate fretwork erected right in the morning sky, a melting tower, a spire, doves, angels – no, I don't see so well. Smiling blissfully, eyes clouded by happiness, Alexandra Ernestovna moves along the sunny side, moving her prerevolutionary legs in wide arcs. Cream, a roll, carrots in a net bag weigh down her arm and rub against the heavy black hem of her suit. The wind had walked from the south smelling of sea and roses, promising a path up easy stairs to heavenly blue countries. Alexandra Ernestovna smiles at the morning, at me. The black clothing, the light hat with clicking dead fruit, vanish around the corner.

Later I came across her sitting on the broiling boulevard – limp, but admiring a sweaty, solitary child marooned in the baking city; she never had children of her own. A horrible slip showed beneath her tattered black skirt. The strange child trustingly dumped his sandy treasures onto Alexandra Ernestovna's lap. Don't dirty the lady's clothing. It's all right. ... Let him.

I saw her in the stifling air of the movie theater (take off your hat, granny! we can't see!). Out of rhythm with the screen passions, Alexandra Ernestovna breathed noisily, rattled foil candy wrappers, gluing together her frail, store-bought teeth with sweet goo.

Later she was swirled in the flow of fire-breathing cars by the Nikitsky Gates, got flustered and lost her sense of direction, clutched my arm and floated out onto the saving shore, losing forever the respect of the black diplomat behind the green windshield of a low, shiny car and of his pretty, curly-haired children. The black man roared and raced off in the direction of the conservatory with a puff of blue smoke, while Alexandra Ernestovna, trembling, bent over, eyes popping, hung on to me, and dragged me off to her communal refuge – bric-a-brac, oval frames, dried flowers – leaving behind a trail of smelling salts.

Two tiny rooms, a high ornate ceiling, and on the peeling walls a charming beauty smiles, muses, pouts – sweet Shura, Alexandra Ernestovna. *Yes, yes, that's me!* In a hat, without a hat, with hair down. Oh, so beautiful. ... And that's her second husband, and well, that's her third – not a very good choice. But what can you do about it now. ... Now, if she had made the decision to run off with Ivan Nikolayevich then ... Who is Ivan Nikolayevich? He's not here, he's crammed into the album, spread-eagled in four slits in the cardboard, squashed by a lady in a bustle, crushed by some short-lived white lap dogs that died before the Russo-Japanese War.

Sit down, sit down, what would you like? ... Please come

362

visit, of course, please do. Alexandra Ernestovna is all alone in the world, and it would be so nice to chat.

... Autumn. Rain. Alexandra Ernestovna, do you remember me? It's me! Remember ... well, it doesn't matter, I've come to visit. Visit – ah, how wonderful! Come here, this way, I'll clear ... I still live alone. I've survived them all. Three husbands, you know? And Ivan Nikolayevich, he wanted me, but ... Maybe I should have gone? What a long life? That's me. There too. And that's my second husband. I had three husbands, did you know? Of course, the third wasn't so ...

The first was a lawyer. Famous. We lived very well. Finland in the spring. The Crimea in the summer. White cakes, black coffee. Hats trimmed with lace. Oysters – very expensive ... Theater in the evening. So many admirers! He died in 1919 – stabbed in an alley.

Oh, naturally she had one romance after another all her life, what else do you expect? That's a woman's heart for you. Why, just three years ago, Alexandra Ernestovna had rented the small room to a violinist. Twenty-six years old, won competitions, those eyes! ... Of course, he hid his feelings; but the eyes, they give it away. In the evenings Alexandra Ernestovna would sometimes ask him, "Some tea?" And he would just look at her and say no-o-thing in response. Well, you get it, don't you? ... Treacherous! He kept silent all the time he lived at Alexandra Ernestovna's. But you could see he was burning up and his soul was throbbing. Alone in the evenings in those two small rooms. . . . You know, there was something in the air – we both felt it ... He couldn't bear it and would go out. Outside. Wander around till late. Alexandra Ernestovna was steadfast and gave him no encouragement. Later – on the rebound – he married some woman, nothing special. Moved. And once after his marriage he ran into

Alexandra Ernestovna on the street and cast such a look at her – he burned her to ashes. But said nothing. Kept it all bottled up in his soul.

Yes, Alexandra Ernestovna's heart had never been empty. Three husbands, by the way. She lived with her second husband in an enormous apartment before the war. A famous physician. Famous guests. Flowers. Always gay. And he died merrily: when it was clear that this was the end, Alexandra Ernestovna called in gypsies. You know, when you see beauty, noise, merriment – it's easier to die, isn't it? She couldn't find real gypsies. But Alexandra Ernestovna, inventive, did not lose heart, she hired some dark-skinned boys and girls, dressed them in rustling, shiny, swirling clothes, flung open the doors to her dying husband's bedroom – and they jangled, howled, babbled, circled and whirled and kicked: pink, gold, gold, pink. My husband didn't expect them, he had already turned his gaze inward and suddenly here they were, squealing, flashing shawls; he sat up, waved his arms, rasped: go away! But they grew louder, merrier, stamped their feet. And so he died, may he rest in peace. But the third husband wasn't so . . .

But Ivan Nikolayevich . . . ah, Ivan Nikolayevich. It was so brief: the Crimea, 1913, the striped sun shining through the blinds sawing the white scraped floor into sections . . . Sixty years passed, but still . . . Ivan Nikolayevich lost his mind: leave your husband *right now* and come to the Crimea. Forever. She promised. Then, back in Moscow, she thought: what will we live on? and where? He showered her with letters: "Sweet Shura, come, come to me!" Her husband was busy, rarely home; while there in the Crimea, on the gentle sands under the blue skies, Ivan Nikolayevich paced like a tiger: "Sweet Shura, forever!" While the poor man didn't have enough money for a ticket to Moscow. Letters, letters, every day letters for a whole year – Alexandra Ernestovna will show them to me.

Ah, how he loved me! Should I go or not?

A human life has four seasons. Spring! Summer. Autumn ... Winter? But winter was behind Alexandra Ernestovna – where was she now? Where were her moist, colorless eyes directed? Head back, red lid pulled away, Alexandra Ernestovna squeezes yellow drops into her eyes. Her scalp shows like a pink balloon through the thin net. Could this mouse tail have been a thick black peacock tail caressing her shoulders sixty years ago? Had the persistent but poor Ivan Niko-layevich drowned in those eyes – once and for all? Alexandra Ernestovna groans and feels around with her gnarled feet for her slippers.

"We'll have some tea now. I won't let you go without a cup. No-no-no, don't even think about it."

I'm not going anywhere. That's why I dropped by – for a cup of tea. And I brought pastry. I'll put the kettle on, don't worry. And she gets the velvet-covered album and the old letters.

It was a long way to the kitchen, to another city, along an endlessly shining floor, so polished the red paste left traces on my shoes for two days. At the end of the corridor tunnel, like a light in a deep robber forest, glowed the circle of the kitchen window. Twenty-three neighbors were silent behind the clean white doors. Halfway down was a wall telephone. A white note tacked up once upon a time by Alexandra Ernestovna: "Fire – 01. Emergency – 03. In case of my death call Elizaveta Osipovna." Elizaveta Osipovna herself is long gone. No matter. Alexandra Ernestovna forgot.

The kitchen is painfully, lifelessly clean. Somebody's cab-bage soup talks to itself on one of the stoves. In the corner stands a curly cone of smell left by a Belomor-smoking neighbor. A chicken hangs in a net bag outside the window as if being punished, twisting in the black wind. A bare wet tree droops in grief. A drunkard unbuttons his coat, resting his face on the fence. And what if Alexandra Ernestovna had agreed to abandon everything and fly south to be with Ivan Nikolayevich? Where would she be now? She had sent a telegram (*I'm coming, meet me*), packed her things, tucked the ticket away in the secret compartment of her wallet, pinned her peacock hair up high, and sat in an armchair by the window to wait. And far south, Ivan Nikolayevich, agitated, unable to believe his good fortune, rushed to the railroad station – to run, worry, fluster, give orders, hire, negotiate, lose his mind, stare at the horizon enveloped in dull heat. And then? She stayed in the armchair until evening, until the first pure stars. And then? She pulled the pins from her hair, shook her head. ... And then? Why keep asking *and then*, and then? Life passed, that's what happened *then*.

The teakettle came to a boil. I'll make it strong. A simple piece for the kitchen xylophone: lid, lid, spoon, lid, rag, lid, rag, rag, spoon, handle, handle. It's a long way back down the long corridor with two teakettles in your hands. Twenty-three neighbors behind white doors listen closely: will she spill her crummy tea on our clean floor? I didn't spill, don't worry. I push open the gothic doors with my foot. I've been gone an eternity, but Alexandra Ernestovna still remembers me.

She got out cracked raspberry-colored cups, decorated the table with doilies, puttered around in the dark coffin of a cupboard, stirring up bread and cracker smells that come out of its wooden cheeks. Don't come out, smell! Catch it and squeeze it back with the cut-glass doors: there, stay under lock and key.

Alexandra Ernestovna gets out *wonderful* jam, it was a gift, just try it, no, no, *you* try it, ah, ah, ah, yes, you're speechless, it's truly amazing, *exquisite, isn't it?* Really, in all my long life, I've never ... well, I'm so pleased, I knew you'd like it, have some more, please, take it, have some, I beg you. (Damn it, I'll have another toothache!)

I like you, Alexandra Ernestovna, I like you very much, especially in that photograph there with that marvelous oval to your face, and in that one, where your head is back and you laugh with those perfect teeth, and in that one, where you pretend to be pouting, and your arm is behind your head so the lacy festoons will fall back from your elbow. I like your life, interesting to no one else, passed in the distance, your youth that rushed off, your decayed admirers and husbands proceeding in triumphant parade, everyone who ever called your name or was called by you, everyone who passed and went over the high hill. I'll come to you and bring you cream, and carrots, so good for your eyes, and you'll please open up the long-closed brown velvet albums – let the Gymnasium girls breathe some fresh air, let the mustachioed gentlemen flex their muscles, let brave Ivan Nikolayevich smile. Don't worry, don't worry, Alexandra Ernestovna, he can't see you, really. ... You should have done it then. You should have. She's made up her mind. Here he is – right next to you – just reach out! Here, take him in your hands, hold him, here he is, flat cold shiny with a gold border, slightly yellowed: Ivan Nikolayevich. Hey, do you hear, she's decided, *yes*, she's coming, meet her, she's stopped hesitating, she's made up her mind, hey, where are you, yoo-hoo!

Thousands of years, thousands of days, thousands of translucent impenetrable curtains fell from the heavens, thickened, turned into solid walls, blocked roads, and kept Alexandra Ernestovna from going to her beloved, lost in time. He remained there on the other side of the years, alone at the dusty southern station, wandering along the sunflower seed-spattered platform; he looks at his watch, kicks aside dusty corn cobs with his toe, impatiently tears off blue-gray cypress cones, waiting, waiting, waiting for the steam engine to come from the hot morning distance. She did not come. She will not come. She had deceived him. But no, no, she had wanted to go. She was ready, and the bags had been packed. The white semitransparent dresses had tucked up their knees in the cramped darkness of the trunk, the vanity case's leather sides creaked and its silver corners shone, the shameless bathing costumes barely covering the knees – baring the arms to the shoulder – awaited their hour, squinting, anticipating ... In the hat box – impossible, enticing, insubstantial ... ah, there are no words to describe it – white zephyr, a miracle! On the very bottom, belly-up and paws in the air, slept the sewing box – pins, combs, silk laces, emery boards of diamond sand for delicate nails; trifles. A jasmine genie sealed in a crystal flask – ah, how it would shine with a billion rainbows in the blinding seaside sun! She was ready – but what interfered? What always interferes? Well hurry, time's passing. ... Time's passing, and the invisible layers of years get thicker, and the rails get rusty, and the roads get overgrown, and weeds grow taller in the ravines. Time flows and makes sweet Shura's boat bob on its back and splashes wrinkles into her incomparable face.

... More tea?

After the war she returned – with her third husband – here, to these rooms. The third husband kept whining, whining. ... The corridor was too long. The light too dim. The windows faced the back. Everything was behind them. The festive guests died out. The flowers faded. Rain hammered at the windows. He whined and whined and died, but when and of what, Alexandra Ernestovna did not notice.

She got Ivan Nikolayevich out of the album, and looked at him a long time. How he had begged her! She had even bought a ticket – and here it was, the ticket. Hard cardboard – black numbers. If you want, look at it this way, if you want, turn it upside down. It doesn't matter: forgotten signs of an unknown alphabet, a coded pass to that shore.

Maybe if you learn the magic word ... if you guess it; if you sit down and think hard, or look for it ... there has to be a door, a crack, an unnoticed, crooked way back there to that day; they shut up everything but they must have missed a crack somewhere: maybe in some old house, maybe if you pull back the floorboards in the attic – or in a dead end, or in a brick wall, there's a passage carelessly filled with bricks, hurriedly painted, haphazardly nailed shut with crisscrossed boards. ... Maybe not here but in another city ... Maybe somewhere in the tangle of rails on a siding there stands a railroad car, old and rusted, its ceiling collapsed: the one sweet Shura didn't get into?

"There's my compartment ... Excuse me, I'll get by. Wait, here's my ticket – it says so right here." There, down in that end – rusted shock absorbers, reddish buckled wall girders, blue sky in the ceiling, grass underfoot – that's her place, right here! No one ever took it, no one had a right.

... More tea? A blizzard.

... More tea? Apple trees in bloom. Dandelions. Lilacs. Oof, it's hot. Leave Moscow – to the seaside. Until our next meeting, Alexandra Ernestovna. I'll tell you all about that part of the world. Whether the sea has dried up, whether the Crimea floated away like a dry leaf, whether the blue sky has faded. Whether your tormented, excited beloved has deserted his volunteer post at the railroad station.

In Moscow's stony hell Alexandra Ernestovna waits for me. No, no, it's all true! There, in the Crimea, the invisible but agitated Ivan Nikolayevich – in white uniform – paces up and down the dusty platform, digs his watch out of his pocket, wipes his shaved neck up and down along the lattice work fence rubbing off white dust, oblivious and agitated; past him, without noticing, go beautiful, large-faced young women in trousers; hippie boys with their sleeves rolled up, enveloped in transistorized badoobadooms; farm women in white scarves with buckets of plums; southern ladies with plastic earrings; old men in unyielding synthetic hats; smashing right through Ivan Nikolayevich, but he doesn't know, doesn't notice, doesn't care, he's waiting, time has been derailed, stuck midway somewhere outside of Kursk, tripped on nightingale rivets, lost, blind in fields of sunflowers.

Ivan Nikolayevich, wait! I'll tell her, I'll give her the message; don't leave, she'll come, she'll come, *honest*; she's made up her mind, she's willing, just stand there, *don't worry*, she'll be here soon, she's packed, she just has to pick it up; she's even got a ticket: I swear, I've seen it – in the velvet album tucked behind a photograph; it's a bit worn of course, but don't worry, I think they'll let her on. There's a problem back there, something's in the way, I don't remember what; but she'll manage, she'll think of something – she's got the ticket, doesn't she? – that's important, the ticket, and you know the main thing is she's made up her mind, it's certain, I'm telling you.

Alexandra Ernestovna's signal is five rings, third button from the top. There's a breeze on the landing: the dusty stairwell windows are open, ornamented with easygoing lotuses – the flowers of oblivion.

"Who? ... She died."

What do you mean ... just a minute ... why? ... I just ... I just went there and came back. Are you serious? ...

The hot white air attacks you as you come out of the

passageway crypt, trying to get you in the eyes. Wait ... The garbage probably hasn't been picked up, right? The spirals of earthly existence end around the corner on a patch of asphalt, in rubbish bins. Where did you think? Beyond the clouds, maybe? There they are, the spirals – springs sticking out from the rotting couch. They dumped everything here. The oval portrait of sweet Shura – the glass broken, the eyes scratched out. Old woman's rubbish – stockings ... The hat with the four seasons. Do you need chipped cherries? No? Why not? A pitcher with a broken-off spout. The velvet album was stolen. Naturally. It'll be good for polishing shoes. You're all so stupid, I'm not crying. Why should I? The garbage steamed in the hot sun and melted in a black banana ooze. The packet of letters trampled into slush. "Sweet Shura, when will you?" "Sweet Shura, just say the word." And one letter, drier, swirls, a yellow lined butterfly under the dusty poplar, not knowing where to settle.

What can I do with all this? Turn around and leave. It's hot. The wind chases the dust around. And Alexandra Ernestovna, sweet Shura, as real as a mirage, crowned with wooden fruit and cardboard flowers, floats smiling along the vibrating crossing, around the corner, southward to the unimaginably distant shimmering south, to the lost platform, floats, melts, and dissolves in the hot midday sun.

1987

NINA SADUR

WICKED GIRLS

Translated by Wendi Fornoff

> Burn up with desire
> Like salt in a fire
> *Incantation*

AS HE BURST IN, his jacket rustled from the wind and rain.
His hollow cheeks were a little flushed from the wind and
cold. He was a beast. With the face of a beast. Because he
was a German; his German mother had him in a camp in
1947. That means that he's fourteen years older than us. You
couldn't like a man like that – German hair and the eyes of
a beast. A wiry, harsh, wheezy man.

We were drinking; he had raised his eyes and was watching
with his pale eyes. I lowered mine and squeezed my knees
together. But Emmie says to me, "He's mine." Let him be
yours. After all, he's fourteen years older than us. In the
second place, there's something of the fascist in him. Apparently it's because he was born in a camp. A babe in arms grew
up behind barbed wire and turned into a beast.

We were drinking vodka, and he was watching with
limpid eyes. But then rage flashed in them, and I shivered.
But Emmie started acting up, she let down her hair, smiled
and joked, and they went out on the balcony.

And when they returned, he looked at me with a jeer, and
contempt twisted his pale lips. He put his arm on Emmie's
shoulder, and his bony, pale hand from time to time sleepily
stroked Emmie's blouse. There were light freckles on this

hand; I could no longer drink. Emmie rubbed up against him, I squeezed my knees together, and out in the street a blizzard whistled. When they returned from the balcony they were ruddy, very cold, and wretched, the biting snow-flakes glittering in his white hair, like salt.

Then we found out that he would be at Gena Galkin's. Emmie says, let's go to Gena's, I say no. But we went – Emmie's crazy. Everything happened all over again, right up to the blizzard, again something gleamed in his hair and didn't want to melt. Of all the people, he was the only one the snow stayed on. And suddenly they separated from us, like a couple, and started to walk just by themselves, without us, in the wet winter twilight. But Emmie likes to mess around, though she says she won't be unfaithful, but that's for about two years. He has three children and a salary of one hundred forty rubles, and Emmie broke up with her boy-friend for him. As a result he says, "I'm throwing away every-thing for you. My children, my apartment, my way of life. There's nothing for me to lose. If you leave me, I'll kill you." And he's right. What's more, he beats her. Emmie is hot-tempered, she got drunk once and started yelling. And he tells her, "Be quiet. The neighbors will hear." But she yells and stamps her feet. Then he tells her again, "Be quiet. The neighbors can hear." But still she yells. Then he flung himself at her and started to beat her. Emmie fell, shut up, covered her head and just lay there, but he kicks her anyway and howls in German. Until the blood flows. Until she's nearly dead. The beast. They went together half a year, and he beat her three times. Emmie says, "He has pale blood, like water. He cut himself while shaving, and I saw it." She thinks that they will get along. She says, "He won't beat me anymore. We'll get along." But I say, "I know you!" But Emmie: "No, you're wrong. There's something in him that isn't

376

in other men. It always holds me back," And I say, "Come on!"

And there you go. They rented an apartment. They'd already decided everything, officially broken off everywhere, put up with everything and rented an apartment for themselves. Empty. A couch and table.

And a candy box appeared on the table. And in it two chocolate candies. I wanted to take one, but Emmie rushed up to me and wouldn't give me any. I was surprised; I even saw her turn pale. I say, "What is it?" And Emmie says, "Don't eat those." Why's that? I love candy. And this was good candy. Expensive. But Emmie says, "Don't eat them. There's something wrong with them."

Here's what happened: when she and Bern rented this apartment, the box was there on the table, just like this. And all the men got sick from it. We found that out much later. In the box lay exactly two candies. Bern ate one, but Emmie, being diabetic, didn't even try it. Then they began to put the apartment in order, to arrange their things, but after two hours Bern's head began to hurt badly. They went to bed, during the night Bern tossed about in a delirium. In the morning there were again two candies in the box. Each thought that the other had done it. They fought for a while and then figured out that neither of them had sneaked a candy back in. They decided that the landlords had a key, that landlords joke around like that. They changed the lock. Bern ate a candy, his head started to hurt, at night he tossed about and cried. In the morning exactly two candies lay in the box. Now every day the same thing happened. Bern said, "I'll croak, but I'll figure out that candy." They tested the bottom of the box, examined it in every way possible, but didn't find anything. Naturally, any kind of life they'd had ended. Why, Bern was furious. All his strength went to the candy. He abandoned everything. He suffered. He became completely transparent, like a blue flame. He can't do anything. He struggles. He knows his own truth and wants to prove it. He became like the flame over an alcoholic lamp, and everything in him died down.

I went over to this box and opened it, and the stifling smell of chocolate struck my nostrils. The smell was ancient, from far away. The two dark candies lay side by side. Suddenly it hit me. I understood everything. I didn't say anything to Emmie and calmly closed the box.

I looked at Emmie with totally new eyes. She was already pregnant. She stood by the table in her dressing gown, the buttons on the gown already stretched. She looked at me, her face was not made up, but simple, forever simple. I saw that she was no longer my friend. I tried not to walk away from the table. We jabbered, like always, but she suddenly said, "Why are you looking at me like that?" After that I looked down, but Emmie no longer spoke very much, she kept falling silent. However, I didn't leave. I tried not to walk away from the table, and Emmie felt something, she began to breathe quickly, to pull at the buttons on her dressing gown, and her frightened glance ran around the empty room in search of protection.

And then the door slammed, we heard Bern's quick steps. He was literally running. Emmie didn't know what to do, what to be afraid of, her eyes goggled, and tears already stood in them. But until the last instant I didn't make a move, in order not to give myself away. But here he is already running up to the doors, I run up to the table, open the box, grab the candies and gulp them down one after the other, and my throat started to hurt from the big pieces of candy, and I remembered that insult. The sweet taste of chocolate slid down my throat, but I didn't forget that it had hurt, and I will get even. Tears even sprang to my eyes.

He ran into the room, mean, wiry, in his rustling jacket, white, limpid, like an alcohol lamp flame. And he saw two women in tears. And as suddenly as he'd run in, so he stopped. At first he looked furiously with his pale eyes, and we looked back at him through our tears. He looked and looked but suddenly began to understand, to understand. A thin flush suffused his hollow cheeks, and his thin lips parted slightly:

"Oh, what kind of a girl are you . . .?" he hissed.

And then softly, softly as a whitish little rat, I breathed on him:

"Berrn . . ."

1990

MARINA PALEI

RENDEZVOUS

Translated by Helena Goscilo

> "The struggle for life is fiercest
> among similar forms."
> Charles Darwin

... WHICH VIEW FROM the window should he choose?
He'd already smoked half a pack of cigarettes as he'd gone
through God knows how many landscapes.

Strictly speaking, he'd have liked something with the
freshness of unmediated contact with nature ... Say, for
example, Pissarro's "Plowed Land."

In the opening of the window there instantly appears a
stretch of grayish-brown: on the boundary of the cultivated
field, a touch to the right, is a plow or a harrow; to the left,
a few thin birches on a knoll.

No, such naiveté may be pretentious; it's not at all what
he needs now. He'd always connected the state of being in
love with an irresistible desire to combine the object of
adoration with the most beautiful exotic landscape, whether
it be lofty mountains or a bottomless sea; their quality
seemed to intimate the immemorial nature of love, lending
that feeling its only faithful tonality ... In that sense Monet's
temperament was closer to him.

Now an intensely blue sea lapped outside the window, the
lilac rocks congealed ... ("Rocks at Belle Ile").

So the final touch for the proper setting was found. The
background music chosen, flowers on all the flat surfaces.

His priceless one, his love – she was to arrive any moment. That enchanting trepidation!

What will she be like today? ...

He had to admit that he'd never seen her yet in Eve's garb. And what was particularly important for the effect here, he believed, were the buttocks, of course. Optimally, they're usually as musical as the hidden places of the joints ... They say Botticelli was very musical; that's stretching it. Rather, he was constrained and archaic, even somewhat mannered; it was he who started the cult of "relishing" women, but in Botticelli the bottom is somewhat limp, he was more concerned with the line. ... Ingres has a much better line, perhaps – you have only to recall "The Eternal Source." True, there's a certain lack of refinement there, a lack of the last refined touch. Most probably the best female buttocks can be found in the cut of Mona Lisa's dress: it gives sufficient intimation – or rather, sense – of the sought for (and calculated) buttocks; it's no wonder Leonardo was so chaste. Now, the neck can be taken from Botticelli. Of course, the neck should be long, but you shouldn't take it from Modigliani, where it smacks of cast iron; that would be the same as taking it from Picasso. In general, the neck shouldn't have any functional sinewiness, otherwise all the emotions are lost. The hair – best from Rubens; there's a lot of everything there, including hair. The hands we'll take from the Japanese. When you imagine fingers like those caressing you – little worms like that – you won't need anything else. Unless it's the breast: it shouldn't be large, there's simply nothing for a gentleman with self-respect to do with it but get distracted. Also of special importance are those hidden parts which more than anything embarrass anyone who's unprepared, for example, a sinewy groin (a ballerina's), the deep hollows of the armpits, that is, all the places where there are natural joints.

Incidentally, if all these little cavities behind the knees, at the elbows, and in the ears aren't ugly, then a woman may be considered beautiful. You can take the armpit, again, from Ingres; the knees too. The shoulders will take care of themselves. That's the last touch, the icing on the cake, the eye-catcher. The back's more difficult. There's a lacuna where women's backs are concerned. It's an undiscovered continent, it shouldn't be muscled or fat or bony. What should it be like? ... He doesn't know. But he knows for a fact that that's exactly why Velázquez's "Venus in a Mirror" is so vulnerable – the back doesn't say anything. The feet you should take from a Greek sculpture, most likely of Diana. A self-respecting man starts a woman from her feet. The feet set the tone for the rest. That's why they should be light and chiseled, like Diana the huntress's.

He hears her coming, his beloved! Ah, what's the main thing in a woman? – the first and last are the scent; as the great Sernuda said:

> The scent of a lemon flower ...
> Was there that, at least?

Here she is now, his promised one, his sister, his beloved, and he doesn't even need to see her – what's important is the *sensation* of movement; he's prepared to swear that a woman's movement can be so enticing that you cease noticing the rest. The movement should be perfectly free – not constrained, but restrained, not primitively naive, but knowing – while retaining complete freedom.

She sits down in front of him, now, his love ... She radiates the fearful arrogance of youth and the scent of wealth ... Subtle shades of lilac and gray, the lightest dabs of color – here, warmer tones tending to rose; there, colder ones, tending to pale blue – play like a transparent shadow on her oblong face; here is a moment of life, full of light and peace.

"You don't intend to offer me tea?" the viscous, honeyed streams pour forth.

"Do you take it stronger?"

"Yes, if possible."

"Two sugars or three?"

"Two's enough."

Ah, beloved! What wouldn't he do for her sake! She's precisely what his soul has yearned for. In general, he's certain that a woman – the one and only, of course – shouldn't have anything that's particularly expressive, for that's tiring. Here she is, then, his one and only, and that's because she's wonderfully neither this nor that, neither beautiful nor ugly. He perceives her as he does himself in a mirror, she's his creation, the crowning achievement of his many efforts and experience.

She's his, and he can watch her with pleasure as much as he wants. Now she's sad, she's crying, and on the left side of her neck a graceful little vein is pulsing and you can be driven mad by it, torn between insane pity and sadistic desires. Linger, linger, enchantment; how sweet, tormentingly sweet, it is to see her tears; even sweeter to show in front of his beloved that he too can let fall a tear – miserly . . . male . . .

However, he's tired.

Stroking the touching back of her head, he slowly, unobtrusively, moves his hand onto her neck and, locating her seventh vertebra, quickly pushes the power supply button.

The sensory-magnetic joint running along the spinal column instantly appears, the casing showing smooth; he easily removes it, exposing the familiar sight of the internal organs, entangled in the blue-red wiring of the servomechanisms . . . An efficient order is the basis of harmony: the power supply unit, the computing system, the control unit, the memory unit – he lays it all out into labeled safes.

Phew, is he tired. Say what you will, intercourse saps your energy. . . . And only compassionate nature gives us authentic repose without demanding anything in return.

He walks over to the window again, breathes in the sea air. No, the Monet, after all – it's overly saturated, and everything that's excessive can't be completely beautiful. Strictly speaking, he's more an advocate of lyrical and leisurely contemplation in the spirit of Sisley: he pushes a button and the sea through the window instantly slips off to the right, followed by a click as "Windy Day in Vienieau" is installed, to fit perfectly in the opening of the window. Oh, no! Not that empty sky and melancholy. . . . He pushes the button and in the opening Sisley appears again: "La Ville Garenny on the Seine" (a quiet river, a quiet boat, cosy little houses on the opposite bank). Yes, he's always wanted nothing but simplicity and peace. What does he need? A forest, a clearing with a haystack in it . . . Monet again: now "Haystack in Giverny." Besides, stacks – he agrees with this opinion – are an ideal artistic subject for experiments in tones.

But his weariness doesn't leave him. His state now is the same as if he'd been ordered to divide by zero. His protective relay switches off. The servomechanisms under the casing sag helplessly. His eyes fade.

The view from the window fades automatically.

1991

NINA GABRIELYAN

HAPPINESS

Translated by Jean MacKenzie

"OH, GOD!" she sighed. "Oh, God!" and burst into tears.

"What's the matter? What is it, darling?" he said, tenderly stroking her hair and gently pressing her close, close to his beautiful body.

She didn't answer, she saw in his eyes that he understood perfectly well what was the matter. She continued her voluptuous weeping. Then she seized his hand and began kissing it.

He smiled and kissed her wet, shining eyes.

He soon drifted off to sleep, holding her close and responding in his sleep to her slightest movement. She was uncomfortable lying that way. She was no longer used to sleeping next to a man, her arm had gone numb, but she was afraid to move, afraid that she would scare away the miracle that had occurred. He breathed silently, and the pulse in his neck throbbed softly, but she already knew how frenzied this beautiful male body could be.

Her body was beautiful, too. She had always known that she had a beautiful body. Even when her former husband used to say that her legs were too short. But she knew that he said that to get back at her for his failure as a man. He also said she was not his type, that he liked long-legged red-heads. She felt her hatred rise and was about to open her mouth to ask when he would finally gather his strength – his powerful male strength – and pound the nail into the wall, so that he could hang on it the precious gift that his loving

391

mother had given them for a wedding present. How much she must have loved her son to give him for his wedding this amazing print, that must have cost all of three rubles!

She had even begun to utter this phrase, but caught herself in time, remembering that he would undoubtedly answer by talking about her father, who was so filled with love for his daughter that he called her all the time – at least once every two months. No, she was no longer as stupid as she had been in the first months of her marriage, she would not give her husband the chance to catch her out, tease her out from the depths of her private world, and tie her, like a goat to a peg, to some stupid phrase. Especially now, fifteen years after their divorce.

The sleeping man breathed quietly and in his sleep tenderly and firmly pressed her body, her beautiful body, close to his. Her very beautiful body.

... *She was eating strawberries sprinkled with sugar, oozing a thick juice. The strawberries had the taste of happiness and freedom, because she had passed all of her eighth-grade exams with flying colors, and in three days she and her mother would be in the Crimea. And she would lie on the hot bronze sand, and her body, separated from the world by only her new red bathing suit, that they were so lucky to get at the Moskva department store, would absorb the red-hot currents of this ancient, dark part of the South, and would itself become the color of old bronze.*

... *And then she would enter the green sea and swim forever, chasing away schools of hook-nosed seahorses. When she reached the red buoy she would turn over on her back and lose track of the divide between sea and sky, between herself and all of this.*

... *Then her father came into the room and, looking in disgust at her adolescent knees poking out from under her short nightgown, asked why she had again hung her panties and bra in the bathroom where everyone could see them. Couldn't she find some other place to dry them? And she felt how disgusting her body was.*

The sleeping man trembled and opened his eyes a bit. But she gathered all her will power and looked her father right in the eye in such a way that, muttering something unintelligible, he disappeared into thin air.

"Go back to sleep," she told the sleeping man, "Sleep." And carefully laying his head on her shoulder, began to rock him quietly. The sleeping man hugged her trustingly and, smacking his lips like a child, fell even deeper into sleep. She was suddenly seized by a desire to look at her legs. But she controlled herself and whispered again, "Sleep."

She herself could not fall asleep, because her mother came into the room, took her by the hand and led her into the kitchen. There, closing the door tightly after her, her mother nervously adjusted the white bow in her hair, and, looking around fearfully, asked in a loud whisper if she felt any pain in her lower abdomen. No, she answered in surprise, she didn't feel anything like that. You will soon, answered her mother. A lot of pain. An awful lot. And every month. That's the way it is, said her mother.

And then she screwed her courage up to ask where babies come from. "Sssh!" said her mother. "Your father will hear." And then she blushed furiously and explained hastily that a woman has a hmmm, well, in general, and a man has to tear it. And this hurts a lot. And the worst thing in a woman's life is the memory of her wedding night.

She laughed at her mother's words for it wasn't just the first – memories of the second and the twenty-second nights were not all that pleasant, either. She shook her head. Harder and harder. To shake out of it the thing that had already begun to spread through her body, threatening to mutilate it once again. No, she would not allow it. She would never again allow them – her father, her former husband, her mother – to paralyze her body's ability to become bronze, long-legged and happy.

The body of the sleeping man embraced her, giving off a dark, acrid heat. She tensed her nostrils and began to drink in this heat. She drank it in until she was filled with it, until there were no empty spaces left in her being where the past could creep in. Not the smallest hole.

And only then did she allow herself to fall asleep. She slept, trustingly throwing her head back in the darkness, protected by this dark male scent that wrapped softly around her – the smell of love, of happiness and security.

And in her dream the sleeping man came up to her once again and offered her a movie ticket. He smiled slyly, just like he had a few hours ago, and said what a shame it was that his friend had fallen ill. That was why he could give her a ticket. It would be just too bad if such pretty girls couldn't get into the movies. He had noticed them, he said, when they were still in line, and he knew right away that they would not be able to get tickets. He had bought his yesterday. For himself and for his friend. And then his friend had to go and get sick. So, if they wanted . . . But, unfortunately, there was only one ticket. Let the girls themselves decide which of them would go. And since in her dream she already knew what would happen, that it wasn't just a simple ticket, she behaved quite differently than she did in real life. She didn't bother to put on an act, to insist that her friend take the ticket, knowing full well that her friend would persuade her to accept it in the end. No, she didn't refuse, she just held out her hand and took the lucky ticket.

And then the cup of tea in her hand shook and fell slowly to the floor. And he laughed and said that it was good luck when dishes break, and that she had beautiful hands. And then she saw that her body was also beautiful. It was lying on a white sheet, and it was already naked and tanned. And she was that body, stretched out and trembling beneath his kisses, and at the same time she was in another corner of the room, in front of the mirror, watching in it what was happening behind her back.

But since the cup continued to fall slowly from her hands, she could not get a look at the faces of the two people in the mirror, one of whom was she herself. And she tried to get a good look at them, and the tension was a torment, sweet and growing. Then it became unbearable, and she understood that she would now, finally, experience something she had never been able to, not with her husband nor with other men.

And she became frightened. Frightened of her husband. Actually, she was afraid she would remember his pitiful face, so ashamed. And then she would ruin it, again. She ground her teeth and moaned. Loudly. Even more loudly. Tears streamed down her face, and through her tears she gave a mental push to the cup, falling all too slowly. The cup crashed down, hit the floor, and, freed from its overfull contents, smashed into a million shining sharp pieces that flew in different directions . . .

She lay, liberated, empty, happy, and she cried, burying her face in his shoulder, not answering his tender "what's the matter" because she could tell by his voice that he knew perfectly well what was the matter.

And then morning came. Sunday morning, and they drank tea in the sunny kitchen. And he laughed and told her how he had tricked his professor at a university exam. All he did was look him straight in the eye and begin to answer a different question than the one on the test card, the only question he knew the answer to. And he spoke in such an animated tone that the professor was taken in.

Then he said that she looked wonderful for thirty-five, and how nice it was that she had her own apartment. Then he got ready to leave, and, kissing her tenderly, said that she owed him fifty dollars. She laughed at his joke. But he continued to insist. She laughed ever louder and kept laughing until she realized that it wasn't a joke. Then she told him he was a scoundrel. He smiled. She began to choke. He smiled even wider. She got fifty dollars out of the sideboard and gave it to him. He thanked her affectionately, and, scratching some numbers on a piece of paper, said that when she wanted to see him again she could call this number. She answered that she hated him.

She cried for an entire day, sitting in front of the mirror and tearing at her face. Then for a week she couldn't face anyone. Two months later she called him.

1994

LUDMILA ULITSKAYA

ANGEL

Translated by Arch Tait

IN THE SAME YEARS that Humbert Humbert was drooling over his prepubertal poppet and hatching his inhuman plan to marry the ill-starred Charlotte Haze, at the far end of the world Nikolai Romanovich, a lonely professor of philosophy (or at least of a science that laid claim to that name), also stricken by a deviant love bug, married a lady who in her wildest dreams could never have hoped for so dazzling a match. Actually, Antonina Ivanovna hardly qualified as a lady, and it would have been charitable even to class her as a citizen. She was unambiguously an old dear and working at that time as a nursing auxiliary – or, in earlier terminology, the linen keeper – of the cardiological department to which the professor was admitted as an inpatient suffering from stenocardia.

The amiable Antonina, who resembled less a hen than a rather gray turkey, expanded downward from her small head to her obese legs. She was divorced, a secret drinker, and she lived in a room one hundred feet square with her young son.

Her salary was derisory and she readily pilfered what she could, although she was ashamed of doing so. In short, she was a perfectly respectable woman. Early in January, as it was the school holidays, she began bringing the boy with her to work. The fair-haired lad, sitting in the linen room peeping out from behind his mother's back, his brow white as milk and with blond brushes beneath his eyebrows, struck the professor right in his sick and disordered heart.

We shall leave a potential digression here on the connection between sickness and sin – their subtle points of contact and overlap – to the psychoanalysts and reverend fathers, both of whom have grazed to their hearts' content on these treacherous terrains.

Nikolai Romanovich would wander down the hospital corridor for hours and peep in the half-open door of the linen room, catching with a targeted gaze a glimpse of a gawky elbow in a mended blue sweater moving lightly over the table (if drawing something) or just a cursory view of items of institutional laundry, yellowed from sterilization in the hospital's autoclaves. Then again, he might suddenly behold, full height in the doorway, a radiant elegant being, a boy from the harem, perhaps not quite fully grown, just needing another two or three years. Twelve is the sweetest age.

Sometimes the boy was fed in the canteen for patients who could walk, and he would sit at the corner table where the doctors ate their rushed meals. His back was straight; he was grave and frightened. Nikolai Romanovich saw clearly his pale blue eyes, which squinted a little when he looked to the right, and his blond eyelashes, as downy as a ripe dandelion head.

"Tonya! Tonya!" the ward sister would call the linen keeper, looking into the canteen and Antonina would respond in her kind flabby voice, "Over hee-er!"

It was upon hearing that voice one time that Nikolai Romanovich was riven by an insight: Should he not try to arrange a different life for himself? She was, of course, a domestic sort of person, just a linen keeper, a nanny, so why not draw up an honest matrimonial contract? You scratch my back, I scratch yours.

Nikolai Romanovich was approaching fifty-five, a fair age.

The provisions would accordingly include no expectation or assurance of matrimonial delights but would include a room of her own, full board and lodging, and, needless to say, all proper respect. Your own contribution, dear Xantippe Ivanovna, will be to run the household, to maintain hearth and home: that is, to do the laundry, cooking, and cleaning. For my part, I shall adopt your young son and rear him in the best possible way. I shall give him an education, oh, yes, including music and gymnastics. A lightly running Ganymede, redolent of olive oil and young sweat. Calm down, calm down. Don't frighten away a lovely melody. Gradually, miraculously, a tender child will grow up in his house, turn into a boy, a young friend, a pupil, his beloved. In these halcyon days he will weave the nest of his future happiness with his diligent beak.

Linen-keeping Antonina was at first thrown into confusion. How could this be? But happiness, like the wind, comes and goes unaccountably. Here she had landed a two-hundred-square-foot room with a balcony, on the fifth floor, with windows looking into the courtyard, in a smart building on Gorky Street, where your neighbors were actresses and generals and heaven knows who. Everything was good quality and solid. Her new husband was not greedy; he gave her a generous housekeeping allowance for food. And what food it was, from the Kremlin distribution center, no less, though he had said not to tell anyone that. And he never asked for the change. He was clean, changed his underwear every three days, and his socks nearly every day. He doused himself in the bathroom like a duck, and even so went to the bathhouse on Saturdays and spent half the day there. He was smartly dressed, brushed his own shoes, and ironed his own trousers. You wouldn't do it right, said he.

To friends who really very much wanted to know, she

would reply in all simplicity: As far as that goes, no, I can't say there is. But how many years is it since I last saw a live . . .? And anyway, who cares about that? I'm used to it by now. I really don't know why I have been so lucky. He looks after little Slava as if he were the boy's father. To tell the truth, he doesn't have much to say to me at all. But what would we have to talk about anyway, when you think about it? He's very educated, obviously, a professor. . . .

On this point, it has to be said, she was not deluding herself. He was both a professor and educated. Classical philosophers, like pedigreed dogs, did not thrive on the meager fruits of socialism, but Nikolai Romanovich himself had happened upon just the right border to cultivate in that garden, and dug it and watered and manured in it the scrawny tree of Marxist-Leninist aesthetics. On the very eve of the Revolution he managed to complete his university education and almost to defend his dissertation on the topic, "The essence of Plato's dialectic as interpreted by Albinus and Anonym. Vales." It was the magic word *dialectic* that opened before Nikolai Romanovich the royal doors to the new life: namely, the position of Lecturer in Classical Philosophy in the Socialist Academy. There he was the only member who actually knew Ancient Greek and Latin, so he was constantly in demand as a supplier of quotations to highly placed leaders, including Lunacharsky himself.

For decades thereafter he sifted through Plato and Aristotle, Kant and Hegel, looking for the correct scientific resolution of aesthetic questions before which all these pre-Marxian philosophers had been as helpless as blind kittens. He also became so adept in the theory of art and the criteria of artistic quality that not a single decree of the Central Committee of the All-Union Communist Party (Bolsheviks) was compiled without his complicity, whether the matter at issue was Vano Muradeli's opera *The Great Friendship* or Shostakovich's *Katerina Izmailova*. He was not schizophrenic in the least. The flexible dialectic, like a knowledgeable guide in the mountains, led him by tortuous paths through the most insalubrious places.

Alas, however, Nikolai Romanovich was indeed the servant of two masters. His second master, imperious and secretive, was his unhappy predilection for the male sex. From his earliest years it bore down on his head like a migraine, raising his blood pressure and causing tachycardia. The dread Article 120 of the Soviet Constitution hung over him. No enemy of the people, real or set up, no opportunist or oppositionist, experienced the same abyss of fear as those who lived under the threat of this seemingly unremarkable article. Theirs was a real, not fictive, secret society of men who, like freemasons with their secret signs and special handshakes, recognized each other in a crowd by the anguish in their eyes and the anxiety etched on their brows. The Leaden Age that replaced the Silver Age sent on their way the sophisticated youths, smutty schoolboys, and good-looking novices, leaving for Nikolai Romanovich and his ilk dangerous liaisons with heartless, greedy young men with whom you had constantly to be on your guard. They could betray, expose, or slander you. They could have you thrown into prison. Only once in Nikolai Romanovich's adult life did he experience a deep and lasting relationship, with a young historian, a boy from a good family who died at the front in the Second World War and who, before doing so, brutally humiliated Nikolai Romanovich with the derisive letters, full of offensive allusions, of a complete psychopath.

The arrival of Slava opened a new era in the life of Nikolai Romanovich. The professor's cherished dream looked as though it was about to come true. He would rear himself a beloved, and the boy would benefit from the love of a wise educator. Oh, yes, he would benefit rationally. Nikolai Romanovich would mold him in his own image, bringing him up lovingly and chastely. Nikolai Romanovich would be a true pedagogue, a slave not sparing even his own life to protect and educate his beloved.

"I swear by the dog!" Nikolai Romanovich vowed to himself. He leaned over the sleeping boy who now lived in his apartment, if admittedly in his mother's room, on a couch upholstered in pale orange plush. "These things shall be!" he declared, by the flickering light of a bulbous standard lamp. "My little angel," he murmured, as he tucked in the blanket at the sides.

In these evening hours, Antonina was allowed to take a glass or two of something strong to help her sleep, in moderation and under his supervision. He was truly a pedagogue who overlooked nothing.

In that first year of their family life, Nikolai Romanovich sent the boy to music school, to the wind department. Slava didn't become a flute player, but he came to feel at home in music as if that was where he had always belonged. His great gift proved to be an ability to listen to music with godlike discrimination, so that even in this rarefied area Nikolai Romanovich received a partner. Stepfather and stepson now went to the Conservatory together to enjoy that art which least lent itself to analysis from a class standpoint.

The Conservatory's habitués of those years grew accustomed to the sight of this couple, the slender elderly man with large spectacles on his small-boned face and the lissom youth with the neatly cut blond hair, in a black sweater with the collar of his white Pioneer's shirt turned over the round neckline. The Moscow melohomophiles, a correlation as yet unexplained, writhed with envy when Nikolai Romanovich

404

bought two lemonades and two cakes in the buffet. Nobody wrote any denunciations of him, however. They were all too scared for themselves.

In those years a circle of cognoscenti formed at the Conservatory. There was no formal membership, but their faces were recognizable and stood out. Apart from secret coreligionists of Nikolai Romanovich and ordinary music lovers, the circle naturally also included professional musicians and also some of Slava's fellow pupils from the music school, like Zhenya, a young cellist, who usually came with her mother and father. Zhenya was forever whispering in Slava's ear and pulling him by the sleeve over to one side with her.

"A sweet girl," Nikolai Romanovich said to his protégé, "but not at all prepossessing in appearance."

This was not true. She was entirely prepossessing, with dark little eyes and curls restrained by a checkered hairband. It was just that Nikolai Romanovich's heart suffered a pang of dark jealousy for a moment. We can quite do without these girls.

He was granted all that Humbert Humbert ever dreamed of: a golden childhood that developed before his eyes into youth; the respectful friendship of a pupil; and a complete and trusting intimacy, carefully nurtured by one who proved to be a master of affectionate touching, breathing, and mellifluous movement.

In the sixty-third year of his life, Nikolai Romanovich died in his own bed from an aortic embolism. He died suffused with the youthful love of his angel and in perfect harmony with his daemon, never having read the novel charged with Nabokov's high-voltage electricity and recognized his profound relatedness to its unhappy hero.

The orphaned Slava, by now a first-year student in the

philosophical faculty of Moscow State University, was left in a state of complete bewilderment after the death of his mentor. While the course continued, analyzing the logic and propaedeutic of dialectical materialism in the old building of the philosophical faculty, whose windows looked out onto the anatomical theater of the First Medical Institute, he did not have too much of a problem. But then the summer vacation arrived. Slava was used to spending this with his stepfather in Estonia, at a guesthouse in Pjarnu, and at this point he became deeply depressed. He took to his bed in his stepfather's study listening to his favorite records, and had difficulty getting up to turn them over or to put on a new one.

Slava had been done no favors by the old aesthete, whose angel now had no idea how to go on living. Without his mentor, Slava was lost. He had no friends. The scrupulously kept secret of his relations with his stepfather had erected an impenetrable barrier between him and other people. He was remote from his mother and had long been treating her exactly as Nikolai Romanovich did: courteously and manipulatively. For the past four years he and his orange couch had migrated to Nikolai Romanovich's study to escape from his mother's snoring.

His stepfather left what by the standards of those times was a staggeringly large amount of money. There was a whole stack of savings books, some of which provided cash to the bearer on demand, while others were in Nikolai Romanovich's name and had been bequeathed to Slava. One humble little gray booklet with three thousand rubles in it was left to Antonina. Slava passed it to his mother, who threw up her hands in delight. She had never expected to be so rich and went completely off the rails. Instead of the double vodka Nikolai Romanovich had permitted her, she now downed a third of a bottle, and not only in the evening either. By nine o'clock or so Antonina would, as always, be sleeping the sleep of the just, and Slava would go out for a walk, to fill his lungs with the heavy petrol-laden air and to sit on a dusty bench on Tverskoy Boulevard not far from the amateur chess club. As evening approached, it drew those addicted to the checkered board, old-age pensioners and failed chess prodigies. One muggy evening Zhenya from the music school also found her way there.

Zhenya came from a good, thoroughly musical family, whose talents passed from generation to generation in the same way that some families pass on a congenital disorder like hypertonia or diabetes. Among their forebears they numbered an Italian prima donna, a Czech organist, and a German conductor. The main Bach of the family was, however, Zhenya's grandfather. To this day his name can be found in the company of Skryabin, inscribed in the roll of honor of gold medalists of the Moscow Conservatory.

Grandfather's composing was no more than mediocre, in line with the spirit and culture of the times. He was captivated by modernism but had been granted neither the audacity of Debussy nor the originality of Mussorgsky. His fame was as a performer, a cellist, a teacher and public figure in the world of music. He chaired a variety of musical societies and committees and distributed stipends to poor but talented children and allowances to elderly orchestra musicians. He was, in short, a true Russian intellectual of mixed blood – none of it, as it happened, Russian. The family was large, and everything revolved around music. His elder brother was a concert violinist, while his younger brother, less successful, transcribed music.

Zhenya never knew her grandfather. They were separated by three decades, which had included two world wars. Her grandfather died at forty-two years of age on the same day as Archduke Franz Ferdinand, at the beginning of the First World War, while she was born on the last day of the Second.

As an act of rebellion or a sport, the family would suddenly throw up an apostate, like Uncle Lyova, who decamped to the accountants, and Aunt Vera, who was unfaithful to music in favor of agriculture. Zhenya's father, Rudolf Petrovich, was another apostate, seduced by a career in the army. Under the tall Astrakhan *papakha* of a colonel, he pined for music all his life. He was infatuated with it but never touched a musical instrument. He decided, however, to be sure that his daughter returned to the family tradition and chose the cello for her. Their home, already full of signed photographs of all sorts of great people, with dusty sheet music, and with the scores of unburied operas, was filled with the living sound of scales and exercises. The little Zhenya showed promise of developing into a real performer. Daniil Shafran himself took an interest in her and supported her. Her grandfather's renown in the music world put the wind in her sails, but her diligence and assiduousness were entirely her own, and as a girl she spent many hours with her legs spread and a diminutive cello, a learner's toy, clenched between her knees. As she grew older something miraculous grew with her. Her cello proved highly responsive. She had barely to put the bow to it for it to respond with sounds more rich and velvety than anything she knew. And what comparison could there be between the broad sinuous voice of the cello and the scratchy unevenness of a violin, the simplemindedness of a viola, or the glum monotony of a double bass?

That summer she was alone in the city for the first time. Her parents were living out at the dacha, and she was preparing for her first concert program. In the evenings she would go out for a stroll.

They were both delighted by their chance meeting at the bench on Tverskoy Boulevard. Each was feeling lonely. For Zhenya it was an acute but temporary state, since she was alone at home for the first time in her life. It seemed to Slava that for him the condition was absolute and would be life-long. They talked, however, only about music. They had in addition a shared source of memories in the music school on Pushkin Square, which both of them had attended for so long and of which no trace now remained. On its site there rose the hideous *Izvestiya* building. They recalled the lessons of solfeggio, the choirs, the student concerts, and talked till late in the evening.

He saw her home to Spiridonovka Street and told her on the way, to his own surprise, "My stepfather has died."

It was the first time he had said this aloud, and he was struck by how the words sounded. Something in the air seemed to change. Because these words had been uttered, Nikolai Romanovich's death became irrevocable.

Zhenya, detecting something, felt her heart beat faster.

"Did you love him very much?"

"He was more than a father to me."

This sounded so elegiac it would surely have gladdened Nikolai Romanovich's heart.

"Poor Slava. I would go crazy if my father – if something like that happened to him." At the age of eighteen, she was so far removed from death she couldn't even bring herself to say the word *died*. She shook her head to drive away the shadow of death and her lips pursed in sympathy, but she said something silly and childish. "Let's go and eat some ice cream! A whole great lot of it."

Slava smiled, touched by such total fellow feeling. "But where can we get it at this time of night?"

"I've got some in the fridge. My parents are at the dacha, and it's the only thing I buy."

The ice cream was excellent, with pieces of frozen strawberry or icy blackberries. The downstairs neighbor brought it in a saucepan with dry ice. She was a waitress at Café North. Everybody was stealing, provided only that there was something for them to get their hands on. After the ice cream, Zhenya produced from her father's room an imposing record in a black-and-white sleeve.

"Karajan. They brought it back from Germany. You have never heard Wagner like this."

She reverently lowered the gleaming record onto the turntable of the record player. It was the orchestral version of *Tristan and Isolde*. You would have thought the musicians in the orchestra were not human beings but demons. The two of them listened to it twice from beginning to end, and to the accompaniment of the towering music, Zhenya fell in love with Slava just at the point where Isolde dies. She had never, even with her father, listened so discriminatingly, so much in harmony with the perceptions of another person. And he was drawn to her with all his soul, such a sweet girl, so loving, with her dark clever eyes, her lively curls trembling above her forehead.

"What powerful, masculine music!" Zhenya commented, when Karajan had thundered his last.

"Wow, yes," Slava agreed, wondering how she could know that. The tang of the wild strawberry ice cream lingered in his mouth, the blackberry seeds lodged in his gums, and a flavor of something remained in his heart from their shared experiencing of the dark colors of the tumultuous music.

He visited her throughout August. Late in the evening, when the heat had died down and the nocturnal chess players

410

had gathered on Tverskoy Boulevard, he would go back home feeling cheered. His depression had lifted. The combined sensations of the boulevard at night, Wagner, and melting ice cream were firmly associated with Zhenya.

When autumn came and Zhenya's parents returned to the city, it was time to study again and they began to meet less often, although every day they would talk at length on the telephone about a Richter concert or a marvelous album by Somov that Slava had bought at the secondhand shop on the Arbat, following his late stepfather's habit of browsing in antique and secondhand shops with money in his pocket. Nikolai Romanovich had never been a genuine collector but had gradually learned a thing or two about objets d'art from the material world, the payoff, no doubt, for being such a convinced materialist.

By the end of the summer it had seemed to Zhenya that she finally had the beginnings of a real romance, but for some reason everything got stuck at the stage of a delightful friendship and just would not develop further. She very much wanted something more than little bits of frozen strawberry or icy blackberries.

Slava could feel the constant expectation emanating from her, and it made him nervous. He very much appreciated being with her, the admirable home he found himself in, and indeed Zhenya herself, who was so receptive toward literature and music and even toward him. He felt as much desire for her as he might have for a lamppost, and there seemed to be nothing he could do about that.

At the age of nineteen, he was well aware that he belonged to a rare and special breed of men condemned to furtiveness and secrecy because those soft protuberances enveloped in fabric disgusted him. He associated them with a large white sow, its nether side besieged by sucking piglets. The actual

411

structure of women, the hairy nest with the unfortunately placed vertical slit, seemed dreadfully unattractive. Whether he had reached that conclusion himself or whether the professor of aesthetics, Nikolai Romanovich, had subtly suggested the idea, was immaterial. He liked Zhenya very much and she kept him from feeling lonely, but his physical longings had not only not gone away, they were growing stronger.

After bidding Zhenya good night, he would usually go to sit on the same bench on Tverskoy Boulevard not far from the chess players. He would look at the few passers-by, timidly wondering, *Him? Not him?* One time a well-built handsome blond man locked eyes with him and he became tense, because the gaze seemed very pointed, but the man walked on, leaving Slava in a delicious sweat with his heart pounding and seeming strangely to be echoing that other heart, which had suffered from angina. *We share that too,* Slava noted. *Music lovers, dicky hearts, aesthetes.*

He was wrong. The true picture was a good deal more complicated, but the error was perfectly understandable. The age of supermen clad in leather and wearing metal chains, homosexuals with bulging pumped-up muscles, contemptuously looking down on "straights," had not yet arrived. Cowboys were sex symbols to excite the female half of the world, bullet-riddled, lustful creatures, not cow boys, cowherds with rear ends battered by coarse saddles, engaging in same-sex love because of a total dearth of women in their environment.

Slava belonged wholly to the Classical World, as romantically imagined by the superficial scholars of the nineteenth century. Even Marx jotted some nonsense about the "golden childhood of mankind."

No doubt, from the immense distance of several thousand

years, the picture had become distorted, and the reality was totally bloody and unbridled paganism. In its lurid polytheism, all that existed was deified, inspired, and set to guiltless lechery not only as nymphs, naiads, satyrs, and petty gods of puddles and roadside ditches but also as swans, cows, eagles, shepherds, and shepherdesses. All these engaged in an unending orgy of copulation that knew no bounds, and for some reason this heaving paganism came to be called Classical Materialism. This fallacy was what the beliefs of Nikolai Romanovich consisted of. He passed them on in full measure to his alumnus even as he inserted more personal predilections, cautiously and patiently, with the assistance of his experienced fingers, his sensitive tongue with its discerning tastebuds, and his old withered lance.

He was a brilliant teacher and he had found a brilliant pupil, whose hypersensitive body could no longer bear this indissoluble loneliness. His fair youthful hair, his mouth, his chest and belly, his loins and buttocks were begging for love. The Garden of Eden and the Rose of Sodom, Nikolai Romanovich had called them. The trout was truly breaking through the ice.

In early October, on one of the dark but still warm evenings of a long Indian summer, Slava's nights of sitting on Tverskoy Boulevard were rewarded with a new teacher. From a group of dark figures clustered beneath a lamppost that illuminated the chessboards, a man of around forty in a canvas cap came over to him. He had a handsome, possibly Jewish, face and was wearing an old-fashioned checked shirt. He took the cap off his bulbous skull and sat down carefully on the rickety bench. All of him seemed to be pressurized: his eyes were slightly protruding, and his beard was bursting forth with such force that only his nose provided a clearing free from undergrowth. (Nikolai Romanovich, in contrast, had always seemed a bit depressurized, like a slightly deflated balloon.)

The new arrival grasped the edge of the bench with his hairy fists and addressed himself very familiarly to Slava. "I know your face. You don't by any chance play chess, do you?"

Slava's heart pounded unevenly, dancing to sleazy music. Was this him? "I do a bit."

The man laughed. "Even my grandmother did a bit. At least, she thought she did. We'll soon find out."

The man pulled a small leather case out of his pocket and opened it. The chessboard was already set up. Sharp little pins were inserted in holes punched in leather. "Your move."

Slava's hands were trembling so much he could barely take hold of the chesspiece. He made the first move, E2 to E4, and felt a sense of relief. There was no longer any doubt: this was him. The chess player lightly pulled out a black pawn with its sharp prong, held it between thumb and middle finger, and murmured, "It's getting dark so early now," before ramming it into a white square.

That evening the chess player supposed that Slava's eyes were mirror-black, like the sunglasses that had just become fashionable, but it was a false impression. It was just that his pupils were so dilated that the blue iris was pressed out to the edge of his eyes.

"Let's finish our game at my place. It really is far too dark." The chess player folded up the chessboard and pulled his cap over his forehead, and they headed toward the trolley bus.

Slava did not ask how far they were going. His heart was thumping with anticipation, and the chess player periodically put a hand on his shoulder or on his knee. They reached Tsvetnoy Boulevard, alighted, and turned up a dark alley.

414

They entered the neglected entrance of a three-story building, and as they were going up the stairs the chess player explained that he lived with his mother. She had been a great beauty in her youth, an actress, but was now almost blind and completely out of her mind.

The apartment was small and very dirty. From time to time the mother's querulous voice was heard on the other side of the wall, and then she started singing a ballad. They did not finish their game of chess. They made love, strong masculine love, of which Slava had had only an inkling before. The place smelled of vaseline and blood. It was what Slava had been wanting and what Nikolai Romanovich had been unable to give him. It was a night of nuptials, of initiation, and of ecstasy beyond the reach of music. A new life began for Slava.

VALITA WAS buried at state expense, if indeed he was buried at all. It is possible that he was dissected for his organs, that they were doused with formaldehyde and given, to be torn apart, to the students whose windows looked out toward the philosophers, or perhaps to some other students, but it's not very likely. The postmortem established that the body had been lying for fifteen to seventeen days before it was discovered in a secluded corner of Izmailovo Park by a citizen of sporting appearance who was taking his fox terrier for a walk.

It is difficult to explain what made Yevgenia Rudolfovna start a missing persons inquiry. In the forty years and more that she had known him, he had disappeared often and for different stretches of time. The first stretch was particularly long. He got five years, and then in the camps it was extended. That time he disappeared for almost ten years, but not from choice. Then he turned up again, but no longer as Slava. Now he was Valita. Such was the nickname he had acquired. He did tell Yevgenia a few things, but nothing to frighten or embarrass her. He did his best to spare her.

It was not exactly that she loved Slava, of course not, but she loved the memories of her youth and recalled how much she had loved an inspired fair-haired boy, how wonderfully they had listened to music together, and how he had suffered from the imperfections of the recording technology of the time. Karajan had six bars piano and eight forte, but everything was evened out. She had felt sorry for this poor man, a pariah who had lost every last thing it is possible to lose: his property, his teeth, his fair hair, even his right to live in Moscow. He wrested that back from the clenched teeth of the world by marrying some irredeemable alcoholic and getting registered as living with her in a street poetically named Deerbank. Of his former riches, all that remained was his rare talent for listening to music and his aristocratic hands with their oval nails.

For many years he came to see Yevgenia at the theater, in her vast office with its MUSICAL DIRECTOR brass plate on the solid door. The other employees who worked there knew him, and the people in the cloakroom let him in. She would usually give him a little money, make coffee, and get some chocolates from a remote corner of the cupboard. He had a sweet tooth. Sometimes when there was time she would put on some music for him, although he admitted that he had long ago ceased to love it. Now he loved only sounds. She was not entirely sure what he meant by that, but in these matters he was better qualified than she was herself, the director of the musical department of a very famous Moscow theater. Unquestionably. She was fully aware of that.

He didn't stay in her office for long. He embarrassed himself, as once his late mother, Antonina, had been embarrassed by herself.

For a couple of months he did not come to visit her, and Yevgenia thought nothing of it. Then one Saturday evening she went to the Conservatory. They were playing Brahms's opus 115, the clarinet quintet, a piece unbelievably difficult to perform. In the last movement, when the soul has almost expired and you fly away into the empyrean, she suddenly remembered Slava. She remembered him sitting with his recorder in a little corner class being taught by Xenia Feofanovna, a fat, florid, coarse lady in a silk shift, and she, Zhenya, came barging into the classroom for some reason and stopped, shocked at her own impertinence. Forty years ago, in the music school, of which not a brick remained standing. The Brahms ended, and with the last sounds she sensed that Slava was no longer in this world.

She made an inquiry through the information bureau. Slava was neither to be found living at Deerbank nor in any other street, and she rang the police. She got a boorish reply, but a day later they called her in themselves, to identify his body. There was virtually nothing left to identify, just a heap of black rags, almost clay, a particularly dreadful kind of clay. Only the hand was human, with its aristocratic oval nails.

She spoke to the investigating officer. He was past his prime, rather flabby, and so knowing he might have been better off knowing less. Yevgenia told him nothing that interested him. The crime would have been fairly straightforward to clear up but the police did not take much interest in homosexual killings. They would snoop around for a while and then pin it on some maniac they already had under arrest. Anyway, who other than a maniac could have wanted to kill Valita, a man who had nothing other than a desperate longing to be loved by a man?

Back home, Yevgenia searched for a long time through the photographs of her childhood until she found the one she

417

was looking for. All the others depicted a little girl called Zhenya with her cello, but this was a picture of the audience during a school concert. Her father had taken it. In the second row you could see both of them quite clearly: Nikolai Romanovich in his gray suit and striped tie with the twelve-year-old Slava in his white Pioneer's shirt with the top button undone. Such a sweet face, as radiant as an angel. And how Nikolai Romanovich had loved him. How he had loved him.

2002

SVETLANA ALEXIEVICH

From
LANDSCAPE OF LONELINESS: THREE VOICES

Translated by Joanne Turnbull

VOICE ONE

WHEN HE SAID: "I love you," but didn't yet love me, didn't realize how deeply he'd fall in love, I said: "What does that mean? That word?" He hesitated and looked at me with such interest. I guess it was time and he decided he had to say it. Typical story. Classic. But for me love's a strange word ... A short word ... Too small to contain everything that was going on in me, everything that I felt. Then he left. We'd meet again, of course, the next day, but even before the door closed I began to die, I began to die a physical death, my whole body ached. Love's not a glorious feeling, not at all glorious, or not only glorious ... You find yourself in a different dimension ... life is shrouded, veiled, you can't see anyone, can't throw yourself into anything, you're in a cocoon, a cocoon of insane suffering which grinds up everything that happened yesterday, the day before yesterday, that may happen tomorrow, everything that happened to him before you, without you. You stop caring about the world; all you do is this work, this work of love. I dreamed about how happy I'd be when it ended. How happy I'd be! At the same time, I was afraid it would end. You can't live at that temperature. Delirious. In a dream. I'd suffered before him, ranted and raved, been jealous, I'd had a lot of men, I'm no prude, but what he gave me, no one had ... He was the only one ... We were soul mates, each other's whole world. No

one gave me that experience of self-sacrifice, I suppose . . .
He didn't even give me a child . . . Even . . . A child? No, he
didn't . . . And I'm a good mother . . . (Searches for words).
Love throws you into the very depths of yourself, you dig
and you dig, sometimes you like what you find, other times
you're frightened. Love blinds you and makes a fool of you,
but it also gives you greater knowledge. This woman said
hello to him, and right away I knew she was his first love,
they chatted about this and that, very social and what you'd
expect. But I knew it . . . Knew she was the one . . . She didn't
look at me, didn't even glance in my direction, there was no
curious stare: who are you with, how are things? There wasn't
anything except some sweet gestures. But I sensed something. They huddled together, together in the middle of a
big crowd, a human torrent, as if there were a bridge between
them. Like an animal I sensed something . . . Maybe because,
before, when we happened to drive along that street, past
those particular buildings, he always had this look on his
face, this way of looking at those shabby, perfectly ordinary
entrances . . . Something like that, that science can neither
prove nor refute, that we can't understand, can't understand.
(Again searches for words). I don't know . . . I don't know . . .

We were on the metro, we worked together, we taught at
the same college and went home the same way. We were colleagues. We didn't know yet, I didn't know, but it had already
begun . . . It had already begun . . . We were on the metro . . .
And suddenly he said gaily:

"Are you seeing anyone?"

"Yes."

"Like him?"

"Not really."

"How about you?"

"Yes."

"Like her?"

"No, not really."

And that was all. We went into a store together, he pulled an antediluvian string bag – by then they seemed funny – out of his pocket and bought some macaroni, cheap sausage, sugar, and I don't know what else, a classic selection of Soviet products. Lump sugar . . . Cabbage pies in a greasy paper bag . . . (Laughs). I was married at the time, my husband was a big boss, we didn't live that way, I lived a completely different life. Once a week my husband brought home a special food package (they were doled out at work) of hard-to-come-by delicacies: smoked sturgeon, salmon, caviar . . . We had a car . . . "Help yourself, the pies are still hot," he ate them on the run. (Laughs again). I was a long time coming to him, it was a difficult journey . . . A difficult journey . . . His sheepskin coat had been clumsily patched up in back with the thread showing. "His wife must have died and now he's bringing up their child alone," I felt sorry for him. He was gloomy. Not good-looking. Always sucking heart pills. I felt sorry for him. "Oh, how Russia ruins you," a Russian woman I met on a train once confided. She lived in the West, had for a long time. "In Russia, women don't fall in love with beauty, it's not beauty they're looking for and not the body they love, it's the spirit. Suffering. That's ours." She sounded wistful . . .

We bumped into each other again on the metro. He was reading the paper. I didn't say anything.

"Do you have a secret?"

"Yes," the question so surprised me that I answered it seriously.

"Have you told anyone?"

I felt numb: My God, here we go . . . My God! That's how these things begin . . . It turned out he was married. Two children. And I was married . . .

"Tell me about yourself."

"No, you tell me about yourself. You seem to know everything about me already."

"No, I can't do that."

"Why?"

"Because first I'd have to fall out of love with you."

We were going somewhere in the car, I was driving and after that remark I swerved into the opposite lane. My mind was paralyzed by the thought: he loves me. People kept flashing their lights, I was coming right at them, head-on. Who knows where love comes from? Who sends it?

I was the one who suggested it:

"Let's play?"

"Play what?"

"That I'm driving along, see you hitchhiking, and stop."

So we started playing. We played and played, played all the way to my apartment, played in the elevator. In the hall. He even made fun of me: "Not much of a library. School-teacher level." But I was playing myself, a pretty woman, the wife of a big boss. A lioness. A flirt. I was playing . . . And at some point he said:

"Stop!"

"What's wrong?"

"Now I know what you're like with other people."

He couldn't leave his wife for six months. She wouldn't let him go. She swore at him. Pleaded with him. For six months. But I'd decided I had to leave my husband even if I wound up alone. I sat in the kitchen and sobbed. In the process of leaving I'd discovered that I lived with a very good person. He behaved wonderfully. Just wonderfully. I felt ashamed. For a long time he pretended not to notice anything, he acted as if nothing had happened, but at some point he couldn't stand it anymore and posed the question. I had to tell him.

He was sorry he'd asked ... He blurted it out but his eyes were pleading: "Don't answer! Don't answer!" I could see in them his horror at what he was about to hear. He began fussing with the kettle: "Let's have some tea." We sat down and we had a good talk. But I answered all his questions, I confessed. He said: "Even so don't go." I told him again ... "Don't go." That night I packed my things ... (Through tears and laughter). But there too ... Now we were together ... There too I sobbed every night in the kitchen for two weeks, until one morning I found a note: "If it's so hard, maybe you should go back." I dried my tears ...

"I want to be a good wife. What would you like?"

"You know, no one has ever made me breakfast. I'd like you to call me to the breakfast table, that's all, I don't need anything else."

He got up every morning at six to prepare for his lectures. I felt downcast because I was a night person, I went to bed late and got up late. This was going to be hard, it was a hard clause. The next morning, I staggered into the kitchen, threw some curd cakes together, put them on the table, sat there for five minutes, and shuffled back to bed. I did that three times.

"Don't get up anymore."

"You don't like my breakfasts?"

"I see what a huge effort they are, don't get up anymore."

We had a child ... I was forty-one, it was very difficult even physically, I realize now, though at the time I thought: Ah, it's nothing. But it wasn't nothing. Sleepless nights. Diapers. The baby got a staph infection. Which meant twice as many diapers and washing them a special way. I felt dizzy ... There weren't any Pampers yet ... Just diapers and more diapers ... I washed them, rinsed them, dried them ... Then one day I went completely to pieces: the diapers in the stove had burned up, the washing machine had overflowed and the bathroom was ankle-deep in water. I'd flooded it. The baby was screaming and I was mopping up the water with a rag. It was winter. I sat down on the edge of the bath and burst into tears. I sat there and cried. Then he walked in ... He looked at me in this cold way, like a stranger ... I thought he'd come rushing in to help, I thought he'd feel sorry for me. I was going out of my mind. But he just said: "How quickly you 'cracked.'" And turned around and walked out. It was like a slap in the face. I didn't even say anything back, I was so undone. Very hard ... I was a long time coming to him, it was a difficult journey ...

Later I understood ... I understood him ... He lived with his mother, who had spent ten years in the camps and never once cried and always sent jolly, humorous letters home. The letters still exist. In one she wrote: "Yesterday a very amusing thing happened. I had gone to see a flock of sheep during a blizzard. [A livestock specialist by profession, she was allowed out unescorted to treat sheep.] When I got back the guard dogs didn't recognize me – they could barely see me – so they attacked and we had a very funny tussle." She went on to describe how they'd rolled over the steppe gnawing each other. And ended: "But now I'm fine, I'm in the hospital, they have clean sheets here." They'd torn her flesh ... Those guard dogs ... He grew up among women like that ... And here I was wailing because of a broken washing machine ... His mother's friends had all come back from there. One woman had been so badly tortured she had a broken vertebra, but she always looked elegant and erect in her corset. Another woman ... They'd taken her naked to be interrogated. Her interrogator had sensed her weak spot, he knew that by doing that he might break her. Her hair was gold, she was little, fragile. "They took you there naked?"

426

"Yes, but that wasn't the funny part." She had been sentenced not for political crimes, but as a socially dangerous element (SDE). As a prostitute. In a dark alley, as that heavenly creature was proceeding between two armed escorts, one of them, a backwoods boy, whispered: "You really an SDE?" "That's what they say." "Can't be." And he looked at her with rapture. It was a famous camp – the Aktiubinsk Camp for Wives of Traitors to the Motherland – a camp of beautiful women ... They had lost everything in this life: husbands, relatives, their children were dying of hunger in orphanages. That word – "cracked" – came from there. They arrested his mother and he was left with his grandmother. His grandmother "cracked." She beat him till he was black-and-blue, screamed at him. Her son had been arrested, her daughter and her daughter's husband. She had lost face. In his diary, he wrote: "Mama, a-a-a!"

His mother ... She'd come to see us at the dacha, this was many years after the camps ... She had her own room at the dacha. It was a big house. And I decided to clean it. I went in – there weren't any things lying about anywhere – and began to sweep. Under the couch I found a small bundle. Just then she appeared:

"My little knickknacks," that's what she always said: not my dresses or my shoes or my things, but my little knickknacks.

"Under the 'bed boards'?"

"I just can't get used to it."

And what do you think she did with her miserable little bundle? Did she unpack it? Hang it up somewhere? You'll never guess ... She stuffed it under the mattress ...

You could listen to her forever ... I was such a long time coming to him ...

Prison. Night. A suffocating cell. The door opens and in

walks a woman wearing a fur coat and wafting French perfume. I can't remember her name now, but she was a famous actress, she'd been arrested right after a concert. They all surrounded her and began stroking her fur coat. Smelling it. It smelled of freedom and their former female life. They were all beautiful women ... Commissars always married beautiful women, with long legs and good educations, preferably from the formerly privileged classes, the ones who were left, who'd escaped notice. In Persian thread stockings. It was Nabokov who noted that the scratches life leaves on women heal, whereas men are like glass.

How much I remember, how much it turns out I remember ... I was such a long time coming to him ...

Nighttime ... In the barracks ... A young girl with long wavy hair ... From an old noble family ... She would sit by the hour brushing her hair and remembering her mother. One morning they woke up and she was bald. She'd pulled out all her hair, no one had a knife, of course, or scissors, she'd used her hands. They thought she'd gone crazy. What have you done to yourself? They were trying to recruit her, she said, they'd promised to let her go free on condition she become an informer. The barracks wept, but she was smiling: "I was afraid I'd falter and they'd let me go, but now there's nothing they can do, I'm bald. That's it, I'm here to stay."

He grew up among women like that ... And I was supposed to become like them ... Like his mother ... And I did ...

2003

ACKNOWLEDGMENTS

SVETLANA ALEXIEVICH: From "Landscape of Loneliness" translated by Joanne Turnbull, from *Nine: An Anthology of Russia's Foremost Woman Writers* (GLAS, 2003). Reprinted with permission from Galina Dursthoff Agency.

ISAAC BABEL: "Dolgushov's Death" (1926). Translated by Peter Constantine, from *The Complete Works of Isaac Babel* (W. W. Norton, 2002).

NINA BERBEROVA: "The Big City" by Nina Berberova, translated by Marian Schwartz, from *The Ladies from St. Petersburg*, copyright © Actes Sud, 1995. Translation copyright © 1998 by Marian Schwartz. Reprinted by permission of New Directions Publishing Corp. Copyright © Actes Sud, 1995.

ANDREI BITOV: "Geghard" by Andrei Bitov, from *A Captive of the Caucasus* translated by Susan Brownsberger. Translation copyright © 1992 by Susan Brownsberger. Reprinted by permission of Farrar, Straus and Giroux. Weidenfeld and Nicolson/Orion Publishing Group.

MIKHAIL BULGAKOV: "The Adventures of Chichikov" (1922). Translated by Carl R. Proffer, from *Diaboliad and Other Stories* (Indiana University Press, 1972). Copyright © 1993 by Ellendea Proffer.

IVAN BUNIN: "The Gentleman from San Francisco" (1915). Translated by S. S. Koteliansky, D. H. Lawrence and Leonard Woolf. Taken from *The Gentleman from San Francisco and Other Stories* (Hogarth Press, 1922). Penguin Random House, Inc.

ANTON CHEKHOV: "The Bishop" from *Selected Stories of Anton Chekhov* by Anton Chekhov, translated by Richard Pevear and Larissa Volokhonsky, translation copyright © 2000 by Richard Pevear and Larissa Volokhonsky. Used by permission of Bantam Books, an imprint of Random House, a division of Penguin Random House LLC. All rights reserved.

FYODOR DOSTOYEVSKY: "The Dream of a Ridiculous Man" from *The Eternal Husband and Other Stories* by Fyodor Dostoevsky. Translated by Richard Pevear and Larissa Volokhonsky, translation copyright © 1997 by Richard Pevear and Larissa Volokhonsky. Used by permission of Bantam Books, an imprint of Random House, a division of Penguin Random House LLC. All rights reserved.

NINA GABRIELYAN: "Happiness" translated by Jean MacKenzie, from *New Russian Writing* (eds Natasha Perova and Dr Arch Tait) (GLAS, 1994). Reprinted with permission.

NIKOLAI GOGOL: "The Overcoat" from *The Overcoat and Other Tales of Good and Evil* by Nikolai Gogol, translated by David Magarshack, copyright © 1957 by David Magarshack. Used by permission of Doubleday, an imprint of the Knopf Doubleday Publishing Group, a division of Penguin Random House LLC. All rights reserved.

MIKHAIL LERMONTOV: "The Fatalist" translated by Vladimir and Dmitri Nabokov, taken from *A Hero of Our Time*, Everyman's Library, 1992. Copyright © 1958 by Vladimir Nabokov and Dmitri Nabokov.

OSIP MANDELSTAM: "Music in Pavlosk" (1925). Translated by Clarence Brown, from *The Noise of Time: The Prose of Osip Mandelstam* (Princeton University Press, 1965).

Marie Jackson, from *Subtly Worded* (Pushkin Press, London, 2014).

TATYANA TOLSTAYA: "Sweet Shura" translated by Antonina W. Bouis, from *Collected Stories* (New York Review of Books, 2007). First published in English in *Tatyana Tolstaya, On the Golden Porch*, Alfred A. Knopf, 1989. Copyright © 1989 by Tatyana Tolstaya. The Wylie Agency.

LEO TOLSTOY: "The Snow Storm" (1856). Translated by Louise and Aylmer Maude, from *Collected Shorter Fiction*, Vol. 1 (Everyman's Library, 2001).

MARINA TSVETAEVA: "Life Insurance" translated by Jane A. Taubman, from *Recent Russian Women's Writing* (Ardis Publishers, 1995).

IVAN TURGENEV: "Living Relic" translated by Richard Freeborn, from *First Love and Other Stories* (Penguin Classics, 1990). Translation copyright © 1967 by Richard Freeborn. Penguin Books Limited.

LUDMILA ULITSKAYA: "Angel" from *Sonechka: A Novella and Stories* by Ludmila Ulitskaya, translated by Arch Tait, translation copyright © 2005 by Penguin Random House LLC. Used by permission of Schocken Books, an imprint of the Knopf Doubleday Publishing Group, a division of Penguin Random House LLC. All rights reserved.